tiara

A SURVIVOR
PSYCHOLOGICAL THRILLER

Tiara
Helga Zeiner

Published by POWWOW Books Canada
Cover design by Vanessa Ooms
Copyright 2018 Helga Zeiner
All rights reserved
ISBN: 979-8-667658-52-8

tiara

A SURVIVOR
PSYCHOLOGICAL THRILLER

BY
HELGA ZEINER

Copyright © Helga Zeiner
All rights reserved
Published by POWWOW Books Canada

1

I'M in a coffee shop. I should be holding a paper cup with my favorite morning brew, breakfast tea with milk and sugar, and a cinnamon bun in my hands, but that's not possible. My arms are forced to my chest by somebody behind me, holding me real tight, so tight that I can feel how the air is pushed out of my lungs. I can feel the pressure all the way into my heart, and I wonder briefly if my heart can be squeezed like a lemon. Would it burst when the pressure gets too much, with blood squirting out of it like lemon juice, and me dropping dead the same instant?

The somebody drags me away from a body stretched out on the floor between the tables. A woman. Moaning. Like, in agony. I crane my neck to get a better look at her but the crowd of early morning patrons surrounding her has closed shoulders. Their voices carry a curious mix of shock and surprise and delight. I'd love to know what's going on there but my fifteen-year-old stamina is no match for the vice-like grip of those strong arms around my torso.

The last bit of air has gone out of my lungs. I gasp and manage to get a minute amount of oxygen back into

Tiara

this spongy organ. Not enough, though. I wriggle my shoulders to tell the arms that this mini-breath isn't gonna do it, and that the shapes and colours around me are starting to get blurry. If the pressure doesn't ease, I'll faint right here and now. I want to call out a warning but my throat is so dry only a hoarse whisper comes out.

My legs cave underneath me. Before I begin to worry if the arms are going to let me slip to the floor, I'm dragged through the door, out into bright sunshine. There, on the pavement, the pressure around my chest finally eases, and I get a desperate drag of air back into me. My skin tingles with relief. My brain functions again. I realize instantly, the somebody holding and dragging me out of the coffee shop wasn't trying to kill me but saved me from being crushed by a mob-like crowd. I blink a few times to adjust my eyes, and turn around to see who my knight in shining armour is. I take another deep breath so I can thank him.

"Thank you," I want to say but my words get muffled by a sharp command.

"Hands behind your back."

What? Who? Me?

More hands grab me and practically lift me off the ground while they twist me around. They cuff me. Why? Dear Lord, why do they cuff me? The new sets of hands stick out of blue uniforms. Policemen. Why am I being held by cops? Panic spreads inside me like hot lava. Now I can't breathe again. My heart hammers away at a hundred miles an hour. What do they want from me?

"Stop it," I yell. "What do you want from me?"

No reaction.

"I haven't done anything."

They are shouting orders to each other, ignoring me totally. This is a nightmare. Like in a movie, when a bystander gets caught up in some kind of freaky action and nobody wants to tell him or her what's going on. The louder I yell, the harder their grip becomes. Real hard. Unforgivingly hard. Now I'm screaming with panic and confusion, and pain.

I can't hear them reading me my rights over my screams—meaning, I don't want to. I don't want to be here. I shouldn't be here. I don't want to be treated like that. Ignored, pushed around like some kind of criminal. I don't know what they are accusing me of, and they're not saying. A silly idea flits through my mind. I'm ignorant of any wrong-doing, and they are ignoring me. Do those two things even slightly correspond? Concentrating on this thought my voice dies down, as does my resistance. They lead me to a cop car parked inside a cordoned off area in front of the coffee shop. When did that happen? One moment people are peacefully drinking their lattes, the next, all hell breaks loose, and now the cops control a portion of Robson Street busy with morning commuters.

One of the cops places his hand over my head while he pushes me into the back seat of the cop car. He slams the door shut. Click. Locked. I'm locked up.

Tiara

The cop gets into the driver's seat, nods at his partner waiting in the passenger seat.

"Goddamn little freak," he says with a flick of his head toward me. Then back to his partner. "Did ya see all that blood in there?"

"Come on," his partner says. "Give her a break. We don't know what happened. We weren't in there when it happened."

What happened?

2

MELISSA opened her eyes and looked at the alarm. 7:35 am. She slumped back on the pillow and listened into the semi-dark. All quiet. Her shift at the supermarket didn't start until ten, plenty of time to get ready. Dozing off would be nice, for another ten minutes or so.

No such luck.

The metal springs squeaked when she lifted herself off the mattress. She pulled back the curtains, saw the low clouds carry an autumn storm in from the Pacific, and shivered in the dampness of her unheated apartment. Her terry-towel bathrobe must have shrunk in the last wash. Impossible to close the gap. Her bare feet found the fluffy pink slippers under her bed, so adorable years ago, so worn in now. Worn out, more likely.

She shuffled down the narrow hallway into her kitchen, put the kettle on, waited for the water to boil, let her tea steep for exactly sixty seconds, heaped three spoons of sugar into the mug—ah, all right, a fourth—and poured so much cream into it, the tea instantly cooled to drinking temperature.

Tiara

Mug in hand, she settled into her favorite place by the window, facing west, toward the high-rise monuments of downtown Vancouver. She opened the window a crack. The hum of the traffic below was still mild-tempered.

Exactly 8:00 am now.

She turned on the TV, channel set to CTV, not paying much attention until a bright orange Breaking News banner flashed below the female morning anchor. Melissa turned up the volume, took a sip of her sweet, sweet tea, and leaned back.

"We have the developing story of a brutal attack on a customer at the Corner-Cup coffee shop on Robson Street. Our reporter Emily Jackson is at the scene. Emily, what can you tell us?"

The upper body of a reporter holding a microphone in one hand and fighting her wind-swept hair with the other filled the screen. Well, it was October, at least it wasn't raining.

"From what we know so far, a young woman has attacked another woman inside the coffee shop behind me. The identity of the victim or of the attacker is not yet known, and we don't have any information about the attacker's motive. Apparently, she suddenly produced a knife and threw herself at the other woman, screaming at the top of her lungs."

"Do we have any information about the condition of the victim?"

An autumn gust blew hair over the reporter's face. Trying to control the strands, she nearly lost her microphone but fumbled it back into position.

"The victim was transported to the emergency ward of St Paul's Hospital. The hospital is only a few blocks from here—"

The reporter's voice travelled along Melissa's attention span and lost its grip. Background noise. She took another sip of her tea, warming her hands on the mug.

The anchor came back on. Her voice went up a notch, trying to draw Melissa back in.

"We have just received a video clip from one of our viewers who filmed the brutal attack. He was a customer in the coffee shop at the time and managed to film part of the actual assault. We would like to warn you that some viewers may find the content of this clip offensive in nature."

Melissa's eyes, glued to the screen, grew wide.

The coffee shop customer must have held his iPhone high to film the ghastly scene. The video was shaky. It showed two bodies on the ground.

The victim of the attack was on the floor, trying to protect her face with crossed hands. The attacker, wearing a black hoodie, kneeled on her stomach with her right arm rising up in the air and down again, in a kind of wood-chopping motion. Up and down, up and down. She slashed into the woman underneath her with such vehemence even Melissa could feel the force of her hatred.

Tiara

Oh my God, did the knife poke into the woman's eye? Melissa shivered.

The filmmaker must have gone in shock, too. The picture went shaky and lost focus. The ceiling lamp appeared on screen, then part of the wall, then the attacker again, scrambling up and disappearing out of the frame altogether. Finally, the victim on the ground could be seen, face covered with bloodied hands, then the screen went black.

A moment later, the clip continued, now outside of the coffee shop, showing a young girl being pushed into the back seat of a police cruiser. The policeman closed the door, and for a brief second a small portion of the girl's face became visible behind the window.

Melissa gasped. The mug slipped from her hands, dropped to the floor and spilled tea on the cheap vinyl floor before rolling under the table.

It couldn't be. It couldn't be.

The attacker looked like her daughter.

3

BY the time Homicide Detective Pete Macintosh from the Vancouver Police Department and his partner Harding arrived at the crime scene it had been compromised by the first responders and the number of witnesses, twelve in all—eight male, three female, plus one girl behind the counter—who had been present at the time of the attack. Harding got the thankless task of recording their names and addresses while Macintosh went to talk to the only guy who'd been quick-thinking enough to film the attack.

"I need to confiscate your phone," he said to the guy who looked like a clone of all the other male customers in the coffee shop. Black padded jackets, black jeans with holes in them, black work boots, faces covered with beards in various stages of unkempt growth. Fashion statements of affluent city slickers.

The guy handed his phone over without complaint.

Macintosh raised his eyebrows. "Uploaded already?"

The guy grinned. "No law against that. Should make me a few bucks. Man, that was so gross. Super cool.

Look at me, I'm still shaking. Can't fucking believe I've caught it on my cell."

"Calm down," Macintosh said. "Let's move over here, sit down and have a chat. I want to know everything you remember that is not on the clip."

"Huh, I don't know. It was so fast. I heard a chair crash and people jumping up, and then…, well, then I filmed. I got most of it, I'm sure. Can't really remember anything before. I was waiting for my order, the girl serving behind the counter had disappeared into the back room. I'm telling you, people were getting pissed off. The place was filling up, and she has the nerve and disappears for minutes."

"Did you notice if the victim was waiting in line or sitting down?"

"My guess is she was sitting by the window, there, where the chair is turned over. But, as I said, I wouldn't know."

And neither did any of the other customers. Macintosh and Harding interviewed each one before they let them go. None of them remembered seeing the victim before her face was slashed or could speculate on the reason for the attack, it had happened so fast, been so unpredictable. No one even remembered what the perpetrator looked like.

"At least we got their contacts," Harding said when they finished.

Macintosh wasn't surprised by the meagre outcome of their initial investigation. People in crowds were usually self-centered. They blocked out much of their surroundings. He bagged and labelled the knife used in the attack, then they headed back to their station at Gravely Street.

Hours later, after he'd played the video clip about a hundred times, he thought he made out the victim's voice in between the excited screams of the customers. He took it down to audio and had them manipulate the different recording levels. When the nearly buried voice became clearer, it sounded like 'Ayuda…ayuda', followed by "oh Dios mio". He opened his Google translating app. The guys in audio agreed with him, it must be the victim's voice. Only she would scream 'Help…Help…oh my God". To double-check he scanned the list of witnesses but couldn't find a single one with a Hispanic sounding name.

Fairly safe to assume the victim would be Hispanic. In times of crisis one reverts back to one's mother tongue. He made a note to send Harding over to St. Paul's Hospital. The doc on duty had told him he couldn't interview her yet, and to have her picture taken was pointless as long as her face was such a mess, but to check her colouring as well as her height and weight might help to ID her faster. Somebody who claimed to know her would come forward soon, and they could match up descriptions quickly on the phone to eliminate all the weirdos who usually called in.

He looked at the clip a final time. Although it never showed the girl's or the victim's faces, this was a clear cut case. Should be easy enough to wrap up. But the girl was so young, it twisted his stomach into knots. What made a kid like that turn so violent?

"Here you go, Macintosh." Harding dumped a stack of files on his desk. "Those need your signatures. Before we get on to the coffee shop girl."

"You kidding me?" Macintosh pushed the files away. "They processed her already?"

"It's a slow day in paradise." Harding opened the top file, and pointed at the printed sheet. "Tox screen is back already, too."

"Let me guess. High as a kite?"

"Negative."

"Lucky I didn't bet," Macintosh said. "Well, then, let's get this show on the road."

"If you want," Harding said, eagerness in his voice "I can do this one by myself."

"Can't let a dumbass rookie like you ruin a cut-and-dry case."

"Let me handle it."

"Don't argue with your superior."

"You don't like teenage crap like that."

"If I mess up, you can take over." Macintosh forced a grin. "Until then, watch and learn, puppy."

Harding backed off.

They walked across the hallway and stepped into the brightly-lit interview room, where the girl was waiting for them. She wore an orange jumpsuit but was not cuffed and shackled any longer.

Macintosh pulled up a chair, Harding hovered in the background.

"State your name and address, please," Macintosh said.

She didn't say anything, didn't look at him.

"I don't have all day. If you don't cooperate, I'll have you locked up and chuck the key. All the same to me."

The girl didn't move.

He gave her a casual inspection. Sitting behind the steel table made it hard to judge her height, but she was young, small and skinny. Too young to be sitting there, and too skinny for such a baggy outfit. Pretty in a way, with soft round features, smooth and not yet painted by life. Dark hair, cut short without giving it any style, most likely by herself with a pair of blunt scissors. All signs of a concentrated effort to achieve a look that wouldn't attract attention. Make her unobtrusive. Not like his daughter. My God, how she used to love to make herself pretty. At that age, it was all about dresses and make-up and stuff like that, and he loved to come home to her little fashion shows, proudly parading the latest bargains from their shopping excursions. His wife and her, doing so much without him. To think how many family evenings he missed. A thought he needed to shake off.

"Don't make it harder on yourself. We'll find out who you are sooner than you think."

The girl wasn't blinking.

Tiara

Macintosh studied her more closely. He had expected her to be agitated. They usually were, after the physical exertion of committing an act of violence. She held her shoulders straight, her hands folded in her lap, her eyes half closed, her face no expression at all.

"How old are you?"

No reaction.

"Suit yourself." Macintosh motioned Harding to follow him out of the room.

"That's a bummer," Harding said when the door closed behind them. "She's got no ID on her. What do we do with her now?"

"Nothing. Let her stew in there. Eventually they all get bored."

It didn't take them long to identify her. Somebody saw the footage of the video clip the city slicker clone had sent to all major TV stations, recognized her, and called in. Her name was Tiara, the caller said. And he knew her mother, Melissa, who lived on the fringe of the Downtown Eastside. The caller didn't know the mother's last name and couldn't give an exact address, but he'd seen both of them a few times in his corner shop.

"I hope for her sake she's older than she looks," Harding said.

Macintosh felt the knot in his stomach tighten. "Not a day over sixteen, if you ask me."

4

THEY said I've stabbed a woman. Nearly killed her. The people who processed me didn't say it outright, but I overheard them mentioning it. I was so shocked, I nearly peed myself. My whole body tensed until I felt like a statue chiselled from granite.

How can they make such a mistake? How could they think I've done something so terrible? I'm not a bad person. I don't do evil.

Gracie taught me what evil is, what sends people to hell. Stuff like poking needles into insects, or stealing from a blind beggar's plate, that makes a person bad. Inflicting pain and suffering intentionally, like on purpose, with a kind of freaky pleasure inside, that's where the line is drawn. I've never stepped over that line. I don't do such things.

I swear, cross my heart and wish to die, I'm not a bad person.

The thought of Gracie adds another level of unbelievable. She'd be horrified if she could see me sitting in a police station, accused of hurting somebody. She's always condemned violent behaviour, always said, there are other ways to solve a dilemma. If somebody hurts me, she said, I mustn't lower myself to a standard that's unbecoming of a beautiful girl like me.

I wonder what the woman who got stabbed did to deserve this. To be clear, I'm not saying, she deserved it, but my guess is, nobody stabs a person without a reason. Which, again, proves the point that is wasn't me who did this. I can't think of a single reason to stab anybody.

I couldn't tell those detectives what goes through my mind. They had such a couldn't-care-less attitude. They asked my name and then they left me alone in this bright and bare room that's supposed to intimidate me. Me, the seasoned mind-traveler who can hide from far worse that an inhospitable environment.

I close my eyes, fold my hands and start to breathe deeply to calm myself again. I can sit here forever, staring at the table. I've been taught to sit still and be obedient. I learned to bob over an ocean of minutes and hours in an imaginary boat. Far, far away I float, until I see no shoreline, not behind me, and not in front.

I concentrate on the floating, drift and dream along. The room around me changes color. Gray becomes seafoam turquoise and white. The air-conditioner noise transforms itself into an ocean breeze. A sandy beach. A sea-side town. Damn it, I'm drifting into Galveston.

Galveston.

I don't want to. Please, don't make me go there.

It scares me to think of the town I grew up in—going back, even if only in my thoughts, scares me something terrific. My insides scream a silent warning. *Stay away.*

A door opens, and I can feel one of the policemen come back in again.

"I'm Detective Macintosh."

I acknowledge with a tiny bat of my lashes that he introduces himself this time. I hear a click. The tape recorder.

A little curious, I open my eyes and look at him. He's slightly overweight and old, at least fifty. His hair, dark with gray streaks, curls outward. Bad haircut or a bad hair day, I can't say for sure.

"You spend too much time in your office," I say.

"What?" Vertical furrows dig deep into the leathery skin of his forehead.

"You're so pasty."

"My complexion is the least of your concerns," he says. "State your name and address."

I can feel angry vibes pulsing out of his pores, surprisingly not directed at me. This guy is wired. I guess he hates his job, or his life, or both, so badly there's no joy left in him. His mouth is a thin line. He doesn't give a damn, not about me, and not about anybody else.

"You're the policeman. Figure it out."

"We know already who you are, Tiara," he says with a brief twitch of his upper lip, like a smile gone wrong.

I look away.

"Your mother Melissa will be contacted shortly, so don't give me any crap."

Good luck with that one, a great help she'll be.

5

WHEN the doorbell rang, Melissa expected the police but it was her mother. Louise looked like she aged ten years since their last meeting only a few days ago.

"Melissa, did you see?"

Her mother stood a head shorter and was half of her in volume but had the same face, the same gestures and movements. This miniature Melissa barged in and headed straight for the kitchen.

"I came right away."

Of course you did. You could never resist a crisis. Taking over, taking control, bossing around, bossing me around, that was always your thing.

Her mother put the kettle on and pulled tea bags and fresh mugs from the cupboard. "God, I can't handle this. My heart!"

Melissa sat at the table.

"That girl… it was Tiara, wasn't it?"

Melissa folded her arms over her bosom, hands tucked in her armpits.

Her mother didn't even look at her, lunged into the predictable litany of accusations, "I always knew it

Tiara

would come to this. You should never have gone down there," her mother said. "Don't say I didn't warn you."

To say nothing aggravated her mother most.

"You could have gotten that job at the elementary school, it was as good as yours. A steady job. How could you throw your whole education away? All that studying, for nothing. As if that hadn't cost me a bundle."

Melissa could feel familiar anger rise inside her, but this time despair reduced its fire to a smoldering heap of ashes.

"Stop it, Mother. You're not helping."

"What do the police say?"

"They haven't contacted me yet."

"What? Why not? How can they *not* speak to you? You're her mother! This is unacceptable—"

"Mother!"

"I'm just saying. You've got to call them right away." She brought the filled mugs to the table and sat down. "You have to. They need to know."

"Leave me alone. Stop meddling."

Her mother sniffed. Sniffled. Tears welled up.

Melissa envied her. She herself had no tears—such dreadful news, on top of all she had to cope with. This girl on the TV screen, climbing into a police cruiser, how could this be her daughter?

"I'm sorry," her mother said. "But look at it my way. If you hadn't left me, if you hadn't run away with that man, you wouldn't have suffered so much."

"If Mike hadn't died," Melissa said, "nothing like this would have happened."

"But die he did," her mother said. "And you had to bring Tiara up on your own. And now look what's come of it."

Melissa sipped her tea. How could her life have derailed this way? Where had it gone wrong? Was it when she decided to run away from a boring life with Mother, packed her bags and went to Texas to live with her new love Mike, a soldier on holidays in Vancouver she barely knew? Or was it when she was forced to live with his sister Gracie at his family home in Galveston, while Mike had to go fight a war on the other side of the world, leaving her in the care of this overbearing, annoying woman? Were those the first warning signs? Did she feel trapped when she found out she was carrying his baby? No, she'd been ready to put up with his sister, wait for his return and make the best of it. Her life hadn't derailed until she was told of his accident, so unfortunate, so sad. That was when she felt most vulnerable.

"You weren't there," Melissa said. "You have no idea what I've gone through."

"I would have come much sooner if I'd known."

"You knew perfectly well I'd lost a husband. You never called back."

"Can't we leave all this behind?"

"I'm not the one who brought it up."

"You're here now. You're back home."

Melissa turned away and stared out the window. "Then how come I don't feel welcome?"

6

THEIR whole incarceration machinery is pretty well oiled. I'm dragged before a judge the same day I'm arrested. Placed in front of him, I stare a hole in the wall right above his head. He returns the favor and stares into space with unfocused eyes while he reads out the detectives' report, detailing the gruesome crime I'm alleged to have committed. He notes that the investigation is on-going but that he feels there is enough grounds for considering me a suspect. He orders me held in custody until my mental fitness is established, which, he points out to nobody in particular with a weary voice, is normal procedure.

Straight from court, I'm taken to a place with a fancy name, the Burnaby Youth Secure Custody Center, but it's a prison all the same. A place for people considered dangerous to the public but too young to be thrown into the ring with adult offenders who'd make mincemeat out of them.

From what I can see through the window slit of the prison van, BYSC is a modern, low-rise brick building. The driver reverses into a loading bay, shutters go down, then they open the van doors and let me out. Two security guards assist me down the steps and into the building, making sure I won't slip and hurt myself and tell a lawyer later on they roughed me up.

At the processing area I'm told to stand in front of a fishbowl counter. The guy behind the bullet-proof glass asks my name. Jesus, as if he wouldn't know already. I opt for silence again to prove a point. He shrugs, doesn't give a damn, deals with difficult customers all the time, I guess. Point goes to him.

They usher me to the next room. Three different security guards, female this time, no weapons, take off my cuffs, unshackle me, watch me undress, ask me to shower. After I'm dry, one of the ladies points at a stack of sweat suits and says, "Pick a color".

"I don't like purple," I say.

She's got a blank expression on her face.

"Or red."

"You're moved to the IAU. There's no code, so take yellow or green."

Now I get it. I'm transferred to the Inpatient Assessment Unit for my judge-ordered mental fitness tests. It doesn't matter what color I wear. Until proven otherwise, I'm a nutcase and deserve to be treated gently. I smile back at Blank Face and choose green.

The IAU is like a hospital. My room is big enough to accommodate a bed, a desk, and a chair. I stretch out on the mattress, hands behind my head. I'd like to lie here and imagine the scene at the coffee shop as it was read out by the judge, but for the life of me I can't see myself in this picture. When I try to imagine me acting so aggressive, hurting that woman so horribly, I draw a blank. I start a mind movie, with two actors taking over her and my part, but that's not working either. The scene is too surreal, I can't get a grasp on it. However, a strange new feeling seeps into my confusion, a growing sense of hostility. Dark, moody. Gaining intensity.

That feeling sure adds to my confusion, considering I don't know why and against whom I should feel so hostile. Hateful, nearly.

A guard knocks, comes in and escorts me to another room where I'm going to be interrogated by a shrink. The guard called it an interview, but I've seen plenty of psycho movies to know better.

The shrink sits not behind but next to his desk, legs crossed, an open notebook on his lap. He points to the other chair in the room, opposite him, not far enough away for my liking. The whole room gives me claustrophobia.

"I'm Dr. Stanley Eaton," he says without shaking my hand. "I'm going to ask you a few questions to get a better understanding of who you are. Anything you can tell me will help your case."

Like I asked for help.

He fires away, asking benign questions like how old I am, how I feel now, how I feel about being in here, how I felt before I got here, pussy-footing around the all-important, "How did you feel when you did it?"

Those detectives must have already given him my name and everything else they dug up about me by now. What kind of half-wit does he think I am? Great, at least now my hostility found a target. I answer every question the same way. "My name is Princess Tia and I refuse to answer any questions." I think this kind of approach is more commonly used in war movies, but who cares.

The shrink doesn't flinch once. This guy may not be brilliant but he sure is cunning, I give him that. I look him over. Middle-aged, which leaves plenty of room for interpretation.

"You don't have to say anything if you don't want to," he says, "but if I were you, I'd think it over carefully. It's totally up to you, but it might be in your best interest to cooperate with me."

"My name is—"

"I know, I know. Princess Tia. I can't force you to cooperate, Tia, and I won't waste my time if you don't want to talk to me. It's your decision. It's your life."

Before I can stop myself, I say, "My life is over anyway."

He closes his notebook, gets up. "If you say so."

He's at the door.

"They told me I hurt somebody."

He stops, turns back.

I take in a deep breath. "But I know I'm innocent. Why do they think it was me?"

"I can't comment on the police investigation. All I can tell you is that you are a suspect."

"Shouldn't I know if I'm guilty?"

"You don't remember?"

How on earth can I explain to him that I feel innocent? I suddenly feel like crying. Who the hell believes me when I say I'm innocent while a judge says there is enough evidence to hold me locked up? I wasn't overly dramatic when I said my life is over. They will declare me insane and lock me up forever. They don't care to find out what really happened. I don't want to cry in front of him because I'm terrified he might come closer and put his hand on my shoulder, and blink rapidly.

Thank God, he stays where he is.

"The court has asked me to offer an opinion as to whether you're fit to stand trial or are NCRMD."

He locks eyes with me, no emotion showing, not pity, not curiosity, not the slightest interest in me. He's just going through the motions with me. Another nuisance case ticked off the list. This annoys me no end. To make matters worse, he feels the need to explain things to me.

"The court wants to know if they can put you on trial," he says, still standing, "or if you're not criminally responsible due to a mental disorder. That's what NCRMD stands for."

"I'm not a nut case."

"I'm glad to hear that," he says, "I won't be able to help you if you're non-disclosive. I hope you are sensible enough to try and figure out what motivated you to commit this crime."—*So, there it is, the all-important question, neatly packed into an offhand threat.*—"Try hard. It might all come back to you. We don't need to talk about the alleged offense, but I need to understand what makes you tick, or I can't recommend that you get out on bail."

I wish he'd sit. Looking down on me creeps me out.

"I don't want to."

He takes a step toward me. "You don't want to talk?"

I shy back. "I don't want to get out on bail."

"Why not?"

"Bail means I have to stay with my mother until trial starts, right?"

"You are a minor."

"I don't want to stay with her."

The idea of happily living with Mom, even if only for a short period, makes my skin crawl.

"I don't want to see her either."

"You have a right to refuse her visits," he says prosaically, goes back to his desk, takes out another notebook, an unused one, and a pencil from his desk drawer. He slides both across the desktop toward me.

"If you choose to stay in here, and you don't want to talk to me, it might help you regain your memory if you write things down."

"Write what? I don't remember anything."

"About the attack—or about nothing at all?"

That's a good question. I remember Mom, and Gracie, and that we lived in Galveston. "Don't know."

"From which moment on does your memory fail you?"

Good question number two. How do you explain a foggy brain? "Everything is in a mist. Like walking through a forest in heavy autumn fog. Shapes come and go. Could be trees, could be leaves, could be people." Now tears do come. I quickly wipe them away. "It's very confusing. I'm so messed up, I don't know what to think."

He taps on the notebook. "Sometimes things get clearer when writing them down."

"Wouldn't know where to start."

"Start at the beginning. Your first memory, maybe?"

He throws this dog-bone idea at me and I catch it flying through the air. "Like my birth?"

He lifts the corners of his mouth in a solid impression of a smile. "That's stretching it a bit. But a good thought. You can anchor your memory if you structure your thoughts. Birthdays, maybe? You remember your birthdays, don't you?"

It's so quiet in my hospital-like room inside the prison I can hear my mind ticking and clicking. The shrink got under my skin. *Sometimes things get clearer while writing.*

I'm sure that I haven't done anything bad, but everybody acts as if it was me. Why? The scene in the coffee shop is beyond my grasp. No matter how hard I try, I don't remember. If I could at least remember going into the coffee shop, if I could remember me being in there, I wouldn't feel so confused. So angry. Not knowing drives me crazy. But maybe I am crazy. I must be, or I'd know the reason why sudden anger flares up inside me. I'm mad at myself, for not pushing through the fog that covers my past like a wet blanket. Too heavy to lift on my own. Is that what the shrink meant?

For an endless time I stare at the closed notebook. Finally, I reach for the pencil and let it roll between my fingers. The pen is round, has a sharp tip—I'm surprised they let me have it. I could do damage with something so sharp.

I open the notebook. If I find out when and how all this began, that might clear the fog.

My fingers tighten around the pencil. Try. Please, please, try and remember.

Birthday Zero

What happened when I was born?

A hot day in summer, 1998, August 21 to be exact. I was born the same day my father, Miguel "Mike" Rodriguez, got killed. On that day, the US bombed an obscure terrorist camp in Afghanistan. No US soldier lost his life except for my father who shot himself while cleaning his gun to get ready for action.

At about the time he blew his brains away by accident, my mother did what I assume pregnant mothers do while waiting for their bellies to pop. Presumably she was knitting some tiny socks or sewing little baby outfits. I wasn't due for another month, but when she got word of her beloved Mike's unfortunate accident, she went straight into shock. They took her to a hospital in Houston and performed a caesarean to make sure she wouldn't lose me as well.

When she woke up, she couldn't even look at me.

Next day, my father's sister, Graciella—Gracie, as Mom called her—dropped by with a bunch of flowers and a box of chocolates. After they cried together for a while, Gracie placed me on my mom's cut-and-stapled-back-together-again stomach.

My mom said, "At least it's a girl. I couldn't bear it if it were a boy. I'm sure he'd look like Mike and remind me of him every single day of my life."

"It's a blessing," Gracie said. "A girl is so much easier. We can make pretty things for her."

I was right there on my mom's now empty belly, kind of listening to every word the two ladies said. I know that's practically impossible, me not even able to open my eyes yet, but I've heard Mom and Gracie tell that story so many times, it's like me remembering it. That's how it happened, unless of course they twisted their account of my birth to suit their own memories. Could be a figment of my mom's imagination because

Tiara

she won't admit that she didn't want to look at me, the red-wrinkled premature bundle of obligations. Truth be told, she probably cried and lamented and cursed me for being the burden of a young widow. Wouldn't surprise me, the way she always went on about her suffering and how much she'd given up for me and all that blah-de-blah.

7

MACINTOSH waited a few minutes in front of the door to catch his breath. Three flights up, and he was winded. He should have sent Harding. But next-of-kin calls, be they for victim or perpetrator, were always tough to handle, and Harding was still a junior detective.

A woman opened the door. Short. Sinewy. Her mouth a thin line, her eyes piercing.

"I'm Detective Pete Macintosh from the Vancouver Police Department, District One."

"About time somebody from the police showed up," she said.

"Are you Melissa Brown?"

The woman pointed toward the open kitchen door.

He walked past her into the room, looked around. The kitchen appeared clean, neat, with all the signs of low-income suburbia—table and chairs cramped into a corner, cracked linoleum tiles, tea cups that didn't match, seat cushions that did.

The woman sitting at the table looked up. Stunned. Confused. Twice the size of the older woman who'd

Tiara

opened the door. Her sloppy appearance—legs held in by over-stretched spandex slacks, upper body spilling out of every opening in her t-shirt—made Macintosh cringe inside. If she was the girl's mother she had to be in her thirties, but her face was that of a twenty-year-old, with traces of beauty still detectable under the balloon-tight skin, ready to burst at the next mouthful of peanut butter brownies. A delicate nose, full lips, high cheekbones, shiny blond hair.

"Ma'am, I'm here about your daughter. You have a daughter named Tiara?"

She waved away his question. Of course she had, and of course she already knew.

The older woman crept up behind him. "Officer, please, sit down. I'm Louise, Melissa's mother, Tiara's grandmother. Please, tell us what happened. We're so upset. We don't really know anything. My daughter wanted to call you but we couldn't figure out whom to contact."

How difficult was it to pick up the phone if they were concerned about the girl? Macintosh made a mental note of it, sat down, took his manila notebook out and opened it.

"At approximately seven-twenty this morning a young woman we believe to be your daughter attacked a female customer inside the Corner-Cup coffee shop on Robson Street."

He set a mug shot on the table. "Is that your daughter?"

"That's her." Melissa put her hand over the picture.

"A judge has ordered her into custody for psychiatric evaluation at the Youth Custody Center in Burnaby. She'll stay there, at least until her exact age is established."

"Tiara's fifteen." Melissa's eyes got watery. "Dear Lord, how can this happen to me? What else do I have to go through in this life?"

Oh for fuck sake. Her girl was only fifteen. In deep trouble with the law. And there she sat, whining about her own suffering instead of worrying about her kid. Macintosh wanted to slap the woman back into reality.

Louise must have noticed his disapproval and jumped in. "The woman? I mean the one who…well, you know, the one who…is…, huh, she…did she…?"

"The victim is still in emergency."

Melissa recoiled at the word "victim", but he wasn't in the mood to be tactful and considerate. "Ma'am. Is there anything you can tell me that'll help us understand why your daughter committed this crime?"

Her eyes now looked dry, but her face remained distorted in a silent bawl. "How can I?" she said. "I don't know what goes on inside this girl's head. How could she do this to me?"

"Please, ma'am." Macintosh took a consent form out and slid it over to Melissa. "Her being a minor, we'll need parental permission to interview your daughter. And do a drug test." He ignored to mention that processing had done one already, assuming that Tiara was over sixteen. Coming back negative the consent after the fact was only a formality. But now that the mother confirmed Tiara's age to him he had to get her approval to interview the girl. Preferably without her present.

Melissa seemed to hesitate. Louise took over again.

"My daughter will sign it. She's a widow. Tiara's dad died fifteen years ago. He was a US soldier. Got killed in the line of duty."

Tough shit, losing a husband and a daughter. Macintosh could relate to that. He tried to soften his expression, still concentrating on Melissa. "What nationality is your daughter, then? American or Canadian?"

"Both. She was born down there. We got back about three years ago."

"Her father's name?"

"Mike." Melissa hesitated. "Miguel Brown."

"Where did she go to school?"

"I'm home-schooling her. Look, Inspector—"

"Detective."

"Detective. She's a teenager, a bit wild sometimes, but she's a good girl. Always has been. She's going through a phase. If you have kids, you understand."

Macintosh didn't want to understand. His eyes wandered over her body again. Okay, life had dealt her a sucker punch, and she'd protected herself under an extra layer—several layers, to be exact—he got that. He put his hand on his own belly, straightened himself, but compassion didn't come. The woman was nothing like his wife had been, he couldn't sense an ounce of maternal instinct in her. Christ almighty, so close to retirement, and he had to deal with a nutcase teenager and an egotistical mother as his possible last homicide case. If it came to be a homicide. Maybe Tiara was lucky and it would finish up as assault with bodily harm only.

"My Tiara is bright and beautiful," Melissa said. "She always got top marks on all her tests. I home-schooled down in Texas already. Every single day I sat with her for hours, read to her, practiced writing and counting. I always insisted Tiara speak properly, so she wouldn't adopt that dreadful Texas drawl, and she didn't. My little girl's such a quick study."

"Did you register for home-schooling when you got back here?"

Melissa's voice took on a higher pitch. "I didn't get around to it. I'm a working mom. There's only that much I can do."

"She's a widow," Louise said. "Raising a child all by herself."

He ignored her, stuck on Melissa. "It's the law, Mrs. Brown."

"So charge me."

Macintosh's face turned to stone. "What about your daughter? Didn't she want to go to school? Meet kids her age?"

"She was twelve years old when we left Texas. She's never lived in Canada before, left her whole life behind her. I can understand why she refused to go to school. Can't you?"

Tiara

"That's not my position, ma'am," he said.

"And that's not the point, right? The point is, what happens now? What will happen to her? What will happen to me?"

"I really can't say, ma'am."

"Then find out, for crying out loud!"

Melissa fisted her hands, shook them like an angry child. He watched her go all sour, almost believed her anguish, her motherly worry. Would it surface now? Would he see a flicker of honest passionate distress for her daughter?

"Get your supervisor on the phone. Talk to somebody who knows. You can't leave me hanging like this. How do you think I feel?"

"Tell you what, ma'am," he said. "I call my superior and see what can be arranged."

Both women looked relieved. He called Sergeant Tong at homicide and read out what he'd written, which wasn't much.

His boss didn't sound too happy. Macintosh listened to the sergeant, trying hard to keep his growing irritation in check. "Too bad. That's too bad," he said. He hung up.

"I'm sorry." He closed his notebook. "With your daughter being under-age I thought we could keep the lid on this. The press won't be allowed to mention her name, and I didn't think it would be a big news item with the victim not—"

"So she didn't die?" Louise said.

"Her condition is still critical."

"So, that's good, isn't it?" The two women exchanged glances of relief. "Nobody will know Tiara's name. Nobody will know who she is."

"Wrong," he said. "The story's all over the internet. Somebody posted the clip from inside the coffee shop on YouTube, together with a comment of somebody who knows her, mentioning her name, and it's gone viral."

"Oh My God." Melissa drew a sharp breath. "Everybody will know I'm her mother. I need to go and see her right away. I bet the TV crews are there already." She straightened her hair, then wiped her hands on her thighs. "You need to take me to her, immediately. That's what they'll expect of me. To rush to her side."

"Again, ma'am, I'm sorry," Macintosh said. "Can't be done."

"What are you talking about? You have to. I'm her mother. I have my rights."

"I understand, ma'am, but your daughter has rights, too. And right now, she refuses to see you."

8

I'M back at the shrink's office, fending off his second attempt to get me talking. Knowing he doesn't give a shit about me, I'm on edge. Best not to show how afraid and confused I am, I stare straight into his face and support my effort with appropriate body language. Crossed arms are a childish gesture, I know, he'll see right through that if he's worth his money, but I can't help it. I'm trying to establish an insurmountable barrier here.

He pretends not to notice and carries on with his monologue, yet all this talk is an attempt to gain my trust. He wants me to open up to him so he'll understand what drives me to do bad things. That's what he's after. As soon as I give him the tiniest clues of my emotional state, he'll twist them into a confession, regardless of the truth. What truth?

If I knew that I wouldn't have to untangle the twisted fibers of my childhood and moor some of their frayed ends—or beginnings—in the notebook he gave me for exactly this purpose.

"Leave me alone," I say. "I told you, I don't remember a thing."

"Nothing?" he says. "You know who you are, don't you?"

"Maybe."

"Tell me about your childhood. Let's talk about where you grew up."

"I'm no good at talking. That's not my thing."

Will he understand that? I can't drag fragments of memories to the surface and explain them to him at the same time. Writing them down seems to work a lot better. The moment I grab a pencil, my thoughts appear much less threatening than all those tumbling words. I keep my arms crossed, press my lips together, and wait for his reaction.

With a casual shrug, he closes his own still empty notebook.

"I'm sorry, then. You leave me with no choice. My assessment will state that you are unwilling to cooperate. I'll recommend that you be remanded at BYSC until the police complete their investigation. I'll forward my recommendations to the court in the next few days. This means bail is out of the question for the time being."

Hallelujah. I won't be sent back to mom.

"It's over," he says. "You played your card, and you wasted it."

After the interview, they take me back to the prison part of the complex.

I have to surrender my green sweat suit and am given a purple one. I can't believe this—purple, the color I hate even more than pink. I shouldn't have told them I hate purple.

They dump me in a cell block they call a living unit. This messes with my brain again. I mean, really? A living unit, as opposed to a dead unit, or what?

According to the instruction booklet they gave me along with a hygiene pack (toothbrush, medium, toothpaste, okay, soap, revolting) and one set of bedding (stiff, sterile), this prison is partitioned into a lot of living units. For security reasons each unit is isolated from the others. I'll have to share my living unit with up to seven other girls.

Lucky for me, due to the current low adolescent crime level in our province, I'm the only inmate, in this particular living unit. For now. They tell me this might change any day. Pray my luck will hold indefinitely, I can't stand other girls around me. If another inmate does arrive and they pair her with me, I'll get myself locked into solitary faster than the speed of Flash himself.

My cell is similar to the one in the medical assessment ward, except for one rather disgusting element. Next to my bunk bed is a stainless steel toilet. Yikes. The door to my new home has a narrow glass window at eye-level, and there's no way to cover it. Guess the guard will have a pee-peek whenever he or she feels the unappetizing urge to watch my private moments.

I own nothing. That's why, I guess, there's no closet in here. There's a small desk with a chair in front, and a window to the outside between the bed and the desk. I can actually look through the metal bars if I stretch my neck. The outside is segmented into neat squares.

Lying on my bunk bed, I study my rights and responsibilities in the instruction booklet. I am a Level One, which means no privileges. For me it's lights out at 8:30 every night.

A very faint Vancouver night shines into my cell. Thank you, city lights. I can't sleep yet, way too early for me. A conversation forms in the dark, and hard as I try, I can't stop asking questions, knowing fully well I have no answers to give. What a bloody vicious circle, a merry-go-round of nonsense.

Calm down, Princess Tia. To find the truth you need to dig deeper than question what happened. Deep, deep down, way underneath the painful surface, lies the answer to the riddle. Go ahead and start digging.

I take my journal and scribble along in the semi-dark.

Birthday One

According to Gracie—and to make this quite clear, everything I write down here about my early years are not things I remember, they are things I remember Gracie telling me—this birthday was a break-through birthday of sorts. My mom turned around on that day.

Until then, she'd been deeply depressed, which is understandable for several reasons. Her husband didn't leave her any money because he hadn't really been her husband (first reason). In all the excitement of their youthful passion, this formality wasn't on their priority list. And now she had this baby at home (second reason) which wasn't even her home (third reason) but belonged to my aunt. Tough luck, mom.

In that first year, and for many years to come, Gracie was much more than an aunt to me. She told me many times how much joy she got out of feeding me, bathing me, dressing me. She sang me lullabies, and took me for stroller outings along the ocean front, next to the highway, where the noise of the cars racing by gets lost in the seagulls' fierce battle cries over the surf's decaying spoils. Where the smell of the salty breeze overpowers the stench of the car fumes. Galveston is considered a seaside town when in reality it's a freeway-side town. All the houses and shops are on the northern side, south of the four-lane concrete snake lies only the beach and a few forlorn tourist attractions.

Lovely walks Gracie took me on, stopping whenever she met somebody she knew. Who would suspect the handy little bags of white stuff underneath my pretty pink pillow to be anything but baby powder? Every time Gracie told me about our baby-stroller outings she laughed her head off about those good-natured fools. Those little packets of goodies helped get you and your mom through the tough times, she said often. We would have starved if I wouldn't have taken care of us.

Tiara

Above and beyond her struggles to provide for me and Mom, Gracie gave me her heart. While I write this down, I can feel her love. Gracie loved me with everything she was capable of. She adored to tuck me into the pink stroller with a pink foldable roof framed with pink ruffles to keep me protected from sun and wind and seagull shit, my naked legs paddling in the fresh air, and show me off to her friends. Gracie's torso must have darkened my vision often when she bent down to go *tickle, tickle, my mija*—she always called me mija, which means something like sweetie in Spanish—her generous bosom dangling in front of my happy pink face. Pink was Gracie's thing. She loved that color, and she loved me. I was her pink baby, and she couldn't have been happier than in that first year when my mom felt so miserable.

On my first birthday she dressed me in my best pink outfit and took me to a photographer. Gracie didn't mind spending money on me. She always made enough money for the three of us to get by, and for the upkeep of our drab but homey single-story structure in the third row north of the all-domineering oceanfront freeway. In those days neither I nor my mom cared where the money came from—although Mom might have snapped out of her depression faster if she'd taken on the responsibility of providing for her infant.

When Gracie came home with me from the photo session she was so excited she forgot how catatonic my mom usually was when it came to her daughter.

"Look, look!" She waved the picture in front of Mom's impassive face. "Look at her! She's an angel!"

The photographer had done me up with fluffy wings made of plastic feathers sprinkled with silver glitter. I've seen this picture often. Every time we looked at it, Gracie gushed about how talented the photographer was. How he captured an expression in my puffy baby face that was for sure a fluke but made me look almost grown up. I could see purity and goodness in that face—unspoiled beauty.

When Gracie brought this picture home, my mom stared at it for the longest time. I don't know what crossed her mind but I like to imagine something snapped. *Is this child really mine?* Even better: *That child is Mike's gift to me from heaven.* Or better still: *I love this little angel of mine.*

Gracie gushed on. "He didn't take any money—imagine, the photographer refused to get paid. He gave me money instead. Here, fifty dollars he gave me. All I had to do was sign a form that he could use the picture for his front window display. My mija is so beautiful, he said, people should see her. He wants to take more pictures, he'll pay for those, too. He said I should come back. Next week I'll go—"

"No!" my mom shouted.

Gracie stared at her, dumbfounded.

"You can't take her. She's *my* daughter."

"You could've fooled me."

Tiara

"I don't believe people pay so much money for baby pictures."

"Then come with me and find out for yourself."

So the path of fate was corrected. Mom had woken up and joined the living again—realizing for the first time the power she held over Gracie.

9

I WAS supposed to go to class this morning—who knew prisons have schools—so I told them I had a splitting headache. They let me stay in my cell, but only because it's Friday. I'll have until Monday to dream up a new excuse.

To be stuck in a room with a bunch of other inmates to do whatever they do in a class freaks me out badly. I've never gone to a real school. The idea of competing with girls my age scares the shit out of me. Some of them might be smarter than me, and I don't know how I'd handle being shown off as the class dummy.

Since I have the day to myself, I open my journal again. Might as well write down what's on my mind, as little as that is. Maybe doodling numbers and letters on an empty page will get the memory juices flowing.

Nothing comes easy. The glaring white of the page hurts my eyes, my head starts to throb in earnest. Proves the old proverb—lies always come back to bite you. I close the journal again without a single stroke of my pen, move back on my cot, arms folded behind my head, and enjoy the pain. Keeps me from thinking.

Tiara

Before I can fully withdraw to a place where only my headache reigns, my cell door opens, the shrink strolls in and asks, "How are you doing?"

I thought he was done with me. Didn't he gave up on me after two lousy tries and sent me back in here, in a sweat suit the color of rotting plums?

I want to reply with an *eff-you-too*, but I can't. Shit, shit, shit. This is so pathetic. I'm supposed to be a murderer—crazy, unhinged, out of control, a total nutcase—but I can't say the eff-word.

All I can do is grunt.

"Just wanted to check how you are."

I want him to ask me why I'm not in the mood for idle chit-chat, why I'm not getting up. Can't he see the pulsing vein on my forehead? The tremor of my hands? I want him to feel my frustration over not being able to get the eff-you out of my parched throat.

"Go away."

The shrink shakes his head and bids me goodbye. Before I can wave to hold him back, he's gone. I'm left steaming, furious, my anger directed at him. Why did he bother to come? To punish me with his indifference, show me how worthless I am? Trash, puking from the insult. Damn you, you smart-ass, you no-good shrink-freak, you goddamn cheat. I rant inside until I've exhausted myself.

Hours later I've calmed enough to notice that my head-pounding has turned into a dull ache. I'm limp and weak, my body spent from the burst of red hot anger, my mind clearing. Before the residue of my anger flares up again, I search for something else to focus on other than the stupid shrink I can't call an effing asshole.

My eyes fall on the journal on the small desk under my window, pen next to it. I heave myself off the cot, still wobbly inside, wipe my face dry with my bedsheet, drink a large gulp of water from my stainless steel inmate-suitable water bottle, and sit down on my desk.

Before I have time to think, my pen starts to scribble away.

Birthday Two

Another birthday I'm too young to remember, but an image of Gracie pops up that is closely related to this age. It's Gracie who helps me now making her memories my own. Gracie, always Gracie by my side, even here in prison. What would I have become without her?

She has an album on her lap, full of pictures of me, studies them intently, an adoring smile on her lips. She collected every single shot her photographer friend had taken of me throughout the first year of doing the shots, and by the time my second birthday came around, there were so many, they filled a whole album. When she realized that, she stuck a big pink Number One on the cover. She would stick a new number on every new album.

Tiara

Some years she filled more than one album. Part of my childhood was this stack of albums with colored numbers.

Some evenings, Gracie pulled me up on her lap, squeezed me between herself and an album and turned the pages for us to study me together. There I am, page after page, chubby and adorable, in all sorts of outfits and in the cutest poses Gracie and her photographer friend found creative. Dressed like a cowgirl, holding a toy gun in my right hand. Then on my tummy, little tutu skirt straight up in the air. Or with plastic apples dangling from my ears, sitting in an oversized wooden bowl, surrounded by plastic fruit. Stupid pictures like that. Gracie told me everything I needed to know about my earliest years, and she told it so intently, I can recall them now and make them my own.

"Look at that one," she once said over my head to my mom, "How she smiles at the camera. How beautiful she is. She loves having her picture taken, my little darling-angel."

Mom rarely commented on those praises other than shaking her head silently, or murmuring something like, "Stop giving her ideas."

Truth was, Gracie adored me, and Mom didn't. Gracie loved me, and I loved her back with all I had. I could feel her love like a warm blanket when I was a child. Gracie was my life, she gave me what Mom couldn't, back in the small square house in the third row behind the highway that was our home. The one with the low ceiling to keep the cool air in, and the iron bars on the windows to keep the bad stuff out.

Gracie adored me and spoiled me, her little angel, while Mom cleaned the house and cooked and left me in Gracie's care. Every afternoon Mom withdrew to her room, not to be disturbed. Especially not by me.

"Don't go in there," Gracie said, "she's sleeping," while in fact all Mom did was lay on her bed and stuff her mouth. Meanwhile, Gracie took me on stroller and photography trips.

Mom, true to her word, came along to that second photo session, right after she snapped out of her I-Miss-My-Mike-Melancholy. She watched how Gracie and her photographer friend fussed over me.

"This is ridiculous," she said. "It's taking forever. I'll never understand why anybody would want to be a model."

"Many models become superstars," Gracie's photographer friend said.

"It's not so easy to become famous," Mom said. "You need to be really beautiful."

"You think she's not pretty enough?" Gracie asked in a slow voice.

The photographer friend tried to please my mom.

"Let's take a picture of the two of you, mother and daughter together."

My mom agreed but complained non-stop about the way he was setting it up and how long he took.

"Tell you what, Melissa," he said, "Gracie and I can handle the pictures by ourselves. We don't want to waste your time."

"Who the hell do you think you are?" Mom said. "You can't tell me what to do."

"There go the extra fifty bucks," Gracie said.

"See if I care," Mom said real fast. "If you want to waste your time, go ahead, I got better things to do."

And that was that. Mom refused to come along to the following sessions, out of sheer principal, but she also didn't forbid it. She liked the extra income. It was only Gracie and me, and her photographer friend, I don't remember his name but I vaguely remember a short man ferreting around us, too busy to look me in the eyes. I think Gracie was very upset about Mom behaving so stand-offish. Once I found her in tears, and when I asked her why she was crying, she told me in a hushed voice that Mom had said those picture taking sessions were useless because she thought I was too ugly for that. I wasn't pretty like she had been at my age.

"It hurts me when your mom says you don't have it in you to be famous," Gracie said when I started to cry because she was crying. "I know better. I love you so much. You're my girl, and I know you'll be a star one day. My beautiful angel, I'll see to that. I'll make sure of it. It doesn't matter when your mom gets mean to me, I can handle it. See, I stopped crying. But if she ever gets mean to you, you come to your Gracie and she'll take care of things. Because you're Gracie's girl."

Mom got mean to my Gracie a lot. She didn't get it that I had stardom in me. But Gracie did, and I repaid her devotion with stoic obedience and a smile that drove her and her photographer friend bonkers with delight.

The one picture from this year of me with Mom shows her still reasonably shapely, a little smile contradicting the sadness in her eyes. There are loads of pictures of me and Gracie. She's all southern comfort. Her breasts are cushions, she radiates, glows, gives, is a buffer to the outside world, the way she folds herself around me.

When I was little, I drowned in her love.

10

TIARA's case was a slam dunk. Regardless if the victim regained consciousness or not, her guilt was beyond reasonable doubt.

So, why the hell couldn't he get it out of his brain? The missing motive, that's what bugged him. Without a motive, nothing made sense. She was so young, without him producing a credible motive, the judicial system would target her mental health, label her unstable, get her into a half-ass program designed to keep her away from the public until she was of age. She'd be back on the streets in no time, same as the scum-bag five years ago. He thought he'd gotten rid of the image of the one that got away. The bad one. His malicious, victorious grin when he had walked past him in the court room, a free man although everybody knew he was guilty—a technicality they called it—still haunted him.

Five years gone, and he still felt the pressure on his chest every time he thought of him. Still felt the anger over the injustice every time it entered his mind. Which was about all the time, day and night, clouding his judgment when he should keep an open mind.

Tiara

Fucking bastard. Your motive had been killing for pure joy.

What was Tiara's motive?

Forget it. Stop obsessing.

He got up early, uptight and miserable from lack of sleep and the senseless effort to control his obsessive anger. When the milk carton slipped out of his hand, Macintosh felt another bad day lurking. A rancid smell was no fun to come home to. He should get a cat, not only for spilled milk. The moment this crossed his mind, he could hear Kathy saying that cats shouldn't drink milk. Well, he didn't have one, and she wasn't here, so his imaginary cat could drink beer as far as he was concerned.

"See what mess you got me into," he said, paper towel roll in hand. "Now I'm gonna be late and get stuck in rush hour." He got down on his knees to mop up the puddle. Splashes everywhere, as far as the kitchen cabinet doors. Bloody carton. He mopped, bunched up the soaked sheet, ripped another one, soaked again—damn this.

Where the hell are you, Kathy? Why aren't you here? Why did you have to go? I can't handle this life without you. Didn't you know? My heart was broken too, when our Danielle died.

Pain shot into his heart. He doubled over, body convulsing, breathing labored, his forehead to the floor. The pain hit him hard. Why the hell wasn't she around to take care of things? Of him. Why did she have to leave him with all this shit called every-day-life? The tray in the hallway stacked with unopened mail, the laundry basket overflowing. Dirty dishes in the sink. The bathroom sink, Jesus, she'd tell him off all right. Dried toothpaste, and all those razor clipping, what kind of pigsty was that?

God, how he missed her. She had kept this kind of nuisance away from him, cleaned up after him, organized his life with the deftness of a juggler. And what had he done to thank her? Stayed in the office until he was too tired to ask how her day had been. He'd come home to a gentle smile, a warm meal, a made bed.

The pain passed. He took a few deep breaths, forced himself up, finished the job, wrapped the milk soaked paper sheets in a plastic bag and threw them in the garbage. His knees felt shaky when he left his tiny apartment.

In the car, he sat still to collect himself. The five years of loneliness twisted into deep regret. Robbed him of making things right. If she were still alive, if she'd be around to share his golden years, he would tell her every day how much he loved her and how grateful he was for everything she did for him. But she wasn't. And he couldn't. That suffocating feeling threatened to choke him again. He filled his lungs with air, took off to work.

The day didn't get any better once he arrived at Graveley Street. All morning he shoveled files around. Tedious paperwork at best, but today it performed a strict alibi function. Anything to keep his involvement in Tiara's case to a minimum. But as foul as his mood was, he could only handle so much desk work. He looked around to distract himself. The department seemed unusually quiet. No new homicide in the morning brief, not even a measly brawl with bodily harm to break the monotony.

When Harding strolled by his desk, Macintosh closed the file he'd been fiddling with.

"Enough," he said. "Time to hit the field."

From there on, his day slid further downhill.

First, he and Harding drove to the coffee shop, where they inspected the scene again and interviewed the manager on duty if any additional witness had come forward. Macintosh figured some onlookers, possibly regulars customers, might not want to talk to the police but would brag about their knowledge to other regulars. The coffee shop was crowded. Apparently the place had acquired a morbid kind of celebrity status, and the manager pestered them for more information. His customers wanted to be fed coffee, muffins and details.

"Waste of fucking time," Macintosh said as they left, "he hasn't said a thing we don't know already."

They drove around the corner to St Paul's Hospital, learned from the doctor on duty that there was no chance the victim would regain consciousness in the foreseeable future—if ever. In all likelihood, if she did wake up she'd have permanent brain damage. For one thing, she suffered severe blood loss. For another, she'd gone into cardiac arrest on the way to emergency, which shut down the oxygen flow to the brain for a dangerously long period.

Macintosh summed it up. "A vegetable. And we still don't know who she is."

"Maybe the shrink who's assigned to the girl knows something," Harding said.

Macintosh radioed in for information on the psychiatrist handling Tiara's assessment and was given Dr. Eaton's name. His heart missed a beat. Not him. Not Eaton again.

"Shall I text you his contact number?" staff asked.

"No need," he said.

They drove over to Grandview and dropped by Dr. Eaton's office only to be told the doc couldn't see them. He was over at BYSC. Macintosh felt cheated. Half of him wanted to keep the contact with Eaton at a minimum, the other half wanted to confront the lazy, incompetent bastard. Poor Tiara, she was thrown to the wolves.

"Let's go see Melissa Brown again," he said to Harding. "I can't shake the feeling that she's been hiding something from me. Let's rattle the cage."

When they drove into her street, two things caught their attention. A mobile TV unit drove around the corner at the same moment Melissa and her mother stepped out of their building.

"Hit the brakes," Macintosh said to Harding.

Tiara

The car stopped right next to the women. Macintosh rolled down the window and waved at them. They looked startled at first, then they recognized him. He didn't waste any time explaining, gestured for them to get in the backseat.

"What's going on?" Louise asked after Harding sped off.

"Sorry about that," Macintosh said. "We didn't want the press to see you."

"We should have given those assholes a ticket for speeding," Harding said.

Macintosh gave him a shut-up glance and turned to the backseat.

"Sorry, ladies, but my partner has an intense dislike for the press. Can we take you somewhere?"

"Sure." Melissa leaned forward, her face so close to his he could smell her hair spray. "How about to my daughter?"

Macintosh withdrew. He noticed Melissa's mouth pressed in a tight line, same as he had seen on Louise. Lemon mouths seemed to be an undeniable family trait. He also noticed Louise held her daughter's wrist. A grip, not a touch. A claw.

"We were going to the corner store to pick up a few things, then maybe see a movie'" Louise said. "We wanted to get out of the apartment for a while. You know, being cooped up like that gets pretty boring after a while."

"Not enough excitement for the ladies?" Macintosh said.

"Well, since we've got you in the car," Harding said, "why don't you come to the department with us?"

"Why's that?" Louise said.

Macintosh bit back another pointed comment. "We can get a few questions straightened out and won't have to bother you later on."

"I certainly won't talk to the press," Melissa said. "Not until I've been allowed to see my daughter."

"How come those press people know where my daughter lives?" Louise asked.

Macintosh stuck his head between the seat rests again. "I told you about the video clip. Tiara's name was all over social media. Remember the Vancouver riots after the Stanley Cup loss? The public knew about the whole mess faster than we did. That's the way it is nowadays. Everybody's connected."

"But what do they want from us?"

Melissa yanked her wrist from her mother's grip.

"Oh, for God's sake, Mother, what do you think? They want to talk to me."

"And I'd advise you not to speak to them," Macintosh said.

Melissa drew in a breath. "Is that a gag order?"

He wished. Women like her did more damage to a case by talking to the press than a false confession by a criminal could do. "Sorry, but yes. That's the rule. As long as the investigation is ongoing."

Harding didn't miss a beat. "They only want to get as many gory details as possible. They probably already secured interviews with the eyewitnesses who will miraculously remember all sorts of crap that never happened, loving all the media attention."

Melissa looked hurt. "So everybody can talk but me?"

They drove on in silence. When they arrived at the police station, Macintosh directed the women to an interview room on the fourth floor.

"Can I get you anything?" Harding asked the women when they were seated.

Melissa looked at her mother. Louise said, "Coffee would be good."

"I'll get you some. We'll be back shortly."

"Now that we've got them in there," Macintosh said once they had closed the door behind them and stood in the hallway, "they won't go anywhere soon. I want you to dig into Melissa Brown's background a bit before we go interview her. She grew up here, there should be records all the way back to her birth. Check out Tiara, too. I doubt there will be much about her in the Canadian system, but check anyway."

"Should I contact the US authorities?"

"If you have three months or longer to wait. Cross border communication is a bureaucratic nightmare for any request we make, even if it involves a US citizen. And what have we got here? The perpetrator is Canadian, the victim's nationality is unknown, the assault happened here on Canadian turf, and the whole incident might not even finish up being a homicide."

"You can always ask Josh if we need help," Harding said. When Macintosh didn't reply, he went over to his computer to start his research.

Macintosh decided to give Harding at least half an hour before they'd go back into the interview room. Time to grab a bite to eat, and, more than anything, to gather his thoughts. Sure he could ask Detective Josh, his friend at Houston Homicide, for information on Tiara but Josh had as much on his plate as any overworked detective on any police force, he shouldn't waste his time on checking how a fifteen-year-old potentially deranged Canadian girl had grown up in Texas. Not if he could get this information from the mother next door.

He could feel a sour taste in his mouth again. He disliked the mother, and the grandmother. And, on a sudden vitriolic impulse, the girl, too. Why couldn't she have lost it after he retired? His thirty years on the force shouldn't be crowned by a violent crime involving a girl of Danielle's age.

He shook off the thought and walked over to the canteen where he picked a pre-wrapped mayonnaise-laden triple-decker BLT. Good choice, my man. Help those arteries clog up faster. Walking back, he saw Harding still working his emails.

Macintosh brought his lunch into the room adjacent to the interview room where he could observe mother and daughter. He got settled, unwrapped his sandwich and took a bite, not caring that the white sauce dripped on the table, and looked into the room. Were the ladies aware that it had a two-way mirror and audio? He thought by now everybody knew that, yet these two certainly didn't appear to suspect someone was watching them.

They sat next to each other, silent. Jesus, that kid's mother made his skin crawl. He had no patience with people who let themselves go to pieces like that. Truth be told, he had no patience with anybody any more, but some bugged him more than others.

This was all wrong. The fucking sandwich tasted like shit. He put the rest of his sandwich back in its cellophane wrapper and threw it in the waste paper bin. Then he took it out again. Kathy was a stickler for separating garbage.

The door to the interview room opened. An officer carried a tray with two mugs filled with coffee, a milk carton and a few sugar packets into the interview room.

Macintosh saw Louise jump up. "How long are we supposed to wait in here?"

"Someone will be with you shortly," the officer said and left.

Louise slumped down again, ripped a sugar packet open, poured its contents into one of the mugs, stirred it, slid the mug over to her daughter, who came out of her stupor and pushed the mug with an irritated I'll-get-my-own gesture back to her mother. It sloshed and spilled a few drops of coffee on the table.

Her mother raised her eyebrows but didn't seem offended. She added some milk to the mug, stirred again, straightened in her chair, took a swallow or two.

Melissa took the other mug, ripped open one sugar packet after another, he counted five, stirred them in, prompting Louise to shake her head.

No love lost between those two.

The silent exchange peeked Macintosh's professional interest. He leaned forward. Give me a lead. Give me a goddamn lead. I still got fuck all to go by.

Silence. The women stared holes in the table. He stared at them.

"Fuck this."

He got up, sandwich in hand, to find the proper waste bin outside when he heard Melissa break the silence.

"Whatever they ask, Mother, don't tell them anything. You hear me? Keep that blabbermouth of yours shut, understood?"

Macintosh jolted to attention. A shiver of anticipation sharpened his senses, same as when he was out hiking in the wilderness, listening for the sounds of danger. A moose. A bear. A cougar—you never knew. Had to respect nature. Had to pay attention to the finer nuances.

He left the room, found the right garbage bin, dumped his sandwich, and strolled into the interview room.

Tiara

"Sorry to keep you waiting, ladies. Louise, if you'll follow me to the next room, please. I have Detective Harding waiting to take your statement. And you, Melissa, wait in here. I'll attended to you shortly."

He saw Melissa's quick glance at the mirror, eyes narrowing with sudden fear.

Gotcha.

11

MACINTOSH settled in his chair opposite Melissa Brown, took the two pages Harding had handed him out of a folder and began reading.

"Detective," Melissa said "I really—"

"In a minute," Macintosh said.

"… I really don't know what I can tell you. I got nothing to tell you. I told you everything I know already when you came to my apartment. What else could there be?"

Macintosh put up his hand, finished reading the meagre information Harding had been able to gather on Melissa and Tiara Brown in the short time, slowly placed the pages back in the folder and looked up.

"Where did you and Tiara live before you came back to Canada?"

"We lived in Galveston, in Texas—"

"Address?"

Melissa drew a breath. "It's been a while. It was 358 or 357, I'm not so sure anymore, Carolina Road, I think it was."

Macintosh let his eyes bore into her. "Where did you work?"

Tiara

"Huh? I worked at different places. Supermarkets, you know, wherever I could get a job. It's been tough, being a single mother and all."

Macintosh asked her if by now she'd come up with an idea why his daughter had attacked the woman in the coffee shop. He watched her squirm in her chair, huff and moan as if this question created her physical discomfort.

"As I told you already, I got no idea. No idea at all. Can't imagine what made her do it. That's what's driving me crazy—oh, I didn't mean to say that. A figure of speech, that's all. It doesn't mean you are, right?"

He waited.

Melissa swallowed hard. "Tiara has never, never, I mean never, shown any aggression toward anyone. You can ask anybody."

"Who?"

"What do you mean, who?"

He waited again. Kept staring at her.

"Well, you can ask people in our neighborhood."

"Didn't she have friends here?"

"Friends? Here? You mean in Vancouver? I can't really say. My daughter kept mostly to herself, she's more the quiet type.

"That's strange. A girl her age."

"If I think about it, now that you mention it, sure, she had friends."

He took an empty page out of his folder and slid it over to her. When she frowned, he let his pen follow and smiled at her. "Their names, please."

"Huh? Oh, well, I will, sure I will. Later. I can't think straight now. How could I write anything down now? How can you treat me like that? My daughter is in prison, you want to punish me for that? How dare you?"

After that, she refused to cooperate. But he didn't consider the interview a waste of time. Tiara had friends. Great. He'd find them, talk to them, get their take on what made Tiara snap.

When he went back to his desk he saw Harding sitting at his already. "How did yours go?" he said.

"Sorry." Harding's cheeks went pink. "I tried my best, but I couldn't get anything out of her. She shut down as soon as I asked her why her daughter didn't come back after Tiara's father had died. Should have eased her more gently into the interview. It was over before I could ask her a second question. She only repeated one statement." He looked at his computer screen and read from his interview transcript.

"I can't say anything. I'm only the grandmother. I didn't know Tiara until she came back to Canada three years ago. We haven't been close. Talk to my daughter, she'll tell you everything you need to know."

That evening, Macintosh was restless. He zapped through the channels to find a decent hockey game, but when he saw that his favorites, the Vancouver Canucks, were three goals behind after the first fifteen minutes, he turned off the TV. He got up again, threw the left-over pizza he'd micro-waved for dinner in the garbage and cleaned his plate. He took the Steve Job's bio from the shelf and settled to read it but couldn't concentrate.

At 9:00 pm he gave up and opened his lap-top. An email from his sergeant, with three documents attached, was waiting for him. Transcripts from the interviews they had conducted earlier on, and a copy of a memo from Dr. Stanley Eaton.

Macintosh got a beer from the fridge and settled into his seasoned leather recliner. Its faint tobacco odor dated back to the times when he still enjoyed the occasional cigar. The patina it had developed after many nights of sitting and pondering—on some of which he'd fallen asleep and woke up with a cramped neck—only increased its sentimental value. It was the only piece of furniture he would take with him into his retirement retreat up at Squamish. Him and the old chair, sitting out what was left of his life.

He leaned back, lifted the footrest, lap-top on his thighs, and opened Stanley's memo. In it, the psychiatrist stated in his typically detached brief style that the alleged suspect remained non-disclosive throughout the psychological evaluation, refusing to cooperate with case manager, psychologist, or social worker. Without further assessment it would be impossible to establish the degree of her amnesia, and one would have to speculate if her uncooperative conduct might be self-serving. Point of interest, when asked, she stated her name is Princess Tia.

Princess Tia? Really? That was all you got out of her? Useless, as always.

Forget him.

Next, Macintosh glanced over the interview transcripts, then put the lap-top aside, lowered the recliner a notch, closed his eyes and thought about the one simple word, loaded with hidden meaning, which made it impossible to disregard the interviews. *Blabbermouth*. He couldn't close this case until he understood what it meant. He had a curious nature. Inquisitive, Kathy had called it. You're a prying old goat, Mac, she'd say, that's why you're so good at your job. And right she was. That's why he'd become a detective, won all those citations with medals tucked away in his desk drawer.

The girl was guilty, and he resented her for messing up his final months on the force, but he couldn't close the case without doing his job. Police work didn't establish guilt or innocence. His job was to gather the facts so higher powers could sit judgement. Damn it, he needed motive. He needed the victim's ID.

Something about her mother and her grandmother didn't sit well with him. He couldn't put his finger on it. A hunch, but one that wouldn't let him rest until he figured it out.

The interviews hadn't shed any light on what those two were trying to hide, he'd have to dig deeper. He had a feeling the grandmother would crack first, spill the beans on their precious secret involuntarily. Her own daughter had called her a blabbermouth. Should he zero in on her, then Melissa? Or maybe the other way around was more effective? Before Louise could warn her daughter of his methods. She'd only give Melissa instructions what to say. She'd want to be the boss.

A sigh escaped him. Fuck all those deliberations. Before you bring out the guns and shoot at bystanders, do your job, step by step. Go see the girl. Go figure out why she did it.

Show the loser shrink how it's done.

12

SUNDAY night in the big city. All the people out there can move around and do whatever they want while I'm locked up in a cell of maybe eight by eight feet. Does it bother me? Not really, I wouldn't know what to do with myself out there.

Which doesn't mean I'm on top of the world happy being stuck in here. I'm dealing with the possibility of being guilty, as ridiculous as it seems to me, by pushing the mere thought of it back into the dark spaces of my mind, locking it into a room called rejection. Don't want to know. Instead I concentrate on the day-to-day bullshit of prison existence. What I find most disturbing about this is the thought of having to sit in a classroom tomorrow morning, with other girls next to me. That terrifies me so much I won't be able to sleep all night.

After the third control round by the security guy who shines his flashlight into my room and probably smiles when he sees me wave at him from my bunk bed like a dolphin flapping its fin, I get up, open my journal and fish for new images from my childhood. It really is like fishing. Thoughts appear on the surface of my memory, and when I try to grab them, they slip through my hands and wriggle away. I remember the shrink's advice to anchor my memories.

Birthdays. Right. We're at number three. On many later birthdays Gracie raved on about the special cake she got for me for my third. The cake wasn't like one you see on a birthday card or in a bakery window, the cake says Gracie the way I like to remember her. Very much, Gracie. A flood of images surrounds the cake-picture, a little shaky and blurred at first but gaining clarity fast. I'm sure those images were born out of stories re-told, but I hold the copyright to them now.

Birthday Three

The cake has pink icing decorated with silver candy pellets. Mom lights the three candles, and I'm supposed to make a wish. What does a three-year-old wish for? Not what grown-ups assume. Kids that age live in the moment.

Gracie says, "Don't you want to have a pretty little doll? One you can dress up? I'll make her a dress like yours, and the two of you can look like sisters? Do you want a new dress? Shall I make you one? With a matching bonnet?"

Mom lets out some air, says, yes, that would be lovely. As long as she doesn't have to do it.

Gracie always makes stuff for me. She's so good with her hands—better, much better, than Mom. Gracie spends a lot of time and money on me. I'm grateful for all she's done for me, later on I was, but at age three I didn't understand the concept of grateful yet.

Now I want cake. I grab for the pellets, and Mom slaps my hand, very lightly, but still. I start crying.

Gracie jumps up. "How often do I have to tell you, don't slap my little girl!"

"Oh, it's your daughter now?" Mom yells back to overpower my screeching.

"I want cake."

"See what you've done? You've upset her!"

"Tia want cake!"

That does it. Gracie swoops me up. I stop crying because I can't breathe, she shushes me and tells me her little angel will get cake as soon as she says I'm sorry. All I need to do is say two little words. So sorry.

Gracie is always kind and gentle with me. Teaches me how to get around Mom's wrath when she was in one of her moods. She lets go a little, enough for me to breathe.

"So…"—gasp, sniff, gasp—"so…soddy!"

She gives me cake. I'm on her lap, protected by her softness.

"My poor little mija. Don't cry. Gracie loves you."

Mom starts to say something but the words seem to crumble in her throat. No, 'I love you too, Tia'. Instead, she apologizes to Gracie. Gracie cuts a big slice from the cake and hands it to Mom. Now I've learned another thing about the value of apologizing. This lesson be-

Tiara

comes part of all my birthdays, and every single day in between my birthdays.

There's always something to apologize for, and the fastest way to get the cake, or whatever else I want, is to say, I'm sorry.

Of course Gracie makes the dress, in lime green with white ducks printed on it, and the bonnet, too. For me, and for a doll with a painted porcelain face. I don't recall what happened to the doll. I think I put it in a corner and never touched it. I'm not one for playing with pretty dolls. Plus, and that upset Gracie so much, she brought it up a lot, I spilled grape juice on my new lime green dress on the first day they made me wear it.

My flow of writing stops. I can feel anger coming up again. The anger pushes the words back into the place I have no access to. The words are dying and with them so do I. A slow death. What would my shrink say to that? He'd have a field day with that all right.

No time to think this through. The door opens and he drops in for yet another visit. Freaky.

"Didn't expect you back. How come?"

"After receiving my rather inconclusive assessment of you—in which I have expressed my opinion that I find underlying issues along with my suspicion that your uncooperative conduct might be self-serving—the court has now asked for a full assessment of your mental capabilities."

My anger bursts open. "Self-serving? What's that supposed to mean? You think not talking to you is a trick to make sure I can stay in here? You think that's what I'm after?" My vocal cords are stretched tighter than my nerves. The guy must be nuts if he thinks I'm holding back on purpose. "You think I remember and won't tell?"

To his credit I have to say he mulls over his answer. Gives me time to calm down enough to study his expression. That's what's different today. Not only that he smiled, he looks concerned.

"I think your memory loss is genuine," he says, "but not as extensive as you make out. You're hiding certain aspects of your life."

"How can you think that, if I haven't told you anything?"

"You might not be consciously aware of it," he says, "but I strongly suspect your lack of cooperation is because you don't want to go home."

Oh my, he actually thought this through. Could he help me figure out the rest? Could he? I do need help, but I can't admit that much right now.

"That wasn't hard to figure out," I say. "You know because I told you I don't want to go back to my mom."

"I know as much as you allow me to."

I refuse to say anything to that.

"As I said, the court asked for a full assessment, and your time here will go a lot easier if you're responsive." He pauses again. "I hope you choose to cooperate."

Tiara

I bet they move me back to the IAU for this. They wear green in there. This purple suit gives me the creeps. Of the this-color-seeps-through-my-pores-and-poisons-my-insides kind of creeps. Plus, when I'm in the IAU I don't have to attend morning classes. Now, that's a big deal.

"Depends. What's involved in this full assessment?"

"A comprehensive assessment includes psychiatric interviews, full psychological assessments with IQ and personality testing, interviews, as well as a psychosocial assessment by a nurse and social worker."

"You've got to be kidding me!"

"I kid you not."

"Not done by you?" My voice goes up a pitch. This is not good. "You mean a bunch of strangers will want to check me out?"

"I usually don't do those kind of assessments. Your lawyer will ask for an independent assessment, and, if you can afford it, a private psychologist."

He wasn't joking when he said I played my card wrong. I don't want another shrink. I can barely handle him, but at least he doesn't invade my space. Even in my compact living unit he leaves as much space as humanly possible between us. He smiled, and he understood the part about my mom.

"I don't want a stranger. Please. Can't you do it?"

"You have a right to refuse and to choose."

"I do?" Who would have thought? "If that's true, you can tell them I won't talk to anybody but you."

13

MACINTOSH spent the bigger part of a sleepless Sunday night to persuade himself that it would be a total waste of time to see Tiara, achieving nothing but throwing his five-year-old hard-fought emotional balance back into turmoil. She'd never confess. With a girl so young, the damage done by her upbringing must be irreversible. She was ruined for a normal life and would never admit to her mistakes.

Come Monday morning, he went to see her.

When the warden brought the girl in, she looked every bit as sullen as last time in the interview room at the station.

"I'm Detective Pete Macintosh," he said.

"No need to say that every time."

"You remember?"

"Only what's happening right now. Sorry to be such a disappointment."

The back of his neck itched. He scratched it. "Disappointment is tied to expectations," he said. "I didn't exactly have high expectations when I came here."

She didn't contradict him or try to explain or—God forbid—start to defend herself.

"Why bother to come, then?"

"I'm the one to ask questions here," he said. "You're the one to answer."

"Make me."

He smirked.

"The shrink told you," she said, "but you can't admit that because he isn't supposed to give out information. Right?"

"Depends."

"On what?"

She asked too many questions, but this round went to him. He got her talking, involved her in a conversation. Before she'd realize, she'd open up to him.

"If it helps our investigation," he said. "Dr. Eaton can inform me of anything you say to him."

"So all the movies and TV shows get it wrong? About the confidentiality, I mean."

"Not entirely. Dr. Eaton doesn't inform me while an assessment is ongoing, but once it's done, he hands his report over to the court, and us." He paused to give his next comment sufficient weight. "He's finished his initial assessment. It's been forwarded to me."

"What does it say?"

Nice try. Macintosh leaned back.

"That you like to call yourself Princess Tia," he said. "Aside from that, there isn't much in it that'll help me."

"Help you with what?"

"Anything to speed up the investigation. The sooner I can wrap up this case the sooner I can get on with my life."

"But that is your life, interrogating criminals, right?"

Her face lit up with sudden interest. Was she baiting him? He had to smile.

"I'll be done with this soon. Talking to criminals won't be part of my life much longer. Once I'm done with this case, I head north to my quiet little place in a small country town, start my new life and forget about all the bad things I had to deal with in the old one. And all the bad people."

She smiled back at him, with a sadness that dulled the little spark in her eyes. He had to look away.

"You mean me, don't you? I'm one of those bad ones. You think you know what I've done and can't wait to have me locked up. On top of that, you resent me because I'm not helping you solve your case quickly. But even if I wanted to, I can't help you. I don't remember anything."

"That's what you say."

"No," she said, kicking her right heel hard on the linoleum flooring. "That's how it is. I wish I'd remember, even the bad stuff, but I'm not like you."

What did she mean by that? Him, dwelling over the bad stuff? Stuck in the past? Hadn't he just told her his plans for the future? Forgetting the life he led, with everything in it. She couldn't mean him. She meant herself.

"Are you saying bad things have happened to you?"

"If there were bad things in my past, I've forgotten about them. I wish I hadn't. Not like you. I'm sorry for you if you want to go away into that country place and forget all the bad stuff that happened in your life. You shouldn't. The bad stuff is part of you as much as the good stuff."

Nice, a fifteen-year-old philosopher. But this could be an angle to draw her out.

"Don't make this about me. I'm interested to hear what's gone on in your past. What you call the bad stuff. Can you elaborate on that?"

She didn't flinch, sat there with her arms crossed.

He considered another approach. Should he tell her that he bought his house by the coast years ago, when Kathy was still alive? They wanted to retire there. It was never meant to be an escape from reality, not then anyway. He couldn't bring himself to open up, so he asked again, "You remember nothing about your past?"

She didn't acknowledge hearing his question, seemed frozen in the private retreat she'd created for herself. He wouldn't be able to break through her barrier, at least not today. He stood and left without another word.

On his way to the station, he went over their conversation—you couldn't call it an interview by any stretch of imagination—and got seriously annoyed. Her comment about him wanting to forget had hit target. A lance, gone through layers of decaying skin and flesh until it hit the center of his pain. Jolted him into pondering the question he thought solved and eradicated: Was it really so bad to forget? How else would he be able to carry on living and get some enjoyment out of his final years if he didn't at least attempt to forget the sadness of his own life? He pictured himself on his porch—sitting on what Kathy always called the old couples bench—with the sun setting behind the cluster of fir trees on the opposite hill. Its last rays were supposed to warm his bones but all he could expect in future was sitting there shivering from the hollowness inside him.

The anger shifted, turned to blame. First at fate, then the girl. To hell with her, she'd touched a nerve that wasn't hers to fool with. She had no right to talk to him like that. Make him question his well laid out plan. His whole future. How dare she tell him he was a sorry ass? Giving up on himself to avoid facing the inevitability of life. Who was she to judge? All very well when you can't remember a goddamn thing.

Two things hit him simultaneously. First, he began to believe that she couldn't remember what she'd done, and second, she was right wanting her memories back, good or bad. She was so damn right.

If he kept his own memories alive, he'd have them to take with him, and he wouldn't feel so goddamn lonely, on that old couples' bench in the sunset.

14

THE moment the detective left, the shrink—now officially my very own shrink-doc, I won that battle—shows up. I'm sent straight from the visitor's room to a small office inside the prison unit for our first full assessment session.

"For the time being, there's no need to move you back into IAU," he says. "We'll do morning sessions here in this office until I've assessed your mental health."

Phooey, I'm not allowed to change from purple to green. At least I'm avoiding school.

"Penalty for my refusal to see anybody but you?" I ask.

"Do you feel guilty about that?"

"You didn't answer my question."

"It's not penalty," he says. "It's procedure."

"I don't feel guilty."

"Never?"

This is our first real, doc-to-patient session. If I answer this question, he'll think I'm easy to trap. We do a staring-sparring match for about a minute, until the loneliness of our last brief meeting comes back to me. How desperate I was for him to figure me out. I cave in like a sink hole.

"Stop staring at me."

"Don't think you've lost," he asks as soon as I shut my mouth again. Which of course is precisely what I'm thinking. "When you're silent, you lose, when you talk, you win."

I dwell on this for a moment. The point is, I've got nothing to say. The stuff I do remember by now is nothing but second-hand. Whatever people, Gracie mostly, told me about my childhood surfaces, but nothing else. Like I have a safety valve that blocks all of my own memories and allows passage only to unreliable recollections. What good is that?

"Are you making progress with your memoirs?"

Clever. He makes even the cheapest crap sound important and classy. Like Mom always wanted to be, and never was. *Sorry, Mom, did I hurt your feelings?*

"Not really," I say. "A murderer is not a writer."

He has a white beard in a white face which nearly swallows this gentle smile of his. His eyes are hidden behind his glasses, so I can't tell if they are as kind.

He shifts in his chair and opens his notebook. "Are you ready to talk now?"

"What do you want to talk about?"

"What do you want to talk about?"

"How about, why did you come to see me today?"

"What do you think?"

"Because you want to know why I did it," I say.

"Why did you?"

He makes a face like a dog in front of an empty bowl, expecting to get it filled. Sorry to disappoint you, doc.

"I can't for the life of me think why I would want to hurt anybody."

"Have you never hurt anybody?"

"Hurt? They say I tried to kill her."

He writes something down. I wish I could see what it is. I don't know if I could hurt, far from kill, somebody. But I can't be sure. It's his job to find this out for me.

"Will you help me figuring this out?"

He stops writing. "My job is to assess your mental state."

I must look disappointed, because he quickly adds, "You'll have to figure it out yourself but I will guide you toward cognition. Look at it this way, you feel lost now, like a blind person, groping around in a void, and I'll be by your side and describe the landscape you're in until, bit by bit, you start recognizing certain points."

That's how it must feel when one wants to hug somebody—if one could stand to touch people. I let out a long breath to show him how pleased I am with his answer. He's given me something to hold on to. And there is more.

Tiara

"I've talked to the doctors at St Paul's Hospital," he says. "Do you want to know what happened to the woman you stabbed?"

"Yes."

"She's still alive."

I should be pleased about this, too, instead, I feel disappointed.

15

THE past days had been the worst days of her life. Ever since she stumbled through that stupid interview at the police station, she'd been on edge. It didn't help that a small but excited press mob practically camped in front of her Eastside building, harassing her the moment she stepped out, as if she was a celebrity. *Melissa, how's Tiara? Has she confessed yet? Why did she do it? Come on, Melissa, talk to us.*

But she wasn't allowed to.

Her mother offered to keep her company, but Melissa couldn't stomach her constant all-will-be-sorted-out-just-let-me-handle-this take on the situation.

Nothing would ever be sorted out again. Nobody could sort out this mess, not even her mother. I need to be alone, she said to her mother, ignoring her hurt look.

She couldn't go back to work at the supermarket, and she couldn't go outside if she didn't want to face the mob, so she spent the days wandering up and down the hallway, stuffing herself with chocolate chip cookies. Her little princess didn't want to see her. Tiara should be seeking the comfort only a mother could give. But does she beg the authorities for a visit? No. Worse, she tells this terrible detective that she doesn't want her mother by her side. Nothing was as it should be. If she could only see her and talk some sense into her.

If only.

Melissa hadn't turned on the TV for days, but she couldn't go to sleep and needed something to take her mind off all the trouble. What a mistake. Tiara was still a news item, although this time as part of a report on the shocking rise of teenage violence. They aired the coffee shop clip again on the late news, showing the attack in slow-motion, making it even more horrific, merciless, inhuman in its brutality. The shape of the woman on the ground seemed somehow vaguely familiar. Melissa moved closer to the screen and tried to make out her face but there was either too much movement or Tiara's arm or the victim's hand was in the way. Oh my God, did the knife poke into her eye?

The anchor said the victim was alive but in critical condition. The police had not yet been able to identify her, and the alleged suspect could not be named, being a minor, but their—the TV station's—very own and super professional investigative team learned that she was a fifteen-year-old Canadian citizen who lived most of her life with a single parent in the States. And that they would follow that lead because their viewers had a right to know.

That did it. Melissa turned off the TV.

Sleep was impossible. Her mind ran the news report on endless loop. Over and over again it ran and mocked her. Tiara was a criminal. Tiara was the daughter of a single mom. So it must all be her single mom's fault.

To hell and back with your gag order, Mister Bigshot Detective. First thing in the morning, I'll go downstairs and tell that press mob camping outside my entrance that Tiara's father would have married me if he hadn't died.

She could have sworn she was awake all night, but when the phone on her bedside table rang, the clock showed eight-thirty.

Detective Macintosh asked if he could come over and see her. He'd like to talk to her again. Had a few more questions. Around noon, then?

What choice did she have? Now she couldn't even set the record straight with the press. Not until he'd been and gone.

She got dressed and made herself a mug of tea. She took the mug to her kitchen window spot and looked into the morning sun, wishing it would rain. A thunderous, out of control rainstorm to keep him busy with other things. To keep him away.

The sun shone right in her face. Oh Lord, what had she done? Why had she promised the detective she'd prepare a list of Tiara's friends? Now he'd insist on getting one. But she couldn't tell him the truth, could she? If he found out the truth, he'd really go after her. Dear

Lord. Dear Lord. Nobody must know the truth. Too awful, too shameful. Her heart began to hammer, she broke out in a cold layer of sweat. Breathe. Calm down. Keep it together. Puddles formed under her breasts and soaked though her blouse. Change clothes, rinse your wrists with cold water. Her legs wouldn't carry her, she couldn't move an inch. All she could think of was, *go away*. Leave me alone. I got nothing to do with what happened. I'm the innocent one here. Go, ask the ones who are guilty. Not me. I got nothing to say. No list to make. *Please*.

By the time the doorbell rang she was a sniffling, snorting, bawling mess.

The detective took a step back. They both needed a moment to gather themselves. His moment was faster, but she caught the disgust. The repulsion.

She opened the door wider and waved him inside.

16

WHEN Melissa opened the door, Macintosh noticed her face looked swollen, all wet. She'd been crying. But her eyes were cold, her mouth hard.

"We need to talk," he said.

She asked him into the kitchen, excused herself and disappeared for at least five minutes. When she came back, she appeared more composed, her face still a blotched mess, but dry.

"So Tiara wants to see me now?" she said.

He took a seat at the kitchen table. "No."

She paced, wringing her hands, puffing in her effort to find the right words. "I didn't get around to doing that list of Tiara's friends yet. I can't concentrate on anything. All the heartache and stress I have to endure, you got no idea what I'm going through."

What list? Tiara's friends? Right. He'd forgotten all about it. Must be important, then. Why that? He watched her closely. Her nose flared, small pearls of sweat on her quivering upper lip. She reminded him of a rabbit in a cage, taking in the scent of danger. Her distrust of him was so obvious, he decided to soften her up a bit.

Tiara

"You can do that list later, Melissa," he said, all buttery tone and gentle expression. "I'm here for a different reason. I've gone over the statement you made at the station again, and I have a few more questions."

"I don't know how I could help you. I told you already, I don't know anything."

"Oh, but you do. You know more than you're aware of, and we need to find out what it is if we're going to help your daughter."

She finally sat down. "What do you want to know?"

He opened his notebook, pretended to read. "To start with, you said you don't know the victim. How can you be so sure?"

"I didn't say I'm sure. I said, I have no idea who she could be. Her face was never shown on TV, at least not clear enough to really see her. It was all so shaky. And you never gave me her name. So how would I know?"

"You've got a point there. Unfortunately we're a bit stuck on that one. She had no ID on her, and so far nobody has come forward with a missing person's report to match the victim. We think she could be Hispanic. Not sure on that one, of course. Her face is not recognizable yet, we need to wait for the swelling to go down before we can take and circulate her picture. If she survives, she'll most likely lose one eye. We'll have to wait for her to regain consciousness which could be a long ways off."

He studied her reaction, thought he detected a faint widening of her eyes when he mentioned Hispanic. What was she trying to hide?

"So, you got any ideas on that? Could it be somebody your daughter might have known?"

"No."

"Listen, Melissa, we're not getting anywhere with this attitude of yours." His voice stayed smooth. "You're not helping."

"But how could I, if I don't know anything? I told you, I can't imagine who that woman could be. What makes you think she could be Hispanic?"

He crossed his arms in front of his chest. "When she was attacked, she yelled something in Spanish."

Melissa didn't miss a beat. "So? I don't understand what you are getting at."

"We find it a bit too much of a coincidence that your daughter, who grew up in Texas and comes back here only three years ago, would stab a woman of Hispanic origin totally unprovoked and in broad daylight, and that this woman is a total stranger to her. Way too much coincidence, in fact."

Melissa nibbled on her lower lip as if she were mulling over what he'd said. "No, honestly, I can't imagine who that woman could be."

"Why don't we try and work on the wider picture then. Maybe we can come up with something together. Why don't you tell me a little bit about your daughter?"

"Like what?"

"To start with, why she calls herself Princess Tia?"

Melissa looked astonished. "She told you that?"

"Yes."

"Oh, I'm surprised she'd even remember that. It was a child's game, that's all. Most children give themselves fantasy names, play names, you know. With Tiara it was Princess Tia whenever she wanted to be somebody else. Play names for play time."

"She's not a child anymore. Is she a bit slow? I mean, for her age and all?"

"Of course not. I told you before, she has a good mind but she always liked to play games." Melissa's eyes clouded over again.

"Describe her to me," Macintosh said. "Anything that comes to your mind."

"The last years haven't been easy for her. I'm not trying to make excuses for what she's done, but don't you think a judge should take that into consideration? That she was a bit like a fish out of water. I tried my best to help her adjust, but at that age it's tough to get into their heads. To help them. Surely you know how tough that is. If you have kids, you know."

"I don't." My girl Danielle. None of your business.

"Lucky you," Melissa said. "They are nothing but trouble. When Tiara was born, I was glad to have her, but now—"

He could see her drifting off again. Fifteen years back.

"So, you think Tiara wanted to stay in Texas?"

"Oh, sure. Yes, of course. She had so much going for her. She was a child model, you know, made lots of money doing it."

This was new.

"Can you tell me a little about that?"

"She was posing for lots of different agencies, for posters and advertisements and such. She had the face for it, and the attitude. The camera loved her. Honestly, she was one of the best-looking little girls in the whole country. She was a natural, until... "

Macintosh leaned forward. "Until what?"

"She grew out of it. Grew up, I mean. Lost her baby face. All that cuteness, gone. Even I had to admit that she wasn't that adorable any more, and I'm her mother. Maybe I should have better prepared her for it."

Now her eyes started to fill with tears again. She fought them, swallowed, her composure wilting fast.

"I was so busy, caught up in this whirlwind of … of … of happiness, activity, luck. I hadn't had much luck till then, you know, but Tiara was a blessing to me back then. Oh, listen to what I'm saying. Then. I mean, she still is. I have to stand by her, that's what I need to do. That's what any good mother would do."

After a few more questions that yielded more motherly self-pity, he decided to call it a day, but he made a mental note to ask Harding to research into Melissa's claim of Tiara's fame.

"You'll hear from me again," he said. Then, at the door already, he remembered how much she had fretted over the list of Tiara's friends. "And don't forget to make me that list."

17

THE shrink didn't show up this morning. Rotten luck. I'd rather take another session with him than attend morning class, even if his end game is to crack me open and pick the juicy bits out my shell. To be totally honest with myself, I want him to get through to me. By now I have to admit to myself—and really only to myself—that I need help. I can't figure out on my own what makes me tick.

Attending school is certainly not helpful in this process. I plead a headache again, but they only give me a Tylenol and escort me out of my living unit to the classroom. Every time we turn a corner, there's a heavy metal door that opens only when my guard touches the electronic lock with a special key that looks like a credit card. Once we step through the doorway, it closes all by itself with a noisy clunk. Now I understand the faint clunk-clunk-clunk that travels all the way into my cell. Doors closing, one after another. All day long the clunk-clunk goes on. I guess the guards are used to the sound, but I flinch every time I hear a final clunk behind me.

Many clunks later they deposit me in a small room with four other girls who pretend to take no interest in me.

Tiara

They're all my age, all in purple, moping, apathetic, clearly not wanting to be here. That's something we have in common, I guess. I sit down and sulk with them. What a gigantic waste of time. What would I, or any of them, do with an education? Do they think I'll be the Prime Minster of Canada one day, or the Premier of British Columbia, or the Mayor of Vancouver? I won't even get a low-level job in a fast-food diner when I eventually get out. I'll be an ex-convict, my past being public property. They'll wallow in the filth they dig up about me. Instead of a scarlet letter A branded on my forehead, it'll be a big fat F. Filth, eff-ing filth, that's how I'll be marked. I'll be an old woman before they let me forget what I'm supposed to have done.

So I sit here, as far as possible from the other four girls that have to go through the same education motions as me, and try and think about more important things than grammar rules and mathematical equations (which, by the way, are far below my level of knowledge, *thank you, Mom*). Like birthdays. Think of birthdays. I need to figure out what kind of filth the F stands for.

They won't let me write in my journal while the teacher goes through her curriculum, and I certainly won't open my secret weapon in front of girls with pea brains. Sitting so close to them gives me hives. I start rubbing the skin on my arms to relieve the discomfort, thinking back to other girls my age I've come into contact with. Woohoo, the class room fills with pretty girls. I can't wait to get back to my cell to keep their images alive.

Birthday Four

A few months ahead of my fourth birthday, the photographer friend told Gracie about a local beauty pageant. They had a section for girls of all ages, but the important one was for ages four to six, the Pretty Princess category. He showed her pictures from last year's winner, pictures he'd been commissioned to take, and both he and Gracie said I outdid this pudding-faced Plain-Jane in every aspect. I had the best of both of my parents. I had my father's dark eyes rimmed with long black lashes and my mother's elegant bone structure. A combination of Dad's bronzed skin and Mom's porcelain complexion resulted in a perfect sand colour that allowed me to tan golden brown without ever burning.

"It's not too late to enter her," the photographer friend said.

He didn't need to do much convincing to persuade Gracie.

"The Pretty Princess winner goes on to National American Miss. Your girl can become famous. You can make a lot of money."

Gracie checked through the competition rules. I wasn't even four yet, so obviously I don't remember how this pageant thing came about, but my God, Gracie talked about it often enough. As it turned out, nobody asked for my birth certificate. Only a parental signature was needed. Truth be told, Gracie could have signed it herself. Mom had been so out of it when I was born she

Tiara

never noticed the name on my birth certificate. It read Tiara Rodriguez. Gracie had faked her brother's signature, and because his death had not yet been officially registered, she got away with it. For the authorities, Graciella Rodriguez was my mother.

But Gracie knew she couldn't keep my participation in the contest a secret, so she went home with the forms and told Mom everything the photographer friend had told her. The winner got a crown, a banner, a trophy, roses—and one thousand dollars. She could advance to national competition, a modeling contract, scholarships, traveling opportunities, God knows what else. The contest was the stepping stone, the door opener for an amazing career. One little stroke of Mom's pen could change my life, her life, the life of the three of us as we knew it.

Mom hesitated. "Like that girl JonBenet? You know, the one who was in all those beauty pageants, and then got murdered? The media crucified her parents. It was in all the papers."

"But that had nothing to do with it," Gracie said. "The girl was murdered in her own home, not at a beauty contest."

"Oh."

Mom liked the idea of her little daughter being admired on stage. That was a totally different matter from those boring photo sessions with that arrogant photographer friend of Gracie's. Lots of people in the audience, maybe even TV cameras. The moms of those little girls were key to their success, nothing happened without them. This sounded exciting. Gracie told her, we'd be staying in hotels, getting roses and chocolate and money—and sparkling crowns.

"Maybe that's why I called her Tiara," Mom said. "Maybe fate knew that all along."

"You have to sign here. That's all you need to do. Don't worry about a thing. I'll handle it, same as the photo sessions."

Mom must have thought of the glory. "But I'm her mother. People will expect to see me there."

"You want to be in charge?" Gracie said. "That's fine with me. You fill out the whole registration, all five pages of it, and pay the fifty-dollar entrance fee."

"No, no," Mom said when she heard it cost money to launch my career. "You go ahead, register her. I know how much this means to you. But I will come along to the pageant."

My shrink had to change his schedule. From now on he can see me only on those afternoons when he comes to the center anyway.

There go my school-free morning hopes, but I have no say in any of his arrangements. I'm the non-paying customer here, free-loading on his legal-aid generosity. As the center admin can't be sure when he'll show up, I'm excused from all the afternoon activities I would normally have to attend, which sweetens the bitter pill a little. The company I'm forced to keep at morning classes drains me enough. I can at least hang out on my own in my cell every afternoon until I'm called to the small office reserved for his visits. I spend my solitary hours wisely, I write in my journal or stare at the wall.

Today he shows up late.

Since I decided to use his skills for self-analyzing the mess called me, I take great care to watch his tactics. So far, he hasn't used pressure, made no demands. He explained he's supposed to do a few tests which are designed to establish the degree of my madness, but that's a bit difficult with me not cooperating fully. Which is not an act and not by choice. Honestly, I wish I could give him more than the memories that feel like washed out hand-me-downs.

Being non-disclosive, as he calls it, empty-headed, as I call it, means I contributed little to his efforts up to now. Today, though, I have something on my mind. I open our session with the question I have mulled over since his last visit.

"When you gave me the good-news shit about the woman still hanging in there, you seemed pleased. Why?"

"It would take quite a burden off your defending lawyer if she survives. That, and you being a minor, could swing things in your favor. We might be lucky."

He says we as if he's my partner in crime. That pisses me off, and I'm not sure why.

I try to imagine her alive. Nothing comes to mind. My pissed-off feeling intensifies. I want that woman to get out from under the covers of my amnesia blanket. I resent her existence. I hate resenting a stranger. I hate her.

He gives me an odd look.

I shouldn't dwell on hating people without a face and a name. Won't open doors for me. I blow out the hate with a strong breath, change the subject.

"What's this about a lawyer? I didn't know I had one."

"You don't, yet. Your case worker has been in contact with your mother, but she has no funds for a private defense, so the juvenile court will appoint one for you."

"I don't need one," I say, and I mean it. I don't want one of those mediocre, bored, underpaid legal-aid types who don't give a shit about me. I want to figure out if it's true what they accuse me of, and if so, I want to know what drove me to act like a crazy person. I want to figure it out with the help of my shrink and nobody else, and once I've figured it out, we can both forget about it and I can rot away in my cell in peace and quiet.

By the way, I won that first contest. The pageant crowned me Miss Texas Princess, age four to six, at the age of three years and ten months. Mom came along that time, and to all the future contests. She and Gracie had come to a silent understanding—a cease-fire of sorts. Mom would bask in my pageant glory in front of a live audience and let Gracie handle the tedious photo sessions in a stuffy studio.

Tiara

"I wouldn't come along if you paid me," she'd say to Gracie. "I don't know how you can stand it—there's nothing to do but sit and wait."

Little did Mom know that Gracie stopped attending the sessions soon after the first one. She took me there, and waited until the photographer who insisted that relatives shouldn't be present for the shoot, got me set up, then she left the room. I guess Mom was right. There was nothing to do for Gracie except sit and wait.

That first pageant victory was really special. I was told many times what a day of utter joy it had been, with Gracie and Mom so happy that they hugged each other and cried for the rest of the day. They took the roses and the thousand dollars. They told me how proud they were of me and what a bright future lay ahead of me, and them.

18

AFTER Macintosh left, Melissa stayed in the kitchen, fuming.

This pit-bull detective wouldn't let up. On anything. As if this list of friends was so important. If she didn't give it to him, he'd come back, and back, and back. But how could she give him what he wanted? Tiara didn't have any friends.

She'd always been a loner. She'd never been close to anybody in Vancouver, and growing up in Texas she never sought out friends. It wasn't for lack of opportunity, she'd come in contact with lots of girls her age down south, at every beauty pageant, but she never started a friendship with any of them. Once—she'd been four or five then—a girl in a contest came up to her in the hotel lobby holding a teddy bear with a heart-shaped pendant dangling over its fluffy tummy. When the girl was close to Tiara, she extended her hand with the teddy bear—a generous gesture, delivered with a generous smile. *You want to be my friend?*

Tiara slapped the little girl's hand so hard the teddy sailed over the carpet in the hotel lobby, bounced off a stainless-steel rubbish bin, the heart-shaped pendant clink-clonking against the metal, and landed on its tummy next to a suitcase with rollers. The owner of the suitcase, the mother of another contestant, picked it up. Thinking it was Tiara's (everybody always centered their attention on Tiara, she had this air about her), she went to hand it back to her. By then, the generous little girl had lost her smile—children can change their moods so quickly. She tried to grab the teddy back, and at the same time she tried to hit Tiara. The two of them were slapping at each other, trying to hit, not targeting properly, but still. The grown-ups had to separate them, screaming and kicking.

"What on earth possessed you?" Melissa asked Tiara once they were back in their room. "You could have said, No, thank you. The other girl only wanted to make friends with you."

"Mom, you are soooo stupid," Tiara said with those airs. "She probably sneezed on that stupid bear so I'd get sick and lose the next time."

She could never tell Detective Macintosh about this. He would only turn it into *so, your daughter always had a tendency to violence?* But aside from that long ago and in hindsight rather harmless incident, Tiara had never been aggressive. That she had now flipped out in public and attacked a complete stranger in that coffee shop was an isolated, out-of-character rage thing. Chalk it down to teenage confusion. It was a phase, nothing else. Sure, she'd been a touch unbalanced when they left Texas three years ago, but that was to be expected. And anyway, didn't most kids that age go through rough patches? Entertainment Tonight often featured young stars who went through difficult times and then had a fabulous comeback.

Melissa could feel another wave of depression coming.

Tiara at eighteen in a flowing evening gown, with a smile brighter than the sun, lighting up the auditorium, waiting for the crown to be placed on her proudly raised head. Her daughter, Miss America at last. All those dreams, all those hopes for the future, where were they now?

She should make an official complaint about this detective. She'd seen it in his face, he hated her. He'd been pushing her to say the wrong things. But she'd held her own. Even when the name came up. Princess Tia. Really. None of his business what Tiara called herself. For the police, she was Tiara Brown.

If only the detective would stop pestering her. Her explanation sounded pretty plausible, but maybe she could do better than that. She looked at her watch. Twelve-thirty. She called her boss at the 7-Eleven and asked for another week's leave.

Now a whole week lay ahead of her. Enough time to convince Tiara to see her and make her understand what to say and what to keep mum about. Why did she refuse a visit from her own mother? Did she still pine for Gracie?

Gracie had always been jealous of her being Tiara's mother. Typical for barren women. Sometimes they even stole babies out of hospitals, that's how much they wanted one of their own. With her being so weak and desperate after the birth, Gracie stole her child and turned that girl against her from day one. It was Gracie's fault that Tiara never respected her as a mother. Tiara would have to understand that she was in charge now.

Melissa went to the window and looked down. A white van was parked on the curb opposite her block. She couldn't read the logo on its side, but it could be a press vehicle. Sure enough, a man with a camera around his neck got out and looked up to her window. As soon as he saw her, he raised it and clicked away. Melissa darted aside, then, after a brief moment, she positioned herself in full view again. She raised her hand. The guy dropped his camera and stared at her.

She waved at him.

His head jerked from left to right, making sure he was the one she meant, then he put his thumb up, climbed in the van, came back out carrying a much larger camera and a tripod. He shouldered the equipment and raced toward her entrance as if he was in a gold medal trial.

19

THE food at BYSC is plain but acceptable. That's okay with me, I don't care much for food anyway, not since I outgrew my childish cravings for sugary comforts. Ice cream and cookies? Not any more, not for me, thank you very much. I'm one for a slice of pizza or a burger with onions and ketchup if I get hungry at all. I'm a rather small person, in height and size, I don't need much to keep me going. Would hate to turn into a flesh-mountain like some people I know.

After lunch, I have an unexpected visitor.

The visitor is the director of this facility. A woman. They put a woman in charge. I force my face into neutral but shit almighty, am I on guard the moment she stands at my cell door and tells me to come join her in the community area of my unit.

The lady prison boss sits down in an easy chair opposite me, legs together in a straight line, hands clasping a file on her lap. My uncomfortable feeling increases. I feel a prescient warning in having somebody sit opposite me, assessing me with eyes sharp as precision instruments.

Tiara

She breaks her inspection, looks down, opens the file, looks up again with a smile, and tells me that she has a concern. Her voice is clear and light, warm. My muscles relax a little and I start breathing again.

"The center functions by giving the residents rights and responsibilities," she says. "You earn points through good behavior, and the more points you earn, the higher your level will be."

"I've read the manual."

"You're currently on level one."

"The lowest."

"I've been informed by your psychiatrist, Dr. Eaton that you find it difficult to interact with other inmates. I have therefore issued instructions that new admissions will be moved to other living units first as long as we have space available."

I feel a surge of warmth toward my doc.

"He also mentioned that we should keep the afternoons free for his consultations with you. I've agreed to his request. As you can't participate in our extracurricular activities, you won't earn extra points."

"I'd only use them for the vending machine."

"We can't make too many exceptions. I'm willing to excuse you from those afternoon classes, but you need to understand the implications of it and indicate that you accept them."

"I read in the manual that you have a gym in here."

She's already up.

I jump up quickly, too. "Would it be possible for me to work out there? On my own, I mean, without others around?"

"I'll discuss this with Dr. Eaton."

Audience over. She leaves me sitting there, pondering rights and responsibilities. But she smiled when she left, and I can't help thinking that she'll make it possible for me to work out in privacy, without sweaty gossiping peers next to me.

About rights and responsibilities I know plenty, probable more than most grown-ups. From my days as a beauty pageant contestant, I know that the responsibility part of the equation usually outweighs its so closely connected counterpart. The rights part is the later twin, the one that didn't get enough oxygen to develop properly.

Thinking about beauty queens takes me back with a vengeance. A flash-back, ready to be recorded. I relax in my now visitor-less home, pull up the chair still warm from the lady boss, deposit my legs on it, journal on my thighs, and start jotting down what comes to mind.

Birthday Five

After winning the Miss Texas Princess, everyone expected me to win the National American Miss four months later.

I didn't.

Gracie and Mom cried foul. The winning girl was not nearly as beautiful as me. How could the judges, those hypocritical blockheads, those astigmatic amateurs, not have seen this?

I remember small, fleeting parts of this strange pageant—a glaring light, adults confusing me, arguing—the rest is filled in with Gracie-talk. She told me how we drove in our beat-up old car to Austin the day before the pageant, and got settled in a motel room the three of us shared. Twin beds, me and mom sharing one.

The two of them were really nervous. She said I acted up because I could feel the tension in the car which only got worse in the stuffy room. Grown-up nerves mean they ignore me, snap at me, tell me to be quiet and stop fidgeting while they both fidget around as if they're sitting on hot stones. Then I pout and cry until one of them responds with soothing gestures and promises of ice cream and cookies. It only works when they're not in competition anxiety.

That evening, they went at each other like roosters in a cockfight, all beaks and claws and ruffled feathers.

"Damn it, you know how important glitz is. That dress is way too frilly. It looks cheap, and it's pink." By now Mom hated pink, she hated the 'trashy and childish' designs Gracie came up with. "It makes her look dumpy, not cute."

"Oh yeah? If you'd picked the right hair style the dress would work so much better. Her hair needs to be pulled up, with pink ribbons. See, here—" Gracie grabbed my hair and yanked it up. I already knew that throwing a tantrum at this stage wouldn't bring the desired result. No cookies and ice cream while they were at each other's throats. So I got away, crawled into bed, hid under the covers and sulked.

Next morning, they hadn't made up but had to work together to get me ready for competition. They must have succeeded, because the picture taken after this pageant shows me with the Most Photogenic Miss crown on my perfectly coiffed dark curls, standing on stage, still pouting my lips. Adorable Mini Drama Queen.

But photogenic sulking doesn't pay much, and to get a lesser title than at least Mini-Supreme is the same as losing. All those alternate titles—Prettiest Eyes, Best Dress, Prettiest Smile, Best Personality—have duct-tape function. Little girls don't cry when they get something, and the organizers make sure no girl leaves without some sort of crown, trophy, title or prize. Keeps them happy. It's the grown-ups that cry, because they know how meaningless those cheap giveaways are.

Driving home, my grown-ups argued over the money they'd spent, how it had been spent, and what they'd done wrong.

This could have been the end of my budding beauty queen career, and nearly was, but soon after the Austin flop, Gracie brought home a visitor. A lady who was always on the look-out for pretty girls who had the potential to become the next Disney star.

Tiara

On the day of the scheduled visit Gracie cleaned the whole house, placed scented candles in the living room and bought fresh flowers to show her appreciation of the honored guest. She got Mom nervous with her fussing, although Mom refused to help her in her preparations. But she did put on her best dress for the visit, and Gracie was really grateful for that. She introduced the visitor to Mom, then to me.

"This is my friend Inez."

The lady patted my head—*aren't you a pretty one*—and kept talking to Mom and Gracie as if I didn't exist. I didn't look at her, either. Her deep voice scared me.

"I can see what you mean, Gracie. She's got good bone structure, nice hair. Yes, quite adorable. But it'll take more than a cheap polyester dress to make a mini beauty queen out of her. We need to turn her into something sensational. As lovely as she might be, it's not enough to capture the ultimate supreme title of Young Miss America. That takes professional styling, ballet classes, dresses with matching shoes, jewelry. It takes money. Lots of money."

Mom must have paled when hearing this. Gracie of course knew all of it already. She'd brought my benefactor into our square little third-row-behind-the-highway home. With the help of her photographer friend, my first true admirer, she had spread my pictures around his circle of friends and acquaintances, talking me up with glowing prophecies of the spoils a famous child beauty queen could garner, and she had actually managed to get somebody interested.

So now I had my first sponsor.

I saw the generous lady with the avuncular voice only a few more times, and each time she ignored me. But I know Gracie met with her often.

"She's a great businesswoman," Gracie said. "We're so lucky to have her."

Indeed we were. The money flowed freely for hair stylists and make-up artists and outfits, designed for all the different categories of all the different pageants I attended in the following months.

A year later, I'd won the coveted title of Grand Supreme twice, in different competitions. My career was well on its way, and Mom and Gracie—and the sponsor, I suppose—were pleased.

I liked being on stage, but I was happiest after I'd done really, really well. Then I jumped off stage straight into Gracie's welcoming arms. When I didn't do so well, when I forgot to smile or missed my next move? No hugs. But she didn't punish me. Gracie never punished me. Gracie loved me.

In the midst of this hectic pageant activity, Gracie told Mom that the sponsor wanted to accelerate my popularity. She wanted to see a decent return on her investment, which was only fair considering she'd spent heaps of money on me. Gracie and the sponsor bonded over their mutual interest—me—and hatched a plan for how to make the most of my photogenic talents. The photographer friend would do a very special photo shoot for my birthday, an artistic one this time, and they could sell those pictures to advertising agencies.

"I don't know," Mom said to Gracie. "You really think those sell?"

"Like hotcakes. You'll see. She's adorable. Lots of people will spend money on her."

"Maybe we should get a different photographer. A better one then Carlos."

"Good luck finding one who doesn't charge up front."

"I don't have time for that," Mom said. "See if I care. Have that amateur Carlos take those pictures. It'll only be that once, anyway."

Gracie took me to that special photo shoot. On the way there, she fussed over me and kept telling me what a pretty girl I was and how proud she was to have such a good girl for a mija. She couldn't stop talking, and her hands shook badly when she handed me over to the photographer. "This is the most important picture taking session ever," she whispered into my ear. "Do exactly what Carlos says. Don't argue with him, my little darling mija. He knows what he's doing. He'll make you famous." Then she left.

The photographer had trouble undoing all the buttons on my dress. But he managed, and finally, there I was, in my birthday suit, not really feeling embarrassed,

I was too young for that. Gracie had told me to do what he said, so it must be all right.

Gracie's photographer friend placed me on a swing they set up in the studio. He moved my arms and legs in position until he was satisfied with the arrangement. He told me not to swing, to sit perfectly still, to keep my hands on the swing ropes, to keep my legs spread, and to smile—smile, for heaven's sake!—until the many, many pictures he took of me were done.

Before we went home, he told me not to tell anybody anything about the pictures because it was a big surprise, and if I ruined the surprise Gracie wouldn't be able to take me to Disneyland. Soon, we'd go there.

In the car, Gracie showed me a pamphlet with all the attractions and talked about Magic Mountain and the rides, and by the time we got back, I'd forgotten about the picture-taking. All I could talk about was Disneyland.

My dear shrink-doc drops by. Yes, dear, I'm slowly growing fond of him. He's all I got in here. I close my journal, try a timid smile which makes him break into a big one (how easy he is to please), and tell him about the director's visit and my request to train alone.

"Do you think she should reward you?" he asks.

"It's not a reward." Why on earth would he even think that? "I don't like being close to other people. If she doesn't grant it, I won't exercise, that's all there is to it. No big deal."

Tiara

"I've asked her to make certain times available to you." *Of course you did, sweet doc.* "She has granted the request. She does find it commendable that you want to look after your physical health. Many of the girls in here don't care—they've given up on themselves."

"I need another favor. You're a big shot here. Can you get me a TV and a computer? I'm stuck here for God knows how long, and I need something to do outside of morning classes and exercise."

We argue for a while. He thinks internet is out of the question. But TV, maybe.

"When?"

"I'll see what I can do." And as an afterthought, he hits me with it. "Of course, privileges must be earned."

"What do you want?"

"I want to read your journal."

Get lost. No, wait. What would it matter if he reads it? Could anything I've written be turned into a disadvantage for me? Hardly. Some of the stuff might be a bit embarrassing—it always is when one is honest with oneself, right?—and I wouldn't want a total stranger to see it, but doc is no stranger no more.

"But only you can read it," I say, "and only when I'm ready."

This evening, a guy in a white nurse's suit hands me the remote for the TV in the community room. Until now I hadn't even noticed the flat screen on one of the walls above the arrangement of easy chairs. Since I'm still the only inmate in my very own living unit, I have free choice of the channels available. The warden-nurse informs me that certain programs will be blocked. They screen them carefully to make sure they're suitable for us in here. I'm curious what this means. Suitable for fifteen-year-old wannabe murderers? Which programs would those be? I'm too pissed off to ask him. He also tells me I'm allowed to watch for one hour per day.

I would have much preferred a computer.

20

THE reporter was very polite. Not what Melissa expected at all. He wasn't pushy or opinionated like most of those interviewers come across on television, and he gave her all the time in the world to collect her thoughts.

When he sat down at her kitchen table she realized how unprepared she was. What to say? How to get across the agony she went through? How undeserved her suffering was, how unfair to judge her so cruelly.

"I want to tell you about my daughter, about her life," she said. "About who she really is."

The reporter asked her if he could film the interview and if she was willing to sign a release form that allowed him to air the material. That was standard procedure, he explained, a formality, but still, it bugged her. Why did everybody want her to sign forms?

"And here is a form to guarantee you five hundred dollars for the interview, plus a hundred each time it's repeated."

"Who keeps track?"

"Don't worry. It's all regulated. If they make a special out of it you'll get even more. Look here, the fine print on the contract makes it quite clear."

Tiara

"A special?"

"At least for an afternoon talk show."

"Huh, I don't know about that. I know I'm not important," she said, signing all the forms. "I'm only the mother."

"You're very important," he said, "probably the most important person in the case, aside from your daughter." What a sweet boy. His name was Andy. He was in his early twenties, still a bit chubby, with big friendly eyes and soft lips. Her anger dissipated in the gentle breeze of his kindness. She felt in control again.

"My daughter has done something terrible, no question about it. I have seen this horrible news clip, it was the worst moment of my life."

"Things often look a lot worse on screen, you know." With this, Andy turned the camera on. "They get distorted."

"I guess so." Melissa looked straight at the red light, the way Andy instructed her. "You'd know better. All I can say is that my Tiara has never shown any aggression, nothing aside from the usual tantrums toddlers throw. It's not fair to brand her as an anti-social dropout kind of girl. Like one of those druggies who loiter around Main Street and have no home to go to. My Tiara had a good childhood, and me being a single mother had no detrimental effect on her upbringing. She has enjoyed a good education, has been brought up with all the love and care a child needs. I want the world to know this."

"Mrs. Brown, tell us about your daughter. We'd like to hear it from you."

"Where do I start? Oh my, Tiara was such a beautiful and popular girl." Melissa checked herself, then went for it with a smile. "She had loads of friends, mostly girls who wanted to be like her. Her friend Luna always copied everything she did." She could see Andy losing interest. He wanted to know more about Tiara and her. "Tiara and I had a bond. From the beginning we were best friends. As a little girl she was most happy when she made me happy. You have to know we were on our own, the two of us. Her father had died, killed in action before she was born, before he could marry me. He was a hero, you know. You can imagine how devastated I felt after that. Looking back at it now, I might not be here if it hadn't been for Tiara. She saved me."

"What do you mean by that?"

"I remember the moment I saw her for the very first time. I'm sure you've heard that before from mothers. Your eyes fall on this tiny bundle in your arms, and you understand that it's part of you, an extension of yourself." Melissa closed her eyes, smiled, hand resting on her ample breasts. After a meaningful pause, she looked back at Andy. "But anyway, that's nothing unusual. It happens every second of every day. When I had Tiara, my broken heart was mended. I still missed my Mike an awful lot, but I had a new purpose in life."

Again, a pause. *I'm the one hard done by here. I'm the one who's miserable. I'm the one who's sacrificed her whole life to bring up this ungrateful brat.*

Tiara

"You can imagine how precious she was to me."

"How was she as a child?"

"Growing up, she was so easy to handle. Hardly ever complained. Such a sweet personality. Quick to understand, too. She was like a sponge soaking up everything I taught her. I didn't go to work, didn't have to, my Mike's pension provided me with enough to support the two of us for a while. I could afford to concentrate on home-schooling her. I preferred that because the schools down there in Texas, you know, they aren't like here."

"Why didn't you take her back to Canada, then, after her father died?" Andy said.

"I was still in love with Mike, although he was dead, and I felt it was the right thing to do to let his daughter grow up in his home town. Surely people understand that."

"Of course."

He must tell the world what a brave trooper I am, single mother and all.

"We had a lovely home. We lived in Galveston. A great place for a holiday. Before Hurricane Katrina, I mean. After the big storm, it didn't look so good. There was so much damage to the city, you can't imagine. Before the storm hit, my Tiara had never been scared of anything. After Katrina, I had to keep a light on in her room every single night, that's how afraid she was of the dark. She was a lot more timid after that. It's, really, it's inconceivable that she'd even touch a weapon, let alone use one—"

Melissa started to weep. She didn't want to, she had to.

Andy didn't pressure her, and didn't switch off the camera.

"How could my Tiara change so much in such a short time? Maybe somebody slipped something in her drink when she was at that coffee shop. That happens, doesn't it? I've read about drugs like that, mind-altering ones. Something like that must have happened, don't you think?"

21

I'M settling into the daily routine of my jail existence: Mornings at school—where I make it crystal clear that I need to be left alone—solitary lunch in my living unit, an afternoon hour at the gym, scheduled around my shrink's infrequent visits, watching an hour of kid's programs on TV, writing until lights-out.

That hour in the gym is my favorite time of day. I do the full sixty minutes on the stationary bike, working up a lather of sweat while sifting through the debris of memories that are swept onshore by continuous rolling waves. It's amazing how the brain works when the body does repetitive movements. The first ten minutes are excruciatingly painful—I hit the pedals hard and fast, and I count the seconds to make sure I don't give up. I have no time to think of anything, but around six hundred, my synapses begin to fire up. Soon after, my mind travels back to events in my past. A journey begins, of good and bad moments, things that were done and said, accompanied by muted colors and sounds. Shapeless feelings brush along the hidden edges of those moments, making them more defined. Some I remember as if they happened yesterday, others drift through my alpha waves with nebulous confusion, around twists and turns and along ups and downs, never on a straight line. I try to connect the scenic points of the memory-vista until the path I'm on becomes clearer.

An excellent exercise, the bike-pedaling as well as the mind-wandering. It structures my past, which makes it that much easier to record in my journal later on.

Birthday Six

Not long after that first, very special artistic photo session Gracie announced the sponsor had arranged for another one.

"This time, I'm coming along," Mom said.

"Why?" Gracie said.

"Didn't you say those photo shoots can further her beauty queen career. I need to be involved in everything that will make her famous."

Gracie threw her car keys at Mom.

"Then you drive her there. I'm fed up being your chauffeur anyway. No need for both of us to go."

Mom had not applied for her American driver's license and depended on Gracie to take us to all the pageant towns from Arizona to Texas, New Mexico, Mississippi, all the way to South Carolina, practically all over the southern states.

"You know I can't drive."

"Take the bus."

Mom realized she'd pushed too far.

"Come on, Gracie, that's not what I meant. I don't want to go without you."

"And I don't want you to come along. Your constant complaining makes the photographer nervous, and then the pictures won't turn out good. I'm doing all this for us, you know, for Tiara and you, so you can have a good life. God knows I'm doing all I can, and this is the thanks I get."

Gracie's voice quivered, which made me run to her to make her happy again.

She folded me in her arms. "Come here, my mija. Come to your auntie. There you are. That's it. A big hug full of love for my most favorite girl in the world."

Mom pulled a face as if she'd stepped on a cockroach, which made me laugh.

Then Gracie laughed too, and now both of us were happy again. I so adored to see her happy. Gracie grabbed my current glitz outfit and the make-up and hair kit, then took me to the studio to do that special shoot the sponsor arranged for me.

On the way, she explained a few facts of life—*my life*—to me.

"What we do at the studio is our little secret, okay? Carlos said you may not always like what he does, but small children don't understand what needs to be done to get ahead. I want you to be famous, and Carlos promised me that he will take pictures that bring in a lot of money and make you a star. That's what Miss Inez wants, and we want that, too, right? Your mom doesn't want that. She doesn't love you as much as I do. She's always so mean to me. If she hears that Carlos takes such nice pictures of you, she'll be upset and will take you away from me. You'll never be able to be with your Gracie again. Do you understand?"

I tried, but I didn't really. Gracie could see it in my face.

"Your mom mustn't know, and if you tell her the good Lord will make me sick. Then you have no more Gracie. Imagine, nobody to love you like I do."

That scared me. Now I understood.

While she did my hair and make-up, she told me how proud she was of me.

"That's my mija. Such a good girl, and so pretty. We'll do some nice pictures for all the fans you've got. They want to see more of you. Let the photographer do his magic and he'll make you into the most beautiful girl in the whole world."

She sat me down in front of the camera and fiddled with my pageant outfit. The photographer turned to Gracie.

"Come back in two hours."

Before she left the room, she gave me a big hug and whispered in my ear.

"Be a good girl now. Remember, if you aren't, the angels won't protect us and bad things will happen."

After she'd gone, he started all over again, pulling the shoulders down and the skirt up as if he couldn't decide what was right.

I still had Gracie's words in my ears, "Let him do his magic. I'm so proud of you and love you to pieces." And she had promised me Disneyland again. I sat still while he clicked away.

Soon after, somebody else came into the studio. Somebody without a face. Now, I was very scared. This was the person who would tell the angels if I didn't behave.

The photographer saw may scared face, laughed and said: "Let's do real art. Get rid of her dress."

The somebody without a face undressed me completely. I let it happen, way too scared to object. Then, the shadowy ghost-like somebody who didn't say a word, arranged me in some sheer material, twisting me into many different poses, as instructed by the photographer. The shadow figure helped him make real art. Some of the pictures had me partly covered, some not at all. I had to sit still for a long time for each shot, the camera staring at me until the picture was art.

I have a very clear memory of feeling out of place, feeling not me. Not wanting to be me. Although it wasn't really cold in the room, something made me shiver. I started to cry, very quietly, because I wanted my Gracie back.

The photographer friend clapped his hands together in delight.

Tiara

"This is perfect! She looks so sad and lost. Those pics will sell like goddamn hotcakes."

"I don't want to go to Gracie's photographer friend anymore," I told Mom when we got back to our square house.

"Why not?"

I didn't really know how to explain how I felt because I didn't understand it, so I said, "he always takes so long with his pictures and I get so cold and I still haven't been to Disneyland."

Gracie said, "If we don't let him take pictures of you, we'll all be very poor and we can't move to this wonderful house where each of us has their own room."

Mom looked sad and said, "and I was soooo looking forward to this house," and I said, "but I'm always soooo cold."

Then Mom turned to Gracie. "Why the hell doesn't that idiot turn the air-conditioner down, if she's cold?"

"I'll make sure he does, next time."

From that session on, I started feeling like two kids. One who hated artsy picture-taking, and one who wanted to do it right to make sure Gracie was proud of me and kept on loving me.

After a few more photo sessions, we moved into a house perfect for us. A detached bungalow at the end of a cul-de-sac in a good neighborhood called La Marque, with a covered porch in front where we could sit in the shade, and flowerbeds on either side of the driveway.

My room was fit for a princess, but right next to it was a larger room that was reserved for my practicing.

Gracie seemed happier then she had ever been. "We have to take it up a notch," Gracie announced when we moved into the house, "Miss Inez said with the extra money coming in from the pictures we can afford to hire a choreographer to come to the house and teach her routines."

That made Mom happy, too, but not me. The practice room became my hate room. Mom home-schooled me in this big empty room with the wooden floor every morning. Texas law required kids to go to school or be home-schooled from age six, but Mom decided it would be better to start a bit earlier since we'd lose so many days preparing for and attending pageants.

I didn't miss going to school. I had no contact with the outside world beyond my family, so the concept of having friends was not on my radar. My world was Gracie, and to some extent Mom, and the crowns I was supposed to win for them, and the pictures I was posing for to make sure the three of us could afford the house.

Gracie kept telling me how lucky I was to have all this, but I didn't feel lucky when I posed for the pictures—although I didn't dare tell her how confused this made me—and I never felt lucky in the afternoons. The choreographer came and tortured me in the hate-room,

Tiara

no escaping him. He poked me with a wooden stick when he wanted me to do a new step sequence and made me practice for hours. I had to learn my routine. Dance steps, posture, different routines for different contests. I was now at the end of the all-important age group 4 to 6—the one that would catapult me into the pre-teen category—and there the judges looked for personality, poise and confidence, not only appearance.

My stage name was Princess Tia. The other mothers and their daughters always shunned us, jealous of my incredible feat: I'd won the Grand Supreme and the Ultimate Supreme four times in the last five pageants before I even turned six.

We finally went to Disneyland. Gracie joined me on all the rides. We stayed in a suite with a princess theme, of course, and Princess Tia wore her sparkling tiara all day long. Every picture Gracie took on this trip shows me grinning from one ear to the other, eating hot dogs and ice cream, carrying a larger-than-Tia Mickey Mouse, having the time of my life.

Disneyland made up for the photo sessions, which I had to do nearly every week now.

22

"SHE can't be serious. She gives an interview without talking to us first?" Macintosh felt more surprised than annoyed. "What's the matter with that stupid bitch?"

He and Harding stood around the computer, watching a replay of last night's CTV interview with Melissa.

Harding shrugged. "She'll be on a talk show later this week."

"Great, that's all we need. We're running in circles here, chasing our tails, and the press has a field day with the mother."

"Your little ruse didn't last long." Harding put his hands behind his neck and stretched. "She knows we can't stop her talking, and now she's not taking us seriously."

"Was worth a try." Macintosh slumped into his chair. "Got her out of her comfort zone. And now I can question her again about some of the stuff she told the reporter."

"Like what?"

Macintosh grinned. "Stuff that doesn't add up with what she told me before. Stuff I'll confront her with in due time." He got serious again. "Any news on the victim?"

"Still comatose." Harding glanced at his notebook. "Medical records indicate she had her appendix out and she's diabetic. Aside from that, we got nothing. So far, nobody's missing anybody of her description."

"What have we done to establish her identity?"

"We can't fingerprint without her consent, or that of a close relative, but we gave the data as we know it—physical attributes like approximate age, height, weight, her speaking Spanish—to all hotels, the cruise ship currently in the harbor and the TV stations. They've been good about it, mentioned it several days in a row."

"And still nothing. That's odd."

"Yeah, especially considering she was right in the center of busy downtown Vancouver when she was attacked, so she wasn't exactly hiding."

Macintosh thought about the ridiculous law preventing him to take fingerprints. Protecting civil rights was sometimes a paradox to him. The victim was in a coma, how the hell could she give her consent? Without knowing who she was, he couldn't contact next of kin. Judicial confusion dreamt up by those damn lawyers who had the common sense of vegetables. "What are the chances she'll come out of it so we can question her?"

"Slim," Harding said. "Lousy odds, but nobody will say for sure."

"We might hit a break there. The bank across the street just sent their surveillance video over this morning," Macintosh pressed a button on the computer console. "Fingers crossed it will give us a clear view of the victim. Something we can print and distribute."

They set the surveillance video at half an hour before the crime happened, increased the speed and concentrated on the fast moving images. At ten to seven, a shapely woman dressed like the victim walked down the street, unfortunately from the wrong side, considering the position of the video camera. They slowed the video down to normal speed.

"Turn. Turn," Macintosh said. Her face stayed hidden. She entered the coffee shop.

"Damn. But that's definitely our victim. Entering at 6:52 am, going to table four."

At 7:02 a girl in a black hoodie arrived, coming from the same direction.

"That must be Tiara," Harding said.

Height and built was about right. The girl opened the coffee shop door and walked in. Macintosh ran the clip the witness had taken with his iPhone in his mind again, filling in the part between entry and the attack which had not been on the clip. The alleged suspect would have come through the door, looked around, maybe pretending to choose an order on the menu above the serving counter, saw a woman sitting at table four and then … then what? Lost it, walked straight up

Tiara

to her and stabbed her without any prior provocation? The witnesses had all agreed that no argument had preceded the attack.

Next they saw a few customers run out of the coffee shop, then the police cruiser arrived. All stuff they knew already.

Macintosh closed the video. Dead end. Everything was recorded, everything was obvious, every detail clear except the victim's identity and the suspect's motive. As long as the victim remained unidentified, he should concentrate on the motive. The girl had to have one. Of course he'd come across cases where the suspect was obviously deranged, guided by voices that told him to kill, or was a psychopath who loved killing for the thrill of it, but those were rare. Usually the perpetrator had motive. If his judgment of human nature wasn't totally off the mark, this tiny girl with the quick mind wasn't a spaced-out weirdo but had a real good, solid motive. Something so unique, so messed-up, that she couldn't admit to it, not even to herself.

Macintosh sighed. "Now, what about Melissa's comment that Tiara was a sought-after child model?"

"We checked with all major talent agencies down south, but she hasn't been registered with any of them. We'll keep at it."

"I know her initial drug test came back negative, but maybe she was on something we don't know yet. They come up with new crap all the time."

Hardin's notebook lay on his lap but he didn't need to consult it. "They've done hair analysis. If she was using, she hasn't done so for a long time. One interesting aspect though, court asked for a more comprehensive assessment of her mental health, and apparently the shrink at the Youth Custody Center in Burnaby is doing it."

Of all the shrinks in the system, why did it have to be Eaton? "That's rather unusual. He's already handed in his report. Usually another psychiatrist is appointed after that. Why is Eaton still on it?"

"From what I understand, she insisted on keeping the same shrink. Maybe he'll crack her."

"A fat lot of good that'll do us. He won't give us anything until he's finalized his report.

"We're looking at another month at least," Harding said.

"We have to dig deeper into the suspect's background," Macintosh said.

Harding pulled a face. "That's what freaks me out most. So far, we've found nothing. Not on her, or her mother. I checked online, the Texas vital records office doesn't list a birth certificate for a Tiara Brown."

"You saying she's a ghost?"

"I found no record of a Melissa Brown or a Tiara Brown anywhere. Tiara is homeschooled, so no school registration, no marriage certificate or driver's license for Melissa Brown, no nothing for anything or anybody. The address Melissa gave us, Caroline Road in Galves-

Tiara

ton, is odd, too. Number 357 doesn't exist, and she hasn't been registered under any other number in that street."

Macintosh digested the news. "If those two lived in Galveston, they flew so low under the radar, their stay there was practically illegal. Follow up on it. They had to live on something. Keep digging until you find a trace."

"I think I already did," Harding said. "Since we know from the mother that Tiara was born on August 21 1998 I checked the birth records of that month. On August 21 that year a Tiara Rodriguez was born at Houston General Hospital. I know, Melissa said her name is Tiara Brown—"

"—but we have to take everything Melissa Brown tells us with a grain of salt," Macintosh completed his sentence. "We know her lover's name was Miguel. I bet Tiara's father was called Miguel Rodriguez. See what I mean with stuff not adding up? Melissa didn't only lie about Tiara's name. She stated in my initial interview with her that she worked in Galveston at different supermarkets, but now she says in that interview that Tiara's father left her enough money when he died." A nasty afterthought hit Macintosh. "Did you check the talent agencies only for a Tiara Brown?"

"Shit." Harding's cheeks turned red.

"Check again and ask about a Tiara Rodriguez." Macintosh's fingers drummed on his desk top. "I don't get it. Why the hell does the mother make such a secret out of the girl's background? Why didn't she give us her real name?"

"Maybe you should try once more to talk to Tiara. Get her side of the story."

Macintosh glared at him.

"Sorry," Harding said. "I know, it's tough for you. But as it's probably your last case—"

"Right. You're right. They'll soon move me into a corner and bury me under even more shit-house files."

"They certainly won't put you in charge of a new homicide."

Macintosh could already feel emptiness creep into his bones.

"So, make the best of this case. I mean, maybe the girl couldn't help herself. Maybe she had a reason."

"Like what?"

"She's so young," Harding said. "I'm not saying she's innocent, but we both know something's off here, and neither of us knows anything about her background. Give her a chance to do some explaining."

"She had her chance."

"She's had time to think by now. Let her shed some light on her motive. Look, I know she's about your daughter's age—"

"Leave Danielle out of this." Now Macintosh's cheeks were burning like hell fire. "And don't you worry about me doing my job. I'm going to see that girl again, but in my own good time. I'll give her a chance to explain herself and that stupid goddamn crime she's committed if it's the last thing I do on this earth."

23

ANOTHER week has drifted by, barely noticed but for the falling leaves outside my cell window. The old trees out there are tall enough for me to see a few stubborn leaves still attached to their bare branches.

I'm staring a lot out this window, and at the empty page of my journal. I have too much time on my hands but I still refuse to leave my cell for anything other than the dreaded morning classes, the bike riding, the shrink's visits. He hasn't been back for a few days—I guess I'm not high on his priority list.

My stubborn-like-an-autumn-leaf attitude persists every time the case worker assigned to me shows up to do her job. She has a lot on her plate and only checks with the center's admin to see if I'm finally willing to talk to her when she drops in anyway. In return she gets my heartfelt thanks, but no thanks, sent via the admin channels.

Can't do that with the detective, though. He's back and demands to see me today. Police trumps social worker. I protest all the way to the visitor's room, to make a point, and my warden ignores me, to prove hers.

Tiara

"Wait in here." Sounds like an order not a request.

A little while later Macintosh barges in, puffed with cop-like determination. Or has the long walk down the center's hallways exhausted him beyond his advanced age? He doesn't look to be in the best shape. I glance at his tight fitting belt. Aren't policemen supposed to keep fit and trim?

"Tell me, where do policemen go when they're old?" I say.

He gives me a not in the mood for banter look. "To a desk job."

"Shouldn't you be there, shuffling papers or something?"

The look deepens, gets as close to pissed-off as I've ever seen on anybody. "Believe me, that's where I'd rather be."

"So why did you come back?"

"Maybe because my partner doesn't see a lost cause when it pokes him in the eye?"

I giggle.

"What's funny?"

"The 'poking in the eye' thing."

He studies me with intense interest. He knows his comment made me remember what they told me about stabbing somebody in the eye.

"Sorry," I say. "I know it's not funny."

"You remember what you've done?" he asks quickly.

"Only what I've been told."

"So you still keep up the pretense?"

This is so exasperating. "I told you, I don't remember. But you don't want to believe me. You want to believe I'm pretending."

He finally takes a seat, settling in for his interrogation. This makes me giggle again. I can't help it, I always giggle when I don't know how to react.

"This is no laughing matter," he says. "Convince me otherwise."

Now, here is an opportunity I should not let pass. "What makes you so sure it was me?"

His eyes muster me without much curiosity. "We got a tape showing a girl in a black hoodie entering the coffee shop."

"Many people own black hoodies."

"We have witness statements confirming it was you. We have a video clip of the assault. We got your fingerprints on the knife you used."

His words hit me in the stomach. I gasp. I can feel the facts he listed like individual blows. Wham, wham, wham. What he is saying rips me apart. Not because I suddenly understand how guilty they make me, but because I still don't feel guilty. All the words in world can't change that. I don't feel guilty. I don't remember.

"And why should I have done this?" A lump in my throat muffles my voice.

"That's why I'm here," Macintosh said. "To figure out your motive for stabbing the victim."

I clear my throat, close to tears now. "If I had a reason, I don't remember."

"Who was the woman you attacked?"

"If I knew, I'd tell you."

"Have you met her before?"

"If I did, I don't recall."

"What were you doing in the coffee shop so early?"

"I don't even know what time it was."

"Did your mother know that you'd go there?"

My body stiffens. "Why would she know?"

"Did you leave your home and go straight there?"

I'm pondering this question. "I guess so."

"Did you take a bus?"

Again, I need time to think. He doesn't give me a second. "Or did you walk?"

Somehow that makes more sense. I can picture myself walking the streets of Downtown Vancouver. "I prefer walking."

"So you remember how you got there?"

I realise now that he is trying to draw me out, make me contradict myself. "I only know that I like walking, and that I dislike rubbing shoulders with people. I wouldn't go on a bus."

"What did you order in the coffee shop?"

"No idea."

He fires one question after another, and in the end I get tired of insisting that I don't know or remember or recall anything. I cross my arms and shut down.

He gives up, too. Shakes his head in a waste-of-time manner and looks so miserable I actually feel a little sorry for him. A tiny twinge of sympathy.

"Why did you even bother to come here?" I ask. "You knew I can't help you."

"I told you."

"No, you didn't."

"My partner thought coming here, seeing you again, would be good for me."

Isn't that an interesting twist? Suddenly the focus shifts to him, and he allows it.

"Because?"

"To heal a nasty wound."

Even more surprising that he's so honest. A policeman with an open wound. Macintosh is not here because of me. He's doing this interview so he can be angry at somebody other than himself. I feel a little better knowing I'm not the only one trying to sort through things. Except, he probably knows perfectly well what caused his wound.

"How did you get hurt?"

His body language displays the inner fight my simple question evokes. Fists opening, closing. Shoulders hunched, straightened. Neck muscles twitching. His hurt is raw, his shield is damaged. He takes a while to get his guard up again. Finally he looks at me, his face frozen.

"Doesn't matter." He takes a deep breath. "Look, Tiara, I want to make some kind of sense out of this senseless goddamn crime you've committed."

Tiara

My mind is spinning. Another concept of bad to look at. A new level of evil. "You think what I did was senseless? That I had no reason at all? That I'm a monster who runs amok, stabbing indiscriminately?"

"If you can't explain it, it doesn't make sense."

He's got a point. But, dear Lord, it couldn't have been like that. If I did it, I must have had a reason. The mere thought of admitting any kind of guilt gashes my intestines. To have no reason makes it doubly horrific.

I gather all the courage in the world. "Detective Macintosh," I say, "Can I ask you a favour?"

His face is all scrunched up, but his eyes light up.

"Will you please find out my motive for the terrible thing I'm supposed to have done?"

24

WHEN Macintosh got back to the station, Harding walked straight over to his desk, nibbling a granola bar.

Macintosh winced.

"I like the crunchy taste of nuts and oats," Harding said.

"Sounds like a commercial." Macintosh watched him take another bite. A few flakes landed on his desk. He wiped them away.

Harding finished his nutty twigs and seeds bar. "How did the interview with Tiara go?"

How did it? Macintosh motioned for Harding to sit down. He wasn't sure how to sum it up.

"She still sticks to her amnesia story. And I tend to believe her. But I also believe that she starts to come around. Like, deep inside, she knows she's committed a crime. She's all over the place. First she had a giggle about stabbing the victim in the eye. Then, when I confronted her with a few facts, she withdrew into her not-remembering-a-thing mode."

"Did you ask her if she remembers anything about the victim?"

Tiara

Macintosh threw him a look.

"Sorry," Harding said.

Macintosh thought for a moment. "Finding motive," he said. "The girl is either a psychopath in the making or she'd been driven by one monster of a motive. And if the later is the case, she needs our help to bring it out in the open. A motive that pushes a young girl into such a savage frenzy has to be serious. No, more than serious, catastrophic. A trauma of epic proportions."

"You mean something so horrible happened in her past, she's blocked it from her memory?" Harding said.

"I think so, but I could be wrong. Only motive will give us a clear answer."

"Won't the shrink find out…?"

"Dr. Eaton? Do me a favour and don't mention that name. His index finger won't find his nose without guidance by a bureaucratic rule book." Macintosh took out his cell and scanned the contact list for Detective Josh Grant from Houston Homicide. "I'm not gonna wait for Eaton's assessment to shine light on the darkness inside Tiara. It's about time for a shortcut on all this cross border agency communication bullshit. I'm gonna ask Josh to dig up everything he can on Tiara Rodriguez."

He dialled Josh's number on his private cell. Within seconds the connection was made and Macintosh put his Texan colleague on Facetime. Josh was about twenty years younger and twenty pounds lighter than him.

"I need a favor, my friend," Macintosh said, "which requires you to kick your underutilized brain into gear, work a few quick miracles and keep them out of your report sheets."

Josh moved closer to the screen and exposed his whitened teeth with a big grin. "Unofficial business then?"

"Don't do that," Macintosh said. "You look like a horse."

25

NO question, I've hit a nerve with Macintosh. Not sure yet where the center of his pain sits, not sure if I care to know, but he's vulnerable, and that I should care about. If he thinks nothing can heal him, he'll be beyond giving a shit. About anything.

But Macintosh also got to me. Since I talked to him I'm dragged down by undefined feelings that feel a lot like guilt. Loads of guilt, a sack full of blame and shame, strapped on my back by people I don't remember.

I hate to carry that load. Nowadays, I hate a lot of things, but most of all I hate the emptiness within the hate. It's such a powerless feeling, like falling into an imploding star.

Without warning, I'm in the hate-room again. I spent a lot of time in there.

Birthday Seven

The Stick had been to ballet school, he knew all about grace and poise. When he was young and flexible, he'd been able to do all the moves he poked into me with that dreaded stick of his. He knew what a human body was capable of.

"He can't help being so demanding," Gracie said at the end of one of the more grueling sessions that left me crying with exhaustion, as if that would explain and excuse The Stick's cruelty. "When he was younger, he had a terrible accident that smashed his leg."

With his dreams of gracing the world's stages ruined forever, he had to settle for kids like me, and some days his pent-up frustrations over my shortcomings burst out with a vengeance.

So what do I remember? An afternoon like many before, the air-conditioner rattling at high speed, the music from the stereo blasting the same happy tune in an endless loop, The Stick yelling at me to pay attention, to move my arms like this, to lift my leg higher, to turn faster, to smile. Me, tired, irritable, confused. Not understanding what I'm doing wrong. Wanting to do it right. Most of the time I wanted to please the grown-ups because if I wouldn't, we'll lose our home or they'll get sick and I might end up all alone in this world.

Another miserable afternoon. The Stick yells, I cry. I stand in the middle of the room, he stands in front of me. I know what comes next: the end of his awful stick pokes me in the tummy.

I feel warm urine run down the inside of my legs. I press my legs together to stop it, I'm six years old, not a baby any more, but my panties are soaked and a small puddle forms around my dancing shoes.

That's all I remember.

When my dear shrink-doc finally does show up for another afternoon session, I'm still in this don't-remember mode, which drives me crazy. But he never asks me about my childhood anyway. We pass our time together doing silly tests and quests. Last time we did an IQ test. I finished it in no time. Doc didn't tell me the score. Maybe I should have taken more care, but concentrating on logic is tough when a large part of your brain is a foggy void.

Today, he asks me stuff like my preferences for colors and activities and things like that, and I answer semi-truthfully. My favorite color is black but I say blue because I know that color is less threatening. I haven't developed a hobby until now and haven't been doing any sport activity outside of dancing, which naturally I despise, but I say I like ballet when he asks me what I enjoy doing. What girl my age wouldn't? Plus, I still have the posture to prove that I've done my share of dancing.

For sure those are catch questions, but without a psychology background I can't tell which ones are traps. All I know is, if I don't cooperate, he'll give me a bad rap, and they try me as an adult and lock me up in a real prison with real hard-core jail birds—movies with greedy grown-up bitches in shower cubicles come to mind—and that is not a favorite hobby of mine.

If I want to avoid such harsh punishment, I have to prove that I wasn't born with a criminal mind. Does this

Tiara

mean I have accepted that I've done the crime? Yes and no. Acceptance without understanding is like one of those painted Easter eggs. A fragile shell with its inside blown out. I need to find out the truth. Not for that detective, not for the shrink, only for myself.

"I'll cooperate with you, if you promise to show me your final assessment of me."

He says although it's unorthodox he'd let me read it if I stick to my promise and let him look at what I've written so far. Now.

I rip the pages out of my notebook and out of my soul and hand them to him.

He leaves, holding the pages like a precious china cup from which he plans to drink in delicate sips. Mouthful by mouthful he will devour my soul.

What have I done?

I'm trying in vain to recall what I wrote so far. He's caught me in one of my bad moments—a good one for him—when my soul is splintered into parts that refuse to blend together. Since being interrogated by Macintosh, I feel chagrined and proud. Yes, proud. I'm struggling hard to stop this inner turmoil. What the hell should I be ashamed of? But is my pride a fight for dignity or an outburst of arrogance? Is my shame born out of guilt or is it disgrace? Where have I failed? What have I done? I'm in for another lonesome-loathsome night.

Doc comes back next day. He didn't take long to analyze what he believes to be my soul.

I'm still in a confused state of mind. He sits down, as usual, on the chair next to his desk, adjusts his glasses, smiles at me.

"Bad night, huh?"

I really had a bad night, a nightmare-night. I'm in a speeding car, racing along an empty highway, golden statues crashing down from great heights, burying the car, me trapped inside, snakes crawling all over me. Senseless scary stuff.

"Just a headache."

"The court-appointed lawyer contacted me to make an appointment with you."

"For the zillionth time, I'm not talking to anybody but you."

"You can trust him. He's part of the Youth Forensic Psychiatric System."

"Nice description for a loony bin set-up."

"I'll let him know," he says. "But you may want to reconsider. He's not your enemy. He will become your closest ally."

That's exactly what I'm worried about. "I can't think straight today. Maybe I'll change my mind later, when I'm better."

He adjusts his glasses again, a signal that we will continue with my analysis. "May I ask you about something you wrote in your journal?"

Tiara

I shrug, a little curious to what part of my ramblings caught his attention.

"When you lost control of your bladder after an exhausting dance rehearsal, was that an isolated incident or did it happen again?"

"No, never," I say.

I don't know why I bother to lie, considering that he'll read everything I'm writing as soon as I'm pathetic enough to hand it over to him.

For the moment, I don't want him to know that many nights after that dance rehearsal incident I woke up deeply ashamed, feeling warm wet between my legs and under my bottom. Lying there motionless until morning, always hoping the spot would dry up enough so nobody would notice. The wetness felt worse when it got cold. Much worse. The air around me smelled pungent when Mom came in and told me to get ready. By the time I came out of the bathroom she was already gathering the sheets in her arms to take them to the laundry. We both didn't look at the large area of different shades of piss-yellow on my mattress. My shame was never mentioned. It didn't exist.

26

MELISSA arranged the Danish pastries her mother brought. Seven sugar-coated blueberry apologies on a cake platter, one for each day they hadn't seen each other.

Her mother wanted to talk about the interview aired last week on her favorite talk show. Melissa didn't.

"Don't get me wrong," her mother said, "it was a good interview. You came across well, I must say. People liked you and felt for you, but I don't think it was a good idea to talk to the press. The police—"

"They lied to us. Andy explained that to me. They have no right to stop me talking."

"Still, no need to wake them up."

"I had to do something." Melissa poured two cups of tea. "People believe what they see and hear on TV. They judge me on that awful clip if I don't set the record straight."

"All you told them was what a great childhood Tiara had."

"Exactly."

"But that doesn't explain why she did what she did. As I said, you came across real caring, being a great mother, and I guess public opinion swings your way, you having such a tough life as a single mom and all. I must say, I wasn't keen on you mentioning that you had nobody to fall back on, considering I've been there throughout all your childhood, and I was a single mother too, giving you the best upbringing possible. But never mind that. Gratitude has never been your strong point."

"All my life?" Melissa said.

Louise placed a Danish on Melissa's plate. "I still think it was wrong to give that interview."

"I had to explain things."

"But you didn't really. You don't know anything."

Melissa shut her eyes, rubbed her forehead with three fingers, keeping them there as if that would help her focus.

"Melissa, you don't know why she did it, do you?"

Melissa lowered her hand and opened her eyes.

"Of course I don't. What are you thinking?"

"I don't know what to think." Her mother sipped on her tea, put her cup down again. "I haven't seen you for so long, and I've only known Tiara for, what, barely three years now?"

"And whose fault is that?"

"Melissa, please, don't start again. Stop dwelling on it. We need to look forward."

"That was exactly what I did when I gave Andy that interview. And by the way, it won't be the last."

"Oh dear, don't do that."

Melissa bit into a Danish. "And why not? Are you worried they'll ask me where my mother was when I was all alone in a foreign country, with a new baby and no husband? Are you worried I might tell them the truth?"

The Danish was gone, leaving drops of berry-blood on Melissa's chin.

"I came as soon as you called me, didn't I?" Louise said.

"You dragged us back here before I had a chance to think."

"You begged me to come and get you. Have you forgotten that?" Her mother frowned. "Besides, Tiara might have done something radical anyway. Her father was a soldier. Our family isn't violent. His sister was a piece of work, too."

"Don't you dare mention Gracie!" Melissa felt herself bristle. "I told you, I never want to talk about her again."

Her mother reached over and placed a second Danish on her plate.

"I'm only saying this because your judgment isn't always perfect. Look how you leaned on that woman, how much you relied on her and trusted her. I'm sure what happened never would have happened if you hadn't let her run your life."

"I was so young. I had nobody else. But once I got stronger, I started to realize what was going on." She could see her mother wasn't buying it. "I'm not the pushover you think," she said. "I can tell you that."

Should she tell her mother how she'd found out about Gracie?

Tiara

A sunny day in February, a mild fifteen degrees—Celsius, she couldn't bring herself to think in Fahrenheit, never made sense to her—a gentle breeze carrying blooming scent through the open windows.

Little Tiara was practicing with Tony, and Gracie was out somewhere, meeting people she didn't know and didn't care for. Her sister-in-law ran with a strange crowd. They were polite in a haughty way, like *Good day, Melissa, if you'd be so good and leave us alone now*, and wore over the top expensive clothes that didn't go well together—white business shirts with purple velvet jackets, two-tone shoes, gold watches with sparkling rings around the dials and the like. Screaming nouveau riche. She'd asked Gracie what her business with those people was, and all Gracie said was, "None of yours."

On that particular day, while Gracie met with her flashy friends, Melissa was doing a real Canadian job of spring cleaning, the way her mother taught her. Move every obstacle and clean behind and under it. Turn the mattress from winter-side to summer-side.

Melissa flipped the mattress in Gracie's room and saw a green plastic bag on the coils. She balanced the mattress against the wall so she could turn it later, picked up the bag and opened it. Curiosity, nothing else. If Gracie had private stuff in there, she shouldn't make it so accessible.

The bag held a tight, fat bunch of bills, rolled up and secured by a rubber band. She slipped the rubber band off and counted them. Forty-six-thousand dollars. God! So much money. They had plenty to eat, could travel to all the pageants, could pay their rent and all expenses, and she usually had a few hundred dollars left over every month, which she tucked away under her own mattress for a rainy day, but they had no bank account, paid everything in cash. Gracie said she felt more comfortable that way. Melissa had never seen that much money in one heap.

She was still shaking when Gracie came home. Deep inside, she knew the money belonged to Tiara. It couldn't be from the pageants, so all the pictures must be bringing in a lot more than Gracie said.

"You're stealing from us," she said. "From me, and from Tiara."

"Leave me alone," Gracie said. "You don't understand a goddamn thing. Look around you. You really think all this is paid for by a few pictures? One day maybe, when she's famous, then it'll be rolling in, but right now we'd be starving if I didn't supplement our income."

"Supplement it doing what?"

"See what I mean? God, you're such a selfish woman. You just sit back and wait for me to provide. Like it's my responsibility. If it weren't for Tiara..., but never mind. If you have to know, I'm doing business with my friends—this money here is investment money. It belongs to them, I'm only safekeeping it. But if you think I'm short-changing you, just say so."

Tiara

"I'm sorry," Melissa said. "You know I don't understand all that stuff. Cleaning up, that's all I'm good for around here."

Gracie broke into a big forgiving tease-grin.

"You're a pretty good cook, too. Even if your chili tastes like Canadian socks."

They laughed together, but from that day on their relationship, rocky to begin with, felt tinged with suspicion.

"…and I never trusted her after that fight," Melissa said. "I knew she cheated me."

"Whatever," her mother said. "But you're walking on very thin ice if you give interviews. One tiny crack and you land in cold water, believe me. Best if we both keep our mouths shut about what happened down there. No need to dwell on hidden money or how that money was made or stuff like that. That'll help Tiara more than anything. She's under age, they'll be lenient with her. But if the press or the police dig into her past, and into yours, it'll only make matters worse."

"A past that could've been avoided." My God, had she eaten the entire second Danish pastry already? "If you'd acted like a mother."

Her mother leaned back, moved her head sideways but kept staring at her. "You shouldn't eat so many sweets."

Melissa picked up a third Danish and smiled back at her. Small victories.

27

HIS Houston detective friend was reliable like clockwork. Macintosh had to smile when he saw Josh's request to Facetime him at 10:00 am. On his private line, of course. That's how they communicated since five years ago when Josh had found out that the Vancouver Police Department had booked a suspect, a Texan-born rich-kid Josh had been after for years. The scumbag had drugged and raped unsuspecting girls in night clubs and at parties in Houston for years but his parents had moved him to Vancouver before Josh could close in on him. Macintosh had not been officially involved on this case but was updated on it by his colleagues and had made unofficial contact with Josh to assist in bringing the scumbag to justice. Unfortunately, they had not succeeded. Exchanging important documents via official channels was excruciatingly slow, and a barrage of lawyers had put up endless hurdles to protect the rights of this scumbag.

10:00 am. Macintosh got him at the first ring. Josh confirmed Harding's research. No Tiara Rodriguez or Tiara Brown or Tiara Rodriguez-Brown registered anywhere in Texas in 1998 except for the birth certificate of said Tiara Rodriguez.

"But I found something else that might interest you," Josh said. "A Tiara Rodriguez participated in one of those kiddie beauty contests in 2003. She won the Miss Texas Princess title, crowned as Princess Tia. She was five then, so the age should be about right. I've emailed you the link to the contest. Check the winner's picture, she might be your alleged suspect, if she still looks remotely like that, which I doubt."

"Hold on."

Macintosh opened the email, opened the link, moved the cursor until he came to the top line of pictures, and there she was. A little girl, head proportionally larger than her body, reminding Macintosh of the famous Disney directive on how to draw proportions: *Comparatively larger heads appeal to our inborn desire to protect the weaker members of our species. That way the characters become instantly more lovable.*

He had to admit, it worked.

The girl was adorable. Big round face with a mass of curly dark hair, wide eyes, dark and shiny, long lashes. The smile came across a bit timid, which increased her loveliness. But there was something disturbing about that smile, too. She wore a midnight blue velvet dress with sparkling rhinestones along a low cut neckline. An evening dress designed for a grown woman with cleavage. Her eyes looked heavy with matching blue eye shadow, her lips bright red, dangling earrings. She looked like a beautiful miniature adult.

Macintosh couldn't take his eyes off the screen. The caption underneath the picture read: Princess Tia. Tiara Rodriguez. Winner, age 4 -6.

"Is that her?" Josh said.

"Princess Tia? Yes. No question. That's Tiara." Macintosh's eyes fell on the picture of a blond girl next to Tiara, titled: La Luna. Luna Vargas. Winner, age 6 – 10. Luna. Wasn't that the friend Tiara's mother had mentioned in her interview with the TV reporter? If this friendship was real, and not just a figment of Melissa's imagination, Luna might be able shed some light on Tiara's character.

"Can you do me another favor, Josh? Can you get me the contact of the winner of cat 6 - 10, Luna Vargas? I'd like to get in touch with her."

Josh promised without asking the reason. That's why he liked this guy so much. Willing to bend the rules for the greater good, and damn competent in doing so. Not many detectives were like that nowadays, most were too interested in keeping their jobs secure.

But Josh only let him off that easily on the professional stuff. "How are you holding up, my friend?"

"Getting ready for retirement."

"Still planning to move into your cabin in the mountains?"

Macintosh had told Josh about his plan to sell the house he and Kathy had bought up the coast, in

Tiara

Squamish, because he couldn't stomach the thought of living there without her, and that he might move into the tiny cabin in the mountains his family owned for generations. From Josh's unresponsive reaction at the time Macintosh gathered that Josh never thought much of the idea. He'd be happy to hear of his change of heart. "That's too remote," Macintosh said. "Even for me. I might go there for the occasional fishing trip, but I'll keep the house in Squamish, spend my final days there and wrestle the ghosts."

"Glad to hear that. You'll do fine," Josh said. "Take care."

Macintosh was relieved Josh hadn't come back with a platitude like 'time heals all wounds'. Then he would have to admit that this new concept of living in Squamish had been born only very recently. Tiara's fault. She had pointed out how wrong he was trying to push Kathy into obscurity. He'd place her picture on his bedside table, sit on the porch, and recall the good times they had together. He finally understood why he had never been able to sell the Squamish house.

Harding strolled over, looked at the open screen. "Is that—?"

"Child beauty pageant winner Tiara Rodriguez."

"Well, at least we know she was a child model of sorts, like her mother said."

"Like hell." Macintosh studied the picture again and felt his stomach acid rising. He burped. "Call the mother and tell her to get her fat ass over here, pronto. I want to know why she's so secretive about Tiara. Why didn't she give us her real name? Why tell us Tiara posed for pictures when she was a participant of a kiddy contest. The winner, even. Which, by the way, I don't like one little bit."

Harding reached for the phone.

"I was already pissed off with that woman, but this takes the cake." Macintosh downloaded the picture into his case file and renamed it the Princess file. "How can anybody in their right mind dress up a child like this?"

28

MY journal is becoming my lifeline. While I'm awake—on the bike, in the shower, eating breakfast, cleaning my cell, whatever—I think about what I will write down later on.

It seems my whole life is devoted to trying to remember my whole life. One hell of a job. Especially when this life of mine holds a secret I don't want to discover. Each passing year I describe in my journal brings me closer to this horrible, horrible moment when I have to face the fact that I have done something terrible. With that I don't mean the attack on the woman. I begin to accept the idea that it was me, although I still don't remember anything about the attack. Once I, or the detective, or the shrink, will figure out why I've done it, we will, together or individually, discover the secret beyond it. Knowing there must be a reason, I also know that I must be hiding something that is deep inside me that made me do it. Something that is part of my character. Something disgusting. Revolting. A flaw, so sickening, it makes normal people puke.

I dread the moment I will have to face this secret. It makes me want to rip the journal into tiny shreds, but then I'll never find out why I stabbed the woman. The attack and the secret are connected. Every time I think of the attack, I feel as if I acted on a quest I had to fulfill. Rid the world of an evil monster.

Princess Tia the dragon slayer.

However, underneath this noble act, buried deep under a mountain of rotten garbage, squirms the secret, wormlike and blind. The worm is coiled around my ankle and holds me down. If I don't dig myself free—and that means dragging the secret up with me—I'll suffocate under a ton of stink. I'm torn apart because I need to know, and I don't want to know. I have no choice. I must carry on searching, writing.

So be it. Going over my notes I realize I haven't even mentioned my seventh birthday. Here I am, already in the year leading to my eighth. Well, it couldn't have been very memorable, my

No-Birthday-Year

What happened that year? I was old enough to remember most parts of the domestic life Gracie, Mom, and I settled into.

Gracie was the center of my world—everything revolved around her. Mom was supposed to provide for me but she never did. Left it all to Gracie, except the home-schooling bit. She liked to correct me, scold me, train me like a parrot to make sure I wouldn't adapt the more colloquial expressions Gracie or The Stick used, the only Texans close to me.

In preparation for my future beauty queen career, Mom made me recite long passages from some of her library reading material. I'd have the advantage, she said, when the movie moguls knock on our door. I'd be able to memorize scripts much faster, and they'd like that. What did Mom do when she wasn't home-schooling me? No idea, except she took my soiled bed-sheets away and complained to Gracie how much work she had to do for my career.

Fact is, Gracie did everything that was necessary to make me into a big star, and that without any complaining, that's how much she loved me. I was her girl. She kept telling me how proud she was of me.

I never did complain either, although I didn't like a lot of the things Gracie made me do. Like the endless make-up sessions. When I was seven, she began to paste false eyelashes on my lids. Or experiment with hair pieces—she parted my real hair, pulled it tight over my skull and fastened the piece in the parting with long clips. Sometimes I cried because it hurt so much, then she loosened the clips a bit. Yes, this definitely started when I was seven, and like the lashes it became a routine procedure I had to endure.

One of the first things I did when I came here was chop off my hair. I wear it really short now, no more than an inch, and I don't wear make-up these days, none whatsoever. Can't stand the feel of cream or paint on my skin.

Tiara

Gracie told me countless times how beautiful and special I was. I was her whole world, her reason for being—she said that often. And if I ever stopped being good, horrible things would happen to us. The angels would turn into devils and punish us all. I never questioned that when I was little. Every word Gracie directed towards me, be it praise or reproach, counsel or condemnation, was axiomatic. My childhood baggage was the instinctive understanding that I had the power to destroy my two grown-ups. Gracie handed me that power along with its imbedded guilt.

That made me worried and angry at the same time. Is it possible to love someone and at the same time be really, really mad at them? To be so torn?

I decide to ask the shrink today. I don't want to wait until he reads about my emotional see-saw in my journal.

"Listen, doc, I've got a question."

"Go ahead."

"When I was young I remember being worried that something bad would happen to my mother and my aunt." I hesitate, almost don't tell him the next part. "I had fantasies of Mom slipping and falling down the stairs, and Gracie being run over by a car. Those thoughts felt good, yet at the same time I was terrified it would really happen, and I'd be all alone."

"I would need to evaluate this more in depth to figure out where the feeling originated."

Now, that's peculiar. Doc being evasive? Normally he is straightforward to a fault.

"I don't know enough about your upbringing to fully understand."

"There isn't much more to know," I say. "I had a fairly normal childhood and it isn't my mom's or Gracie's fault I blew a fuse."

"What about the other people in your life?" he asks.

"What other people?"

"Friends?"

I shake my head.

He rubs his eyes underneath his glasses.

"I didn't need friends."

He stops rubbing. "What about the other kids at those pageants?"

I think of Luna. Would she qualify as a friend? "What about them?"

"Didn't they have playgroups where the kids could play together while they waited until it was time for their performances?"

That takes care of Luna. She certainly wasn't a playmate.

"I'd never have played with any of them. Or they with me."

"Why not?"

He can't be that stupid. He's trying to make me lose my cool. I put on my best Gracie imitation. "You can never trust any of those children. They want the Grand

Tiara

Supreme crown real bad and they'll do anything to get it. They, and their mothers, the lot of them. They're your enemies. Don't you understand, Doc, those kids were my enemies, they'd have stopped at nothing to hurt me."

He smiles. "Do you realize you never call me by my name? You know it's Dr. Stanley Eaton, and you have my permission to call me Stanley if it makes it easier for you, but you don't seem to be able to address me by my name. Same with all the others who aren't your direct family. It's 'the photographer friend', 'the sponsor', 'the Stick'—none of those people have names."

With that he leaves again. I'm stew in a slow cooker. Lid on my bubbling anger. Mixed into the anger is the troubling question: Why don't they have names?

For three days I don't move from my cot. My anger rotates in a room full of balloons. When I try to grasp one with a firm grip, it bursts. Every eff-ing time. When I don't touch them, they bounce off my anger, disturbing and distracting me. I don't want that. I want to concentrate on one feeling only.

The anger.

I was seven when the anger started. The childish tantrums I threw until then had been harmless compared to the bitter frustration I felt at that age. Those had been mere top-of-the-lungs, little-fists-pounding, feet-stomping attention seekers. They only worked as long as I could be pacified with ice cream and cookies.

At seven, this wasn't enough anymore. I was confused. Strange demands, and no control to change anything unpleasant would do that to anybody, not only to a child.

I guess it wasn't a conscious reaction to withdraw into my own world. Not exactly a safe haven to fall back on. More of a dark hole to crawl into. I built myself a shelter with strong walls, curled up inside and made sure nothing spilled out. If the grown-ups noticed my confusion in the darkness—how badly I wanted for things to be different, how angry I got over my inability to say so—well, Gracie told me often enough what would happen. I was so confused. All my anger went inward and settled like mold, greenish-black speckles on the mortar that held the bricks of my seven-year-old wall together. My wall was still shaky. Every now and then my fearless self peeked over it and demanded to change the world. But what can a seven-year-old do?

Once I rebelled openly—oh, look at this, one of those elusive balloons, a bright red one. It floats right in front of me, doesn't burst when I get hold of it. I must be careful now, let the air out ever so gently—there you go, I can see myself, in the photo studio. I see Gracie, always Gracie. Then I see her photographer friend and another, one that takes over when Gracie leaves me alone with him. It's somebody clouded in a haze … I can't make it out … it's nothing but a purple shadow, faceless and voiceless.

Tiara

The photographer friend says Gracie should go now. I don't want her to, but she always does. To be left alone always feels wrong. I want Gracie there, fussing over me and explaining why I have to do what I have to do.

I hold the opening of the balloon between my fingers and make sure the air escapes very slowly. I need to go with the flow, don't disturb me now.

The Purple Shadow tries to take off my panties. It happened before, but this time I really don't want to. I wriggle and pout. When that doesn't work, I rebel.

"No! No! Leave me alone! I won't! I don't want to!" I want Gracie back.

Gracie. GracieGracieGracie.

The photographer friend rolls his eyes and goes on about me being a silly little girl, and then he tells the Purple Shadow to go and get Gracie. She comes back and says I'm a silly little girl, and I should be good and do what grown-ups want me to do. She doesn't know what grown-ups want me to do, she's never there.

I rise up on my toes and peek over the wall surrounding me. I start yelling *I don't want to, I don't want to, I don't want to!*

Gracie yells back at me, but no matter how loud she gets, I don't stop. Jeez, I'm proud of myself now, watching what escapes from this balloon. She takes me by her hand and drags me out of the studio.

On the way home I'm still defiant, and confused. Gracie keeps her eyes on the road, staring ahead, not saying anything, but eventually she starts sniffling and then I see that she's crying.

"I don't understand why you have to be such a bad girl," she says between sobs, "after all I do for you. Now something very, very bad will happen. We will have no money. We'll be evicted. We'll starve. The angels in heaven will weep and the dear Lord will punish all of us. And that'll be all your fault. Little girls should do what the grown-ups want, or terrible, terrible things might happen. We're all in danger now because of you."

"I'm sorry, I'm so sorry."

A quick turn to look at me, then back to the road.

"Maybe we can still avoid the wrath of the angels in heaven. Do you want to avoid the danger you put me and your mom and everybody else in this town in?"

Yes. Yes. Yes. Of course I do.

"First thing, you say nothing, to nobody about what just happened. The sponsor mustn't know."

I never had, but then again, I'd never rebelled before.

"Not a word, not even to your mom, that's very important. If you're a good girl again, then maybe, just maybe, the angels will forgive you."

Yes. Yes. I will.

"And then, next time, you do as you're told."

The air is nearly out, the deflated balloon hangs limp over my hand. There's a little bit left. I put my other hand over it and press very gently—

Tiara

I remember now.

My seventh birthday didn't happen *because a hurricane rolled in from the Atlantic*. We'd planned to go to a seaside restaurant, for cakes and ice cream, but all the restaurants were boarded up. Hurricane Katrina was coming.

When Gracie and I got home from the interrupted session, Mom looked frantic. She'd heard the forecast and tried and tried to reach us, not knowing where we were.

I remember thinking, good, she doesn't know. She must never know, then the angels won't be angry and nothing bad will happen to me and Gracie and all the others.

A few days later, soon after my seventh birthday, we were all huddled together in an underground shelter when Katrina hit. It was a majestic storm, one the world would acknowledge later on as the biggest, most devastating hurricane of all times. Galveston was not flooded as bad as New Orleans, but the storm did a lot of damage in my home town, too.

Everybody in the shelter held on to each other, grown-ups and children alike, terrified by the horrific noise Katrina made outside—a furious noise, like it was desperate to get in—and by the infectious angst wafting through the shelter like poisonous gas. Gracie held me real tight when she saw me shivering with fear.

She brought her mouth close to my ear and whispered, "See? See what you have brought upon all of us?"

29

MACINTOSH rushed over to the interview room as soon as he heard that Melissa had arrived at the station. He was already in position, drumming his fingers on the table, when they brought her in. Harding arrived at the same time, bent down and whispered into his ear.

"Another email came in from Josh."

"Not now."

Macintosh could barely wait for Melissa to sit down before he took his first shot.

"You lied to me!" He slammed his fist down. He meant to startle Melissa, but she barely flinched.

"The address in Galveston you gave me, number 357 on Caroline Road, doesn't exist!"

"Oh, that. I realized later I must have given you my old address, the one where we briefly lived when I moved to Texas. That whole block got destroyed by Katrina, so it wouldn't surprise me if that house is gone."

"So what was your last address?"

Melissa scratched her head. "Huh, let me think—"

"You forgot?"

"Yes."

"You told me all sorts of crap. Like you worked for a living down there."

"Well, I did, for a brief while. Since when is that a crime?"

"With all the money Tiara's father supposedly left you? Since when does the army pay for unmarried partners?"

"An inheritance. I was in his will."

Macintosh's eyebrows shot up. "Great. An official document."

"It wasn't a legal thing. He left me cash. Through friends."

"What a trusting guy he must have been." He changed directions when he saw her squirm in her seat. "You told us your daughter worked for various modeling agencies. We checked with all major ones active at that time. None had a Tiara Brown registered."

Melissa didn't miss a beat. "She had an agent. She handled all the bookings and everything. I wouldn't know which agencies she worked with."

"The agent's name?"

"Oh, I can't remember that."

"How convenient. Looks to me you're bad with addresses and names."

Melissa looked up to the ceiling, rolled her head as if she needed to loosen her shoulder muscles, looked down again, mumbled, "I think it was Margarita…, huh, Rios. Yes, that's it. Margarita Rios."

Macintosh jotted down the name. "You gave me a cock-and-bull story about Tiara calling herself Princess Tia. Why didn't you tell me that this was her stage name for beauty contests?"

"She gave herself that name, and I liked it, so I used if for the contests I booked her in."

"I thought she had an agent?"

"Only for the photo shoots. I did the contests."

This woman wasn't as stupid as she made out to be.

"Why didn't you tell us that her father's name was Rodriguez?"

"She's never met her father, he wasn't important to her," Melissa said, all innocence. "And anyway, Tiara's name is Brown, not Rodriguez. If you accuse me of lying, you have to prove me wrong first."

"Lady, let me tell you something: I don't have to prove anything to you. Your daughter is accused of a serious crime. Your attitude is not giving me the impression that you want to help her, which makes me wonder what else you're trying to hide from us."

Melissa leaned back in her chair as much as her bulk would allow, crossed her arms.

"I'm not hiding anything."

"Yeah? Nothing, huh? Nothing at all?" Macintosh pressed a button, his computer screen lit up. He pressed another button. "How about that? You know nothing about that?"

She made a face, moved closer to the screen as if her eyesight wasn't the best.

"Sure I do. I told you she was a child model."

"You were responsible for dressing her up like that?"

Melissa straightened. Hand up on her chest, covering her heart. "Oh my, how lovely. I did all that, not only prepping her like that, but coaching her for every contest as well. What a princess she was. So pretty. Everybody adored her. A natural beauty."

Harding jumped in, "I got to say, that doesn't look very natural to me. But I'm only a guy. I guess you'd know more about how to fix up a kid for those shows."

Macintosh shot him a look but let him carry on.

Melissa rewarded his partner with a big smile. "A lot of children enter those contests. A lot of them, what am I saying, all of them, are really good-looking. We needed to enhance Tiara's beauty so she'd stand out from the others. And look at her, she sure deserved this crown. I seem to remember it was the Miss Texas Princess, right?" She moved close to the screen again, squinting. "Yes, I'm sure it was. I remember that dress. Adorable. She blew them all away."

"And after that, did you enter her into other contests?" Harding said.

"Of course." She listed a few of them, Harding scribbled them on his pad. "But I don't see what that's got to do with what happened the other day. In fact, I'm getting rather annoyed with this questioning. If you don't give me an explanation, a good reason for this, I'll get myself a lawyer. Don't think I won't because I can't afford it. In that case people are entitled to court-appointed legal counsel."

Macintosh gave her his best cat-ate-the-canary expression.

"Oh, do threaten us, Melissa Brown," he said. "I'll be delighted to discuss a few things with your counsel. Like how you withheld information from the police."

Melissa lifted herself out of her chair, breathing hard.

"I did no such thing. Stop accusing me."

Harding was close to the door. He didn't step aside when she tried to leave the room. "One more thing, Mrs. Brown."

"What?"

"Did it never cross your mind that dressing up your daughter like this attracts child molesters?"

"How dare you!" Melissa pushed him out of her way. "Now I certainly will get myself a lawyer!" She stormed out, slammed the door behind her.

"Holy crap, Harding, what was that all about?" Macintosh said.

"Open your mailbox."

Macintosh wondering why Josh had used the official department channel to send him any information with the subject 'T. Rodriguez' until he read the message.

Tiara

"Have run the Princess Tia picture through face recognition. The attached has come up. Please open attachment and call me." Macintosh did.

Another picture of Princess Tia popped up. She looked a bit older than in the first picture, maybe six or seven, but she wore the same sparkling crown. She posed on her stomach on a white fake fur rug, propped up on her elbows, looking straight into the camera with big innocent eyes, no smile. Aside from the crown and all the make-up, the girl was buck naked. Her little butt up in the air like a Playboy Bunny pose.

Macintosh dialled Josh's department number and waited for the staff sergeant to connect him.

"It's from a pedophile sites we closed down some time ago," Josh said when he got on the phone.

"Good grief." Macintosh let out a shaky breath. "How many more of those pictures are out there?"

"We only found that one so far, but they're really digging now. We think we'll find more."

Macintosh fought down instant rage. Damn. Sick bastards. What kind of person makes kids pose for such pictures? What kind of man spends money on such images? What kind of mother enables this?

"I'm glad I didn't see this earlier," he said to Josh. "I just finished interviewing the mother, a certain Melissa Brown. It all starts to make sense now. Why we couldn't find any records of her living in Texas. Why Melissa gave us a wrong address. Why she and her mother wanted to hide things from us. They sold images of Tiara—God knows at what young age—to pedophiles, that's why!"

"With that history, no wonder the girl is messed up," Josh said.

Macintosh got up, paced. He had to keep his rage in check, had to stay level-headed. "We're getting closer to motive."

"Doesn't give her the right to go around cutting people up, though," Josh said. "A lot of those kids turn our all right. At least they get their chances. Like Tiara's friend Luna you asked me about."

"The one who was a winner in the same year as Tiara? What about her?"

"She did okay. Was an upcoming star, even got a contract for a movie in her pocket. I mean, her mother did—"

"A movie?"

"It never came to that. For some reason Lionsgate cancelled the contract. I'm not sure why. I'll get you the contact info for the mother, Camila Vargas, who's also been her agent. Let me know if you need anything else."

"Thanks. You're the man."

Could be of value. Depending on how well Camila and Luna knew Tiara. He'd deal with this information in due course. First, he needed to get a grip on himself. Get rid of the disgust he felt for Melissa before it exploded out of him with the force of an atomic bomb. Blast her sky high. He'd like nothing better than make

Tiara

her accountable, but for what? Aside from a picture of untraceable origin, he had nothing on her. Not yet. Focus. Follow the leads. Keep your repulsion in check, make it work for you. For the case. For the poor little thing on the white fur rug.

"Harding," he said. "Let's get serious. I want every sordid detail about Melissa's life in Texas dug up, examined, turned over, recorded. I want to know everything, the minutest crappy detail, you understand. Do your online checks, a Google search, whatever. And ask Josh to send you anything he can find out about her—", he paused, looked at his notes, "and about a talent agent named Margarita Rios. She must be involved. Forward an official request, just in case Josh can't justify the time spent on it and needs his ass covered. I won't get back to Melissa until we're sure about her role in this fucking shit child exploitation drama. Let her feel safe for now. Let her talk to a lawyer. And let's check out Louise just as thoroughly." He remembered Melissa warning her mother to keep her blabbermouth shut. "She's involved, too. I want to know every goddamn detail about those two sleazebags. You understand me?"

"Even if it's not a homicide?"

"I'll show this picture to the sergeant and get his approval to involve Sexual Offense Squad. Trust me, when he sees this, it'll take less than a second to get the ball rolling officially."

Harding rushed off.

Macintosh knew, without the sergeant's explicit approval they'd be balancing the investigation on a tightrope. For the first time he saw a distinct advantage in being close to retirement. He wasn't going after a promotion anymore, and nobody would demote him if he didn't stick to the book.

But what a nightmare. What he had seen on that computer screen distorted his whole take on the case. The poor girl. Growing up in an abusive environment, unable to understand that this wasn't normal. To use kids as pornographic models—who'd sink that low? Her own mother of all people, how sick was that? The thought made him want to horsewhip Melissa.

He had to go outside, take a walk, get back his mojo, then face Tiara at the center again.

30

MELISSA sat on the narrow bench of the Boundary Road bus stop, the one closest to the police station. She had to wait twenty minutes for her bus, enough time to calm down and get a grip. What devil possessed her to threaten the detectives with legal counsel? She couldn't afford a good lawyer, and one of those legal aid fools would only mess things up even more. This whole business was spiraling out of control.

She needed to speak to somebody to get some solid advice. It would have to be her mother, the only person in the world who had some understanding of the events in the past that led to this current disaster. The idea of having to involve her yet again was not something she relished. Her mother would throw a fit when she heard the latest, and then, after composing herself, would barge in like a storm trooper and take over. How often had she been steamrolled by her mother and deeply regretted it later on. Last time three years ago, when she'd been desperate enough to finally, finally phone her.

Tiara

"It's me."

Her mother was never speechless, not even after twelve years without any communication between them.

"Christ, Melissa, I can't believe this. What on earth—"

"I can't talk long, so listen. The child I had twelve years ago is a girl. Her name is Tiara. Your grandchild and I, we need your help."

"You need money?"

Melissa heard the accusing undertone in her mother's voice, and gasped. This was a mistake. A terrible mistake. But then her mother surprised her. "I mean, sure," she said, "whatever. Tell me what you need."

"We need to get away from here. My girl's in trouble. It's too dangerous for her here."

"What kind of trouble?"

"You know, drugs and stuff. I need to get her away. There're some bad people here."

"You want me to send you money for the bus?"

Money. She needed more than that from her mother.

"You want me to get on a Greyhound with your grandchild? Do you have any idea how often we'd have to change bus? How long this would take?"

Her mother was silent.

"Can't you get us?"

"Give me a day or so to organize a few things," Louise said. "It's a long drive. I call you when I leave."

Melissa didn't even want to think about the enormous task of organizing a rescue mission thousands of kilometers away, but she knew her mother was capable of doing whatever was necessary. They'd agreed to meet at a pre-arranged spot in front of the NASA Space Center—the only place Melissa could think of that was easy to locate. Her mother would find it.

Three days after the phone call, Melissa took the morning bus from Galveston to Houston. She sat on the long seat that stretched across the back of the bus, next to two voluptuous Mexican women who never stopped talking for a single second. She stared out the window all the way from Galveston's main station to the bus change at the NASA bypass. Industrial landscape connected the two cities, nothing but concrete box buildings and parking lots, crossed by countless hydrolines. So ugly.

The bus moved at a slow but even speed, getting her closer and closer to the woman she had managed to ignore for so long.

She arrived nearly two hours before their prearranged time. Her mother had to drive all the way down from Canada, God knows when she'd get here. She might even be late. The wait gave Melissa time to think. What on earth was she doing? How could she bring her mother into this mess? She'd only make it worse. Melissa felt another anxiety attack coming. Nerve-racking. She reminded herself how efficient her mother was. Annoy-

Tiara

ingly bossy. Wasn't that what she needed now? But what if her mother didn't believe her story? Brush it aside with one of her famous don't-be-a-fool-Melissa-you're-always-imagining-things strokes. She wouldn't do that. Not in this desperate situation. She'd have to take her word for it, even if she didn't understand it all. She'd have to help. Her mother owed her. Big time.

By the time Louise finally showed up, at about three in the afternoon, Melissa was beyond worrying. What an unbearably hot afternoon. Even in the shade of the ample oak trees on the space center's eerily empty parking lot, she knew the temperature had to be over thirty degrees Celsius. She couldn't sweat anymore, not a drop of fluid left in her, even with the super-sized bottle of Coke she'd gulped down since she arrived. The soda evaporated right out of her, she hadn't needed to pee even once.

A silver Honda Civic slowed toward the main entrance. Melissa stepped out of the shade, waved. The car changed direction, headed to the treed area. Melissa walked to the car, dragging her swollen feet, her inner thighs already raw from rubbing together. She had to suppress a sudden wave of hostility. Damn it, Mother, where have you been the last twelve years?

Louise stepped out of the car, leaned back, eyes wide.

"Good Lord, Melissa! I hardly recognize you."

"My weight is the least of my worries right now."

Louise made one of her tsk-tsk faces which meant *there's absolutely NO excuse for letting yourself go like this*. But at least she didn't say it.

"Where's my granddaughter?"

"At home, in Galveston."

"But—"

"She wouldn't come. Tiara's a headstrong girl, and if she doesn't want to go somewhere there's nothing I can do to change her mind."

A fleeting smile lit Louise's face.

"Guess she got that from me. They do say character traits jump a generation."

31

WHEN Macintosh thought of that innocent child made into a grown-up fantasy figure with definite sexual insinuations his heart seized up like a rusty old motor. He hated to admit to himself that he didn't want to connect the image of the little girl on the white rug with the suspect waiting for his next interrogation. Offenders weren't supposed to turn into victims. He didn't want to know.

But the picture stuck in his mind and didn't want to let go. He tried, by God he tried, but it was like rubbing chewing gum off his sole. No way could he continue to classify the teenager that this girl had grown into as a juvenile criminal who'd lost her mind, be it temporarily or permanently. Every time he pictured fragile Tiara in the orange prison suit, he wondered what kind of twisted path, what type of adult manipulation led her to self-destruct in such spectacular fashion. She must have suffered terrible abuse, and now he would be instrumental to give others leverage over her future. Some uncaring judicial system would determine her punishment.

What if he couldn't find plausible motive that was related to her screwed-up childhood? What if she couldn't remember in time? Then everybody would assume she simply lost it, and nobody would care why.

Macintosh called it a day, got in his car, headed south. Before he knew it, he steered into the center's parking lot. Once inside, they made him wait for ten minutes.

When Tiara was brought in, he didn't have a clue what he would say to her. Should he ask her point blank about that awful picture of her on his computer screen? Did he even have the right to confront a fifteen-year-old with the filth grown-ups subjected her to when she'd been little? Why was he here, if he didn't?

She wasn't as upbeat as last time; in fact, she seemed broody.

"You look like shit," she said.

"That's exactly what I need after a rough day."

"You want sympathy, go home to your wife."

"She's dead."

"Shit. I mean, sorry."

"Forget it."

She stopped talking for a moment. Studied her toes. Gave him some time. But then she attacked from an unexpected angle.

"Is that why you hurt so much?" she asked. "How did she die? Did she get killed?"

The words alone had the ability to inflict pain. "Your social graces need some polishing," he said.

"Not a lot of opportunity for that in here."

"Nobody ever taught you manners?"

She looked thoughtful for a second, seemed to contemplate his rather insensitive remark. "I guess not," she said. "From the little snippets I remember, we can safely assume my upbringing wasn't exactly a high-class affair."

He shook his head, disgusted with himself, but at least it gave him a new opening. He took out his notebook. "Do you mind telling me what you do remember?"

"You mean about my childhood?"

"Yes."

"That's easy. Next to nothing. All I know is that I don't know how to behave. Proof given."

"And you still don't remember what led to the attack?"

"Honestly, I don't."

She held eye contact, didn't flinch, the glance directed at him hard as steel. This girl had built herself some armor, had been forced into it by the cruel circumstances of her childhood. *Circumstances?* Was he serious? Call the spade a spade, detective. Kids don't end up naked on fur rugs by accident. People put them there.

"Do you remember where you grew up?"

"Please. By now you know I'm from Texas. You know probably more about me and my upbringing than I do, and if you don't, you're one hell of a lousy policeman. I won't repeat stuff you already know. You're after stuff connected to the attack, but I keep telling you, I don't remember anything about it. And for the record, I would like to be able to tell you more. I would, I honestly would, if I could." She took a deep breath. "It's pretty tough not knowing what makes you tick."

He waited.

"Don't you understand?" She forced every single word out through gritted teeth: "I... do... not... remember... anything!"

"If this is an act, you're quite talented."

Her lips, her whole expression, relaxed again and she started to giggle. It came naturally, from deep inside, bright and melodic, much different from the nervous giggle she'd fallen into before. Hers was a sound he hadn't heard for so long, it turned a metal screw in that locked-up heart of his.

"If I could fool a guy like you, I'd be a contender for an Oscar."

He was fighting sudden mellowness. A softening inside that made him not only pity her but like her. Now he had a new conflict to deal with.

"Don't think for a minute you can fool me. Or your psychiatrist. Or the judge."

"I don't." She wrinkled up her face. "Can I ask you something?"

He shrugged, still caught in the sound of her teenage giggles. So harmless. So much like Danielle. Made him realize yet again how empty his life had become.

"If it wasn't your wife who got killed—?"

He stiffened. "Why do you want to know?"

For a long time, only the clock on the wall ticked away time. Then Tiara got up, looked down on him.

"I guess I'll never know, then."

"Why's that?" he asked, but he could see that he'd lost her.

"Because I can't answer your question," she said. "I have no idea why this is important to me." She shuffled to the door, shoulders down, feet dragging, knocked.

The guard opened the door to let her out.

In a low voice he said to her back, "It wasn't my wife who got killed. It was my daughter. A scumbag at a party slipped a pill in her drink. Turned out it was bad stuff." For a moment he wasn't sure if she heard him. "She was your age when she died."

She stopped in her tracks and turned around. Her face mirrored the pain he felt.

"I'm so sorry for your loss."

She was genuine. Sincere. He understood the honesty and the deep compassion in her words. He understood that she wasn't lying, about anything.

32

THE last of the leaves has fallen. One shriveled brown leftover of colorful autumn has finally given up clinging to Mother Nature and drifted to the pavement. I stood by my prison window and watched the wind play with it before it touched the ground.

Now I see only bare branches scratching a dull sky with spindly fingers. November in Vancouver is like bathing in gray water—without a scent, a color, a candle.

Dreary.

Like me.

Going to Birthday Eight

I'm bloated with anger and angst. Angst. I like that German word better than fear—it sounds dark and threatening. Angst is deviated from its original meaning Enge, which means tightness. My life is controlled by those two emotions. The moment I get angry over the things I don't want to do, I tense up, turn rigid, and everything inside me tightens. My lungs constrict, I can't breathe, my mind goes blank, which leads to one of my

Tiara

anxiety attacks, which in turn results in my complete surrender. I do what I'm told without question or complaint.

What they make me do needs me to be a puppet without a brain.

Because of the devastation Katrina caused, all pageants were cancelled a week after my seventh birthday. People in southern states had to rebuild and reshape their future, they had to set priorities. To watch beautiful and talented kids perform on stage wasn't one of them. Gracie had to fire The Stick. The photo sessions continued. I didn't need a dance instructor for those.

August is really hot in Texas, but on that particular August when I turned eight, the ocean breeze carried cooler air, and we decided to celebrate my birthday in the famous Hotel Galvez on Seawall Boulevard (on the wrong side, of course, like everything in my home town). Although nearly a year had passed the hotel was still under renovation from Katrina's damage but the lobby restaurant with its elegant stucco ceiling and pillars had opened again. There they served huge ice cream cups with chocolate sauce, topped with colored beads and cute little glass monkeys holding umbrellas.

The three of us sat together in the lobby. Mom craned her neck to catch a glimpse of the Gulf of Mexico, when Gracie announced that the first pageants were opening up again. She wanted to enter me in all of them. Truly Unique Pageant, Model Search Pageant, Miss

Heart of America, Midwest Fabulous Dolls—all catering to age group eight to twelve. She planned several years of hectic pageantry for me.

"What are you thinking?" Mom said. "That's way too many."

Gracie crossed out the Bella Latina Pageant. "That won't work. Tiara's got an important photo session that day."

"You can't seriously plan all those contests *and* do photo sessions."

"The photo sessions pay for the contests, in case you've forgotten," Gracie said. "But what's it to you? You can stay home and stuff your face while I earn our keep."

"That's unfair. I'd come along, but you said the photographer doesn't want me there."

"And right he is because mothers are always a pain."

"And aunts aren't?"

"Exactly."

"You're jealous because you'll never be a mom."

Gracie's face clouded over.

"If I had a daughter, I'd be a hell of a better mother than you."

"You always think what you do is so important. But you are wrong. Those sessions aren't getting her famous, it's the contests that do it. Tiara spends way too much time doing those pictures. She needs more time for dance lessons. I insist. I'm her mother. I won't allow such excessive picture taking any longer. I'm telling you, no more photo sessions."

I got all excited when I heard Mom say that. I jumped up and down on the giant lobby couch, nearly knocking over my humongous ice cream cup on the low table in front of me.

"Yes, yes, please!" I squeaked like a piglet. "I'll do all the pageants, I'll study hard, I'll practice my dance lessons, I'll learn all the poems by heart, I'll let you put those false nails on me."

That was a huge concession on my part. When they put acrylic powder with a chemical solution to my nails and held them under a heat-lamp it burned like hell.

Gracie turned on me.

"What's the matter with you? You want to complain about a few photo shoots? Don't you know what happens when you do that?"

All I wanted was for the photo sessions to stop. By now I had a deep aversion against sitting in front of the one-eyed monster, the large black round hole on the camera that was so dangerous because it always swallowed me up whole. Left no trace of me.

"Mom, please?"

Mom didn't look at me. She looked at Gracie who went on telling her, and me, how bitterly disappointed she was in the both of us. After all, last year hadn't been easy. With no pageants lined up, how would I ever become famous if it weren't for the exposure those pictures gave me, and how would we all survive if I didn't do my duty? The pictures had always been the back-up plan, and thank God we'd had them the past year. And thank God for the sponsor, who knew best how to manage the sessions—a meaningful side glare at Mom—without mothers.

Mom stroked my back although I didn't need soothing, I had already given up.

"Tia, Gracie is right. We need the money. I'm sure we'll find enough time between the pageants and the pictures to keep your lessons up to date."

When my shrink—oh, all right, it's silly to keep calling him that—when Stanley showed up again, I had a burning question on my mind.

"Stanley," I say, "back in my ninth year, I was pretty messed up. I felt so confused all the time. Either I was mad like hell, or I was scared. Sometimes even both at the same time. Why did I feel like that? And still do so often?"

For once he doesn't reply with another question.

"Well, let's start with the anger. What was it about the sessions that made you so angry?"

"I never said the sessions made me angry."

"Then what did?"

"If I knew, I wouldn't have to ask you."

"Okay. Why don't you tell me about those sessions anyway?"

Tiara

"What do you want to know?"

"Whatever you tell me. Who was there?"

"Gracie's photographer friend. And Gracie of course."

"Was she always there?"

I had to think hard. My memories are not an open book where I can flip through the chapters.

"Usually, yes. But only in the beginning."

"Was there anybody else?"

"The Purple Shadow."

"But you don't know who that was?"

I look at the ceiling. Nothing there.

"It's all blurry. All I can make out is a shape. And a color. I don't know why I'm thinking of purple. Maybe it's because I don't like it."

"Quite possible. Because you didn't like what was happening in the photo studio, your repulsion by association makes sense. What was this Purple Shadow doing there?"

"Watching."

"Watching what?"

"Me. Having my pictures taken. Helping the photographer do art."

"I see. How did you feel about that?'

"About what?"

"About being handled by the Purple Shadow."

"Oh, I don't know. Okay, I guess."

"Did you get angry then?"

"No."

"Did you feel angst?"

"No, you've got it wrong. I wasn't angry or scared when we did sessions. It was at all the other times. Before I went to the studio, and after. I got mad at Mom, or even Gracie, about I don't know what, and then I couldn't breathe. Sometimes it got so bad, I'd faint."

"You never fainted when you had a session?"

Here comes the feeling again. This Stanley guy is nuts. He doesn't get it. Why the hell doesn't he understand?

"Of course not. Why should I faint? I didn't *feel* anything!" I'm yelling now. "I wasn't there, that wasn't ME!"

Now I'm crying. I cry because I don't understand. How can I make him understand what I don't understand myself?

Stanley gives me a tissue, gives me a smile.

"Wow, we've made huge progress today."

I'm so mad, I could kill him.

33

MACINTOSH enjoyed puzzles. Not only crossword puzzles in the Sunday papers, picture puzzles, too. They relaxed him.

By now, his Princess file had turned into an oversized puzzle made up of information he and Harding had gathered. He kept studying the pieces and tried to make them fit. Not a single one fell comfortably into place.

Josh had called again, told him Camila Vargas had moved out of her original address about two years ago.

"She left the country?"

"Must have. No known address, and she hasn't filed a tax return since. That's all I know about her. But at least I have some interesting news on Margarita Rios. She never worked as a talent agent. She was a married home maker, had never held a job in her life."

Macintosh could feel it in his gut that this piece of the puzzle mattered. He asked Josh to find out the address of Margarita Rios, please.

Josh hesitated, didn't do his usual sure thing reply. Macintosh's antennas went up immediately. "What's up?"

Tiara

He could picture Josh rubbing his cheeks, mulling over his answer.

"Spit it out."

"About that Margarita," Josh said. "She had a run in with the law. Got probation. After that, she's off the radar, too."

"What run in?" Before Josh could answer, he knew. Drugs. Always drugs. And always this attempt to cover him in cotton wool when it came to that. He couldn't blame Josh. He knew how hard he had taken it when Danielle's killer walked. He meant well.

"Drugs," Josh said.

"When did she disappear?" Again, his instinct knew the answer. "About three years ago?"

He heard Josh click on his computer. "Close enough. Two years, eight months."

After he hung up, he tried to fit the two new puzzle pieces – Luna's mother Camila Vargas and Tiara's agent Margarita Rios—into the picture. Both couldn't be located. Weird coincidence, except, he didn't believe in coincidences.

Other than interviewing her, Tiara herself was impossible to investigate. She didn't have a cell phone. She didn't own a computer. He had double-checked on line—she must be the only fifteen-year-old in British Columbia without a Facebook or Twitter or Instagram or other social networking accounts popular with teens. She was cooperating with the court-appointed shrink but refused to see her lawyer or her case worker.

His last visit had left him fighting inner turmoil. Being convinced that she wasn't lying when she said she couldn't remember who she'd attacked or why, he should leave it up to Eaton to make some progress on her memory front, but that line of thought left him with a bitter aftertaste.

Would Eaton be capable to figure out what drove her? He should, he dealt with juvenile criminals all day long, but would he care enough? Would he put justice for a victim above judicial procedure? No way. His assessment of the scumbag who killed Danielle had not been completed when trial started. It might have changed the outcome if the judge would have seen what a psychopath the guy was. Without it, the scumbag's lawyer had used a loophole to get his client released. Eaton should have had his priorities right, but he hadn't cared enough.

If Eaton now assessed Tiara's mental state without considering her exploitation, she'd be swallowed up by a soulless bureaucracy resting on a superficial psychological assessment. And if he, the seasoned detective, didn't give this last case his best shot, he'd fail her, too. She deserved that much, and so did he.

Give the shrink a run for his money.

The victim's slow recovery left another gaping hole in his puzzle. Over the weeks the swelling subsided, but the doctors still kept her in a medically induced coma. On his last check at the hospital, the doc on duty told

Tiara

him that they would try to wake her up soon. He promised to inform him as soon as the victim was able of answering a simple question like who the hell are you. Macintosh was keen to ask this question, hoped like hell the poor woman recovered enough to reveal her identity. Her face was damaged beyond recognition—and would remain so forever. If she woke up with permanent brain damage, she'd be another dead end, literally.

You need help there, Macintosh. Don't go this one alone.

Macintosh forwarded the picture of little Tiara on the white shag rug to Sexual Offense Squad, and attached what little info he had with a request to try and match it to their data base. Hopefully they wouldn't be too busy with their own ongoing cases. He pulled his notes from the file, which was in danger of getting buried under other files, all cases needing a mountain of paperwork to succeed in court. Those other victims deserved his attention as much as Tiara did. Very soon he wouldn't be able to justify spending time on the Princess case. He closed the file with a frustrated sigh just as Harding walked by.

"Any new development?" Harding said, with a sideways glance at the closed Princess file.

"I think I'll try the shrink again."

Harding grabbed a chair. Macintosh looked up the Eaton's office number, picked up the phone, put it on speaker and dialed. This time he got lucky.

"You haven't returned my calls, Dr. Eaton," he said. "About Tiara Brown."

"I'm sorry, Detective Macintosh. I have you on my list for this week."

"That's good to know." Macintosh rolled his eyes at Harding. "I'm wondering if you can assist us with some information."

"Please ask."

"I've seen the initial report you've submitted. There's nothing in it that gives us any lead toward Tiara's motive or the victim's involvement with her."

"A mental fitness assessment is usually quite superficial, Detective. At the time I made Tiara's, she wasn't cooperating with me. All it could do was establish that she's mentally fit to stand trial. But you may be aware that the judge ordered a more comprehensive assessment for her next hearing."

"Yeah, we know that. How come you took her on?"

"It's unusual, yes, but she made her resolution to cooperate with anybody but me quite clear. Tiara's an interesting case, especially because certain elements of her story don't match the initial court report."

"Like what?"

"Well, let's say the attack is out of character for her. That's what tempted me to continue working with her."

"Isn't she lucky." Macintosh could hear the sarcasm dripping in his voice. *Tone it down. Get what you can from the pencil pusher.* "No disrespect there, doctor."

Tiara

"None taken. I do believe this case warrants not only my personal involvement but also a closer look by representatives of the Sexual Offense Squad. The situation Tiara has grown up in was exceptionally exploitive. She's been living with her mother and her aunt, and was subjected to emotional and physical abuse by a number of adults, with or without the full consent of her relatives, that is something I do not wish to speculate on. It certainly left deep scars on Tiara's psyche. I suspect early sexualization, conduct disorder, and self-harm, but you can't quote me on that yet. You'll get a copy of my full assessment as soon as it's ready."

Macintosh forced a big long sigh. Let the doc hear his frustration. "When will that be?"

"I don't know. She hasn't disclosed herself fully."

"Meaning?"

Now Dr. Eaton sighed—barely audible, but Macintosh could hear it.

"She's still struggling to uncover the trauma she suffered."

"And you're sure she stabbed the victim because of that trauma?"

The shrink sounded piqued now. "I'm not sure of anything until I've completed my assessment."

"Okay, okay, let's leave it at that," Macintosh said. "We haven't been able to establish the victim's identity yet. Did you gain any knowledge that might help us on that one?"

"Nothing I've learned so far indicates she knew the victim. But again, I haven't—"

"Finished your assessment, I know, I know." Macintosh thanked him and hung up.

"Why didn't you send him those pictures Josh dug up?" Harding said.

"Don't want to get his assessment tainted."

"Christ almighty," Harding said, "you still hate the guy?"

"Tiara's amnesia is genuine. If she is hiding anything from us, it's most likely out of shame. But I want to know if the doc comes up with the same conclusion all by his studied self."

"Is this a pissing match?"

"Um, maybe."

"I bet he can't figure her out," Harding said. "Look at this call—a total waste of time."

Macintosh couldn't suppress a big grin. "I wouldn't say that. Eaton did mention something interesting. The girl grew up with her mother *and* an aunt. How about that?"

Harding snapped his fingers. "Right, he did say that."

"An aunt in Texas will most likely be a relative from the father's side. Miguel Rodriguez was a soldier. Put in a request to the military for personal information on him. Simple family data, should be fairly easy to obtain. Go look for the aunt. She might shed some light on this mess."

34

MELISSA walked up the steep gravel driveway to her mother's house. The front porch with its wooden pillars was rotting away under peeling paint, the roof shingles were buckling. A gutter had slipped out of the drainage pipe—the next downpour would flood the porch, maybe even the house. She never noticed when she'd been a child, but now the obvious neglect bothered her. After all, the house with its great location in North Vancouver would be hers one day.

She paused to steady her breath before she knocked on the warped entrance door. It took a while for her mother to open it, her cheeks puffy from her afternoon nap.

"Come on in," Louise said. "I'll make us coffee."

Melissa followed her into the kitchen and took a seat at the dining table. It was dim and cold inside the house, nearly as cold as the early November air outside. Although the walk from the bus station left her sweating, she shivered and pulled her cardigan tighter.

"You look done in." Her mother poured water into the coffeemaker. "From that short walk? Really."

"I'm here because I need your help," Melissa said. "I think they're on to us."

Louise turned to her and sat down across the table.

"Who?"

"Detective Macintosh. He knows she was registered under the name of Rodriguez."

"So what?" Louise got up again and set out two mugs. "Since when is it a crime to send a pretty girl to beauty pageants?"

"If they find out about Tony—"

"Find out what?"

"You can't be that stupid." Melissa looked out the window.

Her mother poured coffee into the mugs, brought them over, her face tight with guilt. *You should feel guilty like hell, mother, for neglecting me when I needed you. For ignoring me for so long. For being such a stubborn, calculating, cold-hearted witch.*

"I don't want to talk about it."

"Excuse me, didn't you say you came here for help? How am I going to help you if you refuse to tell me the whole story? Nothing makes sense inside my head, and I can't give you any advice if you're not honest with me."

Melissa took a scalding sip of coffee. Not enough sugar.

"I don't know where to begin."

"You could begin by telling me the truth. Once and for all, did you have an affair with that man?"

"Tony?" Melissa whispered. "Look at me. What man would want me?"

Her mother's eyes wandered down. Melissa clamped her thighs together. Her knees didn't touch.

"Tiara was about five or six when he started to give her lessons, right?" Louise said. "That would have been about nine years ago. I assume you weren't in such bad shape then, and some men—especially southern men—like their women curvy."

"All right. If you must know, Tony and I did have a relationship. It started about a year after Gracie hired him."

"Why the hell did you lie to me?"

"Do you want the truth or not?" Melissa said.

"Yes, but—"

"Then shut up and listen."

"If I'd have known—"

"I said, shut up. It wouldn't have changed anything if you'd known. Tony betrayed me. I trusted him totally, even with my child, and he betrayed me. He didn't do what he did because he wanted me, he did it because he is a sick and greedy bastard. You said so yourself."

Melissa noticed how Louise pursed her lips. That sour mouth was her mother's favorite expression—always had been. Whenever she brought home bad marks, slept in on Sundays, begged to see a movie with her school friends—her mother pulled that face. It bugged her even now, after all those years, although

Tiara

now Louise's eyes seemed filled with compassion. Maybe she did her mother injustice. Hadn't she, too, been strict with Tiara because she wanted a better life for her girl? One that would spare her a boring existence in a mediocre milieu. Glitz and Glamour, that's what she wanted for her. The gold at the end of the rainbow, that's why she'd pushed Tiara. For no other reason.

"It went on until a few weeks before we left." Melissa said. "We were very careful. I wanted to tell Gracie many times, but Tony said Gracie had recommended him to many of her rich friends, and if she found out he'd never get another job as a dance instructor."

"But you told me Gracie fired him after Tiara stopped doing pageants," Louise said. "Why keep it a secret then?"

"He was still worried. He taught rich kids, and rich husbands don't like to think their wives might be fucking their daughter's dance teacher."

"Which they'd only know if Gracie told them."

Again, those lips. But this time, judging others. Yes, mother, shift the blame to where it belongs.

"Trust me," Melissa said, "Gracie would have."

"So you had an affair with your daughter's dance instructor. Not very smart, but what's the big deal here? What's it got to do with Tiara?"

"Don't you get it? Tony was poor judgment on my part, they'll say I acted like a bad mother."

"It was Tony, wasn't it?" Louise said. "Tony gave Tiara drugs. Right? I bet it was him."

Melissa squirmed in her chair.

"But that's all in the past now," Louise said. "The less said about that unfortunate time, the better."

All in the past? On the bus home, Melissa thought back. To the beginning. She leaned back and remembered the day Gracie brought the brother of her good friend Inez into their home, the day she met Antonio Alvarez. Tall, lithe, hips thrust forward—Tony asserted his superiority with every move he made. Similar to her Mike in appearance only—with that smooth dark skin, sensuous mouth, the graceful lean body—but so different in character. Sensuous. Masculine. Desirable. So breathtakingly desirable.

When Gracie introduced them, he took her hand—not a handshake but an intimate clasp, his fingers slipping into her palm, sending all sorts of sensations up her arm. By the time she sat down to watch him dance a brief routine, she was madly in lust.

He came by the house twice a week. She craved those afternoons like an addict. To see him, to watch him work, to listen to his voice when he guided Tiara through the moves, she couldn't get enough of that.

Nothing happened for one whole year.

Then, The Day, etched into her memory like yesterday. Tiara came back from a photo session unusually upset. She'd stopped throwing tantrums some time ago, now when she came home and was in one of her moods, she crept into bed and pulled the blanket over her head.

Tiara

Gracie left as soon as she dropped off Tiara—said she had some errands to run. "Call Tony and cancel the lesson," she said on her way out the door. "The girl is spent."

Melissa clutched the piece of paper with the scribbled phone number in her hands as if it was the Holy Grail, drawing out the moment she would speak to him. When she finally got the nerve to dial his number the call went straight to his answering service. Shortly after that, her doorbell rang.

When she told him Tiara was too tired for a lesson, Tony looked disappointed—but only for a second. Then his face lit up.

"Never mind." He lowered his eyelids. Lashes so long, they threw shadows on his cheekbones. "I'll teach you instead."

Again, he took her by the hand, this time leading her into the training room. She told him Gracie wouldn't pay him for today. He told her he didn't expect to get paid.

"I'd love to dance with you. It'll be my pleasure."

They were alone for the first time ever. She was so self-conscious of her bulges that she didn't want him to touch her. She was hot with excitement and worried about wet armpits, moist hands, glistening cheeks and frizzy hair. She felt clumsy, heavy, graceless.

He didn't seem to mind her uncoordinated attempts to sway her body with the rhythm of the music. He was pulling her strings. Then at some stage, he roped her in. Pulled her closer. It was the most natural movement to swing her into his arms until there was no space between them. She had no resistance in her, would not have wanted to resist, wanted only one thing, to crawl under his skin and stay there forever. Everything around her and in her stopped, including her pounding heart. It didn't matter. Her lungs didn't need air and her blood stopped flowing.

He kissed her on the mouth.

It was a moment she had not expected, had not imagined, had not hoped for. Yet she accepted it totally, succumbed to it with her whole being. She had never felt so grateful in her life.

His lips slid down her throat, he unbuttoned her blouse. Once her breasts were fully exposed, he cupped them with his hands, took a step back and admired them with hungry eyes. She didn't feel self-conscious—they were his to do with what he wanted. He kissed them tenderly first, then sucked her nipples hard until she couldn't stand it any longer. Heat shot through her pelvis in her first orgasm since Mike. She doubled over with the pleasure.

The bus stopped.

Melissa checked herself. The memory of that afternoon left her dizzy, panting. She stood up and moved toward the door, got off, felt the driver's eyes on her.

35

STANLEY being so damn pleased about the huge progress we made at the last session gave me a shit-fit. I was so mad at him it drained all my energy. Next day I got the flu, and I got it bad. My head throbbed, my throat constricted, my nose blocked, all my mucous membranes worked themselves into a frenzy. For several days and nights I was too busy sneezing, spitting and coughing the ugliness out of me to even think about why Stanley thought we'd made progress. *In my ninth year I was full of anger and angst* stuck in my feverish mind. Couldn't imagine why, could only repeat it over and over.

In my ninth year I was full of anger and angst in my ninth year I was full of anger and angst in my ninth year I was full of anger and angst.

Repeat it until I've run dry. I lie on my bed, drink the tea and chicken broth the overworked nurse supplies at regular intervals, and lazily muse over a suitable line for my tenth year. What would be appropriate to sum up those twelve hectic months?

Tiara

Birthday Nine—or is it Ten?

The beauty pageants were on again. They dominated the year leading up to my tenth birthday. Everything revolved around them. Tony was back. I had to do my routines non-stop, and he poked his stick into me harder than ever to make up for lost time. Being away from the hate room wasn't any better. Mom and Gracie and I spent endless hours cramped in our car, always in a rush to motels with stuffy rooms, only to hang out in the corridors in front of hotel ballrooms, forever waiting to be called on stage.

When Mom and Gracie weren't yelling at each other, they fussed over me or my dress or my hair. Not my nails, though. I had made a deal with Gracie. If I let her photographer friend take his pictures, she wouldn't put those nails on me ever again. I think she was glad this could be a point of negotiation, although she didn't give up much with that promise. She tricked me. Nails weren't essential for winning a crown.

But I tricked her, too. When I was on stage I always smiled, that's very, very important. The judges want to see how happy you are doing your routine. For the pictures Gracie's photographer friend made me do, I refused to smile, no matter how often he told me to look like I'm enjoying myself. Even the constant fear that the angels would make Gracie ill or strike us with a terrible disaster didn't make me smile.

It had been two years since Katrina. I still believed I was responsible for the destruction the hurricane had brought upon my home town. If I'd done what was expected of me, Galveston would have been spared.

Stanley comes visiting.

"Feeling any better?"

I quickly close my journal and hide it under the covers.

"Still angry?" he says.

"At you?"

"Were you angry at me?"

Oh Christ, here we go again. I don't know what this line of questioning will achieve, but I decide to play nice.

"It's not your fault for not getting me. I don't get me, so how could you?"

"Do you want to talk about it?"

The flu must have drained me real bad. No energy left, no barriers up.

"Where do we start?"

"You were telling me about the time you were eight, when your internal anger had started to establish itself."

In my ninth year I was full of anger and angst. Did the fear and the fury ever subside?

"Let's move on. I was already thinking of a catch phrase to sum up the following year."

"And, did you come up with one?"

Tiara

"I'm working on it."

I begin to describe my year when I was nine. The crazy schedule, all the pageants Gracie booked for me after the storm and its aftermath, when things returned to normal. I tell him about the fake nails, and while I'm talking, something fundamental hits me. Once I was back at the pageants, I never won. Stanley notices my perplexed pause and digs his heels in right away.

"You didn't win any contest?"

"Not a single one. How could I forget that?"

"But you won just about everything before, hadn't you?"

I'm still confused by the splinter images piercing into my consciousness.

"Why do you think that happened? What went wrong?"

A lot went wrong that year.

I'm leaning against the wall of the auditorium of the Holiday Inn Express Hotel in McAllen, next to Mom, who's holding my hand. I dislike this immensely. Her hand feels clammy and wet, like a used diaper. I know what those feel like. Since the dance rehearsal incident I wet my bed so often, she's made me wear a diaper at night. Nine, and still a baby, she muttered sometimes when she put a fresh box on my bed.

We're waiting for the announcement.

It's my first contest after the year-long break. I now belong to the difficult nine-year-old group. Difficult because at that age the girls are not considered children any more, although deep inside they still are. They don't know how to move, they develop little breasts, shoot up, need braces. Most, like me, feel awkward, the few who don't are the winners. I was called out right away, a shock to Mom and Gracie. Got the Miss Prettiest Smile title, crap without prize money attached to it. I didn't even get a crown, and we couldn't leave because contest rules specify every participant has to stay for the crowning ceremony. I didn't understand what was happening. All those years I'd made it at least to the Supreme titles, a few times even to the overall Grand Supreme, and once I captured the coveted Ultimate Grand Supreme. I thought they'd call out my name later again, but they didn't. Mom already crying, Gracie too stunned to cry. She stormed out of the room, leaving Mom and me standing against the wall.

Later, days or weeks later, I can't quite place the memory flashes on a timeline, Gracie and Mom are fighting.

"She lost her moves. So many months without ballet training will do that," Mom said.

Gracie pulled a face. "I couldn't justify keeping Tony on the payroll when there were no pageants. Inez would've made me fire him."

"Don't be ridiculous. Her own brother."

"They're not close. And anyway, she's not the only one to decide. She's got business partners who have a say in it."

Tiara

"You should've insisted. You should've known when you booked the contests that we can't do without him. Tony can't do miracles in such a short time. But you think you know everything. You're so full of yourself, you think the sun shines out of your ass!"

"Oh, shut up," Gracie yelled back. "He's lucky they let me book him again. But if she keeps losing, he's out again like a flash. Christ, you know, I'd give anything to see her win."

"Then give Tony more time with her."

Gracie's shoulders slumped.

"It's not that easy. Sponsors want to see a return on their investment. They're tired of putting a lot of money in and getting so little back."

Mom's bitter laughter made her bosom jiggle like jello.

"Oh yeah? Those greedy bastards didn't see enough green yet? Every month you have her picture taken, and I never see any of that money. Oh, forgive me, I don't see it because it's hidden under your mattress. Getting rid of Tony? How ridiculous is that?"

The fight goes on, or maybe they get in all kinds of fights and I muddle them all into one. Always about money. And Tony. Gracie insists that every dollar earned has been reinvested in me, and that times are harder than Mom realizes. Mom keeps harping on getting me back on track with my pageant training—especially those all-important dance lessons. She wants more of those. More of Tony. A lot of it doesn't make sense to me while I'm listening to them bickering and bitching. Tony's stick makes me jump and twirl until I pee, that's all I know. I cover my ears, only to drop my hands in the hope to hear the two words that would release me from my agony. No more.

But neither Gracie nor Mom say those words.

"So we finally got a name," Stanley says.

"A name?"

"Tony. You said Gracie couldn't justify keeping Tony on the payroll."

Did I say that?

"Tony. The Stick." It's kind of a relief to be able to say his name out loud. "At the end of the year, after I lost all the contests, Gracie fired him again."

Stanley shifts in his chair.

"You're aware that you've been brought up in an abusive environment."

"Nobody hurt me."

"I believe you were emotionally abused. Correct me if I'm wrong, but all signs point toward this. You wet the bed, at nine years of age—"

"I'd appreciate if you could keep this out of your notes."

"Sorry, can't do that."

"Who will read that crap?"

"The courts get a full report that outlines the information I've used to reach my conclusions. A copy goes to the Crown and the defense."

Tiara

"Shit!"

"I told you that when we moved on to the comprehensive assessment. You have committed a serious offense, and it's my job to find out what made you do it and how responsible you are. Tiara, my report will determine whether you should be tried as a juvenile or as an adult."

I know. He needs to establish the degree of my madness so others can decide how long I should be locked up. He needs to understand me and my motive.

"Do you think you'll ever find out why I did it?"

"Not if you don't want me to."

"So, to help you, I have to let you dissect my childhood like a corpse in a morgue?"

"More like a living human being," he says.

"You can't dissect a living human being. That would make you a murderer."

His expression doesn't change but he takes a second and clears his throat. "Let me correct myself. I need to dissect—meaning to examine, not using the literal context of cutting apart piece by piece—the childhood of a living human being to determine if there has been trauma."

This is interesting. What trauma? "Trauma that might lead to committing a crime?"

"In your case I suspect there has been more than one trauma."

"Wouldn't it help me remember things better or faster if you give me a little heads up on what you suspect?"

He ponders, takes out a handkerchief, cleans his glasses and puts them on again.

"You need to come to your own conclusions. Look at all the people who were around you when growing up. Question their motives. You're already doing a great job piecing things together. It'll all come back to you eventually."

"How much time have I got before a judge slams down his gavel on my life?"

Stanley looks at me through clean glasses.

"As much as I say." He hesitates. Clears his throat. "To a point."

I hadn't noticed until now that his eyes are green like a lake after rain.

"Good," I say.

He studies his notes. "You told me your mom accused your aunt Gracie that she and 'they' made money with you posing for pictures. Who are 'they'? I thought you had only one sponsor?"

Now that's a good question for a change. Unlike him I don't have written notes in front of me, so I study the fly on the wall and he lets me.

"Gracie always said the sponsor had partners. People, who were in the business of selling all the art pictures Gracie's photographer friend took of me."

Stanley crosses his legs, he does this with elegance, smiles at me to prove he's got all the time in the world. We both wait.

Tiara

A memory invades my diligent study of the fly on the wall. The picture in my head shapes into words that want to, need to, come out. I start telling him a story I had long forgotten—or had never been aware of until now.

After a string of losses which had started with my disastrous loss at the McAllen Holiday Inn, my sponsor comes to the studio. Gracie finished doing me up, and I'm sitting on a chair, trying not to move. The sponsor hands a bottle to Gracie and tells her to let me drink some. It'll stop my fidgeting. She calls it dream juice and says it'll calm me down. My hair is hardened by hairspray, my heavy eyelashes darken my vision. When I blink, I can see them moving up and down. I try to blink the sponsor away, but she comes closer. I don't like her.

She stands right in front of me and says in her husky voice, "We need to do something about her." She inspects me like I'm a prize calf. "Look at her. She's growing too fast. She doesn't look like a kid anymore, she looks like a teenager." She takes my face in her hand, lifts it up, turns it left and right. "She's still pretty, though."

"Tony's working with her again," Gracie says quickly. Her voice quivers. "She'll win again, I promise."

The sponsor drops my face.

"And for how long? Another year, maybe two?"

"Come on, Inez, you know the pageants are important. Now more than ever."

"Sure. If she wins in spectacular fashion. There's a lot of competition out there. She needs to be a celebrity. I can't market her as the fabulous Princess Tia if she isn't a winner, so you better make sure she wins. Her pictures won't be worth a dime if she's the ordinary girl next door."

"That was a one-time slip." Gracie sounds unusually apologetic. "It won't happen again."

"It better not. If this becomes a habit, and quite frankly that's what I expect, we won't waste any more money on her."

Gracie and the sponsor walk away, I can't hear what they discuss. I've already forgotten the sponsor's face, but not her words. Gracie looks terribly worried when she comes back, and I'm sorry that she's so upset, truly, but it doesn't change that I feel amazingly good. Kind of mellow, and at the same time happy—like a cat basking in the sun. If I don't win, they won't market Princess Tia any longer, isn't that what the sponsor said? No more pageant wins means no more photo sessions. No more. That's exactly what I want. No more.

And that's exactly what Princess Tia did. I forgot a dance step or a line to recite. Walking across the stage, I smeared my mascara or messed up my hair. I discovered so many ways to lose.

When I'm telling Stanley about my silent resistance, he asks me how I felt doing that. Good, of course, really good. By the end of that year, when my tenth birthday came up, Gracie informed me that my career as a child

Tiara

beauty queen had come to an end. She wouldn't enter me into another contest. The Stick—Tony—also lost. He was not needed any more.

Mom cried, told Gracie it was all her fault. If she'd only kept Tony on while there were no pageants, if she hadn't been so miserly, I would have won. She sniffled like a toddler denied her favorite toy. Gracie blew up and called her every bad name under the sun. By now I knew quite a few of those words, none of them flattering. Most had to do with Mom ballooning out of proportion.

For once, their squabbling didn't bother me. I was happy. I danced a little jig until Gracie got mad at me, too.

"Stop doing that. Don't you know what you've done? You've ruined your career. From now on it's a lot more photo sessions for you, and you better not complain about those."

36

ANOTHER awful night. How Melissa hated those nights spent tossing and turning and worrying about things she couldn't change or influence one bit. Trying to get her problems into perspective only made them worse. What would the police think once they found out that Tiara had disappeared for days and weeks at a time, doing god-knows-what on the streets of Vancouver?

They would think she was a bad mother, they would condemn her, the most innocent one in this tragic mess. Easy for them, they didn't know how she suffered, didn't want to know. Nobody cared for the reasons why a teenage brat left the safety of her home to roam the streets. So easy to blame the mother.

Finally, the first daylight peeked through the curtains. Best to get up and face this latest worry before she'd lose her mind completely. She had to give the police some kind of explanation they could accept. Not able to come up with a bright idea herself, she called her mother.

Louise offered one of her usual quick patch-up solutions.

Tiara

"Tell them Tiara stayed with me," she said.

"But what if the detectives ask Tiara?"

"Who cares, nobody will listen to her."

Melissa didn't buy it. "What about your neighbors? Won't they say they've never seen her?"

"Don't be silly, the police won't bother them."

"They'll want to know about my home-schooling her."

"Why on earth did you bring that up in the first place?"

"Kids are supposed to go to school."

"A lie by an overprotective mother," Louise said. "Stick with that."

She cut her mother short and hung up. No help there. Time to get ready for work.

Back at the 7-Eleven she stood idly at the cash register. With very few customers to break the monotony of her job, her overtired mind got stuck on the most pressing question again. Where had Tiara been when she wasn't in the apartment?

Melissa didn't have the strength to stand up to her once back in Vancouver. My God, all those dramas she had to cope with then. Her heart broken, the upheaval of leaving her home, the embarrassment of having to crawl back under mother's apron, even the change from the hot and dry Texas weather to the rain and cold of Vancouver, all that robbed her of the last bit of energy.

How could she be expected to put this aside and supervise the movements of a headstrong teenager at the same time? No wonder so many parents were desperate. There's no mechanism to control kids that age, once they decide to do their own thing. Nothing in the world will stop them, short of locking them up.

Those hot-shot detectives would be delighted to poke the finger at her. *Melissa, how often did Tiara slip away? Why didn't you supervise her properly?*

True, she should have paid more attention to Tiara's development. But fighting Gracie's maternal instincts would have meant a constant power struggle. She didn't have the strength for that. Gracie liked to play mom, she should have done a better job. She was the one who spoiled her princess rotten, and then complained when she started to act up. Like the times when she'd scratch at her skin. Gracie was furious when she noticed the attempt at self-mutilation the first time.

Tiara must have been about eleven, sitting on the porch swing Melissa didn't dare use anymore for fear of breaking the chains. Tiara was scratching her arm with a broken branch, blood dripping on the wooden planks. When Gracie came home she went into a God-almighty rage.

"How can you let her do that?" she yelled at the top of her voice. At her, as if it was her doing. Gracie even raised her arm to her. When Melissa took a step back, Gracie lowered her arm but raved on, "What kind of

Tiara

mother are you? Look at what she's doing to herself. Her pretty arms. Don't you have a speck of feeling for your daughter? Letting the poor girl suffer like that."

With that she folded Tiara into her arms and walked her into the house, comforting her with "poor little mija" shooing. Melissa heard it a million times before. She probably bad-mouthed her the second they were out of earshot. Gracie put the blame on her for everything that had to do with Tiara. In fact, for everything that went wrong, period.

It wasn't right for Gracie to treat her like this. But it also wasn't right for Tony to do what he'd done. It wasn't right for Mike to die and leave her in Gracie's care. Nothing was right in the world, then or now.

Melissa decided not to care anymore. Nobody had ever cared for her. Mike left her, Louise abandoned her, Tiara despised her. As much as she wanted to be accepted as a good mother, she was sure her daughter didn't give a damn. Tiara still refused to see her. She'd rejected her mother three years ago, wandering the streets of Vancouver instead of staying home with her, giving her the company and comfort she'd missed ever since her Mike had left her.

A customer approached the register, loaded her items on the conveyor belt. Melissa smiled at her and scanned the first one. She'd carry on living and working and not caring any more.

Let the detectives think what they liked. She had done nothing wrong.

37

MACINTOSH stuffed a file into his briefcase. "I'm off to see Tiara," he said to nobody in particular.

"Bye Mac," one of the newer recruits yelled from a corner of the room.

"Piss off," Macintosh said to the loud-mouth. Nobody called him Mac. Nobody, except Kathy. The familiar wave of anger at the inevitable flared up inside him. He still yearned for Kathy's gentle "Mac, honey" when she was sweet with him, or the more forceful "Mac, do this, Mac, do that". Even the "Mac, for Christ sake, stop being such an asshole" she used when he annoyed the heck out of her was worth an arm, or a leg, or his heart. Only she was allowed to call him Mac, nobody else.

"Shut up," Harding said to the rookie. "That's your boss, you're talking to."

The anger died down again. Suddenly, Macintosh couldn't be bothered. He waved at the recruit. Harding followed him out into the hallway. They walked to the elevator together and waited for a lift.

"Will you ask Tiara about the aunt?" Harding said.

Tiara

"Don't know yet. It's tricky. We know too little, and I don't want to put words into her mouth. I'll improvise."

"Want me to come along?"

The elevator arrived. Macintosh stepped in and pressed a button.

"No need. I'll tell you all about it later."

"You better," Harding said to the closing doors.

Tiara looked pale and exhausted, her cheeks abnormally sunken for a girl her age. Macintosh could feel a sting in his heart when he saw her brought in. Young people didn't usually show the same signs of stress as adults did.

"Are you getting enough to eat in here?"

She sat down. "Don't you know, they're fattening me up for the big slaughter?" When he didn't reply, she said, "My trial."

Her off-hand joke didn't fool him. She was scared of what would become of her. "The trial will turn into a mere formality if we manage to establish grounds for you not being criminally responsible. I wish you'd give me something to work with." When she opened her mouth to object, he stopped her. "I know, I know. You don't remember. And I believe you, Tiara. I truly do. But I have to keep digging. I know you're talking to the shrink, so I guess there must be something. About your background, your upbringing. Anything you two talk about might give me a lead."

Her drawn face brightened. There it was again, the giggle coming from within.

"Can I tell my shrink that you're fishing for information? Shouldn't he be here if you do?"

"You can ask for a lawyer to be present, but my understanding is you don't want one."

"No, I don't. And I didn't want to talk to you, either, but they forced me to come here."

"I'm not forcing you to say anything, Tiara. But I'm sure you know I've come back for one reason only. It's because I want to help you."

She considered this for a moment, then she widened her smile.

"I know you mean well, but please understand, although talking to the doc makes me think back a lot, nothing is in perspective. Nothing makes sense. I can't figure out why I feel a dark cloud hangs over my years in Texas. Why I've been feeling so empty since I've been in Vancouver."

"Do you miss being back there?" Macintosh asked quickly.

All color drained from her face again, and he bit his tongue. Fool, don't you know what kind of childhood she must have had.

"Miss what?" Her glance turned inward. "This talk-therapy with the doc only brings up a lot of confusing stuff that's messing with my brain. Not what you're after. Trust me, it's all in shambles up there." She knocked on her left temple. "One gigantic mess."

Tiara

"That's too bad," Macintosh said. "I've been talking to your mother—"

He stopped. She looked unsteady, like she might faint any second. He reached out to steady her.

"Please don't touch me."

He pulled back. "Sorry."

They sat quietly while she composed herself.

"Can we talk about something else?" Tiara finally asked.

"Sure. What do you want to talk about?"

"You."

That surprised him so much that he had to laugh.

"About an old man like me? What's interesting about that?"

Her eyebrows pulled together.

"Talking about me and my life, my feelings and all that shit gets pretty boring after a while, I can tell you that. The doc and me, we're talking non-stop, and when I'm not talking with him, I'm thinking about what to write in my journal. Me, me, me—all the time. I could do with a little break from this ego routine."

"Okay, if that's what you're after. Here goes nothing. I was married and my wife is dead. I was a father and my daughter is dead. I was a policeman all my life but soon I won't be any more."

"Shit," she said. "And I thought it sucks to focus on me."

Now they both laughed.

"My daughter," Macintosh said, "she had a laugh like you." He got serious again. "Wish I'd spent more time with her. But the office always came first."

Tiara looked like she understood.

"What will you do when you're not a policeman anymore?"

"Retire at my place up north, in Squamish. Nice house. When it gets too big for me, I'll go stay a few days at my cabin in the mountains, about two hours' drive from the last hydro pole. It's nice there, quiet. Very remote. You can only reach it by foot. You have to cross a lake and then hike up the mountain path. My wife and I…, well, I guess it's only me now, so I'll make the best of it."

"Must be nice to have a place where nobody bothers you."

"Tell you what," he said. "When you get out of here, you come visit. I can take you out into the country, show you the beauty of our hinterland. Wilderness, untouched by mankind."

She studied her shoes.

Oh shit, what was he saying? To her, of all people, a girl with a history of abuse. He sounded like a perv or, at best, like a desperate old man. "I mean, don't get me wrong, I'd take you same as I used to take my daughter. She loved hiking and fishing," he said. "But you don't have to. Fish, I mean. A lot of people don't like fishing. Find it boring as hell."

Tiara

"I think I'd like that," she said. "Really. I've seen it in movies. People stand in the water with rubber trousers up to their chests. You wear those, too?"

He had to grin. "God help me, no. I don't fly-fish. I sit in my aluminum nutshell of a boat, with a can of beer in my hand, listen to the waves hit the boat. Watch the eagles fly over me. Peaceful. Like I said, boring."

"How big is the boat?"

The question took him back. Then he understood. "Large enough. You can sit on one end, me on the other."

"Good. Then I'd like to go there." She frowned. "But you might be dead by the time I get out."

For the first time in ages a belly laugh burst out of him. It shattered the hard crust of pain inside him into a million pieces. They would remain there, would never leave, but now that they were broken up, they could let other feelings, better ones, maybe even good ones, in. And out.

"I'll make sure I live a long and healthy life," he said, once he got his breath again.

"You should." A shadow crossed her face. "Not because of me. We both know this fishing trip will never happen. I don't count. But you do. You're a kind man. You deserve better."

38

NO more birthdays

I'm scraping and scratching at the bottom of my being-bowl, trying to loosen and wash out the hardened memory-bits. God, what a painful, useless process.

I've gone over the first ten years of my life again and again, trying to sneak into my eleventh year. Stanley is coming today, and with all that wonderful progress we've made, he'll expect more than what I have to give.

Since I've been opening up to Stanley, I've developed writer's block. The moment I take the pen in hand, words elude me as if they're punishing me for spilling my guts earlier on. Try as I may, I draw a blank.

I don't remember much beyond the beginning of that elusive eleventh year. My tenth birthday, yes, I can recall what happened on that day. No big party, there never had been one, but a cake in the afternoon and quite a few presents. Mom gave me a stack of books I'd need for studying, Gracie gave me a thin gold chain with a sparkling flower-shaped pendant dangling from it. I hated it, didn't wear it a single day.

Tiara

Mom launched into an argument with her as soon as I unwrapped the jewelry box. She said, "I thought we have to save?" to which Gracie replied, "Nothing's too good for my favorite girl."

Neither bothered to ask me if I liked what I got. While they bickered on about how hard times were (Mom) and how much I deserved a little treat (Gracie) and how she denied herself any small treat (Mom) and how much harder it would be without me earning the money (Gracie), I said thank you, ate a slice of the cake and went to my room. I was fed up with those arguments. Heard them all before. Gracie always saying how grateful she was for me doing all the photo-shoots Mom didn't need to know about. How much she loved me. And Mom always going on about Gracie being a self-centered egotist, keeping stuff for herself, stuff her daughter worked for so hard. All their arguments sounded lopsided. They never talked about the same thing.

I was beginning to understand that the only two important people in my life were engaged in a non-stop tug-of-war, with me fastened at the middle of the rope. Sometimes I felt so torn apart, I could have screamed.

Stanley comes to see me after I refused to go to his office. I'm slumped on my bunk bed, unable to move. He takes one look at me and says with deep concern in his voice, "What's wrong, Tiara?"

"Go away."

He turns to the door. Jesus, get that guy. His shrink training sure was worth the shitload of money it must have cost his parents.

"Wait."

When he sits down, I close my eyes and start. "I feel like kicking and screaming but can't. I haven't got the strength to even sit up," I say. "I keep thinking about Texas, and a lot of stuff pops up. Stuff I've told you about. It goes as far as my tenth birthday, and then I remember that horrible storm we had a few weeks after my birthday. Then, nothing. Like my memory is a train entering a tunnel, somebody hits the emergency brakes and then it derails in total darkness."

I can't help it, tears of frustration well up in my eyes. Stanley is swimming in milky fog.

"Which storm? You're talking about your tenth birthday, so you can't mean Katrina, right?"

"Katrina was long gone. I mean Hurricane Ike. Actually, by the time Ike made landfall it was downgraded to a cat two, so in truth it wasn't a hurricane anymore but it still was one major nasty storm."

"Why don't you start at your birthday and take it from there. Tell me all you remember about those weeks leading up to that particular storm."

So I tell him. About the birthday presents (the books, the golden flower), the arguments (money, me, money), and then, the weeks after.

Tiara

About two weeks after my birthday, Gracie took me to do another photo session. I should have known that this one was different. Gracie told me how much she loved me, and stroked my back every time she walked past me. I cringed inside. I couldn't bring myself to tell Gracie that by now some of those sessions were physically painful to me. By this I don't mean the sitting down for hours or the often painful applications of my make-up—pulling my hair too tight, or stinging my eyes with lash glue, or rubbing too hard with the remover—it was more a dread I had before a session started. My stomach contracted into a hard ball the moment I got in her car. The photo studio was in Texas City, a suburb by the ocean, and in the fifteen minutes it takes to get there I always felt this hard lump forming inside me. Mom didn't give me anything to eat or drink a few hours before each session because I'd thrown up more than once when getting me ready. Gracie then started to give me a few sips of the sponsor's dream juice to drink before we arrived, and that helped.

"The juice calmed you down?" Stanley asks. "What kind of juice was it?"

"I don't know. Gracie wanted me to feel good. She always said, 'I want you to enjoy what you're doing. It hurts me more than you can imagine when you don't enjoy a session, but we need the money from these sessions to survive. I'm so proud of you, my mija, and I love you so very much'. The juice was like medicine, she said, it helped me relax. I didn't like the taste but I didn't want Gracie to fret so much over me, so I always drank it."

"Do you know why you felt so uptight?"

"Sure I do," I tell him. "I had to do all sorts of artsy things that made me feel very uncomfortable. I hated doing them."

"Can you describe one to me, so I understand better?"

Most of it is lost in fog, but that one especially bad session after my birthday raises its ugly head and invades my memory.

I see myself, already fully made up, when the photographer tells the Purple Shadow to undress me completely. "We're doing a very special art piece today." When I hear that, I wince. The Purple Shadow hands me more juice. I'm sitting there, with no clothes on, drinking, and then the Purple begins to dress me up for the shoot, but this time the costume isn't a fancy fantasy creation. The photographer friend holds a few ropes in his hands. I see me starting to cry because I felt more embarrassed than usual—I had come to feel embarrassed about everything they made me do, I guess that's normal at that age—and because the ropes were put at places that cut painfully into me.

"They *hurt* me." I'm surprised at the sudden revelation. "All I had on was ropes. They tied me up like a goddamn parcel and made me sit and lie on those ropes for hours."

"How did Gracie react when she came back?"

I shrug, trying to collect myself again. Talking about it is still embarrassing me, after all those years. I should have kept my mouth shut.

"Didn't you tell Gracie what they did to you?"

My memory quickly colors in the fine lines of the emerging scene. When Gracie came back in I was fully dressed and sobbing like crazy. She ushered me out of the studio and into her car. There I showed her one of the welts on my thighs where the ropes had cut into me. She gave me a Kleenex to dry my tears and told me it wasn't that bad. Just a few red streaks, they'd disappear in no time.

"But she was upset about it," I say to Stanley. "Honestly."

He doesn't believe me.

"No, really. It's like this, she couldn't show her feelings so well, sometimes not at all, but for sure, she loved me. Life isn't always a bed of roses, and no matter how much we wish for our loved ones to be happy, it isn't always working out like that, right?"

"Is that Gracie talking?"

"In the end she told me to stop whining. She explained to me what the session was all about. Taking pictures like that is called art, she said. My pictures don't sell because I'm a cute little kid, they sell because they're art. It's my own fault for having messed up my chances to become a famous beauty queen. I'm too old for that now, there's no way back, and unless I prefer that we all starve to death, I better do as I'm told. I shouldn't be such a baby. I'm nearly grown up and have to take on my responsibilities like everyone else. You get the gist."

He does. "Looking back at it now, did you realize then that they took those pictures for a certain purpose?"

"Of course I understood that. Pictures like those are considered art. But I was at an age when I didn't give a shit about art."

"Do you still think they were art?"

Why does he harp on about art?

He leans forward in his chair. "Tying up a naked young girl—doesn't that strike you as odd when you think back now?" he says.

"Not really. Of course that's a bit freaky, but I've seen those type of pictures before."

"Where?"

"Here in Vancouver. I often crashed at a girlfriend's place—"

"I thought you didn't have any friends."

"She wasn't really. I met her when I started to stay away from home, when I couldn't handle being close to mom. Her name was Candy. She had one of those coffee table books full of bondage pictures. By Madonna. You know Madonna?"

"The singer, yes, of course."

I have to laugh. *Me*, digging into *his* brain all of a sudden, now that's hilarious.

"See? She's famous and had those artsy pictures taken." I say. "Are you surprised I know the word bondage? You look a little freaked out."

Now he starts laughing, too. It's good to be on the same level again.

"You've never let on how much you know about sexual practices," he says.

My laughter wilts in my throat.

"That wasn't sexual."

Every fiber of my insides is screaming *but it was it was it was*.

"Tell me about your girlfriend," he says.

"I met Candy about a year after we came back. I took to wandering around the streets, not going anywhere in particular. We got to talking. She told me to go home, said I'm too young to be on the streets, and I guess she took pity on me when I told her why I didn't want to spend much time at home."

"And why was that?"

"I told you, I can't stand being close to my mom."

"And your friend Candy, she accepted this reason?"

Damn, he's good.

"Okay, I lied to her. I said my mother is trying to make me do things I don't want to do, you know, with men."

"So, Candy took you in."

"She said I reminded her of her little sister. I could always crash at her place. Wasn't much, but it was comfortable and peaceful there. We hung out together, not doing anything in particular, watching silly shows and a shitload of movies on TV, then talking about what we'd seen and having a few laughs together. She's been easy to chill with, never bugged me, never touched me, never demanded anything of me."

"Okay, let's go back to the time after your tenth birthday, to that terrible session. Can you tell me more about it?"

This question annoys the hell out of me. Now I can see two black holes, two cameras. One that went click-click and another producing a constant humming noise. A movie camera, a goddamn movie camera! Two black eyes staring at me.

"As always. After Gracie left, the photographer and the Purple Shadow took over…, and then two black holes sucked me in."

"Did your sponsor never show up at any of those sessions?"

"No, never."

"And you have no idea who the Purple Shadow was?"

"No. All I remember is that they get me ready and then purple fog swallows me up. I know they're there but it doesn't matter what they do. Or what I do. Be-

Tiara

cause I'm not really there. I'm far away. The next thing I know is me sitting in the car with Gracie, driving home. Anything in between is… it's kind of … um, I don't know… it's just not there. I'm soaked in purple liquid, swimming in it … drifting … drowning … um, I really can't describe it." It's so frustrating not to get a clear picture. I must look so stupid. What kind of fool forgets stuff like that?

Stanley feels my desperation and guides me away from self-reproach. "Did you tell your mother about the rope session when you came home?"

I sigh and explain for the umpteenth time that I never-never-ever talked to my mom about those sessions. Why should I mention that particular one? Sure, being tied up like that felt so bad, even floating in purple fog couldn't quite take the pain away. And the embarrassment. On that day, I guess I was more sensitive, more irritable, more touchy, more whatever.

But that wasn't the moment the train stopped and derailed. That came about another week later. It was early September, and I'm pretty certain about this because I know when Ike hit. Everything that happened to me, had to do with the storm. Now the memories roll in, so powerful I stumble over my own words to make sure I get them all out. Anything worse than the rope session might slip back to be forgotten.

Stanley doesn't interrupt me once.

Hurricane Ike raced toward the Gulf Coast, and Galveston and Houston sat in its direct path. The authorities warned the people living in the low-lying houses on Galveston Island that they faced "death from flooding" if they didn't evacuate. For several days it seemed like there was nothing else on radio and TV but those warnings. The forecasters predicted a wall of water so high it would flood the whole coast.

Ever since that scary night in the shelter when Katrina hit the Gulf coast I was terrified of storms. Strong winds and rain turned me into a gibbering nitwit. In the days leading up to Ike's landfall, clouds darkened the sky, driven by furious gusts. I wanted to hide in my room, in my bed, under my blanket, but couldn't handle to be alone.

So I spent the hours when the storm approached curled up on the sofa, shaking…, couldn't get myself to stop shaking. I couldn't articulate what I felt, but I had nowhere to hide. I'd never felt such numbing fear.

Mom sat glued to the TV. To hear those constant warnings and see frantic evacuees packing their belongings as fast as they could didn't exactly calm her down either. She'd been packing all morning, waiting for Gracie to get back.

When Gracie finally came in, she laughed at Mom. "Have you lost your marbles? The mandatory evacuation order is only for the Island, we live off the coast, we've got nothing to worry about."

Tiara

Mom told Gracie what she'd heard on TV. They were evacuating more than a hundred thousand people, so it couldn't only be Galveston Island. Mom looked like I felt. Panicky.

"Sure," Gracie said, "we'll go if you feel so strongly about it, but I've got an important session lined up for Tia this afternoon. I can't cancel that one. We leave when she's done."

The wind rattled our tin roof when she said this. I thought its power would rip off the roof, then suck me out. The gusts would hurl me into space, then drop me to the ground. I would crash and burst like a pumpkin.

Mom stood her ground for all of ten minutes. She argued that it was way too dangerous to wait much longer, and if Gracie took me out there for a session as if no hurricane was approaching, she'd be stuck in this house all by herself, with no way to leave if things got worse.

"I'm the one with hurricane experience," Gracie said. "Hurricane Carla in 1961 was much bigger than Ike, and my parents hadn't left then, either. And what about Hurricane Gustav earlier this month? That blew over with hardly a dent. God, the authorities always issue panic warnings, they have to so they won't get sued later on. We're safe here."

"But the studio is in Texas City," Mom said, in a last desperate effort to change Gracie's mind, "that's even closer to the coast than La Marque. We need to get inland. Fast."

I held my breath waiting for Gracie to see Mom's point. Inland, not to the studio. I'd die, we'd all die, if Gracie takes me through the storm and forces me to sit still for a shoot. *Please, Gracie, if you love me, don't make me go.*

"We're not doing it at the studio," Gracie said. "We're doing it not far from here, so stop your worrying."

Gracie got her Princess Tia bag, took my hand to drag me out of the house. The short distance to the car felt like a walk to the gallows—I'd seen those old movies where guards drag the innocent man to his death, and he goes limp halfway there, accepting his fate. After the initial half-hearted struggle, I went limp, too. Gracie had to drag me the rest of the way to the car.

We drove out of Azalea Lane onto the highway, turning south. I can still see all the cars bumper to bumper in the north-heading lanes, our lane deserted. Everybody except Gracie and me was trying to leave the coast. Gracie didn't have the radio on. She didn't want to know.

She stopped at the Island View Motel, told me we'd be doing the session inside. The motel smelled moldy like all cheap places close to the ocean, all the windows boarded up with plywood planks, so dark inside. Only dim lights guided us to a room at the end of a hallway.

The pattern of the carpet, entwined gold leaves and vines on solid burgundy, was only recognizable along its borders—the middle part, the part I stared at while

Tiara

trudging along, had long ago faded into a dirty brown beaten path.

We got to our room, which looked as shabby as the carpet, dominated by a large bed with a purple spread so shiny it looked like plastic. Same entwined gold leaves. Gracie said I should sit on it, she'd do me up for the session now. I looked around. No photographer yet. I was hoping he'd be too scared to leave his home. I saw a double door with a slide lock. Gracie unlocked this door and explained that the session would be done in the next room. Such a pretty setting, such amazing art. How lucky the photographer was such a genius, coming up with all those brilliant ideas.

I could hear the wind rattling the plywood safety-shutters, a wild creature, trying to get to the hidden prey.

Me.

Most of what Gracie said while she changed my dress and slapped some color on me got lost in a raucous cacophony of screeching and whistling and rattling. The storm-beast got stronger and stronger, determined to dig into my lair.

Gracie hurried to finish.

"You stay here now and wait until he comes to start the session."

I started to cry. "Don't leave me, Gracie."

"You be a good girl." Urging me with a brisk voice. "You be a good girl, and it'll all be over before you know it."

"Gracie, please, please, don't go." I threw my arms around her.

Gracie stiffened, then pried herself out of my vise embrace. My thin arms couldn't hold her.

"Pull yourself together," she said. "You're a big girl now. My pretty mija. You'll be fine. You'll like it. I'll get you some more juice, and you won't be so scared any more. Wait here until I'm back."

Then she left me. I'm all alone. Who will get me? The storm? I wait, shivering and more scared than before. Then—

A huge bang, like an explosion, like thunder, really close. The light on the bedside table goes out. Total darkness.

Now I cry. Stanley touches my arm, I recoil. The unexpected caress is more than I can handle. I sob even harder.

"She left me alone in the dark. I couldn't see anything, not even a shape. Pitch black. I was, I was—" I can barely speak. "I was all alone in the dark."

In his most gentle voice—without touching me—Stanley tells me to take my time. But I can see it in his face, he wants to know what happened next.

So do I.

"I don't remember anything after that," I say. "It's all black."

39

MACINTOSH wasn't overly surprised when the morning brief detailed a new homicide. Vancouver was like every other big city, crimes never stopped. Another shooting, in South Vancouver this time. Two rival gangs spiraled out of control. They shot at each other in broad daylight, and plenty of people witnessed the attacker's car speed off after fatally wounding one gang member. What did surprise him, however, was that Sergeant Tong assigned him and Harding to the case.

"You're still on the force," Tong said.

"But not much longer," Macintosh said.

"Long enough to single out the shooter and book him. Harding can finish off the paperwork."

"What about the Princess case?"

Tong waved it off. "Harding can finish that one, too. Or drop it. Who cares? It's a done deal."

Tiara's case slipped into obscurity faster than a politician caught cheating on his tax return. Deep in his heart, Macintosh knew he could not let go of the Princess case. Tong or not, Tiara deserved better than being branded a juvenile criminal by a sluggish judicial system. Harding was a decent detective but he still ranked junior, he couldn't override Tong. To hand over this half-baked file to Harding meant he'd send an already troubled girl into an uncertain future. How could Tong suggest he should do that?

Macintosh was pissed off. He flipped through the fast growing stack of documents on the new case while wondering where to find the time for Tiara when Harding approached with a notable spring in his step, placed a file on his desk and sat down. The chair creaked as though complaining about the weight.

"Shit, you got to do something about this chair before somebody breaks his neck. I'm a featherweight in comparison to your average detective around here."

Macintosh opened his hands like a saint and smiled.

"Don't worry, if you break yours, you get early retirement."

"Is that all you ever think about—retirement?"

"Gone fishing. That's what's written on my door. Nine months, three days and counting." He tilted his head back and looked up at the ceiling. "I'll get up to Squamish, start breathing fresh air, go for long hikes in the mountains, see the sun rise and set again, eat fish I caught that day with vegetables grown in my own garden. Don't envy me, your time will come."

"And until your time comes, let's concentrate on the job at hand." Harding said with a big grin.

Macintosh grimaced, pointed at the stack. "What the hell do you think I'm doing?"

"Fuck this." Harding's grin widened. "Gang losers. Who cares? I'm talking the Princess case."

When Macintosh's eyebrows shot up, Harding confirmed, "I found the aunt."

"Took you long enough."

Harding opened his file. "Come on, I had to call fifteen times and sweeten up the nice lady at military records to give me the plainest of personal information on the deceased soldier Miguel Rodriguez. His name came up under the same address Melissa Brown gave us initially—you remember, the Caroline Road one that doesn't exist anymore. She told me to contact his next-of-kin, a sister named Graciella Rodriguez, for further information."

"Ask Josh—"

Harding held up his hand. "Already done. Josh ran it and came up with a few very interesting facts."

Macintosh settled back in his chair.

"After she moved from the Galveston home, her driver's license states her address as 4341 Azalea Lane, La Marque." Harding tapped on the address written on the top sheet of his file. "That's a town north of Galveston, south of Houston. No official record shows Melissa or Tiara Brown residing at this address, but when I checked the registry of the Little Miss Texas Beauty Pageant online for the years 2000 to 2010, I found a Tia

Rodriguez listed as a participant in 2006 with the La Marque address. She didn't win that year, so there's no picture of her online, but it's fair to say that Tiara and her mother lived there with Graciella, at least in 2006."

"It's a good start."

"More than a start. I told you Josh ran Graciella Rodriguez's name through the system, and guess what, she was under suspicion for drug trafficking in 2002. Wasn't convicted, though, not enough evidence. Nothing after 2002. She must have been especially careful or exceptionally lucky, unless she stopped altogether. And you know as well as I do, that's unlikely."

Macintosh scrunched his face. "Hang on a second."

After a full minute, Macintosh's face opened up. "The victim. In St Paul's."

"What about her?"

"Just an idea." Macintosh grinned. "What if the attack wasn't random? After all we know by now, Tiara had good reason to take revenge on somebody close to her. We know the victim wasn't her mother. What if she is Graciella Rodriguez?"

Several hours later they waited at the reception area in St Paul's Hospital. Macintosh studied the station's head nurse who marched toward them to defend her territory. Up in invisible arms, protected by an armor of discretional powers, she, and she alone would decide who'd be permitted to speak to the patient in her care.

"The doc told us he'd try and wake her up soon," Macintosh said.

"So?"

"So, did he?"

She made her yes sound like a rebuke. Like it's none of your business. Like don't waste my time.

"We have a few questions," Macintosh said.

"Being out of a coma doesn't mean she can be put under stress. She's lost a lot of blood, suffered a cardiac arrest, and had major surgery. Her vital functions don't need to be supported any longer, but we don't yet know the extent of possible brain damage. CT is scheduled later on this week."

"Has she said anything at all?"

"Of course not. I told you, she's not coherent yet. And even if she were, she can't speak. She's got an endotracheal tube."

"How much longer?"

"You'll need to consult the physician on duty."

"Can we at least take her fingerprints?"

The armored guard of hospital patients made a head-nurse face. "Is that normal procedure?" she asked. "Her file doesn't classify her as a suspect."

"It would help us identify her."

"Can't do. Not without her permission."

"Damn it, you said she's incoherent."

"Then bring a next of kin."

"Don't know any—"

Tiara

"Or a court order. You know the rules."

Macintosh gave up. A long shot, and not really that important. If Graciella Rodriguez had never been arrested, her prints wouldn't be on file anywhere.

"The doctor on duty, where do we find him?"

"Down the hall, third door on the right. But he's doing his rounds now. You'll have to wait. He could be a few hours."

Macintosh took a card from his pocket and handed it to her.

"Would you be so kind as to give this to him? I'd appreciate if he calls my cell when he's free."

She pocketed the card. Of course she'd give it to him, she promised, and of course the doctor would call, today or tomorrow, as soon as he found a minute.

They left the hospital, crossed the street and walked into the Throw & Catch Sports Bar. High time for an off-duty beer.

"We're going in circles here," Macintosh said. "There's no saying when the woman will be stable enough to be interviewed—even after they remove the damn tube."

Harding took a sip of his beer and wiped his mouth. "Then wouldn't Tiara know who she stabbed? I mean, her own aunt?"

"That could be the reason why she doesn't remember," Macintosh said.

"But why would she attack her like that?"

"She held a grudge against her because of all those weirdo modeling jobs they made her do. So far we suspected only the mother to be responsible, but considering they were all living together, the aunt could be involved, too."

"You think Tiara is one hell of a pissed off teenager?" Harding said. "Payback time for having to work as a child model?"

"You've seen the pictures. Who could blame her?" Macintosh paused to get his thoughts in line. "We should interview Melissa again, confront her with what we know. Ask her why the fuck she didn't tell us about this precious aunt."

"How're you going to justify the amount of time we spend on this damn case? Tong's just about pulled us off. Not surprising, it's not even a homicide yet, and if she does pull through it will only be aggravated assault with bodily harm. Tong is right to shift focus."

Macintosh's brain raced through the options. Not much there. "How about child exploitation?"

"Not our domain either. Those beauty pageants are freaky but they're not illegal, and as far as those pictures on the internet go, that's Sexual Offense Squad. Who, by the way, are overloaded with stuff that's way more serious."

"It seems pretty goddamn serious to me," Macintosh said. "Tong doesn't need to know everything. I'd be willing to put in some extra time."

"Anything to save Tiara?"

Or myself. "You got something better to do with your evenings?"

For a while they both sat in silence, drank their beers, watched the pretty waitress behind the counter polish glasses and wipe the counter tops when she wasn't smiling and serving. It was still early, she did a lot of cleaning.

Macintosh's cell announced an incoming text. He took it out of his pocket, clicked on it and read it.

"I'll be damned." He lowered the mobile. "You're not going to believe this."

Harding cocked his head.

"It's from Josh. I texted him on the way to the hospital to check if Graciella Rodriguez still lives at the La Marque address."

"And?"

"It's worth another beer. You paying?"

Harding waved at the waitress, showed her two fingers. She acknowledged the order with a nod.

"I'll read it to you: 'Graciella Rodriguez's last known address is 4341 Azalea Lane. The building located there burnt to the ground three years ago. Fire of unknown origin, but suspected failure of an electric heater. No indication of arson. One body recovered. Call me.'"

Macintosh did not even glanced at the two beers the waitress placed in front of them. Neither did Harding.

"Guess we owe Josh a six-pack," Harding said.

Macintosh was already dialing the Texas number. He got connected fast and listened for what seemed like a long time.

"Great work, Josh," he said finally, hung up and filled Harding in.

"The body they recovered was burnt beyond recognition but was female and matched in height and approximate age that of the woman living there. The autopsy revealed blunt force trauma to the her head which matched the shape of a metal table next to the deceased, leading to the conclusion that she was overcome by smoke, fell and smashed her head on the table corner. No dental records were available of the tenant but neighbors confirmed that they'd seen her at the house on the day the fire broke out. The deceased is listed as Graciella Rodriguez."

Harding took a large pull on his beer. "Then who the hell is our victim?"

They contemplated the question when Macintosh's cell pinged for another incoming text. Josh again. He forgot to mention that Margarita Rios and her husband, a certain Carl Heider, had flown to Toronto nearly three years ago. No record of re-entry.

40

MELISSA felt instant excitement when Dr. Eaton called to tell her he'd like to pay her a visit on his way home. The psychiatrist evaluating her daughter wouldn't drop by for no reason. Maybe Tiara was finally willing to see her.

She called her mother right away.

"I bet he's got bad news," Louise said. "I bet Tiara's been saying bad stuff about you."

"Like what?"

"Oh you know, like you dragging her to all those pageants."

"That's not bad. She loved doing them. Every little girl loves the attention they're getting. Tiara was very competitive, she liked being on stage."

"Until she started losing."

Damn it, why had she told her mother the bed-wetting?

"Well, at least she had a great time until she was about ten. What other girls do you know who've lived the life of a princess, I ask you?"

"Maybe the detectives found out about the money you stole from Gracie."

"Oh, stop it. How could they? Tiara never knew about that."

"In my opinion—"

"Sorry, but I got to go. Dr. Eaton will be here any minute. Call you back soon as I can."

Melissa waited. Lately she always had to sit and wait for something. Maybe this time things would move in the right direction. Since she'd decided not to care anymore, she spent most of her free time thinking about the past in an effort to avoid the horribly confusing present. The good times with Tony, when he made her feel so special—as rare as those moments had been—dominated her last years in Texas. They were all she had to treasure. Until Tony, her whole focus had been on Tiara's career. Tony managed to widen her vision. She'd still been there for her daughter, of course, but Tiara kept her distance, was remote, preferred to be alone. Especially after Ike devastated Galveston.

As if the approach of the hurricane had been easy for her—stuck in the house all by herself after Gracie and Tiara left for their inopportune photo session—until Tony showed up, frantic with worry.

"I tried to call you but couldn't get through," he said. "That's one fucking crazy storm."

He'd braved the rapidly deteriorating weather to rush to her side, to protect her. She felt so relieved, so happy, she forgot about the winds chasing the rain-heavy clouds inland, upending everything in their path that wasn't solidly anchored.

She was so happy she even forgot about Tiara and Gracie. Tony dampened her euphoria somewhat when she tried to entice him to her room.

"It's too risky, way too risky," he said in a hushed voice, as if he could be heard by anybody but her. "You want to make love at a time like this in Gracie's house? What's the matter with you? Are you out of your mind?"

"Touch me, please," she said, "down there. Please, show me you love me."

Instead, he drew away from her.

"Let's get the fuck out of here."

Even now, with the raging storm outside, he had more fear of Gracie than of the forces of nature. Of course he didn't have to persuade her for long. If Tony wanted her somewhere else, she would go wherever he wanted.

"I'd love to take you up north," he said, "out of danger, if I could only afford it."

The money stash under Gracie's mattress had never been far from her mind. It still bugged her that Gracie would hide it from her, so the devil must have whispered into her ear. *Go and get some—for Tony, and for yourself. Go get it, it's yours as much as hers, you earned it. Tony's your future, not Gracie.*

He acted reluctant at first, but she insisted. When they found the money bag and saw that it contained about twenty thousand dollars, he changed his tune.

Tiara

"Okay, let's make this look like a break-and-enter."

He started by knocking over the lamp and bedside table. He smashed the window in Gracie's room and a couple more things.

"Write a note saying I've come to pick you up to take you north," he said. "You've got no transport."

She wrote the note, stuck it on the fridge with duct tape to make sure it wouldn't blow away from the gusts that already rushed through the rooms, searching for loose objects. She packed a small bag, terrified that Gracie would suddenly stand at the door, asking what she was up to. When they finally hurried outside, Tony left the house door open.

"The more damage, the more realistic it looks. That crap in here isn't worth shit anyway."

Melissa was not afraid of the storm anymore, she loved it. Tony drove to the 45. When they reached the turnpike, it took them over half an hour before they even got on the freeway, and after that it was stop and go. But go they did, all the way past Houston, in pouring rain, with the wind so strong he had to grip the steering wheel and use all his strength to hold the car against the buffeting. How wonderful.

They drove and they drove and they drove. Together. Soon after Houston, barely able to see through the pounding rain, Tony left the 45 and took the Northwest Freeway to Austin. Traffic was no better there, and when he saw the sign to Somerville Lake he turned off and drove along a few side roads. The windshield wipers couldn't keep up with the squally onslaught. But Melissa felt warm and safe with Tony all the way.

Finally he found what he was looking for, a narrow driveway with a beat-up sign, pointing into the property. The cabin looked as rundown as the sign. Tony knocked a few times before he broke open the lock. He couldn't have chosen any better. They found food in the pantry, lots of cans and packets of dried stuff, and the tap water ran clear and clean.

They stayed put in the rural cabin for the duration of the storm, enjoying the privacy and security as if they were staying in a luxury hotel. Melissa thought those to be the best days of her life. Every now and then, a tiny doubt crept virus-like into her bliss. Had she paid for this, for him, with the stolen twenty thousand dollars?

41

THE doorbell. Thank God, Dr. Eaton. She opened the door, taken aback by the way he looked.

"So good of you to see me on such short notice," he said. "May I come in?"

"Of course, of course."

She'd thought he must be well over fifty to have reached the position he held in the medical field, but he couldn't be a day over forty. His voice, though, sounded a lot more respectable and dignified than what his lean frame and casual clothes suggested. Or that hair. Either it was high time for a haircut or he was stuck in his student days. Snow-white curls hanging over his ears, really.

She went ahead of him into the kitchen.

"I hope you have good news for me. Has Tiara sent you? Can I go see her now? Is she getting any better?"

He sat down at the table. "Any discussion I have with your daughter is privileged, so I won't be able to answer any questions regarding her. I can tell you that she still doesn't want to see you, but nothing else."

"Then why did you come here?" Melissa asked.

Tiara

"A comprehensive assessment includes interviewing essentially everyone who dealt with her, anybody I think might be helpful."

"You took your sweet time to contact me, didn't you?"

"We're in no hurry to finalize the assessment. I have a better understanding of your daughter now. An interview at this point will most likely give me more insight than if I conducted one a few weeks earlier."

Melissa's red flags jumped to high alert. This guy sounded, looked slithery. He moved with too much ease and elegance, had a tinge of arrogance about him. He could probably talk himself out of a snake pit with a smile on his face. The eyes behind those frameless glasses gave her the creeps. Green, like a reptile's. Did crocodiles have green eyes? Creepy-Eaton. She would tell him only what was absolutely necessary.

"So what do you want to know?"

"You home-schooled Tiara, so obviously we can't contact any of her teachers—or her peers, for that matter—and you've never given the police a list of her friends."

"I told the detectives about this girl called Luna. They were close."

Dr. Eaton didn't dwell on it. "There's also no medical record," he said. "She's never seen a doctor here in Vancouver? Not even a dentist?"

"She's a healthy girl."

"Right. So it all falls back on your shoulders, and of course her grandmother's. I'll contact her in due course to give me some insight into Tiara's character."

Melissa sat up straight.

"You want to call my mother? She won't be able to tell you anything."

"Well, every little bit helps. If you can provide me with enough answers, we may not need to trouble your mother." He took out a notebook and a pen. "Shall we start?"

This was not good. Not good at all. She tried her hardest not to fidget. Mustn't give away how nervous she felt.

"Good, then," he said. "Do you remember Hurricane Ike?"

She nearly laughed out loud.

"Why do you want to know anything about that?"

"Do tell me what you remember. How did you and Tiara experience it?"

This guy's a real snake, all right. But he'll be disappointed.

"Unfortunately, I wasn't with my daughter when Ike hit our region. We got separated in the days leading up to Ike's landfall, and I took shelter in a small village up north. Sorry, Dr. Eaton, I'm afraid I won't be able to tell you anything useful."

"How did you get separated from her? She was only ten years old then."

Tiara

"You've never been in a hurricane, have you? It's a nightmare come alive. People get separated all the time, because they suddenly can't get from A to B. Roads become impassable, phones don't work, roofs get blown off houses, people can't make it home. I was a good mother, I would never leave my daughter alone if I could help it. She was in the care of a …, um, a relative, when things turned for the worse. I had to get out of the house to get to safety and could only hope Tiara and her aunt would be able to do the same. It was pandemonium. They were saying the storm-wall shielding Galveston from the ocean would break at any moment, and then all low-lying land would flood. There was no time to waste, for any of us."

He made a note. She watched his long manicured fingers glide over the sheet of paper. Spindly spidery fingers. Creepy. No, she didn't like him one bit.

"I understand. You fled the area on your own. Did you drive?"

Stick close to the truth. "I didn't have a license. A friend took me."

He scribbled again. "It must have been very upsetting for you, not knowing what happened to your daughter."

"You've got no idea. I was frantic."

"For how long?"

She frowned. What did he mean?

"I mean, how long did it take until you were reunited with Tiara and the aunt who took care of her?"

"Oh, that. Much longer than I expected. You see, the coastal area did get flooded and the power was down in the entire greater Houston area for about a week after Ike had blown through. Imagine, no air-con, no refrigeration, no lights, no phones—for one whole week. My friend and I were lucky to find a safe place to wait it out, far enough from the devastation. We had power there and watched TV non-stop to get the latest reports. We tried to call every hour, but it took a whole week before we found out that Tiara was safe."

"Was she able to leave the Galveston area, like you did?"

"As a matter of fact, she didn't. But they managed to find shelter in a motel."

Dr. Eaton looked up sharply.

"Tiara spent a whole week in a motel?"

"They got there before the storm hit, and then couldn't leave. Nobody could get out, they were stuck there. At least they were safe. If I'd known, I wouldn't have fretted so much."

Did he understand that? He didn't seem to grasp the agony a mother would feel in such a situation. Did his face reflect disdain?

"I was beside myself with worry."

"How was Tiara when you got back together?"

Okay, back to solid ground. Good. Stick to the truth on that one.

"Dear me, she was a wreck. Imagine, she'd never been away from her mom for so long, and since Katrina

Tiara

she was always scared of storms. When we found her, she was frantic, didn't speak for a month. She spent all that time in bed, like in a stupor, and it took all my love and care to make her better."

"Where did you find her?"

"What?"

"You said: 'when we found her'? Where?"

"Did I say that? I mean, when I found out where she'd been staying and picked her up. That's what I meant."

"From the motel?"

"Yes."

"Who was 'we'?"

"I mean 'I'."

"You mean, when you found them, Tiara and her aunt?"

"Yes, right."

"What's that aunt's name?"

"Uh, um, you mean ... do you mean the one who took care of her?"

He had his pen ready. "Yes. Her name?"

Should she make up a name?

Too fast he said, "Was that Gracie?"

She couldn't hold back her surprise. He knew. All of it? Panic! Stay calm, calm, calm.

"Ah, yes, right, that was her name."

"And you were with…?" Creepy Eaton asked.

She could feel sweat on her forehead. Dripping. For the love of Jesus, it was running down her temples, stinging her eyes.

"You mean Tony?"

"Yes," he said, "Tony. The choreographer. What was his last name again?"

Did he notice? She wiped her forehead, dry as a bone. Pull yourself together, stay calm, he can't know about the week at the cabin. Creepy-Eaton is fishing.

"Tony Alvarez," she said, steadier now. "But you know what, Dr. Eaton, I don't see where this is leading. I insist on seeing my daughter before I answer any more of your questions. It doesn't make sense to me why you're asking me all this." She crossed her arms and put on her best pout. Might as well show him. *You're the creep. I'm the hard-done-by mother.*

He closed his notebook and stood up. "As you wish. I think I've got enough for today. Thank you for your willingness to provide me with answers to some troubling questions. I'll be in touch."

She stood at the closed door, feeling exposed, vulnerable. Stop shaking. Stay calm. You've done good. You've made your point. But what did his parting remark mean? What troubling questions? What did she tell him that he found so useful? She hadn't given away anything of importance, except possibly the slip of her tongue when she'd mentioned Tony's last name. But he knew about Tony already, same as he'd known Gracie's name. This slippery Eaton snake must have read something into what she told him, but what?

Tiara

Did he know that when she and Tony finally did came back to Galveston, Gracie had lost contact with Tiara? Had Tiara told him how she found her?

Tony dropped her off at her home, synchronizing their story one final time on the drive up to the house, then sped off as soon as she got out of the car. The front yard looked a mess, like every yard in the street. Tin sheets from the roof hung over the entrance. The main door was closed, but not for long. Gracie sped out like one of the Furies.

"Where's Tiara? Where've you been? What the hell were you thinking? Why didn't you stay in the house? Where is she?"

It took Melissa a moment to realize that Gracie's outburst wasn't about her or Tony, it was all about Tiara.

"What do you mean—where is she?" She glared at Gracie. "She was with *you*. You should know. She should be with you."

"I'm not your daughter's keeper. You're her mother!"

"Damn this, she was in your care, not mine!"

Their screaming match went on until they exhausted themselves. Then Gracie explained what happened. The storm had taken a turn for the worse while she and Tiara drove to the photo shoot. At the motel, the Island View something-or-other, Tiara got so scared she dropped her off, knowing she'd be safe there, and drive back to get Melissa to safety, too. But that had been impossible. Halfway, the roads started to flood and she had to ask total strangers to take her in. She lived with them for five days, with no food, with only water to drink.

Then, when the flood water finally receded, she'd driven back to the motel. A lot of power lines still dangled from broken poles, and she couldn't be sure if the wires touching the ground were live, so navigating them was really dangerous. But she had gone anyway, only to find out that Tiara wasn't there any more—nobody knew anything, everybody looked out for themselves—and then she'd come back to the house, hoping to find Tiara there.

That was Gracie's story. The three of them had gotten separated. It happened. It was nobody's fault. But where was Tiara?

They both cried, from the shock, the fear, the uncertainty. Everything around them looked like a war zone. It was still dangerous to venture out, but they couldn't stand waiting in the house. When they got in the car, Gracie mentioned that the house had been vandalized, lots of stuff missing. She didn't seem concerned. It was a minor annoyance in the wake of a life-threatening experience.

They drove for hours, circling the streets as much as the fallen debris allowed, until Gracie yelled "There she is!" and slammed on the brakes.

Melissa saw Tiara on the sidewalk, stumbling barefoot through ankle-deep water, soaking wet, hair and clothes stuck to her like a second skin.

Tiara

They both ran up and tried to hug her, but Tiara started screaming and didn't stop until they both let go of her. They pushed her in the car and took her home. She didn't seem to be injured except for a few scratches, already scabbing. Melissa made the bed as best as she could—there really had been looters in the house, most of the bedding was gone—and let her sleep, thankful that nothing bad had happened to the three of them.

42

THE shrink called him. Him. Macintosh nearly dropped his cell when he saw the number. He took a deep breath to reduce the instant pressure on his heart, and answered.

Eaton didn't waste any time with introductory pleasantries, didn't even bother to mention Tiara's name, but came straight to the point.

"I have information that might assist you in finding motive," he said. "Tiara has mentioned several times a person other than the photographer being present when pornographic pictures were taken of her. You are aware of those, aren't you?"

Idiot. Careful. Don't rock the boat. It must have been hard enough for the shrink to dial his number.

"Did she mention names?"

"No."

"What did she say?"

"I can't disclose any information—"

Macintosh couldn't hold back any longer. "Oh for fuck sake! What's wrong with you? I'm trying to help her. To do so, I need information. You're supposed to help her, too. Instead, you let me bounce against rubber walls. You're burning her. Your fucking impartial position results in nothing but unnecessary delays and judicial ignorance." He had to take a breath or his lungs would burst.

"Calm down," Eaton said, making him even more furious. "I understand your frustration. I know you blame me partially for the botched conviction of your daughter's killer—"

You bet, you arrogant asshole.

"—but we need to put this behind us and concentrate on the case we're working on. It may comfort you to know that ultimately the guy has met his fate. I understand he's died of an overdose soon after his release."

"You really think this makes you less guilty of negligence?"

Eaton paused. It gave Macintosh time to collect himself again. Then Eaton said, "I'm not guilty of anything. I am overloaded with cases, just as you are, and you have decided to put the blame on me in an effort to ease your pain. I can live with that. But both of us need to stay focused on Tiara now. I will give you any information that is not strictly under our professional code of confidentiality. I'm already bending it by telling you about the person Tiara calls the Purple Shadow. If I got more, I call you again."

Macintosh nodded to himself. All right. Truce. He let his anger simmer down until his head was clear enough to think. Eaton had a point, damn it. The scumbag had met his maker, and the book needed to be closed, and stay closed forever. Josh was the only one who had shared his grief after the scumbag walked. Who could say how many girls he'd lured into his flat in Vancouver until the fateful night when Danielle became his prey. Macintosh had been forced to sit on the sidelines—conflict of interest, damn it—while others investigated the case, but he'd been working the background as hard as he could. The bond he now shared with Josh was born out of the frustration they both felt over a dangerous criminal walking because the two countries had no fast and effective way to officially exchange information, and because a psychiatric assessment was late. By the time both came through, the scumbag had been released and had done his usual disappearing act.

So many people, so many bureaucratic blunders were at work, he couldn't put the blame exclusively on Eaton's shoulder.

All calm again, Macintosh pondered the question what to do with this new player, the Purple Shadow. Nothing came to mind. Concentrate. Sort through the info you got. You can't just rely on Josh. He's got his own cases to deal with. No point asking Melissa at this stage. If the Purple Shadow was of importance to the exploitation Tiara had suffered, Melissa would deny any knowledge. What about Luna and Camila Vargas? They were the only names other than Melissa's that had come

Tiara

up so far who had known Tiara in Texas. Maybe one of them was close enough to shed some light on what Tiara meant when she talked about a purple shadow.

Suddenly his half-hearted plan to contact Luna and her mother became more pressing. But how get hold of them? Josh had not been able to provide him with a contact address, and he couldn't really pester him for information on something that at this stage was a mere hunch. Think. Come up with a solution outside of contacting the slow moving authorities. What do you know about them? Next to nothing. Hadn't Josh mentioned that Luna had a movie contract? With Lionsgate? Weren't they based in Vancouver? A rather abstract idea came to his mind. Long shot, but didn't movie companies excel in spreading PR on their new recruits?

Macintosh googled Canadian–American movie industry. Immediately 'Lionsgate Entertainment & Media' popped up. He extended his search, added Luna Vargas and found an interesting one year old entertainment blog about the new star Trina Holden of the upcoming teen American-Canadian co-production of 'Roses are Pink', who had taken over from the original cast choice Luna Vargas. Luna had lost the part after compromising pictures of her appeared on social media.

Wow. Bulls-eye. He continued searching, but could not find further reference to Luna. Then he tried the name Camila Vargas. An article about a year older than the first one mentioned that the rising star Luna and her manager mother had moved to Vancouver in preparation for the extensive production period.

What? Vancouver? Could she still be here, two years after Luna had lost the contract? Macintosh didn't think so, but he had to follow that lead. Maybe after Luna was dropped, her momager stayed on, trying to get other, smaller parts for her daughter. A move was expensive. Maybe they had their immigration sorted out by then, got a place to live, got settled, tried to ride the tide of fate. Were too ashamed to go back to the States.

He texted Harding instructions to find out if Camila Vargas had a Canadian address.

43

Still no birthdays

I seem to do nothing but lie on my bunk bed and stare at the ceiling. For two long days I refused to see Stanley. I know my inner turmoil isn't his fault, I can't blame him, he's only doing his job. He nudges me into a dark alley, pointing a flashlight into the darkness, but the light is too dim. I can't see, and I'm scared to venture further all by myself.

But I have to. The answers are hidden in the shadows.

My thoughts keep changing direction, wanting to drift off to more pleasant places, but are inevitably drawn back to this obscure tunnel Stanley tries to open up for me. It can't lead anywhere. It's got to be a dead end.

Deep inside, I know it isn't.

Today, I finally gave up my arduous efforts to not-think about the night in the motel when all the lights went out, to not-worry about the fact that my memory got switched off with those lights. I asked one of the staff to call Stanley.

Tiara

He arrived within the hour, telling me he was really glad to hear I'd be ready to continue our talk. Talk about what? Where we left off last time? The land of Tiara in the Dark?

"Don't get your hopes up. I'm not ready. I don't want to talk about what happened in the motel, but I also don't want to *not* talk about it. Does that make any sense?"

"Perfect sense." He takes out his notebook. "We can talk about something else." When I don't answer, he says, "Why don't we work it from the other end?"

Now, that's an idea. The other end starts today and moves back toward the dark alley entrance. "But I don't want to talk about the coffee shop thing."

"Okay. Why don't you tell me about your life here in Vancouver?"

"Nothing much to tell."

"It was a full three years. There must be something. What did you do? Did you have friends, other than Candy?"

No, I didn't. I admit that I was pretty lonely all the time. Stanley must have guessed this anyway, he's smart enough. The deeper I delve into my Canadian years, the more relaxed I get. Solid grounds here—no black holes, no trip-wires, no murky ponds. Plain and simple. I distanced myself more and more from Mom, to a point where she gave up home-schooling altogether. The first few months she stuck to a schedule and made me sit through the lessons and do homework. She lost the pitiful rest of her enthusiasm to transform me into a model student when she realized that I didn't listen to her, didn't finish the assignments, and even if I knew the right answer might give a wrong one. I must have been such a disappointment to her. No good at studying, no good at winning any crowns. Sometimes, when I sat reading a book, she looked at me with such sad eyes. All her dreams, squashed by a daughter incapable of becoming Grand Supreme.

"Were the beauty pageants important to you?"

"That's unfair," I say. "You said we'd work backwards."

"Sorry."

Assuaged, I throw him a morsel. "I try not to think of them. Gracie always said I had a lot of fun on stage but every time I think back I get a knot in my stomach. I don't even want to remember the contests I won, how that felt like and so on. I guess I must have liked those moments, the winning, I mean. And I guess the performance part was okay, too. I always wanted to do well to make Gracie proud."

Stanley's tactics work. His scribbling can barely keep up with my barrage of emotions long past.

"The contests were so important to Gracie. With every contest I lost she got more desperate to see me with a crown on my head. Poor Gracie got so tense, as if the world depended on it. I don't know what she was trying to prove. Once she took me aside so Mom couldn't hear and said: "Mija, make sure you win this time, I don't want to see you hurting. It's like cutting into my own flesh." She got so frantic, but there was nothing I could do about that. I had to make sure I'd lose, or it would never stop. I was determined to fail—and hey, I sure succeeded in that one, didn't I? Look at me. An all-round failure.

"My self-esteem must have been rock-bottom when we moved here. I couldn't stand girls my age. My grandmother insisted that Mom enroll me in a school, and I lasted exactly one day. Those kids looked at me and asked me a few questions and caught on right away that I was from a different planet. I didn't fit."

I tell Stanley a bit more about my only school day ever, how I threw a book at one of those bullies to make sure I'd get sent home quickly.

"Mom had no choice but to try and steer me toward my GE herself, but that never happened. Once she got the job at the 7-Eleven she was out most of the day and I took to the streets even though I felt the cold. Everything was cold in Vancouver, even the summers.

"After we arrived here, we stayed at Grandmother's first, which was even worse. Her house is a total dump. She lives like a slum dog, at least then she did. I've never been back since we moved out. It's not that she has no money, but she doesn't take care of her home. There are people who're all flashy outside and rotten inside, like they cover their stinky smell with perfume. My grandmother is one of them."

Stanley shifts in his seat and makes another note.

"You don't like her?"

"Of course I don't. I don't like any of them. Mom. Grandmother. Tony. The Purple Shadow."

"What about Gracie?"

"Gracie? She tried her best to be good to me. I know she loved me. Then, I loved her too. Now, I'm not even sure if I like her." When I'm admitting this, it's like I flick a switch. I suddenly realize how much poison I have inside me. I don't like anybody. Well, except Candy, and this doc—and maybe Macintosh.

"I hung out with Candy a lot. I told her very little about me but she kind of figured out what makes me tick. Once she said, "Jeez, it sounds like your childhood has been worse than mine." Imagine, a girl like her, pitying me."

"What was her background?" Stanley asks.

I pause, have to twirl this question around my recovering memory. Seems not important enough to surface. "Not sure. I can't remember much of what she told me. But I know what she said was true because I felt like shit all the time. A shitty, good-for-nothing failure. Miss Useless. Princess Crap."

Back to grandmother. We stayed with Louise all of four weeks, then she paid the two months' rent to set us up in that crummy place we call home. Mom needed to

Tiara

find work to support us. It was weird. Until then, I had always felt responsible for our livelihood. Listening to Mom applying for a job on the phone felt good and bad at the same time, like I'm two people. *Serves her right*, says the mean one, but the other one says, *You're a failure, it's your job to make money.*

My dislike for Mom steadily increased until I spent most days and a lot of nights away from her. The first time I stayed out overnight, she threatened me with the police when I finally did come home. She would report me, and me being underage meant they would lock me up. Candy said that's BS. If anything, it would spell trouble for my mom, not for me. So I told Mom what Candy said, then stayed away a whole week. From then on, she gave up interfering with my life.

But I still wasn't happy. Truth be told, I remained in a permanent state of depression. Honest to God, I got close to slicing my wrists, and already made plans to do so. End this shitty life. I'd do it at Mom's apartment, right there in her kitchen, messy as hell. I got myself a nice sharp knife. I've been carrying it on me ever since. Oh, I was so close.

It was supposed to be my last day at Candy's. My last day, period. She didn't know that, of course, when fate or some other force outside our control interfered. We were hanging out that evening, just bored from doing nothing. Candy was a few years older than me and earned money doing some adult stuff—not what you think, it wasn't like she did the streets or whatever, she said she didn't allow anybody to touch her, which is something I could relate to—but anyway, it made her good money and she lived not exactly in luxury but not in poverty either. She had loads of stuff and was never short of cash. She had this lap-top sitting at her desk, and asked me if I wanted to play with it. Me and a computer. Ha. Fifteen years old, but what would I know about it? Hadn't been exactly in Mom's curriculum. Candy was shocked and made me promise to figure it out. She was a useless teacher, but she knew of a course for Eastsiders, for people like me, roaming the streets, to advance our chances in life. The course didn't cost anything. Candy urged me to go. I'd qualify, she said, and I did.

I postponed my suicide plans to do her that favor, feeling I owed her that much. The course was a piece of cake, literally, a sweet, delicious slice of true education. My first taste of the real world outside the cocoon Gracie and Mom had spun around me. The four other pupils attending didn't bother me, that's the advantage of a computer course, everybody's glued to a screen and doesn't interact with the person sitting on the next chair. After two lessons I tried to show Candy what I'd learned.

"Phew, you're so good at this," she said, "way better than me." She gave me the laptop. "Tia, if you have so much fun with it, you play with it. It's all yours."

Tiara

I wonder now if she hadn't somehow figured out my plan to kill myself, which I shelved until I could finish the course. Kept it on the shelf when an advanced course started, then another one, and then my plan went up in smoke because cyberspace demanded more attention than my depression.

Stanley looks impressed. Here is Tiara, the failure, good at something after all.

On this high note, Stanley wraps up for today.

"We'll work backwards again tomorrow," he says.

Just as well he's gone. I've said enough about me and computers. About the time I learned a real people skillset, one that might come in handy one day, the future began to look quite a bit brighter. I knew I was broken, damaged goods, unable to stand up straight without crutches—except on the computer. In cyberspace I felt capable. A real person. The internet did that for me. It made me feel whole, alive, like I had never felt before. It connected me to a world I hadn't known existed, and let me be in control without having to reveal my identity or being crowded by strangers. Even when my past elbowed itself in, my discoveries invigorated me, securely hidden behind the anonymity the net gave me.

44

THE South Vancouver case took a lucky turn when the shooter placed himself into custody, probably fearing repercussions from the rival gang if he stayed out in the streets. His confession cut a lot of red tape, and Macintosh got a free moment to check his Princess file.

The current status of the investigation was depressing. Margarita Rios' and Carl Heider's entry into Canada had been recorded, showing them landing at Toronto Pearson International airport two years and eight months ago, but after that their trail had gone cold. No further air movement, neither outside nor within Canada. The profession of Carl Heider as stated on the travel document had caught Macintosh's attention. A photographer. Macintosh had felt in his gut that this was connected to Tiara, and had asked Josh to check where Carl Heider had worked. The name of the studio was Photomagic but further research showed that this shop didn't exist. Another dead end.

He still had Luna and Camila Vargas. He walked over to Harding who told him with a resigned shrug that he hadn't been able to locate them yet.

Tiara

Macintosh looked at his watch. Exactly 6:00 pm. "Time to call it a day. I might go see Tiara's mother on my way home, throw the Purple Shadow at her and see how she reacts."

He didn't think she'd contribute anything useful, but he hated to feel so unproductive. While he dialed to make the appointment with Melissa Brown, Harding did a final check on his emails before closing shop for the day.

Macintosh glanced up, saw the color drain out of his partner's face, and hung up again.

"Something wrong?"

Harding pointed to the screen, displaying a video clip of a young girl, no more than nine, being undressed. She faced the camera without recognition. Seemed sleepy, couldn't keep her eyes open.

"Josh sent us this." Harding said, barely audible.

"Oh my God," Macintosh said. "It's Tiara."

The person undressing Tiara expertly avoided the camera. Macintosh could only see hands in black gloves. One garment after another fell on the floor. Tiara stood motionless, let herself be handled like a lifeless mannequin. When she was fully undressed, the black-gloved person moved behind her, again not exposing any details that would make identification possible. All Macintosh and Harding could see was a dark purple cape, the shape of the wearer hidden under the folds. When the gloved hands finished their task they pressed Tiara's naked upper body against the purple material and held her still for the camera to zoom closer. One black leather hand cupped her chin and lifted her head up so the camera could focus on her face, her eyes closed.

For a brief moment the head of the handler became visible. Macintosh gasped. The face was covered with a dark mask with narrow eye slits that made the action even more sinister. The head disappeared again when the camera moved down on Tiara's body. The other hand begun to stroke her lower body.

"Jesus," Macintosh said. "The Purple Shadow."

Harding hit the stop button repeatedly. "Shit! Shit! Shit!"

He kept hitting the keyboard, closing down his computer.

Macintosh leaned forward and pressed the start-up button again.

"What the hell's the matter with you?" Harding said. "You're on your own if you play that again."

"Don't be stupid," Macintosh said. "I'm not watching this disgusting filth again. I'm forwarding the clip to Sexual Offense Squad. This is proof that Tiara has a history of abuse which goes way beyond participation in beauty contests or even pornographic modeling."

"We should send it to the shrink, too," Harding said.

Macintosh dug out Eaton's card and handed it over to Harding. "You tell him," he said. "And we should

Tiara

show it to Melissa. I'd love to see her reaction. The crazy lying bitch must have known all along. She had to know what was going on. She sold her own daughter to those black leather handlers."

Harding typed Dr. Eaton's email address and forwarded the link. Then he dialed Dr. Eaton's office. This time they wouldn't wait for a call back. Harding told the secretary it was an emergency, and was asked to hold.

"I agree," he said, covering the mouthpiece with his hand. "We should surprise Melissa Brown with this. She's in deep shit now."

Eaton came on the phone.

"Dr. Eaton, good of you to talk to me," Harding said. "Detective Macintosh asked me to send you an email link of a pornographic video clip featuring Tiara Rodriguez-Brown. Our Texas connection discovered it and mailed it to us…. Yes, unfortunately I was informed there are more of a similar nature…. No, I'll have them forwarded directly to Sexual Offense Squad. We can't stomach more of these. And anyway, we're homicide. But it does give motive, if we ever find out who the fuck, excuse me, who the victim is…. Oh yes, we assume she must be connected to Tiara's past. We thought we'd identified her already, a woman called Graciella Rodriguez—that's right, her aunt Gracie—but when checking into that lead, we found out she's dead. Died in a fire a few years ago…. Sure, you look at the video and judge for yourself… Okay, I'll keep you in the loop, no worries. And if you ever… I mean, I know your conversations with Tiara are privileged… What's that…? What's his name?" He scribbled something on his pad. "Thanks for this, we'll check into it."

Harding hung up, a smile flitting over his somber expression.

Macintosh took the pad and read the name Harding had written down.

"Who's Tony Alvarez?"

"The shrink said you were looking for names. He found this one in his notes from the time he interviewed Tiara's mother as part of her psycho-social assessment. Melissa mentioned a guy with that name, and whatever she tells him is not privileged. Apparently this Tony guy was the choreographer the mother hired to teach Tiara the moves for her pageant appearances. Now what does that tell you? The moves. He was training her for those competitions. God knows what else he made her do."

As much as viewing the video had affected their mood, Macintosh felt a little better now. Harding looked relieved, too. They had another name. They had a fucking name which was directly connected to the case. It was their first real lead in the case after the victim's identity had gone cold. He sent an email to Josh, thanking him for his help and giving him the name of the dance teacher they suspected to be involved in Tiara's sexual exploitation.

Macintosh thought about Melissa. He couldn't imagine a mother doing that to her child. Kathy would have killed anybody who tried to molest their daughter.

Tiara

So would he, policeman or not. Natural impulse. Unfortunately, some parents lacked the instinct to nurture and protect. Melissa could be one of them. The few times they'd spoken she came across self-centered to a fault, a possible egomaniac. Abnormal to the point of allowing this kind of child abuse? Jesus. He had to find out. Had to crawl into her head to figure out what made her tick.

"If I were Melissa and got confronted with this video," he said, "I'd deny everything. There's nothing that ties me to the crime."

"Except being the abused girl's mother."

"Right, but I'm thinking what have those idiot detectives got on me? They can't prove anything. I made damn sure I wasn't visible in any of the pictures or video clips."

"You really think Tiara's mother was stuck underneath that purple cloak and covered her face with that disgusting mask so her own daughter wouldn't recognize her?" Harding said.

"Why not? Whoever is under that cloak had a good reason to hide. If it was her, she would have been super careful to make sure Tiara didn't know. She'd have been careful all those years, making sure she didn't leave a trace."

"Do you really think Melissa is that smart?"

"She's a lot smarter than we gave her credit for. What bugs me most is the incident with the fire. When exactly was that?"

Harding looked at his notes. "Same month she and Tiara came to Vancouver."

"See. Again, I'm Melissa. Something happened that made it necessary for me to leave the country in a hurry. I pack up my daughter. Before I go, I burn the place where I lived to the ground, destroy all possible evidence. Or I get somebody do it for me. The aunt's still in the house. I might not know this, might not even be aware to this day that Graciella Rodriguez is dead."

"That means they've cut off all ties, otherwise she'd know."

"Right again. But if I do know, I've willingly accepted her death. Maybe I made sure she was in the house and incapable of leaving when I burnt it down. That way I get rid of anything or anybody that might implicate me in the future. I know nothing and I've done nothing wrong. I'll be shocked when I see the video, and there isn't a goddamn thing anybody can do about it."

"Unless we have proof."

"Yeah," Macintosh said. "We have to tread real careful there. Lucky I didn't call Melissa yet. We have to gather a lot more information than this video before we confront her with it. How high would this clip rank on the Copine Scale?"

"I do murder, I don't deal in pedophile pornography."

Macintosh typed Copine into the search engine and pulled up the information. Together, the detectives skimmed the ranks of the scale compiled by the London Metropolitan Police in 1990 in an effort to categorize child abuse images.

There were ten levels, least to worst. The ninth, gross assault, was defined as 'grossly obscene pictures of sexual assault, involving penetrative sex, masturbation or oral sex, involving an adult'.

"Gross Assault. That does it," Macintosh said. "We need to tell the sergeant. It has to be added to our Princess file. Her lawyer must be made aware of this, he can do better for her if the extent of her abuse is documented. And as far as we're concerned, let's see what we can get out of the mother bitch. "

"But if we don't confront her with the video, what are we gonna do?"

"We know Melissa's warned her mother to keep her blabbermouth shut. Louise is tough as nails but she isn't the brightest bulb in the chandelier. Let's see how much she knows and how she reacts if we threaten her with obstruction of justice. If she's covering for Melissa, she might manipulate her daughter to save her own skin. I bet Melissa breaks under stress if the pressure comes from all sides."

45

THE clocks had been turned back to standard time two weeks ago. Now the dark fell way too early. Melissa walked from the bus stop to her apartment building, thinking how the dreary twilight matched her mood. Colored light bulbs began to pop up over storefronts and on neon signs, barely fighting the dull gray dusk. Serious storm clouds pushed in from the Pacific, darkening the sky even more. And it wasn't even five yet.

She didn't have to walk far, but the distance from the bus stop to her apartment took her longer than ever, and she had to breathe deep to manage her already slow pace. Her weight had been climbing constantly since she was back in Canada—well, to be honest, that had started a few years before—but seemed to spiral out of control lately. She could feel the extra pounds piling on her waist, and there wasn't a thing she could do about it.

She blamed the stress. All the magazine articles giving diet advice said so. Avoid stress if you want to lose weight. How on earth should she do that with her making only minimum wage at the 7-Eleven, and her meager savings from the TV interview dwindling rapidly? She wished her fat would vanish like that.

What was she going to do? Her wages never covered her expenses, as careful as she was. Already she was buying marked-down groceries with close expiration dates.

Her biggest fear was that they would cancel her cable. What would she do without her TV shows on all those lonely evenings? Tiara wasn't coming back, not ever. Once they released her, and that could be years away, she wouldn't move back in with her mother. Tears welled up but not out—Melissa couldn't weep any more. No tears left in her, her burning eyes nothing but a figment of her misery.

When she finally reached her apartment, she put her plastic shopping bags full of tins and packets on the kitchen counter, sat down, slipped the shoes off her swollen feet. The phone rang. She got up with a heavy sigh and walked barefoot to where she'd left the phone.

"Thank God you're home." Her mother sounded excited. "I thought you finish work at three."

"It takes a while from the bus stop."

"Guess what, the police called me this morning."

Pause. Melissa's pulse went up. How she hated her mother doing that.

"Why? What did they want from you?"

"I wish I knew. Detective Macintosh called. He asked me to come to the station at Graveley Street for an interview. Tomorrow. He sounded serious. Is there anything going on I don't know about?"

"Like what?"

"Like I don't know. That's why I'm asking."

"What exactly did he say?"

Silence. Melissa could picture her mother squinting in an effort to recall the conversation.

"He said there's been a new development and he has some questions." Silence. Squinting again? "And I might as well tell you, he said I should come alone and shouldn't talk to you about it."

"Jesus Christ."

"What new development is he talking about?"

Should she tell? Why not. Might be important for her mother to know before she faced the detectives. "I had a visit from the shrink who's treating Tiara, and I think I made a mistake. I mentioned Tony's name, and when he asked me for his surname, I blurted it out."

"I thought we didn't want to talk about the past?"

"He tricked me. But that's the only thing I can think of. Nothing else that could be classified as a new development, at least not from my side."

"Then we got nothing to worry about," her mother said. "Tiara knows nothing, and Tony's irrelevant to what she's done here. Don't worry, I'll handle them."

If you only knew how relevant Tony is.

Melissa said goodbye, disconnected, slumped back in her chair, still holding the handset. She fully expected

Tiara

Macintosh to call her, too, about the so-called new development.

Nothing happened. The darkness outside went deeper into the night, and her mood sank to a new low. Tony, always Tony, everything led to him. He, a devilish magnet. She, helpless to resist the draw.

He was the one who made her do what she did. She would have done anything for him, to get the life she so desperately craved. A life with him by her side, a normal life, without Gracie and her increasingly erratic behavior. With Tiara, of course, if she pulled herself together and became normal again.

Sometimes Melissa felt like she was stuck in an asylum for crazy people. Tiara, sullen and silent, Gracie always carting her off somewhere. If it wasn't for the photo sessions, it was for doctor's appointments or therapy sessions, she said. Therapy, my foot. Tiara had no medical insurance, and Gracie was far too frugal to pay for anything unnecessary. Let's face it, Tiara's detached attitude stemmed from her fear of storms. She hadn't been the same since she got lost for days during Hurricane Ike.

Growing up, whenever Melissa was afraid or sulked her mother ignored her until she snapped out again. "Indulging childish conduct only encourages more of it," she used to say. Melissa had soon learned that such behavior didn't get her anywhere. Tiara would learn, too. To get her expensive treatment like Gracie mentioned was ridiculous. Gracie only said so to cover up the fact that so little money was left over, although Tiara had to do a lot of photo sessions ever since their sponsor Inez, who had become Gracie's best friend, had taken control of their lives.

Gracie didn't want to share those earnings with her, that was all there was to it. Collecting and hiding the loot out of her sight. She checked Gracie's room periodically but never found more than a few hundred dollars. Not until that fateful day three years ago, when she was forced to leave her home and go back to Canada.

Melissa tried to shrug off the memory, tried to think about something else, about how she could make do on her salary. There she was, thinking about money again, full circle. The money thing didn't want to go away. Money. Tony. Money. Tony. Tony. Tony. Always Tony. He didn't want to go away. Oh Tony, why did you deceive me?

46

How long to my next birthday?

IT'S the end of November. Nine months to go before I'll be sixteen.

My sweet Stanley tells me my psycho-social assessment, which involves interviewing essentially everybody who dealt with me—medical, school, friends, you name it—is completed, for lack of anybody else to contact aside from my mother. Because I'm unwilling, or unable, to provide further insight, he will finalize his assessment shortly. He has even given me a little hint what his verdict will be.

"In my opinion, you're not delusional. You're also not aggressive. You may not be consciously aware of what triggered the attack, but your subconscious knows, and I'm confident that you'll eventually regain your suppressed memory and uncover your motive. I even think you're quite close to this stage. Unfortunately, it may take too long for the court."

If I'm not aware of what triggered me, he explains further, I can't anticipate or locate the stress that might lead me to commit another aggressive act. This determines whether the judge feels the need to protect society from me.

"If you want to get a lighter sentence," Stanley says with an earnest face, "you need to become more cooperative. The only way to avoid adult sentencing is to open up to people who usually work on an assessment."

"Like who?"

"Your case manager, your lawyer, a social worker, the police. You need to give each one of them anything that might help them figure out the reasons for your actions."

"Like what?"

"It would help if you at least agree to see a psychologist."

"Why? I've already agreed to talk to you."

"I'm a psychiatrist."

As if I would ever let any other soul searcher but my very own shrink-doc infiltrate my psyche. "Sounds all the same to me."

"A psychiatrist has a medical degree and can prescribe medicine. Psychologists put more emphasis on research and testing, and they use talk therapy."

"Isn't that what you're doing with me? All that digging into my past?"

"True. Our sessions are therapeutic."

"So why change, then?" I say. "Does a psychologist have more clout in court?"

"As a psychiatrist I can query their test results."

"Which ultimately puts you in charge when the judge is undecided?"

"Yes."

"I'll stick with you, then, thank you very much."

Is he pleased? I can't read his expression.

"Once I hand in my report," he says, "no further consultation with you will be scheduled. As bail is out of the question, you'll be locked up in here until your case goes to trial. You should make good use of this time. If anything comes to your mind that might explain your actions, now, that would be really helpful."

How will I cope without his visits?

He watches me getting a little scared of the future.

"Your mother has requested to see you. Should you agree, I would highly recommend you let me be present as an observer."

I cross my arms. "I don't want to see or speak to her."

"Good."

My presentiment of the coming months in the center were well-founded. Within a few days of Stanley's last visit, four more girls are put into the eight-cell octagon I had entirely to myself until now. They're hanging out in my so far very private community area. Yikes. I'm expected to live with four total strangers—all of them in purple sweat suits. Inside those sweat suits are breath-

Tiara

takingly common chicks. Listening to their non-stop clack, clack, clack makes my head throb so bad I'm ready to puke.

I need to get out of here. I can't handle such closeness.

But there's no hiding from this unwanted company. I briefly considered a screaming match or slapping one of the girls, but the rulebook states solitary is only good for two to seventy-two hours. I'll only jeopardize Stanley's statement of my fragile but non-criminal mental health with such drastic action. I'm stuck in close proximity to strange purple girls. They automatically assume I'm one of them and ask me what I've done, where I'm from, how long I'll be here....God only knows what else they'd ask if I didn't cut them short.

One of them had the temerity to walk up to me while I was taking cover behind a book and introduce herself.

"Hi there, I'm Alison," she said, extending her hand.

I ignored her, but she persisted.

"I'm fifteen"—aren't we all?—"and I'm only in here for three months. It's okay in here. I should know, I've been in and out since I was thirteen."

What an accomplishment. Really something to be proud of. I turned my back to her, hoped she'd get the message. What it boils down to is that I'm cornered. In a room without corners. The irony of it.

The cell doors are locked for the hours we're supposed to communicate and participate in the mandatory home work that is supposed to help us better integrate into society when the time comes. I don't want to participate in anything, but now that I don't have the privilege of Stanley's visits any more, I have even less opportunity to withdraw into myself.

I feel a little better when everybody is asleep. Alone in my cell, I ignore the hourly flashlight check by security, making sure I haven't escaped or hung myself from the window bars with a ripped bed sheet.

The nights are long. Endless. November days get dark too early, plenty of extra hours to give my nightmares a whole new quality. The dream that tortured me last night was drawn out painfully long, reaching way into my semi-awake state. Started with me falling into an unprotected water drain on a roadside somewhere. I got stuck halfway down, but nobody up there looked into the hole. The rain pelted into the drain so hard it muffled my screams, and soon enough I felt like I was drowning whenever I opened my mouth. I willed myself to wake up, but couldn't.

Made me feel like those times when Gracie gave me that juice. She'd always made me drink the sweet concoction when we were on the way to the studio, moments before we got there, and sometimes afterwards if I became fidgety and whiny. The juice made me lethargic fast, but I've always hated the helpless feeling

Tiara

that came with it. Then, and even more so now, drugs are not for me.

Candy gave me a joint once, and I took a deep drag because she said it would lift some of the burden I carried with me. It didn't. One single puff threw me back to those juice-confused-days. Candy saw my panic, made me drink lots of water, and after I snapped out of it she made me promise to never ever again take any drugs. Easiest promise in the world. Why should I want to feel like garbage?

That's how I felt like in my dream, while I was struggling to wake up. I'm stuck in the wet hole, fighting the drowsiness I hate so much, willing myself into a more alert state. Scenes come and go, with languishing clarity or annoying fogginess, never there long enough for me to grab one and shake it into reality. I drift in and out, lose focus, want to slip into oblivion. One lulu of a nightmare, all right.

Finally, the automated lights go on. It's 7:00 am, I have forty-five minutes to get up, go to the shower attached to the community area, wait my turn, shower, go back to my cell, dress, go back to the community room, have breakfast with my four purple resident-inmates, go back to my cell, make my bed, clean the toilet and washbasin, mop the floor, then wait for room inspection.

While I was doing all that, the nightmare never left me. I had it on a leash, or it had me dragging along, who's to say. I stand by the window, look into the November clouds racing by. Serious rain clouds. Maybe a storm coming. I try not to think about any storm, but the memory of the Big One is creeping in. A scene from my half-awake, half-asleep groping-for-reality gains momentum. The storm. Me. Alone. All alone. The darkness. And suddenly, the doors opening.

I can see. I know.

I'm screaming. My cell door opens and security rushes in.

47

MACINTOSH found a copy of Eaton's completed assessment, constituting his pre-trial report, waiting on his desk. It had arrived at the station over a week ago. This he couldn't blame on Eaton. It wasn't marked urgent, so it could have taken that long for the in-house journey between the mail arrival and his department. Why was all communication with court still done with hard copies? The report, addressed to the Presiding Judge of the Family and Youth Court, Vancouver, BC, was only five pages long, but short was better than not at all. Maybe Eaton finally understood the importance of delivering on time.

His heartbeat accelerated when he sat down and opened it. He took a deep breath to steady himself before he started speed-reading over the introductory part. Once he got to the main part, he highlighted what he found important:

...Tiara Brown is charged following an incident where she was observed by a witness and on video stabbing an older female multiple times without apparent provocation ...

Tiara

...has not cooperated with investigators but has provided information to me up to the time of this dictation...

...was raised by her mother and aunt ... home-schooled and isolated from her peers ... was enrolled in beauty pageants from age four ... put under significant pressure by both her aunt and her mother to succeed in these competitions...

...indicates that beginning at an early age Tiara Brown was photographed ... pictures became increasingly sexually explicit ... at times drugs were administered to her to sedate her for the purpose of taking the pornographic pictures...

...became socially isolated ... refused to attend school ... became increasingly estranged from her biological mother...

...shows some degree of agitation and emotional distress if attempts are made to discuss emotional details of her life...

...psychological testing ... high intelligence ... highly defensive and unwilling to disclose details about herself ... consciously suppressing emotional responses...

...significant tendency towards dissociation ... noted to isolate herself ... extreme reluctance to be touched ... depression with difficulty sleeping and obvious neuro-vegetative slowing...

Macintosh learned few new details, but now that he came to the psychiatrist's all-important conclusion, he put his yellow highlighter aside and concentrated on every single word.

Your Honor, Tiara Brown has been charged with a serious assault, without apparent provocation.

Our assessment has demonstrated significant emotional numbing, withdrawal and dissociation. We do not have significant evidence of a psychotic disorder, but she is demonstrating significant symptoms of depression.

Inasmuch as Tiara Brown herself does not remember and therefore is unable to understand her behavior, we cannot provide the court with any assurance as to her safety or the safety of the public should she be released.

If Tiara Brown is remanded in custody, she will continue to have access to mental health services. She will be seen on a continuing basis by members of the mental health team and will continue to have access to me for ongoing psychiatric care and assessment.

If the courts were to choose to release this young woman, given the history made available to us, it would not be appropriate for her to return to the care of her biological mother. If released to the community, we suggest that she be subject to strict conditions that include regular attendance for ongoing assessment and treatment through Youth Forensic Psychiatric Services, and if released to the public she should be accompanied by a knowledgeable and responsible adult.

Tiara

Until we get a clear understanding as to what provoked Tiara Brown's behavior, final diagnosis and treatment recommendations cannot be made.

I trust this report will be of use to Your Honor in making an appropriate determination at this time. If you have any questions or concerns, please feel free to contact me at Youth Forensic Psychiatric Services, Inpatient Assessment Unit, South Burnaby region.

Respectfully submitted,
Dr. Stanley Eaton, M.D., F.R.C.P.

Good and bad. The shrink opened the door wide for the judge to consider mental and emotional problems, but even with the reference of Tiara suffering sexual exploitation with this evaluation Tiara would never get probation. She'd stay locked up indefinitely.

Macintosh mulled over this rather bleak outlook for the girl when Harding rushed up to his desk. Macintosh put the report aside.

"Good old Josh tracked down Tony Alvarez," Harding said. "The guy is living in Phoenix now, giving so-called dance lessons to young girls again, the sick bastard."

Macintosh laughed. "You never learn, do you? The accused is innocent until proven guilty."

"Sure, the prick deserves to be treated with kid gloves—black leather gloves, I bet. Josh wants to interview him real bad. Unfortunately the prick is in Phoenix, which ain't Texas, so organizing it takes a tad longer."

"They got something on him?" Macintosh was all ears now.

"You bet. They found a number of guys with the name Antonio Alvarez spread over several states, that's why it took a few days to figure out which one is our man. The one in Phoenix is not only a dance instructor, he—now hold on to that—once owned a photo studio in Texas City. Name, Photomagic. Sold it three years ago, about the same time Melissa brought Tiara back here. Nice coincidence, isn't it? Anyway, Sexual Offense Squad analyzed some of the Princess Tia video clips, one of them showed a partially covered window in the background. The prick, excuse me, the accused, wasn't overly careful. They enlarged the window and matched the shape of the building outside to the view from the window of the Texas City studio."

Harding paused but Macintosh waved him to go on.

"It's definitely our man in Phoenix who made those clips. We know it was Antonio Alvarez' studio."

"And we have enough circumstantial evidence pointing to the identity of the photographer. Put out a Canada wide warrant for Carl Heider and his wife Margarita Rios."

48

STANLEY is sitting next to my bed, keeping his distance, not invading my space. I'm so grateful for that. He never pushes me, not even now. When the center staff realized I didn't have anger issues but a plain and simple nervous breakdown, they transferred me back to the Inpatient Assessment Unit.

"Hey, that didn't take you long," I say. "Guess you missed me."

His face goes a nuance softer. "You don't make it easy to say no."

I'd begged the nurse there not to give me a sedative but to call Dr. Eaton because I remembered something that could be important to my case. An hour later he was there.

Outside, the storm clouds gathered right above Burnaby, and, as if to mock me, lightning illuminates the sky at regular intervals, followed by angry thunder. I embryo-curl up under my blanket, but I do so from habit, not to take the fear away. I'm not fearful. The storm has lost its grip on my soul. My soul is safe. Groping for the dangerous words that describe what I remembered, I begin to tell Stanley.

Tiara

He takes out his notebook.

"Please don't write anything down. I'm not sure I can handle the idea of anybody else but you knowing what happened."

He closes his notebook again.

I bring him back to the time when Hurricane Ike was approaching, so I can step into the horror I now fully recall, with him—metaphorically—holding my hand.

"Remember, the hurricane approaching, Mom and me stuck in the house. Mom beside herself with terror, me even more scared, wanting to creep under the table, under a blanket, and hide from Ike, from Mom, from Gracie."

I hesitate, Stanley helps me along. "And then Gracie came home…"

"… and bundled me into her car. She put me on the back seat, buckled me up and told me to close my eyes so I wouldn't see branches and objects flying past the windscreen. I pressed my eyes shut, but the noise of the storm surrounding us made not seeing worse."

I tell Stanley how Gracie groped in her handbag on the passenger seat, took out the usual bottle and handed it to me without looking back at me. Traffic was heavy, stop and go, with everybody trying to get out and get away.

"Here, drink it all," she said. I took the bottle and unscrewed the cap. The instant I put the bottle to my mouth, Gracie had to brake hard. I lost my grip, the bottle slipped to the floor, the contents spilled out. Gracie didn't notice—she was so focused on driving. As soon as the car got going again I picked up the bottle. I could see some of the dream-juice left inside, but didn't want to put the bottle on my lips, not after it rolled on the filthy carpet. Gracie's car had never been very clean. So I let the rest drip on the floor and screwed the top on again when it was empty. If she'd caught on, everything might have turned out different.

When she stopped the car in front of a motel, she got out and opened the back door to help me out.

She studied me, then snapped at me, nervous, hurried.

"Did you drink it all?"

I let my head go all limp.

Thinking back to what happened next has been tormenting enough last night, but to try and find the right words to tell Stanley now feels excruciatingly painful. My mouth gets dry, my lungs tighten, my heart palpitates.

"And then she took you inside and made you up." Stanley assists, probably worried I might withdraw. But I won't, not this time.

"She dressed me in a ruffled nylon creation which looked soft and felt scratchy. Straight from my princess days. She mumbled orders like 'turn' and 'lift your face' and 'up with your arms.' I pretended to be drowsy. She expected me that way, and in those days I always did what was expected of me. I was sitting on the bed, the ruffled nylon skirt arranged around me so I didn't have to sit on it, looking at the golden vines woven into the carpet, as if I wasn't interested in anything. When she was done, or I was done, she packed her bag and then she… she…she said—."

Stanley assists again. "Then she told you to be a good girl."

"Yes, she said, you're a big girl now, my pretty mija, you'll be fine." My heart races. My throat constricts. Labored breathing, shallow. *Stanley, Stanley, she said I would like it*. The horror of those words crush the life out of me. I try to continue between gasps. "She said, I get you some juice… wait here until I'm back."

My lungs, my lungs, they tighten. Shut down. No more air. My head swims. The blackness engulfs me again. I'll drown in nothing. "Oh God—"

"Take your time," I hear Stanley say from far away. "Breathe. Slow, slow… deep… there you go. Don't rush it."

"I'm… scared. I need to tell you what happened… now… before it slips away again."

"Don't worry, it won't go away, and once you've told me you'll feel much lighter."

I know he's right. The picture doesn't disappear because I don't want to see it. Gracie has left me. I'm all alone in the room.

With a barely audible voice, I tell Stanley in simple, tiny words how the dim light went out with a bang, throwing me into pitch black terror. So dark, I can hear my ears hum. I can hear my labored breath—then and now. The terror is back, it swallows Stanley, and the cell I'm in, and the whole world. Darkness with me in its center, not able to run and hide because there's nowhere to go.

The double door to the next room opens. Not Gracie. A man stands in the frame, outlined by a lamp in the room behind him, he's holding a flashlight. The light blinds me.

Where did the light behind him come from? An emergency lamp, one of those portable battery-operated lights people have in their cars. It gives off a bluish shine, cold and distant.

Still, it's a light. I can't look into the beam of the flashlight, I'm half blind and shaking, too confused to utter a word. But he does. He says ... he says ... he says ...

I take a deep breath and make myself say it out loud. He says, "Let's fuck."

I managed the eff-word! The one swear word I could never say before. I say it again. I want to shout it out again, but stop myself. Stanley would understand, no question, but being free of the word doesn't mean I like the word. It's ugly, it's disgusting, and I don't want that word to become a part of me.

The man throws himself on me, still holding the flashlight. I'm ten, small for my age, and this bulky guy pins me down and starts pulling at my frilly dress. Finally, my tongue loosens enough to let the screams out of my throat.

He freezes.

"Hell, what's the matter with you? Shut up!"

I don't, and he muffles my screechy, scared sounds with his big hand. The flashlight slips out and rolls off the bed. We are both in near darkness again. He gropes and fumbles with the other hand underneath my nylon dress. The stiff material rubs against my skin every time I pull it down again. I wriggle and pull with all I've got.

His hand hurts me in places he should never touch, but I can't scream because of his other hand on my mouth and because he buries me with his weight. Then he uses both his hands to hold my head, but I can still feel something hurting me where his hand had been. The pain moves deeper inside me. I pass out.

Later, I'm lying on the plastic bedspread feeling cold. And scratchy inside-out, outside-in. He gets up again. He's still in the room, I can hear him. Getting his clothes in order, picking up the flashlight. He comes back to me.

"Come on, sugar," he mumbles, "that wasn't too bad, was it?" He sighs. "I couldn't wait. This goddamn storm is messing up everything. The photographer will be back soon and we'll do it again, real proper, like a little princess deserves."

He comes closer, lays down next to me, touches me again, not down there, but stroking my face.

"We'll get the whole thing on tape then. Look, it's all set up there in the next room, all ready to go. As soon as the power's back on, we'll move over there and make you all pretty again and then …well, you make me come again just thinking about it. My pretty little Princess Tia. I've seen all your videos. I'm your biggest fan, ever since your first contest. You ask Inez how much money I've spent on you. Years of waiting, years of paying, but now, I get my reward. I've been your first, and you'll never forget me. You're mine. My pretty princess, I've got to have you on tape. I'll have you for the rest of my life then. When you move on to other men, you'll still be with me."

He repeated what he said for what seemed like an eternity while we lay on the bed, waiting for the power to come back on. I was too numb to feel anything but I couldn't help hearing him in the dark. He must have carved most of his words into me, inside my brain, because they're all there now, clear as warning bells.

Eventually, though, he grew tired of waiting. He got up and told me to stay put while he checked out what was going on.

"This power outage is taking way too long," he said, "don't those idiots have a generator?"

He expected me to follow his orders and wait for him to come back. I didn't understand what had happened but I knew if the lights went on again, he'd hurt me again. I was terrified of the darkness, but I was even more terrified of him.

Tiara

The bluish glow from the next room fell on my street clothes. Without thinking, without feeling any pain, I slipped the scratchy nylon thing over my head and got into my cotton dress. I couldn't find my shoes and didn't have time to look for them. I grabbed the portable lamp and saw that the next room had a door too. I opened it to look down the corridor. The man would come back from the reception area, so I stumbled in the other direction. It led to an outside door, the back entrance of the motel. When I opened that door, I was amazed to find that outside was still afternoon. I dropped the emergency lamp and ran and ran and ran into the storm.

For a while Stanley doesn't react. I wait for him to comment, expecting him to try and comfort me. After the silence exhausted itself, he claps his hands together.

"Excellent. You made it."

"I guess so," I say, a bit bewildered. "They found me nearly a week later, and I'm not sure how I survived the storm. I must have hidden somewhere, I had scratches on my arms and remember climbing over a fence and through bushes into a garden shed. I couldn't have stayed there all week but yes, I made it."

"Oh dear, of course you did. But that's not what I meant when I said you made it. You managed to open the lock to stored memories. That is excellent. I'm so pleased with you."

I'm pleased with him, too. Trust Stanley not to feel sorry for me.

"Do you want to continue?"

Enough for today. All I want to do is sleep.

49

Fireworks for my lost birthdays

I slept like a log. Solid, unmoving, undreaming, like a chunk of wood left on the ground, too heavy to roll. Stanley let me sleep, I guess he was making phone calls or seeing other traumatized resident-inmates in the medical unit of this extraordinary establishment until the hourly security check alerted him that I'd woken up.

One would think I'd be drowsy after such a death-like slumber, but I feel as fresh as a daisy. Stanley's face reflects his surprise when he registers how alert I am.

"I see you're ready to carry on."

As always, he reads me like an open book. Yes, I want to keep talking. I turned on a tap and now the memories gush out with enormous pressure. A wild waterfall of words. He settles down and listens, this time with his notebook open, ready to record the things done to me.

After Hurricane Ike passed, the population of southern Texas began to rebuild their lives out of the destruction

Tiara

it left them in. Our small household was no different. For several weeks—or months, I don't recall how long it was—after Mom and Gracie found me on the street I stayed in my room.

Deep inside, I knew that Mom and Gracie should have protected me. I still didn't fully understand what had happened to me in that motel, and resented them both for letting it happen, but Mom and Gracie were the only family I had. They were part of me, like my arms or legs. I wouldn't chop off my arm or leg because they hurt, and for the same reason I wouldn't cut myself loose from Mom and Gracie. It wasn't an option. I was ten years old then, I had been hurt bad and couldn't deal with it. All I could do was withdraw into myself in a desperate effort to forget the pain.

Sure, deep inside I must have hoped Mom would come to my room and demand that I tell her what was wrong with me. She should have insisted that I answer her, tell her the truth. She should have protected me years ago, when I came home and told her I didn't like the photo sessions. But as I lay in my room I knew I was waiting in vain for her to hold me and comfort me and coax from me the horror of what the motel-man did to me.

I slipped into a state of utter passivity—uncaring, unfeeling. I ceased to exist. Another girl got up in the morning, got fed and dressed, sat in front of homework without reading or writing a single line, answered

Mom's simple questions with a nod or a shake of the head. I lost my ability to communicate any other way. Mom tried only half-heartedly to snap me out of it, she had other things on her mind. "Don't worry, princess, next time there's a storm, I'll take you away from the coast before it starts."

She occupied herself with getting the house in order again, arguing with Gracie over money, and hanging around the house waiting for the phone to ring. I knew she waited for that because she never ventured far from the phone and jumped every time it did ring, excited-like, pressing one hand on her chest to hold her heart in, then dropping it resignedly after she picked up the call.

Quite often I could hear Gracie shouting at Mom, but when she came into my room she kept her voice down, asking me if I needed anything. I always pulled the blanket over my head. About two weeks after they found me on the street, Gracie finally sat down on my bed, pulled the blanket down and put her hand on my arm. I tried to tug away from her but she tightened her grip.

"Mija," she said, "I know you're upset with me, but there is no reason to blame me."

I wanted to scream at her. *You brought me to the motel. You left me alone in the dark. You let that man come to the room. You let him hurt me.* But the words couldn't break through the barrier of shame and turned inward instead.

Tiara

"Do you want to tell me what happened?"

I couldn't.

"You got to believe me, I would have stayed if I'd known I can't get back to you."

She started to cry. I turned my face to her. I wanted so much to believe her.

"Please," she said, "please, I'm your Gracie. I love you so much."

She was all I had.

"This will pass, and then one day you'll understand. Bad things happen all the time, to a lot of people, not only you, but I promise you, in future I'll take better care of you. Soon you'll feel like a real beauty queen again. Big promise, cross my heart."

The last bit of rebellion smoldering underneath my shame went cold. Gracie was smiling again, and I knew I would be her good girl again. Gracie was all I had.

Months went by. I stoically accepted Gracie's presence and listened to her chatting about whatever she thought might get me out of my dark mood, but I couldn't react to her. I stayed in my deep freeze and barely registered what was going on around me.

Now that I've broken through the glacier ice that held me captive for so long, everything that happened then becomes visible and presents itself to me—and to Stanley—with amazing clarity.

At the end of those months, Gracie said it would do me good to participate in some photo sessions again.

As soon as she suggested it, Mom agreed. It's about time you do your bit, she said, to get us out of our current financial bind.

"So the photo sessions started again?" Stanley asks me, not really throwing me off track. "When you were still ten?"

"I didn't even put up a fight. I let it happen because I saw no way out. They relied on me—and I didn't have the guts to say no. Mom didn't matter any longer, but I finally understood that Gracie needed me as much as I needed her."

"Do you remember what happened to you in those sessions?"

Of course I do. It's been on my mind since I woke up. The sessions always followed the same pattern: Gracie takes me there, calms me down with her drink and makes me pretty with her paints and brushes, places me on a chair and leaves the room.

The Purple Shadow glides in. I never see a face or hear a voice, stuff flows and rolls, assisted by the photographer who tells me what to do. Sometimes I have to do things to myself, like getting undressed and touching myself in areas and in a way that would feel wrong if I could feel anything. But I don't. Can't. Because I'm not me.

The Purple Shadow films everything. The photographer friend is always there, too, behind the smaller camera, click-clicking away. Sometimes the Purple

Tiara

Shadow comes over to me and does things with me before filming again.

I have no will because I'm not really there.

This happened to another girl, one I knew and didn't like much, my ugly other, who went through those sessions. The original me-part retreated deeper and deeper as time went on. Part of me was ugly and despicable, I felt that every waking moment, but I learned to live with it. With every session it became more acceptable to do what they asked me to, even when their demands got more outrageous.

"What about Gracie? She had promised to protect you."

"Gracie had nothing to do with it. I didn't tell her for fear of upsetting her, and putting her in danger. The sessions…" This is hard to admit. My heart beats faster and my lungs compress again, trying to keep the confession locked in. But Stanley deserves to know. "Over time, the sessions made me feel … I began to feel like a beauty queen again, true to Gracie's promise. They called me Princess Tia when I did good." I think back, try to find the words to explain my unexplainable behaviour. "I wanted Gracie to love me again, be proud of me again. I gave them whatever they asked of me. The smiles. The gestures. The liking it. That went on for nearly two years … until … until one day when …when a session went really bad."

Silence.

Stanley holds my glance, searching behind my eyeballs to find both of me. He's not scared of the ugly other, and I shouldn't be either.

"There is more."

My increased heart rate begs me not to expose my ugly me. I feel my hands cramp into fists. My heart races even faster, cold sweat makes me shiver. This is a lot harder to tell than to think, yet the cascade of my words shoots over the cliff and can't be halted.

The Purple Shadow comes in, moves a sofa behind me and positions the camera in front of the arrangement. I hear a man's voice. I recognize the voice.

"Smile," the motel-man says. His face still eager but clouding over with disappointment. "You've grown." He pushes me on the sofa. I'm limp from juice, and defeat.

"Oh fuck," the man says to the Purple Shadow behind the camera, "start filming. You owe me that one." Then he throws himself on top of me. The Purple Shadow starts the camera rolling.

I… feel… nothing. I'm looking at the black hole, at the hand adjusting the lens, fingers turning the focus on me, making sure I'm sharp and visible and … the man starts … I know I should fight … but I can't … I'm mesmerized by the hand on the camera, I concentrate on that hand so I don't feel the other hand, doing …, the man, his hand.

Tiara

My breathing's still normal, it's only my shame that makes me hesitate to describe what the man is doing to me. What the motel-man did to me again.

Remembering the scene so vividly, a realization hits me like a lightning bolt. Electric charges fire up those parts of my gray matter that have been dormant for so long and lift the fog that has enveloped my every waking moment since I attacked the woman in the coffee shop. In one brief instant I'm catapulted from a hazy part-remembering into the horrific realization that I now remember all of it.

Oh my God. Oh my God. I remember. All of it.

I see what led up to the attack. I see and understand. The image which penetrates my memory shield at nail-gun speed is so shocking I cover my face with my hands. A simple gesture meant to hide the monstrous moment of enlightenment not only from myself but from Stanley. *If I don't see you, you don't see me.* It can't be true. It is.

I know who I stabbed. And I know so much more. I'm not innocent. I began to believe others around me that I've stabbed that woman, but I didn't *know*. Now I do. I see what I've done, and I see beyond the act of aggression. I see who I really am, what guilt I carry, and most shocking of all, I see why I carry this guilt.

I finally know my filthy, wormlike secret.

I want to tell Stanley, right here and there, but I can't do that. I can't. He must never know my secret. Nobody, please, please, please. Nobody must ever know.

I'm still reeling, and can only hope Stanley thinks I'm hiding behind my hands to cover the shame I feel. Let him think so, I need time to hide the truth, I need to deflect from what's happening inside my mind. Time—please, give me time.

"You have no idea who that person is?" Stanley probes, in his gentle way. "The one you call the Purple Shadow?"

I can't lower my hands. I can't look at him.

"I have no idea." After years of being touched and manipulated by the Purple Shadow, I should know.

I need time to think. The implications of what I've dug up from my buried memory are too far-reaching. I can't even comprehend what this means for my future. How to react to all that dirt and filth coming to the surface. How to deal with what I've done. What others have done to me. Too much truth to face. It's not a simple case of crying a little and feeling better—what's inside me is breaking me apart.

Behind my hands, I weep hot tears. I shake with disgust.

He backs off. "Don't worry about it now, let it rest."

When I calm down a little, he gently probes once more, "Is there *anything* you remember about that person?"

I finally take my hands off my face. My expression is stiff with the knowledge I need to hide.

"Only a long cape of sorts that covered the body from head to toe, one like some of those Muslim women wear. It was purple."

Tiara

He doesn't look surprised at all by this description.

"I'm wondering if you'd be willing to talk to the police about it."

The police? "Only if it's Macintosh".

"I'm sure he wants to hear about this person, and about the involvement your aunt had in this."

"Gracie?"

"You realize she's been an accessory to a serious crime, don't you?"

Gracie, an accessory? Dear Stanley, how wrong you are.

50

MACINTOSH and Harding watched Louise for a while through the two-way mirror. Sitting in a nearly empty room with nothing to do unsettles most people. Not Louise. She brought a book and was reading in it. The detectives stepped into the interrogation room.

Louise looked up and smiled.

"Good morning, detectives."

Macintosh pulled up a chair, sat down, close, right in her face.

"How much time have you spent with Tiara, since she was back in Canada?"

"Quite a bit," Louise said, backed up her chair.

"So you know her well?"

"Actually, I don't. The girl was growing up and had her own mind."

They bombarded her with one question after another, giving her no time to think, but she held her ground. No, she didn't meet any of Tiara's friends. No, she didn't know her friends' names, if she had any—hadn't she explained that before? No, she had no idea why

Melissa wanted to come back. Yes, she drove to Texas to pick up her daughter and grandchild—again, a fact known to them.

"When you were in Texas, did you meet Tony Alvarez?" Macintosh asked.

Louise's head jerked up. "Um … no, no I didn't."

"But you know of him?"

"No …well, yes, I've heard his name mentioned."

"By whom?"

"By Melissa, I guess. Let me think, well…yes, wasn't he the dance instructor who taught Tiara for a while? Long before I took them back home. So I didn't meet him, no, never."

"Apparently, he didn't only give dance lessons."

Louise stared at him. "From what I know from Melissa, that's all he taught."

Macintosh stared straight back. "What did Melissa tell you?"

"Well … um … she said he might have gotten ideas, but she wasn't interested. She never got over Mike, she didn't want another guy. Tony didn't take no for an answer, he made some advances, that's why she fired him. That's all."

"What advances?" Harding got closer, too. "Are you saying he was after Melissa?"

"She wasn't in such bad shape in those days. She was still attractive then."

Macintosh never took his eyes off Louise. If he could only stare the truth out of her.

"Are you sure those advances were directed toward Melissa and not Tiara?" he said.

"Are you kidding me? Of course he was after Melissa."

"Let me show you something." Macintosh opened his laptop to set up the video clip. "I'd like you to watch this and then tell me everything you know about Tony, about his involvement with your daughter and granddaughter, and anything else, like the connection they had with Graciella Rodriguez."

Louise's face twitched. So she knew about Tiara's aunt but had so far neglected to mention her existence. What else did Louise hide from them, and why? Macintosh turned the laptop and hit the start button. He didn't need to see the clip again, he wanted to watch her face.

When she recognized Tiara, she froze. It took a full minute of her watching the handler undressing her granddaughter before she processed what was happening, then she broke down. She covered her face, started to cry. Macintosh turned the computer off, closed the laptop and slammed the lid down.

Louise winced at the bang.

"We have reason to believe that the person clad in purple is Antonio Alvarez."

Louise lowered her hands. "He … Tony did that to her?"

"We also have reason to believe that Tiara's aunt, Graciella Rodriguez, was involved in the sexual exploi-

Tiara

tation of your granddaughter." Macintosh softened his voice. "I'm sure you had nothing to do with this, and I'm sorry you had to find out this way, but if you know anything, anything at all, now is the time to tell us."

"I ... I ... oh my God, I don't know. This is too dreadful. This girl has been nothing but trouble from the start. I wish Melissa would never have gone down there. Nothing but trouble. I knew it—"

"Let's be clear on this, Louise, this case started out as a potential homicide investigation. What we've discovered since, what happened to Tiara, surely had an impact on her development and will be taken into account by a judge, but it has also altered our investigation. Our counterparts in Texas, who work closely with us, are now investigating this case. The clip you've seen has been sold via an internet pedophile ring and trust me, any connection to such a criminal organization will be treated with great seriousness here in Canada as well. If you knowingly withhold any information relevant to this investigation, we'll go after you with all the might of our judicial system. Mark my words, I'll personally make sure you land in the slammer."

Macintosh watched Louise turn red, whether from shame or indignation he couldn't tell. She fought hard to hold it together, her hands prayer-knotted so tightly her knuckles turned white.

"When Melissa called me three years ago, I immediately understood that it was a desperate cry for help.

She said Tiara was in trouble with some people doing drugs. That happens with teenagers all over the world, nothing unusual. When I got there, it certainly looked that way. Melissa met me at the NASA Center, the Space Institute, you know, where they keep all the rockets from the scrapped programs, because I'd never been to see her before and didn't know the area at all. But everybody can find the Space Center, it's so…, well, whatever. We met there and drove straight to her house. Melissa was in quite a state, and that's understandable too, considering that her daughter was doing drugs and all. That's the impression I got, anyway. And on the way there she told me she'd given Tiara something to make her sleepy, something Gracie—that's Graciella Rodriguez—always had in the house."

Macintosh listened to the undertones of her story. She sounded sincere. She was picking up speed, feeling more confident now.

"She told me Gracie had always supplemented their income by peddling drugs. That was the main reason she had to get Tiara out of the house in such a hurry. Gracie had to leave town for a few days, which presented the perfect opportunity. Melissa acted really scared, and I said, calm down, even if she comes back, we pack your stuff and leave, Gracie can't stop us."

"Why was Melissa so scared?"

"She told me Gracie would kill us all if she caught us leaving, and I said, no way, I don't believe that. I really

Tiara

didn't. I mean, honestly, I didn't know this woman, but how could she do something as awful as—she was a relative, right?"

Macintosh watched Louise search her memory.

"Tell us everything you remember, Louise. No matter if you think it's relevant or not."

"She was a bad one, that's for sure. Melissa was scared of her. She told me Gracie once kept some cash hidden in her room, money from her deals, and that she'd taken some of it, quite a large amount, and that she suspected Gracie had found out and was really mad at her. Let's hurry, she said—so we did. In case you're wondering what that has to do with Tony, I'm coming to it."

Macintosh gave her an encouraging smile. Now you're talking, lady.

She stopped twisting her hands and let them drop in her lap.

"When we got to the house, first thing Melissa did was carry Tiara to the car and laid her on the backseat. Tiara was so out of it, she hardly noticed I was there, in fact, I don't think she noticed me at all."

"Tiara had no idea that you were taking her back to Canada?"

"No, it was all very hectic and secretive. Nothing had been prepared. When Melissa came back in, I helped pack her things. She hadn't dared before, afraid Gracie might come back while she was out meeting up with me, then her whole plan would blow up. We were in the middle of stuffing clothes into plastic garbage bags when the doorbell rang. Jesus, Melissa jumped like she was hit by an electric current, it made me freak out too. I pulled myself together and said stay, I'll open the door and if it's Gracie I'll give her a piece of my mind. I felt I owed Melissa that, after all, she's my daughter."

"So Gracie came back?" Macintosh said. "Why would she ring the bell?"

"It wasn't Gracie. It was Tony, asking for Melissa. For a second I didn't know what to do, then Melissa pushed me aside. She looked white as a sheet and he didn't look much better. That's when I knew there was something going on between them and later on Melissa admitted … I mean, I asked her about it … and as I told you before, Melissa said he'd made unwelcome advances. Anyway, those two, white as ghosts, glared at each other. Melissa told me to get the last bags from the house while she deals with him.

"That's more or less all there was to it. I didn't tell you I met this guy because it was so brief I'd practically forgotten. Now I understand why Melissa needed to get Tiara away, I bet she suspected something. The trouble with Tiara wasn't about drugs after all. She'd lied to me. All those years I thought she was involved in some shit, pardon my French, some illegal stuff Gracie got her into, when in fact it was … you know …." Louise started to cry.

"You said Melissa told you there was something going on between Tony and her."

Louise looked up sharply. "I did not."

Harding checked his notes. "Yes, you said you thought there was something going on between them, and Melissa admitted it. You stopped yourself, but that's what you wanted to say."

Louise hesitated. "So what if she did?"

"If she had a fling with Tony, she must have been involved in or at least been aware of the exploitation of your granddaughter."

Macintosh leaned into Louise.

"Your granddaughter was molested by a guy who walked in and out of Melissa's house and probably carried on an affair with her to disguise his true inclinations. She must have known, or closed her eyes to protect him. At least until something he did upset her enough to jolt her into action. Maybe he dumped her."

"I don't know about that." Louise frowned, then indicated the laptop with a flick of her chin. "But I don't believe for a minute she knew about that."

"Let's find out," Macintosh said, all nice again. "Do you have a mobile with you, Louise?"

She frowned. "Yes. Why?"

"Can I see?"

She handed it to him.

"Thank you. We'll be back shortly."

The detectives left the room. With no phone in the interview room Louise couldn't contact her daughter.

"Time to have a serious talk with Melissa," Macintosh said to Harding when they reached his desk. "Order her in, but don't tell her Louise is here, too."

The phone on his desk rang. Macintosh picked it up, listened.

"Sure thing, right away," Macintosh said. He hung up and turned to Harding.

"I know we aren't legally entitled to hold Louise, but try and keep her in the building until I'm back. That was Eaton on the line. I got to rush. Tiara had a breakthrough of sorts and is willing to talk to me."

51

WE group around the table in the center's meeting room, with the inevitable plate of cookies placed in the middle. I take an Oreo and bite off a chunk. The black crumbs sprinkle on the table top. Unsure if I should ignore them or wipe them away with my sleeve, I gather them with my left hand and collect them in my right. Then I'm unsure where to put them. Stanley hands me a tissue and points to the basket behind me.

"Thank you for seeing me again," Macintosh says. "I really appreciate it. Dr. Eaton said you have some information that might help us piece things together."

Although he acts more formal in Stanley's presence, today his face looks kinder than on his last visits. The kindness still fights with his usual expression of bitterness and disillusionment, but it's there all the same. People tend not to realize that their thoughts and actions engrave themselves into their features until they mirror their exact feelings. Deep down and unbeknownst to him, Macintosh is kind. He smiles with his eyes, not just his mouth. The lines on his forehead come from thinking, not from worrying, and his energy radiates warmth, not aggression. He's the second man in my life I like. That makes me giggle.

He cocks his head, sets to ask a question, stops. I decide to put him at ease.

"So far, there were only three men in my life who've talked to me more than once. Tony, Dr. Eaton, and you. That made me think of the song 'Two out of three ain't bad.' To set the record straight, I didn't like Tony."

He chuckles as soon as he gets it. Then he asks me what I remembered.

I tell him about the time Gracie left me at the motel room when I was ten, and about the rape. Macintosh stares at the clean table. I tell him that the same happened two years later. Macintosh looks back at me, his eyes pleading for me to stop.

Good. No need for details. I'm prepared to tell the truth, but not the whole truth. Stanley guides me unknowingly away from the oh-so-close-to-the-truth account. He mentions the photo sessions, and I tell Macintosh about some of them until we come to the person who has controlled so many.

Like Stanley, Macintosh asks me if I remember anything, anything at all, about the Purple Shadow.

"I'm sorry." I decide to carefully navigate through the rapids, trying to avoid the obvious hazards. No matter what they ask me, I cannot lie to those two, they are too smart to be deceived, but I will not tell the full truth. "The Purple Shadow has always been covered with a long cloak, and I've never seen a face at any of the sessions." True. Stick as close to the truth as you can.

Macintosh squirms in his chair. Then he comes out with a strange question.

"Could the person have worn a mask?"

"A mask?"

"To hide the face?"

"Now that you mention it, there's a dark hole where a face should be. Like there's no face at all." True.

Macintosh seems pleased with this answer, but before I can figure out why, he presses on.

"Your aunt Gracie, what was her role in those shoots?"

"She brought me there, checked that everything was set up right, then she'd left. After the session was over, she came back and took me home." True again.

"But she knew what kind of pictures and movies were taken."

"I don't think so."

Now he and Stanley look taken aback.

"Why not?" Macintosh asks. "Did you never talk about it?"

I'm getting irritated. "It wasn't something I could talk about."

He backs off right away. "Was your dance instructor Tony ever present at those sessions?"

"No, of course not. He was my dance teacher for as long as I was doing pageants. He had nothing to do with

Tiara

the photo shoots. After the pageants stopped he dropped by the house a few times, visiting Mom, trying to get his job back, but Gracie never took him on again."

Macintosh looks puzzled. He scratches his prickly chin.

"Did you know that he was the owner of the studio where the photo sessions took place?"

What? The implications of this revelation don't hit me right away.

"Tony? The Stick? Are you sure?"

"Positive."

This sinks in. A concrete block of disturbing news.

"But if he was, he'd have known, wouldn't he?"

"I'm afraid so. Your aunt Gracie hired him, and maybe—"

I don't want to hear the end of this sentence.

"Well, you better ask Gracie, then."

Stanley and Macintosh lock glances—a silent consultation that ends with Stanley giving Macintosh, with a minute nod, permission to proceed.

"I'm afraid that's not possible," Macintosh says, his expression all wary. "Your aunt is dead."

Gracie dead? I think my mouth dropped down to my chest. "No way. Gracie can't be dead."

Macintosh tells me she was the victim of a house fire—and enlightens me at the same time that my previous home in Texas has burnt to the ground. The second mind-blowing news of the day. The thought of

Gracie charred beyond recognition is too much to picture. But to imagine that the house is gone is uplifting. It sets something free inside me.

"When did the fire happen?"

"Three years ago. Must have been soon after you and your mother left."

"Pity the studio didn't burn to the ground, too."

This brings Macintosh back to its owner.

"Could it have been Tony hiding under the purple cloak? Behind the mask?"

"I don't think so." The idea seems ludicrous. "But I don't know."

"Does the name Carl Heider mean anything to you?"

Honest to God, I never heard that name. "I know a Carlos."

Macintosh coughs. "Right. What about Margarita Rios?"

"I think my mom knew her. She's been on the phone a few times. I always thought Margarita to be a stupid name." True again. Margarita, the flower? Honestly?

Stanley and Macintosh relax a bit when they hear me giggle. They've been so tense, my two men. They get ready to leave.

"Unfortunately, your aunt, being deceased, won't be able to help us identify the Purple Shadow," Macintosh says, already standing, "but we'll figure it out eventually."

Tiara

"I'm sure you will, you're not just a pretty face."

That's the truth, too. His smile brightens and mellows his serious, chiseled features, making him less of an old grump and more of a kind-looking old uncle.

"Flattery will get you everywhere," he says. "I do what I can. Don't want to wait forever to go fishing."

Stanley looks a bit puzzled but we both ignore him.

I promise Macintosh I'll contact him in case something relevant comes back to me. Off they go. Door closes.

This has gone really well, I didn't have to lie once, didn't even have to settle for a half-truth. I know already that the core of my secret will eventually be revealed, but hopefully not until the trial is over. All I need now is a little more time—long enough for the judge to reach a verdict. After that, who knows what will happen. There's even a chance they might never figure it out. Let's face it, Macintosh never forced me to lie. He didn't ask the one crucial question. He never asked me if I now remember whom I tried to murder.

52

MACINTOSH walked with Dr. Eaton out to the parking lot. He had parked his car way down the private road, before the roundabout leading to Fraser Drive, Eaton had his in a reserved space right in front of the main entrance. They stopped there to say goodbye.

"Thanks for giving permission to let me sit in on the interview," he said, actually meaning it.

"Tiara had given her consent," Eaton said. "Otherwise—".

"I know. I know." Macintosh fiddled to get his car key from his pocket. The conversation with Tiara had unsettled him. He couldn't figure out what it was. Tiara's reactions. The light-hearted banter. Her giggles. Her surprise at Tony's involvement. Gracie's death. The burnt home. Innocent guilt? Guilty innocence? What the hell was played out here?

Eaton opened the passenger door of his car, dropped his briefcase on the seat, closed the door again and turned to Macintosh. "Do you want to talk about it?"

"To a psychiatrist?" Macintosh pulled a face. "Sorry, that was uncalled for. What I meant is—"

"I know what you meant."

Tiara

Don't fend him off. "Tiara's a lot more mature than any girl her age I've come across. I hadn't expected that, not after finding out how secluded her childhood was, how little education she got, and everything she's had to endure."

Eaton leaned against his car. "It was very considerate of you not to mention that we've seen the footage with the mask."

"I'm glad she let it go."

"That would have mortified her. Tiara has a tendency to ignore what she can't cope with."

"Don't I know it." Macintosh smiled. "I guess we can discuss this case now, you and me, right?"

"My assessment has been completed and delivered to the judge over two weeks ago. MCS Homicide Unit should have received a copy—"

"I've read it."

"Good. So we can talk freely," Dr. Eaton said. "What's on your mind?"

"It's beyond any doubt that Tiara was molested as a child. I'm talking seriously, repeatedly molested from a very young age on, right?"

"Unfortunately, yes."

"Has she told you anything about who the molesters could be?"

Eaton hesitated, then chose his words with care. "She tends to forget names in an effort to depersonalize people. So far, she's only mentioned the name of her dance instructor, Tony, but she says he was close to her family circle and not involved in her exploitation—in fact, she vehemently rejects that idea. Of course that doesn't clear him of any suspicion."

"You bet it doesn't. We'll certainly check him out."

"Then there's this elusive Purple Shadow, and you heard yourself that Tiara can't even be certain about the gender."

Macintosh's eyes grew dark. "A shame she can't give us more information on that creep."

"I suspect him or her to be one of the ringleaders of whatever pedophile operation exploited Tiara."

"I agree. Tony and Carl had a sweet thing going. Tony owns the studio. He gets the girls. Easy enough for him to persuade parents who are keen making their little girls famous to have pictures taken. One thing leads to another. The lure of the money comes into it. Carl is the photographer. He takes the pictures. His wife Margarita is in charge of selling them. Maybe she was the one under the cloak. I'll let Sexual Offense Squad in Texas know about this Purple Shadow. It's not much to go on, but there is a chance Tiara hasn't made up the description herself but has heard somebody calling the handler by that name. It might mean something. They might have a record of it in Texas. And hopefully they in turn will keep me informed. When it comes to internet crimes, there are no borders. Everything points toward Tiara having been a star in one of those revolting networks.

Tiara

We've found several videos of her being promoted as Princess Tia." Macintosh shook his head in disgust. "I tell you, I'm glad I'm close to retirement. You've seen one of the video clips—stuff like that seriously freaks me out. I only hope we can catch those bastards. It's a crying shame that the aunt isn't around anymore, I'd have loved to interview her. I still think her involvement wasn't all that innocent as Tiara thinks."

"Tiara was genuinely stunned to hear about Graciella's death, but she's shown no emotional reaction," Eaton said. "One would think after three years her mother would have heard about the fire and told her. But obviously Tiara didn't know."

Macintosh scratched his chin. God, first thing when he retired, he'd grow a beard, same as the doc's, except his wouldn't look so perfectly groomed. "Tiara seemed surprised all right, but she didn't ask how the fire happened or what happened to her aunt. You'd think she'd be curious how she died, maybe even relieved, you know what I mean? But she was blasé, as if this death was a good joke, entertainment. Certainly not closure."

Macintosh wasn't sure if his observation made sense until Eaton confirmed it. "Exactly. But, as you know, Detective, closure takes time. Tiara doesn't believe that it's over. I hope she'll continue a dialogue with me, so I can help her along that road."

"She sure got a tough deal so far." Macintosh extended his hand.

"Truce?" Eaton asked.

"Don't let her down. She'll need a friend when this is over."

Eaton shook his hand. "More than one. I think she trusts you. It may be good if you contact her again. Don't wait until she asks for you. Her social skills are seriously underdeveloped and she may feel she can only ask for your visit if she has another breakthrough in her protective memory shield."

"I will."

Dr. Eaton got in his car. Macintosh walked over to his own when he thought he heard the shrink call after him.

"Detective," Dr. Eaton said. "One more thing."

Macintosh turned. "Yes?"

"Did you get hold of Tiara's computer?"

"She doesn't have one."

"She does. Not at her mother's place, though. She stored it at her friend's place, at Candy's."

"Candy?"

"A young woman who let Tiara stay at her place when things got too difficult at home. From what I gather, she's into adult entertainment. You may want to look into that."

53

DETECTIVE Macintosh called and ordered her to come to the police station, same as her mother. No mistaking his tone, he was seriously annoyed. Oh dear, oh dear. Louise must have been there already. What on earth had she told them?

On the bus to Graveley Street, she left several messages on her mother's cell, trying not to let her mounting desperation seep into her voice.

In the interview room, she checked her phone one final time. No message. Why didn't she call her back? Leave a text? My God, mother, can't I ever rely on you? I need to know what you told them. She looked around. Was Louise still here, maybe as close as next door? Melissa struggled out of her seat. Get out of here. No, no, stay put. Those detectives hated her. They'd chase after her. She'd have to face them eventually.

She held on to the table to steady herself. No dizzy spells allowed, stay calm, no panic attacks allowed. She'd show everyone what a good mother looked like, and maybe they'd let her see Tiara. Just this once, to have a few words of caution with her. The girl needed to

Tiara

understand how damaging her words could be. She, and her stupid grandmother, needed to shut their traps, once and for all.

Melissa slid back into her seat, trying not to think about her mother, about Tiara, Tony, Gracie, not even Mike. All the ghosts she kept at bay for so long. How could she ever think she'd be rid of them?

But the ghosts were right in this room with her, planting silent accusations into her brain to make sure she wouldn't forget that awful day in Texas.

A slow, boring day, like so many of them were in Texas. Intense heat compressed life until everything moved in slow motion, if at all. Melissa spent most of the afternoon prone on the sofa, finally understanding why southern countries often were poorer and less industrious than northern ones. A matter of conserving energy, a matter of movement, or better, of non-movement.

Gracie and Tiara were out. When they came back, she expected Tiara to walk straight past her as if she weren't there and disappear into her room as usual. Gracie would fuss a little over her, bring her some food and medication—nowadays Tiara needed a lot of that, she always had something wrong with her—then disappear herself.

But on this afternoon, the atmosphere changed the minute they came in. Tiara's cheeks and eyes were swollen, red. She'd often come back home in an agitated state, but she'd never been anything like this distressed. Melissa got up, confused. Gracie glared at her and whispered, "We need to talk," in a voice that didn't allow any resistance, then took Tiara to her room. Melissa followed them. Gracie put Tiara on her bed, making soothing sounds.

Tiara started to cry. "Mommy. Please. Help me."

"What is it, princess? What's the matter?"

"I don't want to do this anymore."

Melissa stepped up to the bed, looked at Gracie, then back to Tiara.

"Do what?"

"He hurt me."

"Who?"

Gracie pushed herself between Melissa and Tiara, busied herself with tucking Tiara in. "Stop this now, mija. No point in dwelling on what can't be changed. The pills will work soon. They'll take the pain away. Rest now, I'll talk to your mother. We'll do something about all this, cross my heart, big promise. Rest now, we'll be back soon. You're safe here."

She grabbed Melissa's sleeve, pulled her out of Tiara's bedroom and closed the door.

"What's she talking about?" Melissa said. "Who hurt her? What's going on?"

"You don't need to know. I'll take care of it."

"Care of what? She's my daughter. What's wrong with her? I want to know."

Tiara

Back in the living room, Gracie pushed her down on the sofa.

"No need to get all worked up. Nothing I can't handle. Don't you worry about it."

"Damn it, Gracie, tell me now or I go back in and ask Tiara."

Gracie turned to face Melissa, took a deep breath, then lunged at her like a wild cat, hissing and spitting.

"Did you see your daughter? Did you see how she's cried her eyes out? Do you have any idea what this poor girl has gone through?"

Melissa sat up straight and shook her head. What the hell were they keeping from her? What was all this about?

"Tony, your precious Tony—and don't think for one second I didn't know about your sordid little affair with him—did this to her."

Oh God, oh God, what did he do?

"Tony wouldn't touch Tiara. Never. He'd never do that."

"Really?" Gracie laughed at her. "You really think he's interested in a fat slob like you? Don't flatter yourself. He smoke-screened you, that's all there's to it. Do you honestly think he'd touch you if he wasn't getting rewarded for his bravery? Look at you, you can barely see your feet when you stand up, your sagging breasts and your giant gut block the view."

Melissa froze, her legs like lead, not able to run away. She had to listen.

"God, that's enough to make my poor brother turn in his grave. To open our house to a creep like Tony and let him molest Miguel's own daughter to satisfy your cravings for a good fuck. You're disgusting. It's your fault, entirely your fault, I'm telling you. I never wanted that creep back in our home after I'd fired him first time round. You insisted that we take him back. Even after I got rid of him the second time, you let him carry on with your daughter right under your nose. Sweet Jesus in heaven, how could you!"

Not Tony, no, Tony loved her, told her so, made love to her. The week in the cabin, during the storm.

"No way," she said. "He didn't. He wouldn't."

"You bet your fat ass he did. I caught him. This afternoon."

"How? Where?" Her voice came out a hoarse whisper.

"At the studio. Usually the door is locked until the photo session is over, to make sure nobody interrupts. This afternoon I came back sooner than expected to pick her up. In his sick excitement the bastard must have forgotten to lock the door. God knows how many times this has happened to my poor girl. To think I might have been sitting outside while this pervert ... oh, no, it's too disgusting."

"But ... but what's Tony doing at the studio?"

"He bought that studio a few years ago. I told you but you never listen to me. He's been taking the pictures."

"I don't believe you."

"Believe what you like, you ignorant cow."

"He doesn't have any money. He couldn't have bought the studio."

Gracie started to laugh again. This time, she sounded amused.

"Well, he had the twenty thousand you stole from me. He didn't spend that much on your week-long love fest in the cabin at the lake."

Melissa felt her resistance crack. The only way Gracie could know about that was from Tony himself. If she knew that, everything else she said had to be true. Tony used her to get to Tiara. The shame, the horrible truth, excruciating, unbearable. To feel anything became too painful. No feeling, nothing, not for herself, not for her daughter.

When Gracie left the house, Melissa went back into Tiara's room. She looked at her daughter's face, buried in white bedding with rainbow colored dots on it, for a long time, expecting to feel compassion, pity, something. Any emotion to fill the hollowness inside. But she stayed empty under the layer of shame and repulsion.

Repulsion.

Tiara must have done something to encourage Tony. How else would he get involved in something as weird as that? It couldn't have been his idea alone.

Tiara stirred, opened her eyes, barely any light in them.

"Mom," Tiara said. "He hurt me so bad."

Tramp.

"I don't want to hear any of it. Girls your age should know what to do. Men stop when they're not encouraged. It's your fault if it went too far."

The dull eyes of her daughter grew wide, then closed.

"Don't you breathe a word about this, to nobody. You hear me? Not a word, or they'll all know what a slut you are."

Disgust. Deep disgust.

She turned and left the room. Tony touched her daughter. Now they were both defiled by him.

Melissa winced. The memories came back so strong she wanted to puke. Her stomach contracted, but all she managed was a silent burp. Indigestion. That's all that was left of Tony. If Tiara told the police what Tony did to her, my God, who'd get the blame? Her, always her.

The detectives would never believe she hadn't known about the rape. Not if Tiara told them the scene in the bedroom, when she'd begged her for help. After that, it had taken her almost a week to get Tiara out of the house and back to Canada. Was that too long? No way, that was fast, by anybody's standards. A trip across the whole continent, for crying out loud, leaving her whole life behind. That was something in her defense. She should stress the fact that she took quick action to

Tiara

protect her daughter when the detectives accused her of negligence. Okay, so she did nothing to expose Tony, but what good would that have done? Tiara would have been defiled, and she… she'd be ridiculed. Disgraced. Everybody would laugh at her. Desperate Melissa. What had Gracie called her? A fat slob.

The door of the interview room opened and there they stood, the detectives, glaring at her. She knew it, had known it all along, they despised her. She steeled herself for the inevitable fight.

One of them, the senior one—that hateful Macintosh—looked diabolically pleased to see her in such an agitated state.

"So, here we are again, Melissa," he said. "Do you know why we asked you to come in?"

She took a deep breath. "You've spoken to my mother."

"Indeed we have. She told us what happened when she drove to Houston to get you." He let his words linger in the air.

"So my mother took the money. That's not really a crime. At least part of it belonged to me and Tiara. She took only what was ours anyway."

Macintosh coughed into his fist.

"I doubt your sister-in-law would see it that way. Stealing her money would make her very angry."

"I told you, I didn't take that money. You got that wrong." Melissa felt a glimmer of hope. With her mother already admitting the theft, she might be able to convince the detectives that stealing the money hadn't been her idea. "I only told my mother where to look, I didn't ask her to pocket it. It wasn't much anyway. Five thousand dollars. Please. Gracie owed me more than that. I did all the housework, the cooking, the laundry, everything, and I never saw a cent."

Macintosh grinned at her.

"And how much was it you stole from Gracie before your mother arrived?"

"What? I ... I never ..."

"Yes, you did. Louise told us. She said you'd been afraid of Gracie because of that theft."

Now they had her. Stupid, stupid mother, can't keep your blabbermouth shut.

"Twenty thousand," she said. But for Tony. Should she tell? Could she blame it on him? What happened wasn't her fault. Why did people blame everything on her?

"Look, Melissa, we know already what happened on that day, so why not tell us in your own words," Detective Macintosh said. "Give us a chance to see your side of things. Everybody sees things in a different light. It'll make it easier for us to understand."

He was right. So she told them. The story didn't differ much from her mother's, except for stressing the point that she'd been deeply engaged talking to Tony while her mother went back into the house to look for the money. Her mother had been the one who found it, grabbed it, and hid it in one of the garbage bags. Only after they drove away, with Tiara dozing on the backseat, did her mother tell her what she'd done. She said they sure could use the five thousand dollars, back in Canada. But that scared the daylight out of her. Her mother didn't know Gracie, she had no idea how outright mean and nasty she could be. All the way up north she was terrified that Gracie would follow them or have them stopped at the border.

"Why would you think that?" Macintosh asked.

"Gracie would think I was in on it. She'd think we were both thieves, wouldn't she?"

"Please, you didn't really expect her to contact the authorities over a relatively small amount of money. Not her."

That's when it hit Melissa. They knew about a lot more than that pitiful theft of five thousand, or the previous theft of twenty thousand her mother snitched about. They must have interviewed Gracie, checked the story, and, my God, now the detectives knew everything. Tiara. Tony. The rape. She started to cry again.

Macintosh smiled. Produced a tissue box from nowhere and slid it over the table.

"Now there, no point in crying. Let's start from the beginning. Let's go back to where you said you did everything and got paid nothing."

"If you must."

"Do you mean she never once paid you for selling your daughter into the sex trade?"

"What? I never—"

Harding opened the laptop.

Macintosh pressed the start button.

Melissa watched the video for all of ten seconds, then lowered her head and refused to look at the screen. That was so disgusting, how could they do this to her?

When she looked up again, she saw pure malice in Macintosh's face. Dear God, he thought she knew. He thought she'd been part of this ... this disgusting, horrible ... how could anybody think a mother would ...

That's when she broke down. His humiliating suspicion was the last straw, she couldn't handle any more of it. When she finally stopped crying and shaking, Macintosh lashed into her again.

"You knew nothing of this?"

"I knew Tony had tried to sexually assault Tiara," she said, not able to fight them off any longer. "Gracie told me. But honest to God, I didn't know about ... about what's on that video. That was at the studio, I've never even been there. Gracie took Tiara there—I had no idea. I didn't know anything was wrong, not until the day Gracie brought her home in such a state."

She sobbed in between sentences but soldiered on.

"I called my mother in Vancouver right away and asked her to help me get Tiara out of there. To safety. A few days later we left Texas. I did all I could. I wanted to get my daughter away from a child molester like Tony. To leave him, to leave like that, broke my heart but I've acted as fast as any good mother would."

"Sure, he broke your heart," Macintosh said. "He was your lover. You let him molest your daughter because you couldn't stand to lose him."

"No. Honestly, I didn't know. Nothing. Nothing. NOTHING! You hear me? Everybody always blames me but it's been Gracie all along who always acted like Tiara's mother, always put me down, I never had a say in anything. Talk to Gracie, you're smart, you'll see for yourself."

The detectives looked at each other.

"That could be difficult, Melissa," Harding said. "Gracie is dead."

"What?" Melissa couldn't believe it. "She's dead?"

"Dead, yes," Macintosh said.

The news calmed her a little.

"Well, that's too bad, but it won't change a thing. I've done my duty by Tiara, and that's all that counts."

54

Candles on a birthday cake

Macintosh asked if I would see him again. Poor guy, he can't stay away from me. I'd like to refuse his request. As much as I've enjoyed his company so far, I'm not sure I should talk to him, or to anybody else, while my new-found memory does hula-hoops in my brain. But he asked the prison lady for permission, not me. I was kidding myself, pondering my choices—as always, I don't have any.

I spend all night, alone in my cell, talking to myself to get my story in order. How amazing, every sentence hangs in the dim light, does a few rotations so I can inspect the meaning from all angles, then withdraws into a corner to join all the other sentences I've brought out into the open. Each sentence is a brick. I've said so many, I'm building a fortress.

The morning routine interrupts the formation of my magic structure. I have to conform to their system, suffer through the closeness of my four resident-inmates, eat breakfast in their presence, with them chat-

Tiara

ting away with full mouths and empty brains. Then the guard announces my visitor, and I hope we don't have to share the meeting room with other girls and their eager parents who are probably the reason they landed here in the first place.

We're alone. Obviously nine in the morning is too early to allow family members to visit, while police have access whenever they want.

"Good morning, Tiara," Macintosh says, painfully formal. The bearer of bad news?

He comes straight to the point.

"Detective Harding and I met with your mother and your grandmother yesterday. Very interesting, to say the least. Would you be willing to hear me out on what we've discovered so far, the idea being that you correct me whenever you feel my account isn't accurate, or stop me if it becomes too distressing for you?"

Jesus, there I was, thinking he'd ask me all sorts of questions I won't be able to answer truthfully if I want to protect my secret, and now he'll be doing all the talking.

"As I said, if anything upsets you, let me know and I'll stop right away."

"Shoot." I realize what I said and quickly look at his side. No gun, of course not, he wouldn't come in here armed with a deadly weapon.

"You're pretty daring, talking to me unprotected," I say.

"You pose no threat to me, Tiara."

"Aren't you brave."

"What's the matter with you today? Trying hard to be the bad girl again?"

"That's what I am. So I'm told."

He lets out a labored breath, which instantly turns my stomach into a knot, then gets down to business.

"So you still don't remember more than what you told me so far?"

"I've said all there is to it." I cross my arms. Lousy protection. "Can I go now? Are we done?"

He looks kind of amused. "Your bad girl attitude doesn't exactly encourage me to go out of my way to help you."

"Then why don't you stay away?"

"Because I've got a job to do. And because I like you."

What can I say to that? I go all mushy inside.

"So, how about it? Play nice again?"

We're both grinning now, but he turns serious, ready to get started. Before we do, I need to clarify my position.

"Are you here to tell me who I stabbed? Have you finally figured out who the victim is?"

"I'm afraid we still don't know—"

Cool. One monster worry lighter.

"—we didn't get anywhere with that. Not yet. In fact, we might never. There's a good chance that she won't regain her brain function. If that happens, and you don't remember, we've reached a dead end."

Dead end. That sounds promising. I take in a big breath, let it out slow, slow, slow, to hide my relief. All I can hope is that Macintosh reads it wrong. He does.

"Sorry about that. We do what we can and we'll keep at it. Promise."

"Don't stress yourself," I say with a forgiving smile. "I'm sure you'll figure it out eventually."

"Yeah, I know, not just a pretty face," he says. "Let's get back to the purpose of my visit. Here's what we do know. Your aunt Graciella Rodriguez was dealing drugs when she was younger, and we assume she never stopped. From what we know, she kept a considerable amount of cash at her home. Your mother siphoned off money from those illegal funds, even though we don't think she was aware of your aunt's activities. We're also convinced she didn't know until yesterday that your aunt is dead."

"I bet she didn't exactly break down when you told her."

"Those two didn't get along?"

"Love-hate at best."

"We strongly suspect that Antonio Alvarez, your dance instructor, was involved in your…, huh, in illegal activities. In fact, we consider him the mastermind."

"Who, Tony? The Stick?"

"Yes."

I can barely suppress a giggle. "What has he done?"

Macintosh takes a minute to ponder.

"I'm not so sure Dr. Eaton would want me to go into that."

"Because it concerns my past?"

"Yes."

"If you don't tell me, I can't help you."

"Tiara, it's better if you don't—"

"Look, Mister Detective, I'm not a child any more. My childhood was taken away from me, I was exploited—"

He jerks his head up. What's the matter with him? Has he forgotten what I told him yesterday?

"—and I've been more or less living on the streets the last three years, so please don't hold back any information you got. I've been wracking my brain ever since I came in here to figure it all out. Whatever you tell me will help me as much as I might be able to help you."

"Deal," he says, doesn't extend his hand, thank God. "Your mother and grandmother told us about the day they took you back to Canada. Let's start with that. Do you remember anything about that day?"

"Yes."

"Can you tell me?"

"Sure."

"Do you mind if I record it?"

"No."

He takes out a pocket-size recorder, clicks a button, says, "Go."

Tiara

I haven't left my room for a week, not since Gracie brought me home after the session when they shot the rape video. Whenever Mom comes to my room she pretty much tells me that all that happened is my fault and that I'm a cheap tease. She stands at the door to ask me in this detached voice, if I need anything. As if I've hurt her. As if she's afraid of getting close to me. She never comes to my bed, she never touches me or holds me, like I so desperately need her to. She deposits a tray with food and drink on the bedside table then hurries out as fast as her bulk allows. I hurt in places I never hurt before, and I feel desperate. I don't understand why she's angry with me. I'm a stone in her presence, can't move, can't speak.

Gracie doesn't show up. She's disappeared from the face of the earth. I dread the thought that she might come through the door any minute. God knows what she'll do to Mom.

One day, maybe a week later, Mom ventures as far as my bed.

"Remember what I told you," she says. "You better not breathe a word about what happened—to anyone."

She hands me a glass of the stuff Gracie calls dream-juice.

"Here, drink this. All of it. I got to leave the house for a while. When I come back I'll take care of things. Everything will be okay again."

I must have gone back to sleep. When I wake up I hear two female voices, Mom's and another, not Gracie.

A stranger in the house makes me more alert. When the door opens, I pretend to be asleep.

I hear Mom saying "Shhh, don't wake her, Mother, I'll carry her." Wow. Mother? My mom's mom? What's she doing here? Where does my mom want to carry me? What's happening to me now? I'd like to ask her, but as always, my throat is swollen tight and won't let the words out.

They leave the room. After a few minutes Mom is back, alone, lifts me up to take off my night gown. I go all limp to make it harder for her to dress me. She pulls and tugs and slides until I'm ready, all the while breathing hard, moaning. She lifts me in her arms and carries me outside like she said she would.

I'm kind of dumped on the backseat of a car I've never seen before. Mom puts a thin blanket over me and disappears again. Why am I not in Gracie's car? What's going on? Fear grips me again, and I don't know why. The reason for the fear I've felt all week has flown into the sky, like one of those kites I see other kids play with when we drive by the park. The kite is attached to me, there's no escaping the fear—it's holding me by its string but the kite itself is so far away that it's only a dot in the clouds.

Mom comes back with this other woman. She's shorter than Mom and much, much slimmer. Her face seems familiar. I can watch and hear them because they stand close by the car without paying attention to me, asleep on the backseat. They argue over what to take with them.

Mom says: "I should look for the money, there must be at least a little bit."

Her mother, which must be my grandmother, says she's an idiot for not taking care of this in the morning.

"Damn it, mother," Mom says, "I forgot, all right? You can't expect me to think of everything."

They go back in the house and another car turns into the driveway and stops next to the car I'm in. Tony jumps out, rushes up to the house, rings the doorbell. My grandmother opens, then Mom comes out and drags him along with her, stopping right next to the open car window.

Now those two argue. I don't understand what about, really, with him wanting to know what my mom is up to, and her saying he's a monster and she hates him and crying, and him yelling and stomping his foot and slamming his car door and leaving. This is all too much for my fuzzy brain and I'm getting sleepy again.

A few minutes later, the car starts. I open my eyes and grandmother, sitting in the passenger seat, says "Sleep, sweetheart," so I close my eyes again and pretend. We drive for quite a while before they start talking.

"Did you really take it?" Mom asks, and grandmother must have nodded, because Mom says, "Oh my God, I don't know. Maybe you should've left it there. If Gracie finds out her money is missing, she'll kill us all."

I shiver on the back seat. Gracie will kill us. I must stay very quiet and be a good girl.

The air stands still between us. Macintosh makes no attempt to stop the tape recorder, so I do. Click. No more record.

Quiet again. Macintosh is deep in thought. His face looks distorted, with ice-cold eyes. What goes through his mind must be intense. He's out for blood, and I can feel that his bloodlust is directed at others, to revenge me. Makes me feel special. Kind of protected, like I've never felt before.

"I'm going to get that sick bastard, and all the others involved in this goddamn crime, if it's the last thing I do before I retire."

I chuckle. "You better hurry. You're old. You don't have that many years left."

His smile softens some of his tension.

"Don't you get cheeky with me. I've got only a few months left on the force, but I don't think I need more than a few days to get my report down to Texas. They already have Antonio Alvarez in custody."

I make a face, trying to understand.

"What's this thing you have about Tony?" I say. "What's he got to do with it?"

Macintosh crumbles. "But isn't he the one … I mean, the one who…"

"Tony? How did you get that idea?"

"Your mother told us he raped you."

Disgust made me twist my face. I don't want to go down that alley.

"It wasn't Tony."

He crumbles even more. "How can you be sure? You lost your memory."

"Of course I'm sure. I can remember everything that happened on that day. I'd know if it was him."

"Then who was it?"

I shrug. "A stranger. Who knows? It certainly wasn't Tony."

55

IN the end it wouldn't matter if Tony was the rapist or was running the pedophile ring behind the scene. Macintosh was confident Josh would get him. He'd dig up enough evidence down in Texas to nail the bastard.

However, that still didn't answer the questions who Tiara had stabbed, and why. Macintosh had lied to her when he said they had no idea who the victim was. He had two candidates waiting in line, Margarita being the stronger possibility. Maybe she and her sleazebag photographer husband moved from Toronto to Vancouver, and Tiara met her here by chance. Their reason to go underground three years ago must have been connected to Tiara. Margarita could be the woman in St. Paul's. Wouldn't that be sweet? The second candidate was Luna's mother Camila, again, a woman somehow connected to Tiara, although in a less conspicuous manner.

He was just processing this thought, contemplating if Camila was the right age and what Tiara's motive could have been to attack the mother of a fellow contestant, when his phone rang. Harding. He put him on speaker phone.

Tiara

"Where are you?"

"On my way back from BYSC."

"If you are still close," Harding said, "you might want to swing by Camila Vargas's place and see if she's home."

"You're kidding me? I just thought of her. She's still in Vancouver?"

"A few blocks from BYSC. Her address just came in. I'll text it to you."

Camila less than ten minutes away from here? Macintosh didn't believe in the esoteric principle that everything happened for a reason, but this was a coincidence bordering on fate. He had to sit and collect himself for some time before he could drive over to her address.

She lived on the ground floor of a low rise apartment block close to the Fraser River. He rang the doorbell, hoping for her to be home.

Camila opened on the second ring.

"Are you Camila Vargas?"

She stared up to him with glazed over eyes. He thought he smelled alcohol on her breath.

He showed his badge. "It's about your daughter, Luna," he said.

"She's not here."

"May I come in?" He pushed his way past her. She had no strength in her to object. Good Lord, please make her coherent. "Do you know where she is?"

Camila laughed, then coughed, then wiped her mouth with her hand. "I wish," she said. "She's moved out and left me sitting here with nothing. Still owes me the money for the car I bought her." She walked into the living room. "She doesn't care if I have to take public transport."

Macintosh followed her. Camila went to the cabinet, got a second glass, turned and asked, "You want one?"

He noticed the half-full glass with the vodka bottle next to it on the coffee table. "No, thanks. I'm on duty."

She put the glass back. "Suit yourself."

When she sat down he expected her to take a swig from her glass but she ignored it, leaned back, did her best to melt into the sofa, pulled a cushion on her lap and crossed her arms over it.

"So, you finally got the creep who did this to us," Camila said. When he didn't answer, she added, "Who was it?"

"I'm not at liberty to discuss an ongoing investigation," he said. She accepted that, said it didn't matter.

"What's done is done. It won't give us her career back. After those pictures surfaced, she was done in. Who'd ever take her serious again?"

He watched her moving gently from side to side. Lost in a past he knew very little about. "Yeah, that shouldn't have happened. Social media can be a dangerous place."

She didn't respond.

Tiara

"Must have been so tough for you to lose that contract. I guess Luna took it pretty hard."

Still nothing.

"I'm sure she regrets putting those pictures up on her page."

That triggered something. Camila shifted forward, got hold of the glass, took a sip of the colourless liquid, leaned back and placed the glass on the cushion, holding it tightly. "As if she'd been that stupid. She's an ungrateful brat, but she ain't nobody's push-over. She knew better than to put that stuff out herself. No, no, I'm telling you, I've been telling everybody from the start, but nobody wants to listen to me, somebody did that to her. There are jealous people out there, and they sure didn't like her making her way. If I could only turn time back, I'd tell that bitch Inez to be more careful."

Macintosh took a slow breath to keep his surprise in check. "Inez?"

"You know, Inez Alavarez."

He sorted his memory for the familiar name. "Tony's wife?"

"No, his sister. She'd promised me the pictures would only go to a group of select clients. Hand-picked by her. Very exclusive. I wouldn't have allowed my girl to do those if I'd known every Tom, Dick and Harry can drool over them, would I now? Inez said only her most influential contacts would get them. They'd further Luna's career, she said, but see what it got us now. Empty promises, nothing but bullshit."

"Did you tell the police about Inez' involvement in those pictures when they surfaced?"

"Don't be a fool. Of course not. We still had hopes Inez and her partners would find a solution. A new contract. We couldn't mix her up in this, not officially." Tears fill her eyes. "Doesn't matter anymore now. You're police. Do what you like with this. Lock them all up."

What a stroke of luck. Tony and Inez. Camila handed him a gift he'd need to analyze as soon as he got back. He certainly would get back to Camila again, summons her to the station, all sobered up, but for the moment, he'd take advantage of her confusion. Let her believe he was here about the cyber bullying, done with pornographic pictures taken of her own daughter. With Camila's consent. His stomach turned into a hard knot when his mind recalled the images of Tiara's abuse. What was it with those ambitious women? How could they subject their own flesh and blood to such filth? Promises of a golden career? Fame, money, self-realization? Projection of their own dreams onto others, regardless of the cost to them? Camila, the same egomaniac as Melissa. Or worse?

"Did you know Melissa Brown well?"

Camila thought for a moment. "Melissa? You mean Tiara's mom? Why do you ask?"

"She said you two were friends."

"Oh please. We knew each other, bumped into each other at a few pageants. She buttered up to me every chance she got, trying to pick my brain. Luna was so successful then. I can smell jealousy a mile away."

Macintosh decided to take a shot in the dark. "You think Melissa had something to do with making Luna's pictures public?"

"Not a chance." Camila took another sip. "She didn't strike me as somebody who understand how the entertainment business works. You see, Inez, she was smart, I give her that. Always up to date on the latest trends. She knew fame doesn't come from sitting on your ass. You need to take risks."

Sure. Exposing your under-age daughter to pornography—that's one hell of a way to secure a bright future for her. Ambitious mothers like that had always existed. Roman Polanski. The entertainment industry was full of them.

"Did you know Melissa's sister-in-law, Graciella?"
"Why?"
"I just thought, her living in Galveston, too—"

Camila pulled a face. "I won't go back to Texas, ever. Not with all the people knowing what..., huh, you know..., what with the pictures..." She wiped her eyes dry and finished the rest of her drink. "That bitch."

"Graciella?"

"No, not her. Sure I knew her, we all knew each other. She was a sweet one. Very protective of her niece. Over-protective if you ask me. Always hovering around that bitch. Her niece, I mean. That piece of shit Tiara."

Macintosh bit his lip. No need to break her flow, she was talkative now, letting her thoughts out unfiltered, although her speech pattern began to slur.

"If you ask me, it was her who's done in Luna. Young girls know how to do this social media stuff better than any of us. Her poor aunt tried her best to make her famous, thinking a few pageants would do that, but that won't cut it, not nowadays. Tiara treated her like shit, ignored her most of the time. Stand-offish she was, like a princess. With that stupid name Princess Tia, too. Speaks volumes. Now, my girl, La Luna, that's what I call a name. Perfect for Disney. That would have been next. A Disney movie."

Camila jumped up so sudden, her glass rolled on the carpet. She threw the cushion on the floor, too, steadied herself and walked to the cabinet. There she picked up a silver frame, came back and thrust it in Macintosh's face. "See, here. What a gorgeous girl she's been. My Luna."

He took the picture from her. Indeed, the girl was a stunner. A lovely, delicate young girl with bright blue eyes and blond hair. Smiling demurely. At an age when her world must have been still full of promise. Two golden interwoven letters dangled on a fine chain around her neck. He looked closer. 'C' and 'V'—she was still mummy's girl, then.

"Do you have proof that Tiara put those pictures on the net?"

Tiara

Camila sunk back on the sofa. Of course, she didn't. All speculation.

Something he'd have to address later, too. Much later. Camila closed her eyes and started to hum a tune. She might provide more insight into the pedophile organization, provide further proof of its existence, but not in the state she was in. He got enough out of her for the moment, he should get back and work the leads he had. Tony. Inez.

56

UNDER normal conditions Macintosh could have made it back to the Graveley Street MCS station in about an hour, but when he left Camila's place it started to drizzle. The light, cool December rain slowed drivers to a near stand-still, and, to make matters worse, Christmas was already raising its tinsel-head. Boundary Road displayed all the early signs of shopper's enticement, garish or gorgeous, depending on the merchants' budgets.

He didn't mind inching his way back to MCS. His head spun and he used the stop-and-go to bring order into his confused thoughts.

What he promised Tiara had not been an empty phrase. Even if she didn't hold him to it, he would never be able to look at himself in the mirror if he didn't catch the bastard who'd molested her. God, she was right, he was getting too old for this. How much time did he have left? Was it enough?

Melissa's extreme reaction to the video was an indication that she never suspected Tony to be a pedophile. But she'd lied through her teeth so often he didn't trust

Tiara

her one bit. Maybe it was her who burnt the house down and killed Gracie. If so, why? To get revenge for her daughter? If that was her motive, she should have killed Tony.

She said she knew Tony had raped Tiara. But Tiara said no.

Even if Tony wasn't the rapist, he was still involved. He owned the goddamn studio. And who was this elusive Purple Shadow operating the camera? Was Tony the Purple Shadow? Maybe his sister Inez. There was a thought. Camila had put her finger on it. That's where she could fit in. Tiara wouldn't know, she'd never seen behind the mask.

So many questions, so many assumptions—and still no proof of anything. He was about halfway up Boundary Road when his phone rang.

"Where are you?" Harding asked.

"About ten minutes away on any normal day, a half-hour today."

"Don't bother coming here. You're closer to your home than to MCS. Go home."

"It's not even four yet."

"I meet you there," Harding sounded cheerful. "And don't fret, my friend, I'm bringing work along so you won't feel guilty. Tony Alvarez's interrogation tape came through. Should make for a comfy video evening."

"I'll chill the beer. Don't forget the chips."

"You're right. Traffic's a bitch today," Harding said when he finally arrived at Macintosh's small apartment about an hour later.

Macintosh rented this place a few years ago after selling his Coquitlam house. After Kathy's death, he couldn't stand living in that place any more.

"Tiara insists the rapist wasn't Tony," he told Harding.

"The girl's confused, she can't be relied on. Tony's got to be involved. He owned the studio, it may not have been him but he must have known what was going on."

"Exactly my line of thought." Macintosh popped a can of beer open, slumped into his recliner. "Let's find out what he's got to say."

Harding connected his laptop to the TV, took a beer from the fridge, grabbed the remote, settled in the chair next to Macintosh's, and pressed a button.

Macintosh opened his can, spraying beer bubbles into the air.

They leaned back and watched.

The video started with the usual preliminaries, names, addresses etc. Clear picture, not perfectly focused. Macintosh knew that always happened when a stationary camera high up in the corner of the interrogation room filmed an interview.

A good-looking guy, Alvarez sat ramrod straight on the chair that looked every bit as hard and unforgiving as the chairs in the interrogation rooms of the Canadian MCS.

Tiara

They watched him, minute by minute, giving an account of his life. How he'd wanted to become a professional ballet dancer, how he injured his leg, how he became a dance instructor, how he started to work for Tiara's mother—and how he fell for her.

"Nice going, you revolting prick," Macintosh said under his breath.

Josh conducted the interview. He'd been briefed by Harding and now started to question Tony about his relationship with Tiara's mother. Tony said he'd fallen for her, hard.

"Sure," Harding said, "isn't that called the Lolita effect? A guy weaseling in on the mother?"

Josh asked Tony about his buying and owning a photo studio in Texas City. Tony confirmed this without hesitation. Yes, he did own Photomagic, but in name only. He'd never even set foot in it.

"Oh yeah?" Macintosh said. "Give me a break."

Josh, careful to sound polite, asked how and why Tony would own a studio and not be involved in it.

"It belonged to my sister Inez."

Crucial information. Made Macintosh sit up in his chair. Harding must have picked it up, too. He threw him a side glance of major alarm.

"Inez?" Harding said. Macintosh shushed him.

"She couldn't buy it after she got hassled by the IRS, some huge amount of money they wanted from her. She asked me to buy the studio for her, and of course I did.

Inez put me through dance school a long time ago, I owed her. She paid me a monthly allowance so long as she could use my name for the ownership."

"How long was that?" Josh asked.

"Not long enough. She told me to sell it about three years ago."

Josh then asked Tony why he never set foot in the studio if he was so close to his sister. Didn't he ever visit her there?

"Hell no," Tony said. "We'd grown apart years before she bought the studio. I guess she got tired of me being dependent on her. She hadn't supported me for years, the tight bitch. Rolling in money herself—she's a good businesswoman, my sister is—but didn't give me the time of day when I asked her for support, until she bought the studio. Then she needed me, and she knew it would cost her. Was a nice supplement to my dance instructor's income while it lasted."

"Why did she sell it?"

"How would I know? I wasn't exactly her confidant. We hardly ever spoke on the phone. All I know is, it had to be done real fast. I remembered what she paid for it when I signed for her, so I was surprised she sold it at a loss."

"She gave you no explanation?"

Tony fidgeted in his chair.

"No, how often do I have to tell you, she didn't trust me. Ask this Rodriguez woman. Inez hung out with her a lot. With her or with that other woman, Margarita. The one who did the office stuff for her. Graciella was related to Melissa, and I got the instructor's job through her."

"You were dating Melissa Brown and knew Graciella Rodriguez well, but never spoke to your sister?"

"I never spoke much with Graciella, either. She was a weird one, that one was, always thinking herself above the rest of us. High-and-mighty. She gave me the creeps."

Josh kept asking details about Tony's work at Melissa's house, trying to get him to contradict himself. Either he was the smoothest liar around or he was telling the truth, Macintosh couldn't find a single discrepancy in his account.

Eventually Josh moved on to the day Tony witnessed Melissa's departure.

He seemed to remember it well.

"I was upset. Imagine, for a whole week Melissa refused to speak to me on the phone, didn't pick up when I called. I decided to drive by her place. I'd gotten a job in Arizona, one that was really promising, and I wanted to persuade her to go with me, with her daughter, but without the crazy Rodriguez woman. I thought we could start a life together. So what do I see when I arrive at the house? She's *leaving*. Texas. The country. *Me*. We weren't really together, not in the classic sense, like a couple I mean, that wasn't possible as long as I depended on

Graciella recommending me for jobs. She had a lot of contacts, you know. Shady people she knew from her drug peddling days who'd come into enough money to show off. Private ballet lessons for their daughters and the like. Cash payment, if you know what I mean, but I didn't care where the money came from. Had to support myself, and was too proud to ask my tight-ass sister. But of course, the jobs weren't few and far between, never enough to get me through all my expenses. Anyway, with that new job, I thought I could finally make a go of it."

"With Melissa?"

"You bet. She's the only woman ever to take me serious."

"How's that? Come on, you're a good-looking guy."

"I was also a lame dance instructor, getting jobs by the grace of a known drug dealer. I had no steady income, no home to speak of, and to top it off, lots of women think I'm gay."

"So when you saw Melissa packing up, you got angry."

"I begged her, I yelled at her, and you know what? She accused me of molesting her daughter. Didn't even listen to me when I tried to set her straight. She said her sister-in-law, that Graciella woman, told her. And if I ever came near her again, she'd have me arrested. That's when I knew she was serious. Let's face it, if the police picked me up, it'd be her word against mine, and who'd believe me? So I left. I called my sister that same day and told her about Melissa leaving with Tia, hoping she'd persuade Graciella to talk some sense into Melissa. I know, that was a far-fetched hope, but what else could I do?"

"Did your sister try to intervene?"

Tony crossed his arms. "That's when it got a bit weird. Not a minute later Inez called me back, in total panic. I've never known her like that. She said she needed to sell the studio, things were happening fast and she needed to disappear for a while. I should handle the sale for her, and I shouldn't worry about Melissa, she'd take care of that. I should go to Phoenix as I'd planned, lay low, and wait for her to contact me once she'd sorted out the whole mess. I asked her what mess, but she didn't tell me, so I said if I'm supposed to go away without questions asked, I need some cash. She said I could keep the proceeds from the studio as long as I kept my mouth shut about Melissa and her daughter, whatever stories I might hear about them. I figured her and Melissa and Graciella must have had a business deal go south. I didn't really care, but the money from the studio would come in handy."

"Did she contact you later?"

"Only through her lawyer. I got a letter from him after the studio was sold, with a check and instructions not to look for her. That was it. Since then I never heard from her again, or from Melissa."

Josh continued his line of questioning without producing anything else remotely meaningful before he sent Tony back to his cell. On the way out, Tony groused about his treatment and insisted that he'd done nothing wrong. He'd been cooperative until now, but that was it. He wanted a lawyer. The screen went black.

Harding switched off the video.

"Now what? The guy's slippery as an eel."

"They've got nothing on him," Macintosh said. "Nothing."

"But he admitted he owned the studio. He's responsible for what happened there."

"Tony didn't own the studio, his sister did," Macintosh said, got two more beer cans out of the fridge.

"Come on. He did on paper. They can get him on that."

"I'm sure the lawyer who handled the purchase as well as the sale will have an agreement in place which proves that Tony was acting as a front man. You know what? I believe him. We've been chasing down the wrong alley."

"I don't know, sounds too smooth for me," Harding said. "He can't be that innocent."

"Try and poke a hole in his statement."

"How come he's got a sister all of a sudden? We didn't know he had a sister."

Macintosh considered this for a moment. "We didn't even know about Tony until recently."

"Who isn't involved at all, other than his sordid affair with Melissa?"

Macintosh felt a sense of excitement. "His sister did the dirty work together with the photographer Carlos. Inez Alvarez is the Purple Shadow, and Tiara was raped by a client of her pedophile ring. One of many. She's the one we need to go after."

"Not us," Harding said. "We have to let Texas know. Once they get her, Josh and his men will catch the others."

Macintosh opened his beer, Harding did the same. They saluted each other with a click of the cans.

57

THE following day, their stalled investigative machinery began to rev into high gear.

Macintosh told Harding to order Melissa back to MCS. "Let's put the fear of God into her. If we find the slightest proof of her being involved, we book her on the spot."

Melissa arrived a few minutes after nine. She looked tired, like she hadn't had a decent night's sleep in ages. Hair a mess, no make-up, wrinkled dress.

Before the detectives could start their interrogation, she made a statement.

"I understand now why Tiara refused to see me. Why she left me alone in the apartment so often. I knew what Tony had done to her—I always thought it was just that one time, when he lost control because Tiara egged him on. I didn't know about those horrible pictures. Tiara blames me for those, she believes I knew about what happened at the studio, and so do you. You think I deserve what Tony did to me. So charge me if you want, I don't care if you believe me or not. It really doesn't matter anymore, I've lost everything that was ever dear to me."

Macintosh took the lead. "As a matter of fact, we don't think it was Tony who abused Tiara."

Melissa looked perplexed. "He didn't?"

"No."

"But yesterday you said—"

"Well, we were wrong. I want you to look at part of an interview with him the Texas police taped yesterday."

"I don't want to see him."

"Oh, but I'm sure you do."

Macintosh clicked the pre-set start button, and once more he placed himself so he could watch Melissa's reactions. Regardless of what she'd said, her eyes moved to the screen as soon as it lit up. When she recognized Tony, a deep, anguished breath escaped her, an even louder one when she heard him speak. What he said shook her to the core. By the time he confessed his feelings for her, tears streamed down her face. She didn't wipe them away.

Macintosh switched off the computer, convinced that she was innocent, at least of any active involvement.

After a few moments of silence, Melissa said, "So Gracie lied to me. Why did she do that?"

"We don't know why she put the blame on Tony. We can't ask her any more, but we'll find out eventually. Let's just say by discrediting Tony she gave you a target for your... uh ... shall we call it your motherly rage? Her strategy worked, didn't it? You never questioned your daughter about what had happened on that day."

Melissa looked dazed.

"Quite frankly, why you wouldn't know about all those earlier years of exploitation is incomprehensible to us," Macintosh said.

"What do you mean? I thought this terrible thing only happened that one time."

"Only one time? You got to be kidding me."

She threw her hands in the air. "I never noticed anything. I didn't even know about that particular incident until Gracie told me. I knew of no other. You can't blame me. I never thought anything like this was possible."

"Not even when Tiara came home from those so-called photo sessions, disturbed and withdrawn? You never tried to get through to her and find out what troubled her so much?"

"Gracie told me some people react like that to the dream-juice."

"You knew she drugged your daughter?"

"That wasn't a drug." Melissa sounded firmer now. "The juice was supposed to make her calm. Those sessions took a long time to set up, and kids get fidgety. Gracie told me it was only to help the photographer do a good job. What should I have done? Those photo sessions brought in good money, and Gracie always said Tiara liked doing them. I didn't know there was anything wrong with it. Tiara earned the money we needed to live on, that's all I knew."

"That's all you cared about? The money?" Macintosh could feel the familiar anger poke inside his brain with a red-hot lance. He'd need more than a Tylenol tonight. The woman was guilty of so many things, yet there was nothing he could pin on her. Nothing official that would make her pay for exploiting her only child.

"We are very keen to confirm who the photographer was who took that video we showed you yesterday. I'm sure you can give us his name—"

"I've got no idea."

"—as well as the name of the woman involved."

"You mean Tiara's sponsor?"

"You got a name there?"

"Inez?"

Macintosh glared at her.

"Well, I guess that's the one you're thinking of. Inez paid for all the pageants. She worked with the photographer, set up the appointments, and later on she was in charge of selling the pictures to the ad agencies, that's what Gracie told me anyway. I bet Inez is to blame for all this—who would have thought? But frankly, I never liked her. She's always been a bad influence on Gracie."

Macintosh should feel pleased how it all came together, but he felt sick. Inez was heavily involved in the studio business. She was the one calling the shots from start to finish. She was the sponsor and the Purple Shadow, all in one. And Graciella couldn't be all that innocent, she must have known something. Too bad she was gone.

He took a breath. "Since Graciella's dead, that leaves only Inez to face the consequences. As soon as the police in Texas bring her in, we'll find out who else was involved. Did you know that Inez is Tony's sister?"

"Sure. So what? That's not Tony's fault. Oh my, oh my, Tony. My Tony."

Macintosh realized that she'd shrugged off everything he'd said. She didn't waste a single compassionate thought on her daughter. All she was interested in was Tony. Her face flushed, glowing, she wore a Mona Lisa smile. She leaned back in her chair.

"Oh dear Lord, he didn't lie, did he? He's telling the truth. He's been in love with me all along. I need to see him and tell him that I love him so very much."

After she had left, Macintosh told Harding to check immigration if a certain Inez Alvarez had entered Canada recently. Like in early October. Another crash hot candidate for the victim. In fact, she knocked Margarita off the pedestal big time. Fingers crossed.

He then drove straight to the BYSC without asking for an appointment. They would make Tiara available to him, even on short notice. He had a desperate need to talk to her, explain things to her.

He was twiddling with his phone when they brought her into the meeting room.

"Hi there." She sat down about five feet away from him. Hands on her thighs, chin down. "What's up? You found out who I stabbed?"

"Still working on it," he said, his voice low.

"Then what?"

Tiara

"We still don't know who the guy… I mean, the one who—"

"You mean the motel-man?"

Oh God, she didn't make it any easier for him. Then it crossed his mind that it was a bit selfish to feel sorry for himself, considering the courage it must take her to tell him as much as she had.

"Yes. We don't have his identity yet, but he'll be caught eventually. Texas police will take care of that—it's only a matter of time before they apprehend him, and all the others involved."

She stared at him with her dark eyes.

"But I've got something else for you. We can finally put a name to the Purple Shadow."

Her eyes darkened even more.

"It was Tony's sister. Does the name Inez Alvarez ring a bell?"

Tiara didn't answer right away. She seemed different today, more guarded, more reserved. She looked at the floor, formed fists, like she had to hold back some inner turmoil. Then she looked back at him, let her fingers relax.

"Can you imagine, in all those years I didn't know Tony's last name. But I know Inez, of course. She was the one who paid for everything." She stopped, looked puzzled, as if her mind tried to fit this new information into an existing pattern. "So you think my sponsor Inez was the Purple Shadow?"

"We're pretty sure about that. She either ran the operation herself, as the boss, or worked with some partners. Would that make sense?"

Tiara looked deep in thought. "Sure, it's possible, why not? I don't remember much about Inez. And even if I did, I've never seen the Purple Shadow without a cover, so I can't confirm that she was Inez. Does it matter?"

"Not any more, not to you. We're convinced Inez ran the business together with the photographer Carl Heider and his wife Margarita Rios. We know of one other case already, a young girl you may have known, who'd been exploited by Inez and her partners."

"I don't really want to know."

"Never mind for now. It's up to Texas law enforcement to deal with that case as well as the exploitation you experienced. Out of our jurisdiction." Damn, not again. If Inez or Margarita was the victim, they'd have to extradite her. Their crimes were not committed in Canada. Whoever it was, he wouldn't let her out of sight until he put her on a plane, with Josh waiting at the other end.

Tiara needn't be burdened by this. "Whatever they uncover down in Texas will be shared with us," he said. "It will influence what happens to you. The information they provide will prove that you had more than your fair share of ... I mean ... look, you got dealt a shit hand, kid. Your mother is a piece of work, aiding and abetting a sexual predator, and—"

Tiara

Tiara burst out laughing.

"And my grandmother is a thief."

"What?"

"My grandmother. Louise. She told my mom she took five thousand dollars from Gracie's room. She lied. On our drive back to Canada, we stopped at a gas station close to the Canadian border. It was pretty cold by then, and while my grandmother went inside to pay for the gas, Mom told me to go to the trunk of the car and look for a sweater in the bags there. That's when I came across the manila envelope with a big wad of cash inside. I didn't count it, but it was a lot more than five thousand, believe me. It was all in hundred dollar bills, about two inches thick."

Macintosh didn't know how much that would add up to, but he planned to find out.

"Christ, I bet that must be at least a hundred thousand."

"And she never gave any of that money to Mom." Tiara shrugged. "But then again, Mom didn't deserve it, right?"

Things were looking up. Melissa getting cheated by her own mother, now that was something he could relish.

"Your mom is already making plans to go back to Texas. Hooking up with Tony again."

The blood drained from Tiara's face. Her hands flew to her mouth, her eyelids fluttered. For a second

Macintosh thought she'd faint, but he knew better than to touch her. She lowered her hands, fighting for composure.

"Will I have to go back with her if they let me out?"
"Not if I can help it."
Another promise hard to keep.

58

MACINTOSH was driving from the Center back to MCS when Harding called and told him that law enforcement in Texas had tracked down the last known address of Inez Alvarez. Josh and his boys were on the way over to a judge to get a warrant for her arrest.

How he would have loved to hear that Harding had found her name on the immigration entry list, but it was too early to hope for that. Immigration had their own speed of dealing with requests that didn't scream money laundering or drug trafficking.

Please, merciful God, let the victim be Inez, or Margarita, I don't care which one as long as it gives Tiara motive. Please don't let it be a random stranger. With Eaton's report already on the judge's desk, and their own investigation wrapping up at lightning speed, it was more important than ever to find out fast what drove Tiara to stab that victim.

Could she have attacked a total stranger because something about the person reminded her of the sponsor? The dreaded trigger effect?

Tiara

Stopped at yet another red light, Macintosh fished for the card with the number for St Paul's and dialed before the light turned green. He put the call on speaker and drove on. After a few minutes and several transfers, he got hold of the doctor currently on duty.

Macintosh listened, his excitement rising, to the doc's brief summary of the victim's condition. The CT scan confirmed near normal brain activity so they'd removed the endotracheal tube a few days ago. It was now possible to speak to her, though only under doctor's supervision. She was still weak and should not be subjected to unnecessary excitement, but she'd made remarkable progress.

Macintosh called Harding.

"I'll meet you there," Harding said. "Don't you dare go in without me."

Macintosh changed route and turned left onto Broadway. Ten minutes later he crossed over Burrard Bridge. Five minutes after, he parked close to the emergency-room entrance at a special permit spot reserved for police cars.

He had to summon all the discipline he possessed to wait for his partner. A few minutes went by. While several ambulances drove into the delivery area to unload their patients, Macintosh withdrew into a corner of the reception area to get away from the hectic sounds of saving lives. Way too many things rubbed him the wrong way nowadays. No wonder, he wanted to turn the clock back without having to go back. He didn't want to live through his past again.

That's what he admired about Tiara. Her memories must hurt like hell, yet she did her best to bring them on.

Back to the task on hand. Concentrate. What's needed now? Establish the identity of that woman in there, the victim. Establish motive. Something that would get Tiara a lighter sentence.

Harding came puffing into the reception area.

"Sorry I'm late. I was ready to leave when the sergeant asked for a final brief on the South Vancouver case. Couldn't tell him where I was heading. Had to hang around and couldn't call you."

Macintosh waved it away. "Let's go and find this super-duper important doctor."

They took the elevator to the intensive care unit and had to wait another twenty minutes before the doctor in charge found time to see them.

"I'm Dr. Vanderhoof," he said.

"I'm Detective Macintosh. This is my partner, Detective Harding. Good of you to see us."

"You're lucky you caught me," Vanderhoof said. "My shift ended over an hour ago."

"We don't want to hold you up longer than necessary. We're here to see the coma patient from the coffee shop stabbing. We understand she can now be questioned. It was me you were talking to on the phone earlier."

"Yes, I know that. By the way, we got her name now."

Macintosh's heart skipped a beat or two. He held his breath. Please, God.

"How?" Harding asked. "She had no ID on her."

"It's normal procedure to ask patients for their name when waking them from a prolonged period of unconsciousness," Dr. Vanderhoof said. "That's the first thing we ask."

Macintosh let out air. "And? What did she say?"

"I was on duty the day when she came to. Her name is… hold on, let me double check to make absolutely sure. I wrote the name on my notes."

He went to the reception desk, asked the nurse for a file, leafed through it, stepped back.

"Here it is. Her name is Graciella Rodriguez."

59

THE doctor didn't give the detectives much time to digest the news. He ushered them into the hospital room, said he'd give them ten minutes max, as long as they didn't upset the patient.

Tiara's victim lay connected with tubes to several machines. Heavy bandages covered the left side of her face, the right distorted by swelling. Nobody would recognize her like this, but Macintosh didn't plan on letting her find out. He needed a blitz attack to make the most of this new development.

"Graciella Rodriguez," he said in his softest voice. "How nice to see you coming around."

She cocked her head, struggling with the limitations of a one-eyed line of vision. Macintosh moved in front of her bed.

"Who are you?" she said, her voice still hoarse from the removal of the tube.

Macintosh said, "We're detectives from the Vancouver Police Department in charge of investigating the attack on you."

Her right eye stared at him, watchful, wary.

Tiara

"So?"

"We've been waiting for you to get well enough to talk to us. We'll need to confirm a few details to wrap up the case. I'm sorry we don't have much good news for you regarding your attacker."

The eye clouded over.

"The young person escaped. Obviously a drug addict. So sorry."

Dr. Vanderhoof opened his mouth, but Macintosh gave him a shut-up look. The doc swallowed visibly but kept his lips closed. Macintosh pressed on.

"So if you're up to answering a few questions now—that's standard procedure, I'm afraid—we can leave you to your hopefully speedy recovery."

"What do you want to know?" Careful. Slow.

Macintosh opened his notebook, pretended to read from it. "Your name's Graciella Rodriguez."

"How do you know?"

"You told the doctor when you woke up."

"I did?"

"Yes. You did. You're from Texas?"

"Huh, yes. Yes, I am. On a visit."

"And you were staying where? The name of the hotel?"

"Ah, um…don't remember. Need to think."

Dr. Vanderhoof found his voice. "I really think we should give the patient time—".

Macintosh moved to block him from Graciella's view. "One more minute, please." He smiled at her.

"My note here says you have relatives in Vancouver. I guess you probably stayed with them?"

"Yes. No."

"No, you don't have relatives or no, you didn't stay with them?"

"I don't have relatives. I'm a tourist."

"Sure. Thank you." He closed his book and turned to Dr. Vanderhoof. "We're done here."

"Thank you, detectives." The doc moved to lead them out.

"Very good. Thank you, Ms. Rodriguez."

They left the room together, Macintosh thanked the doctor again, then they parted ways. The detectives walked to the elevators. While waiting for one to arrive, Macintosh watched Dr. Vanderhoof disappear down the hallway.

"What was that?" Harding said as soon as the doc was out of sight. "Why did you stop?"

"Oh, I didn't," Macintosh said. "I called a brief time-out. Come on, let's get back in there, the doc's gone."

"But we can't, we need his permission."

"Didn't he give it to us a few minutes ago?" Macintosh headed straight past the intensive care receptionist, who barely glanced at them. Macintosh banked on her assuming that they had every right to be here. Two detectives who'd just been with the doc, right?

"We can't do this," Harding said in front of Graciella's room. "We'll get into trouble."

Tiara

"It'll only be me who gets into trouble, you won't. I'm the senior here, and I say we go in. You got no choice but to follow orders. I'll write in my report that you objected, and that we had a slight difference of opinion. The doc's shift is over, we need to respect that. No need to have him called back just because I want to check a small detail with the victim. Got it?"

"Got it." Harding's shoulders relaxed.

Macintosh opened the door to feel that hawk's eye on him again.

"Sorry, Graciella, I need to ask you one more question."

"What?"

"How did you kill Inez Alvarez?"

"I ... what are you—"

"We know you set fire to the house in La Marque and stole Inez Alvarez's identity. We know who you are and where you've lived and what you've done. The only thing we don't know is how you killed her. I'm interested in that. I'd like to wrap up this case."

The eye blinked several times. "How the hell did you come up with all that shit?"

"That doesn't matter, does it? You're in a hospital in Canada now, but as soon as you've regained enough strength to be deported, you'll be sent back to the States to stand trial for your involvement in child-abuse allegations Texas MCS is compiling against you, as well as the murder charge—"

"I didn't kill her."

"We got proof. We got statements. From Melissa, Tony, Tiara. We know everything."

Close enough.

"I didn't kill Inez. It wasn't murder. It was an accident." Her harsh voice had shrill overtones but quickly broke into coarse whisper.

Macintosh pulled a chair closer to the bed and sat down. "Tell me."

Gracie blinked and swallowed hard.

"Wait," Macintosh said. "Do you mind if we tape this?"

"Go ahead, I'm only saying how it was. I can explain it all. You'll see, I'm innocent."

Harding took a small tape recorder from the inside pocket of his jacket, turned it on, stated time and day, and asked the suspect if she gave her consent to be interviewed. She nodded but he made her state aloud, yes.

"Good," Macintosh said. "Now let's get started. We know you're Tiara's aunt."

"That little bitch. After all I've done for her. Whenever she opens her mouth, she's lying. Make sure you tape that, you hear me? I'll tell you how it really was. It wasn't my fault." She stopped to clear her scratchy throat.

Harding moved closer to the bed, held the tape recorder in position. Macintosh moved Harding's hand even closer. He had enough trouble understanding her Spanish accent without her damaged windpipes keeping her voice so low.

Tiara

"Tell us everything you remember from that day when Inez got killed, uh, by accident."

"I was with Inez, at her place," she said. "We were yapping about everything and nothing when the phone rang. Inez has a brother, Antonio, her kid brother—Tony, you know—she spoiled him way too much. I always told her he was a no-good, lazy son of a bitch, but she didn't want to hear any of it. Even when he took up with Tiara's mother, who was his employer, Inez didn't cut ties with him altogether. Imagine, the fool was dumb enough to confide in her, even telling her that Melissa stole money from me and gave the cash to him to pay for a romantic holiday. The idiot. He didn't have a clue that I'd been safe-keeping that money for Inez, so he'd actually accepted money that belonged to his own sister. The guy's a total loser. You better not believe a word he's saying."

She had to pause and swallow a few times before she could carry on.

"Anyway, he called on that day, all in a huff about something, and Inez got really pissed off with him. I heard her say he'd better lie low for a while and assumed he'd gotten himself into trouble, but when she hung up she told me my sister-in-law, Melissa, was on the run with her daughter, leaving the country with another woman, somebody Tony didn't know. He said the three of them were packing up when he left their place, and he begged Inez to do something about it. Inez had a quick think and called him back because she suddenly remembered that she wanted him to do something for her…uh, kind of, something personal. Never mind that. Anyway, knowing Melissa had bolted, Inez got worried about the money I was keeping for her at my place. Very worried, I tell you, and so was I. When Melissa stole from me before, Inez insisted I pay her back, so you can imagine how I felt."

Now Graciella started to cough, couldn't stop. Macintosh handed her the glass with tea from her bedside table but she ignored him. Her desire to finish off her story seemed to be stronger than the discomfort of talking.

"So we raced off like two crazies to my house, but we found everything deserted. Melissa and Tiara and that other woman, gone. All the closets empty and the stuff from the bathroom gone. Jesus, I tell you, my heart sank when I saw the door to my bedroom wide open. Inez went into panic mode. She started screaming at me that it was my fault those women took off. I didn't say anything, went to my hiding place, and can you believe it, Melissa cleaned that out all right, too, every dollar gone. All of it, nearly a hundred thousand. I thought I'd die. Inez then flew at me with claws out, like a werewolf on a rampage. She thought I'd put Melissa up to it. And Tiara. She screamed about the money, she screamed about Tiara."

"Tiara?" Macintosh said, the back of his neck on fire.

"What? Yeah, sure, she liked that girl a lot, been like family to her. The money gone, and Tiara, that was too much for her. She hurled herself at me, screaming I'd never get away with cheating her. What could I do? I had no choice but to defend myself. I knocked her over, and would you believe it she fell and banged her head against the brass frame of the sideboard. We had one of those glass and metal things to match the dining table, Melissa's idea, I hated that stupid thing from the start. Anyway, there she was, bleeding like a stuck pig, all over the rug.

"What a nightmare. I didn't know what to do. I wanted to call an ambulance, but Inez knew she was dying fast and with her last breath she said, don't do it. She'd done some terrible things, she said, I guess to cleanse her soul before meeting her maker, no good for nobody to involve the authorities. She hadn't been totally legal in her dealings, they'd only confiscate everything if they found out. She told me to do certain things for her and said I should then disappear for a while, to protect myself. That was Inez, in her last moments still thinking of me."

She had to stop to suck in air before she could carry on with laboured breath.

"It made sense to me then. I mean, I was Inez's best friend, and Melissa disliked me from the start. She's a mean woman. I had a bit of a run-in with her a week earlier, about … well, about all sorts of things, so I spent the week at Inez's place. I was only doing what Inez wanted. I had to protect myself."

"So you set fire to the place."

"Inez was dead. With my little niece gone and all the money missing, the stuff in the house meant nothing to me. Nothing but a rental anyway."

"But you said her business partners would come after her when they found out their money was missing. So weren't you worried to take on her identity?"

Her one eye gazed at the ceiling, then pierced Macintosh with an angry look.

"It was like this. Inez had some cash money stashed at her studio and at a few other places, and I used that to pay the people she owed. Get it? That was part of what I had to do for her. I needed to pay off Carlos and his dumb bitch Margarita so they could leave Galveston, and a few others down in Tijuana—Inez had some pretty solid contacts in the cartel—and to get all this done, I needed to be her. I took care of things for her, that's all there's to it." She closed her eye. "I'm tired now. I don't think I need to say any more."

"You certainly told us enough for today. Thank you very much."

Macintosh motioned to Harding to turn off the tape recorder, and as soon as he heard the quiet click, he came even closer to the bed. He bent low, until his face was right next to Graciella Rodriguez's head.

"I'll come back with a warrant. We know about the whole pedophile operation, and you'll be held accountable, I don't care which name I write on your deportation order, Inez or Graciella. In fact, I might ask Texas police which one they prefer. They'll get proof that Inez and you, you two scumbags, partnered up. We already got a witness statement—"

The eye flew open again, blazing like burning coal.

"Tiara is a liar. She tried to kill me."

"Why did you come to Vancouver?"

"Why do you think? To get my investment back."

"I take it by that you mean Tiara? You came to Canada because you knew Tiara lived here, you found out where, stalked her, watched her movements for a while, followed her, and eventually confronted her in the coffee shop to lure her back."

"Nothing of the kind. I did nothing wrong."

"Oh yeah? You entered Canada illegally by using the name Inez Alvarez."

"So what? I had to protect myself. Melissa's a mean bitch. There's no saying what lies she'd spread to stop me getting my niece back."

"So you admit you planned to kidnap her."

"To take her home, not against her will. Whatever she says is a lie. She was quite willing at first."

Macintosh took a deep breath. He felt a huge burden lift off his shoulders.

"But then you said something that aggravated her, you threatened her, and she lost it."

"The stupid bitch! She's a snake, a lying, two-faced snake. I had no idea she'd trick me like this."

"You got what you deserved."

With that he turned around, left, Harding gathered the recorder, followed him. When he was close, Harding asked, "What did she mean by, 'I had no idea she'd trick me like this'?"

Macintosh hesitated for a second, thought.

"You didn't hear that right. She said: 'I had no idea she'd treat me like this'."

"Yeah." Harding frowned back at the door, then looked at his partner. "That makes a lot more sense."

Back at MCS, Macintosh phoned Josh and briefed him on the latest twist, not forgetting to mention the name Camila Vargas as additional proof in the pedophile case. Josh could shine with that investigation, get the promotion he deserved. He owed him, and it made Macintosh feel good to square his debt.

Josh promised to get the warrant changed to Graciella Rodriguez as soon as he got hold of the judge again. With the original warrant they had forcefully entered Inez Alvarez's apartment and discovered more damaging material than they'd ever seen in any of their raids. Computers full of explicit pedophile pictures and video clips, actual prints of girls as young as four or five in suggestive poses. Best of all, Josh told Harding with a pained voice, hating to have to use the word 'best' in such a context, they found a small book with a long list of names and phone numbers. Incredibly careless, but Inez/Graciella must have felt immune to discovery. This started to make more sense to Josh now. Shielded behind the identity of a dead woman, Graciella must have felt invincible and invulnerable. Or she was one hell of a smug bitch. Or plain dumb.

Tiara

With the evidence collected at the apartment, the VPD would be able to arrest Graciella in her hospital bed.

Macintosh breathed a sigh of relief, told Harding to write the final report that completed the Princess file. A copy would go to Sexual Offense Squad. Within the hour, their detectives were on the way to St Paul's Hospital.

Macintosh sat back in his chair, felt better and better.

Harding said, "I'll go get some coffee", came back with two cups, placed one on Mac's desk and sat down, too.

"Good feeling, eh?"

"Yeah," Macintosh said. "For once the baddies are either dead or arrested. And with a bit of luck, the innocent one gets a new chance in life."

"I wonder what will happen to Tiara."

Macintosh thought a bit. "Somebody's got to tell her that the victim of the attack was her own aunt, and that she's still alive. I don't think Tiara will feel overjoyed, but then again, she's been trying hard to remember who she attacked."

"Are you absolutely sure about that? Is it really possible that she still doesn't remember who she's attacked?"

Macintosh took a long time to answer.

"That's what Eaton said. His report explains that Tiara is unable to understand her behavior, and if it's in that report, it's good enough for me. As far as I'm concerned, Tiara can't be criminally responsible for her action, period."

"Then call Dr. Eaton. He can give her the news."

"You know what," Macintosh said. "I think I'll call it a day. Might drop by the center on my way home and tell her myself."

60

TIARA was brought to the visitor's room. She wasn't as composed as on his previous visits. Her fingers kept pulling on her lower lip, exposing her teeth. When she sat down, her left leg quivered. As soon as she noticed that he noticed, she stopped working on her lip, placed her hand on her knee and pressed down.

"I'm sorry to be the bearer of bad news," he said. "Remember when I told you your aunt died in that house fire?"

Tiara didn't move.

"We had that wrong. The body they found wasn't your aunt."

"I agree, that is bad news."

"What I'm saying is, your aunt's alive, which means, well, this is quite complicated…, the person they found in the burnt ruins is now identified. It was Tony Alvarez's sister, Inez, the one we know to be the Purple Shadow."

Tiara stared at the floor.

"Which means the one in the hospital, that's not Inez. That's Graciella, your aunt. She's been posing as

Inez Alvarez, taking over her illegal business in the past three years—" he halted, not sure how to proceed without hurting her. "I'm not saying she's been involved with your…, um, we don't know about that. What I'm saying is, we're certain she took over once you were gone. She's being arrested as we speak."

"Is she awake? Have you spoken to her?"

"We interviewed her, and she more or less admitted waiting for you at the coffee shop."

"Did she say anything else?"

"Lots of accusations, but we know she's lying through her teeth, so it's of no importance to us. We've heard enough to be able to deport her to Texas. They'll deal with her there."

"You won't talk to her again?"

"I got all I needed."

He waited for more questions, but none came. Tiara looked absorbed in a world of her own. So he asked the one question he couldn't shake off.

"Didn't you know the person you stabbed in the coffee shop was your aunt? You must have recognize her?" He sounded like a sulking child. *You must have known. Why didn't you tell me?* But it did bug him. In front of Harding, he'd presented Eaton's assessment more concisely than the shrink had formulated it. How could she not have known? Why hadn't she told him that the victim she attacked had been her aunt? It could have saved them all a lot of work.

Tiara sucked in her lower lip and moved her head side to side.

"You really don't remember?"

No reaction. Then it hit him. She still couldn't deal with confronting that particular memory. She must have seen her aunt, recognized her, and been instantly terrified. Gracie wanted to take her back to a life of abuse. Tiara must have panicked and reacted subconsciously. Lost all her memory the moment her survival instinct forced her to attack. Shock did that to people. Eaton would be able to analyze this. Macintosh made a mental note to ask the psychiatrist to modify his report to the judge and include a reference to this possibility which should make Tiara's action and her selective memory loss more explainable.

Tiara interrupted his thinking. "What about my mom?"

Hadn't she paid attention to anything he'd said? He tried to follow her train of thought. Gracie, Inez, the attack, the fact that they had solved the case touched her only peripherally. Didn't seem all that important. But her mother? Why did she bring her up now? Was she trying to throw him off track? Hide something she knew all along? To think of her mother when she should react to the rather spectacular development he'd just presented … oh shit! Of course. Since he'd mentioned it yesterday, she couldn't think of anything else but having to go back to Texas—with her mother. That must terrify her all over again. His fault, totally his fault. So insensitive. He must have left her in a terrible state. The poor girl must have gone through hell, imagining that the authorities would send her back to the place of her unspeakable childhood.

"Dr. Eaton was quite specific about the condition of your release if the judge grants you probation. Taking your history into account, he didn't find it appropriate to have you returned to your mother. I'm sure the judge will take his recommendation into account."

"What's the alternative?"

Yes, what? Tiara's attack could be considered spontaneous and not premeditated. With the background of abuse they could prove to the judge, and with Eaton's assessment of her partial amnesia, she most likely would get out on probation.

"A foster home, maybe. You need to discuss this with your lawyer."

Her worried expression changed to abhorrence.

"A strange family?"

"Let's not jump to conclusions. Why don't we wait for the trial," he said.

"When will that be?"

"It's nearly Christmas now, the courts go into recess until mid January, after that it'll take a few weeks before your case can be scheduled. Spring, maybe?"

Her face crumbled. "I have to stay in here until then?"

God, that didn't help. He didn't know what to say, so he said the first thing that came into his mind.

"I'll visit you as often as I can and keep you informed of what's going on out there. If you want me to."

"If it makes you happy."

61

Birthday balloon bursting

I'm looking out my cell window, size two by two feet. Nothing to see but sky. Its color hasn't changed much in the past three months. Vancouver in winter is either dark gray or light gray.

Today I would have liked the sun to shine, but no such luck. Today is what Macintosh calls The Big Day. True to his promise, he's come to see me nearly every week, feeding me information and playing it cool.

He told me when they found Margarita and Carlos living in a Toronto suburb and confronted them with the evidence Josh had collected in Texas, they begged to turn witness against their former employer Inez Alvarez and the other players of her criminal organisation. He tells me what a great bloodhound Josh is, going after all the baddies within the pedophile ring as much as their sick customers.

He never mentions my mom or my aunt, though. I appreciate his efforts—honestly, I do—but I can feel the toll it takes on him to act cheerful and optimistic while

Tiara

the mere thought of my upcoming trial crawls underneath his skin like a parasite that constantly places disgusting larvae into his system. Yet on the outside he pretends all is well. We joke around—our senses of humor in sync.

At least I got rid of purple, I'm now surrounded by the color red. After they downgraded the charges from attempted murder to assault causing bodily harm—thanks to Macintosh's insistence and Stanley's report that I pose no risk to my resident-inmates—I was transferred to a different unit. Red sweat suits instead of purple, I'm moving up in this world. The girls in red—five of them in here—are just as friendly, forever trying to draw me into their closeness. If I want to keep my red status I can't shove them away.

Macintosh gave me instructions on how to behave. So did Stanley, who still drops by occasionally. He has other cases to worry about by now. The psychologist-in-residence keeps pestering me to work with him, but I hold my non-committal position. What is there to treat? I remember everything, and what I pretend not to remember, other people have figured out for themselves, or so they think. They've filled in all the holes, pleased with their conclusions.

Stanley's report has been revised, so has the police report. The Purple Shadow is no more, the sponsor is no more; both of them have morphed into one. Inez Alvarez, they tell me, and because I never saw her face or heard her voice when she was my handler, I'm not asked to elaborate on this. She's dead, murdered by my aunt, so we can close the Purple Shadow chapter, which suits me just fine.

I have no secrets left—well, none except that all-important one I keep from Macintosh and from Stanley and from the rest of the world.

Today, I don't have to clean my cell for inspection. When I'm gone, they'll clear it out, disinfect it, I guess, and get it ready for a new arrival. Should things go wrong at the trial and they send me back to the center—Macintosh said no way is that going to happen, but his voice sounded raspy when he said it—I'll be given a new cell. But I might not come back. Neither of us know.

Wardens usher me through the corridors, into the changing area, reverse arrival mode. Off with the sweat suit, on with the prison orange, the shackles, the cuffs. A bag with my street clothes, the ones I wore coming in, will accompany me. Into the prison truck in the loading zone, and finally, after five months in BSYC, I see the sky and the road and the trees all in one picture and not cut into neat iron-bar-squares.

The van drives along roads I've never been on. Southern Burnaby wasn't my area. It's beautiful, not too many houses, not many cars. I can't get enough of looking. Even when it changes into serious suburbia, one detached house next to another, with a towel-wide space

Tiara

in between, more cars, more noise, pedestrians on the roadside, then high-rise buildings and even more cars and buses and trucks and honking and screeching and blinking and bleeping. My ears hurt. My eyes burn. But I still can't stop taking it all in. I'm a turtle, peeking out under a thick protective shell, ready to retract.

We arrive at the courthouse. I'm unloaded like a parcel and deposited into a holding cell close to the courtroom, where a judge will decide my future. I am to sit here until 10:00 a.m. when the circus begins.

The chair is small and hard, and I realize for the first time that the furniture in BSYC was pretty comfortable. As a whole, the center wouldn't be a bad place for a little while longer. Staff was always courteous, the food edible, the building clean and modern, and there were hordes of volunteers offering different programs for us misguided adolescents. If it weren't for my animosity toward groups and group activities I might have enjoyed my stay there. At this precise moment, I wish I could go back. The idea of being the center of attention in a courtroom becomes close to a horror scenario. My mother will be there. I haven't seen or spoken to her since a few days before the coffee shop incident, as Macintosh refers to it, and I have no desire to do so now.

The key turns in the door, my heart rate goes wild. Short, fast beats. They wouldn't allow my mother a visit against my will?

Macintosh.

"Hi there," he says, overly exuberant. He grabs a chair.

"Big day, today, uh?"

As if we both hadn't known for weeks.

"So, how're you feeling?"

As if he wouldn't know. But I do him the favor.

"Nervous. Confused. Scared."

"Yeah, yeah," he says. "I can imagine. Came to wish you good luck. I mean, I'm sure you don't need luck, it'll all be fine. Judge Carr has a rep for being fair. It's all good, you'll do fine … just fine."

"Stop being such a fuddy-duddy, you're making me even more nervous."

He coughs. "No need for nerves, I'm telling you, the judge—"

I glare at him.

"Okay, okay, but one more thing. In case you're thinking your mom might be in there—"

I hold my breath.

"She won't," he says.

I exhale, slowly, carefully, so he won't know the extent of my relief. But of course he knows me well enough to read my face.

"You're glad about that—well, good for you. She decided to stay away, and though I'm glad for your sake, that pisses me off quite a bit."

My heart rate goes back to normal. A considerable weight lifts off my lungs and my mind, and that makes me giggle.

Tiara

"Don't be mad on my account," I say. "I can't face her yet, I'm not ready, maybe never will be, and her staying away today is the first act of consideration and kindness I can remember in ages."

"Don't be too sure about that," he says. "Apparently she flew to Texas a week ago. Louise told Harding yesterday, so this throws a new twist into the case."

"How so?" I giggle again, realizing that I'm really fond of this old guy.

"Harding told your mother about the money Louise stole. Apparently your mom was livid when she heard how much she's been cheated out of and went straight to your grandmother's place. Louise said she'd only wanted to safe-keep the money, in case there was an emergency—"

"Oh yeah, I can imagine how Mom reacted to that. She had to slave away at the supermarket while my grandmother sat on a small fortune."

"Right. Your mom made her hand over what was left. Louise said it was close to eighty thousand. And with that, according to your grandmother, she immediately checked herself into a clinic for a major overhaul, getting rid of fat and skin and what have you before she flew to Phoenix last week. She must have gone to the airport still wrapped in bandages—again, according to your grandmother."

Interesting. My mind is racing. So is his.

"It's blood money, no question about that. She won't enjoy whatever's left of it for long." With that, he changes the subject. I guess he wants to spare me further thoughts of my mom living in blissful happiness ever after with money I and other pretty little princesses earned for her.

"It's nearly ten. Time to get you in there and out again on probation."

"Into foster care."

"Maybe your grandmother?"

"Never!"

He looks pleading. "I bet probation only lasts until you're of age. Wouldn't be too long. Two years with your grandmother. Couldn't be that bad."

"I'd rather go back to prison."

"But why? She hasn't… I mean, she didn't live in Texas when you—"

The tension of waiting for the circus to begin must have frayed my nerves. I'm close to losing it. "She's a mean woman." My voice is too high pitched. I swallow, cough, lower my voice to a mere whisper. "On the back seat, when we drove to Canada, I heard her talking, about me, about how much she wished my mom wouldn't have run off with my dad. About what a mistake I was, shouldn't exist at all. Bad blood, she called me. Soldier's blood. She told Mom to put me in a home in Canada, nobody needed to know about me. You can imagine how I felt, the state I was in, and having to listen to her trashing me. On top of that, she'll know it was me who told you about the money she stole. She'll hate me even more for that."

Tiara

To make sure Macintosh understands my deep aversion, I say, with tears streaming down my cheeks, "Remember, she never came to see us because my mom didn't do as she saw fit. That's how opinionated she is. Her rules. Her life. I can't handle this kind of dominance any more. People ruled over me long enough. Nobody's allowed to tell me what to do and how to behave—not any more. Not ever again. I rather die."

I've convinced him. I see only raw anguish in his face. "There might be other options. The judge might appoint a legal guardian. How would that sit with you?"

"Why can't I live alone? I can take care of myself." *Candy. Why can't I live with Candy?*

"I'm sure you can, but you aren't even sixteen yet. No way they let you out unsupervised."

My heart sinks again, right down to my twiddling toes. Guess they're nervous, too.

The judge is a woman. Can you believe this? My luck, another woman to rule over me. It makes me more nervous to watch her sitting high above us in her black robe, a raven ready to sink her beak into my quivering flesh.

The morning goes by like a flash. I distance myself from the progression of my exposure by numbing my auditory reception to a point where only muffled sounds penetrate my ears, and thereby, to a large extent, lose their meaning. Doesn't seem right to listen to them talk about me, about the perils of my childhood, about the shortcomings of my family. My court-appointed lawyer, who knows his shoelaces better than me, does a good job reading out different parts of various statements with the sole purpose of making the judge understand how harmless I am when I'm not confronted with a member of my family who has subjected me to sexual exploitation, sedated me, and auctioned me off to be raped by the highest bidder.

Stanley and Macintosh are called to the witness stand to substantiate those claims. Judge Carr scribbles notes while they speak.

But just before noon, she stops writing and listening, looks directly at me, and makes a surprise announcement.

"We needn't waste any more time on this trial. I've heard enough, and I've seen enough. With the statements of the expert witnesses and the video clip I had to watch in my chambers this morning, I'm about ready to rule."

Macintosh and Stanley sit behind me, out of my vision, but I can feel their sudden tension.

Judge Carr keeps looking at me.

"I don't want to subject the accused to any further unnecessary and painful disclosures. I will not be part of exposing more intimate details of her horrendous childhood than absolutely necessary. As I said, I've heard and seen enough, but I'd like to ask you—" and with that she smiles at me, "if you are willing to answer a few of my questions. Do you mind?"

I do mind, but I don't have a choice. So I grin at her.

"Then please step up to the witness box."

I do. It's a bench as hard as the chair this morning. My heart begins to pound when I'm asked if I would be willing to swear on the bible. I place my shaking hand on the book and swear to tell the truth.

Judge Carr keeps smiling, keeps her voice soft, speaks in a slow manner, as if I'm mentally challenged.

"Do you remember anything about the attack on your aunt?"

"Yes."

"What do you remember?"

"I walked into coffee shop to get a muffin. I saw her sitting in a corner. I remember this in flashes. Walking closer, making sure this is really her. Realizing it is. Reaching for my knife. The next thing I remember is somebody on top of me, lots of noise, sirens, people touching me, holding me, me trying to get them off me. That's all."

"Where did you get the knife you used for the attack?"

"I bought it when I planned to kill myself."

"But you gave up on this plan?"

"Yes."

"So why did you carry a knife on that day?"

"I always do, I mean, did. I always carried this knife on me."

"Why? Did you ever feel the need to defend yourself?"

I look straight at her. "Every single day."

Her smile fades. "And now?"

"Not anymore."

"Why not?"

"I understand my aunt Gracie is in custody and will be deported very soon. And my mom is gone, too. I guess I don't need to be afraid of my grandmother."

With that Judge Carr chuckles. "No, I guess not—which brings me to my final point. If I order you released on probation, would you be willing to live under the supervision of your grandmother—"

"No way!" I practically bark at her. It doesn't matter if she gets mad at me. I glare at her to underline my deep resentment of this ludicrous idea. "I'd rather go back to prison. Send me back to the center."

She blows out a long breath. "Calm down. Please understand, I have to make a decision on this. I have an application here for a legal guardian—"

"No foster home either!"

She frowns. "You are not to interrupt me, young lady. This is my courtroom, and you will keep your mouth shut and listen when I speak."

"Sorry," I say.

She looks around. "I understand the applicant is present right now?"

My head jerks around. Macintosh stands up.

"Yes, Your Honor. I am."

I think I'll faint. "But… he didn't… tell me."

"Detective Macintosh, I understand you'll ask for early retirement if I grant you legal guardianship?"

Tiara

"Yes, Your Honor, I can arrange for this. My supervisors have granted me leave with immediate effect if I am to take care of Tiara Rodriguez."

"And how do you plan to do this? The application states you're a widower. It would be highly improper to place a young victim of sexual abuse into the care of a man."

They talk above my head, which twists back and forth between the two of them.

"I know that, Your Honor. But please consider this: I've been serving on the police force for over thirty years, with an impeccable record. I can supply you with a letter of recommendation from the chief of police. In preparation for my retirement I bought a home in the small town of Squamish. The house is big enough, and would give Tiara plenty of privacy. The town has an excellent psychologist for ongoing supervision, recommended by Dr. Eaton."

He pauses, looks at Stanley, who sends enthusiastic nods to the judge.

"Tiara is nearly sixteen," Macintosh continues. "Through no fault of her own, she has problems adjusting to a crowded environment. I believe a secure and quiet country home would help her heal at her own pace. It would be a tragedy if she's placed in a foster home, and she certainly shouldn't be sent to a halfway house. She knows me well by now, I've been visiting her regularly at the Burnaby Youth Secure Center. I think

I've gained her trust. Furthermore, I trust her, I respect her, and I like her."

Judge Carr raises her eyebrows. Scribbles a few notes.

I hold my breath. Macintosh, me, away from here. He'd leave me be, he knows me well enough by now. He respects me. I like him so much, my soul soars into the sky. Perfect. Perfect. Perfect.

Then my soul comes crashing down.

"I'm sorry," Judge Carr says, "but I can't allow that. Detective Macintosh, this is no judgment on your character, quite the opposite. I find it laudable that you are offering to take Tiara Rodriguez in, but—"

Her words drift into the background. My childhood, my miserable childhood is crushing me once again. Because of my background as a molested child, they won't let Macintosh take care of me. I'll never be free of the stigma. Nothing good can ever grow and succeed when planted close to me. Like poison, my past seeps into my present, to destroy and devour. I have no more hope.

Macintosh tried to warn me. A foster home or grandmother. The judge has ruled. Even that goes against me. I can't go back to prison. She doesn't put me on probation. I have suffered enough, she says.

I'm crying. Inside. No tears. Outside.

"Grandmother," I mouth without a voice.

Judge Carr smiles. "I'm glad. Family is always the best option." She looks back at her notes. "Staff con-

Tiara

firmed that Louise Brown is willing to take you in. You're free to go as soon as your grandmother arrives at the court house to pick you up. Won't be long, and you can start a new life with the help of your grandmother."

She doesn't ask why my grandmother isn't present. That she'll pick me up like a piece of garbage only because the court tells her to, because it's the expected thing to do in a fake civilized society. She's willing to take me in on court order, not because she cares for me.

I'm done with people who don't care for me.

Macintosh, the only person in the world who does, says something like he'll sit with me until my grandmother comes. They hand him the bag with my street clothes, take us back to the holding room.

He puts his arm around my shoulders. He knows somebody has to steady me because my insides are empty. All that's left is a bone and skin structure to keep my head up until we're out of sight.

But I'm not the only one crushed by the judge's ruling. Macintosh has been rejected, too. He's lost a daughter all over again.

62

ONCE we're alone, I collapse on the floor, in a corner, arms around my knees, head down.

"We can go to the cafeteria," he says after a few minutes of silence.

I look up. Shake my head.

"If you need a drink, or some food." He knows I can't handle anybody around me now. "Just a thought. It'll be a while before your grandmother gets here."

Maybe I can't even handle him anymore. He should have fought harder.

"I know it's tough. But two years go fast. At your age, they seem endless, but trust me, they fly by if you—"

"Please," I say to him, "please stop. You have no idea how long even a few hours can be."

Here we are again. My past. Catching up to me with lightning speed. No escape.

"You could work with your computer. Learn more stuff. Keep busy."

"My grandmother won't get me a computer."

He stands up heavy, hands me the bag they've given him. "Why don't you change your clothes? Will be good to get out of that orange. I'll get myself a coffee. Sure you don't want something?"

"Water," I say to make it easier for him.

When he's gone, I undress and put on my old jeans, T-shirt, black hoodie, washed, pressed. Won't make a difference.

A few minutes later he's back with a paper cup, a bottle of water and his briefcase. He puts his coffee cup on the table, gets down on his knees, puts the bottle next to me, opens his briefcase, takes out a laptop and places it next to the water. He gets up again and moves over to the chair.

"Too old for this," he says. "Don't know why you kids always want to sit on the floor."

"What's that?" I ask, while I feel my face heat up. I know, right away I know, it's mine. "Where did you get it from?"

"Your friend Candy. I tracked her down, and she gave it to me. I told her it might help get you free."

"How did you—?"

Macintosh has an intense look on his face. Like he hopes I can explain it all away. I can't.

"I met her mother."

"Oh."

"Eaton tipped me off on the computer. I didn't connect it first when I met Camila Vargas, but when she told me that she had allowed Luna to be abused by Inez and her pedophile ring, I couldn't let it go. Checked their immigration application, and guess what I found? The name on La Luna's birth certificate is Candice. I remembered seeing Luna in a picture wearing a necklace with the initials 'C' and 'V', thinking those were her mom's. But they weren't, right? They stand for Candy Vargas. How did you two hook up again?"

"Like I told Stanley. We bumped into each other in the street. I recognized her right away, she was such a star. Until somebody did a smear campaign on her."

Macintosh nods and tells me that in his opinion this would have been Inez' doing. Must have been thoroughly pissed off when lucrative Luna made a break. Can't let that happen in her circles.

I agree with his assumption. "Her mom told her to sleep with some movie guys here in Vancouver to get another contract. That's when Candy left home. She was only seventeen then, but with what she had on her mom, well, she couldn't stop her. As soon as she was eighteen, she went into adult movies. That's all she could do, she said, to make a living. She took me in, let me stay, gave me what I needed to survive without having to do stuff myself. She thought at my age I still had a chance to do better." A bitter laugh works its way up my throat. "Guess I blew that one."

Macintosh keeps mustering me. We're not done yet. I get up, take a seat at the table, stare at my laptop. "Did you look at it?"

"Should I?"

Tiara

My mouth starts to form a "no" when my mind says stop. He looks so hurt. I owe him. The time has come to let him in on my secret. The one secret I managed to hid until now. He deserves to know, and I got nothing to lose. Not anymore.

"I have planned this from the beginning," I say. "I hacked into some pedophile rings, found Gracie as a supplier on the internet, posed as a… you know, a client, until I established contact with her. Then I lured her to Canada."

He straightens. Looks sharp.

"How did you do it?"

"It wasn't difficult at all. A few emails went back and forth, and some time into our exchange I identified myself to her. I told her I couldn't stand living with Mom anymore, wanted to come back to her. Missed her. She offered to send money for me to come back, but I told her to cross the border on my own was out of the question. I couldn't travel by myself as long as I'm still underage. I begged her to pick me up. She should pose as my mom, I said. We have the same surname, so it would be a piece of cake. She agreed without much persuasion, I guess she wanted her girl back, big time. I'm too old for her business by now, but I'm sure she had something lined up for me that would make her money. And by keeping me close to her, she'd gain total control over me. I wouldn't pose a threat to her any more. Of course she was also keen to punish Mom for stealing from her. When she waited for me that morning in Vancouver, she really thought I'd go back with her."

"She entered the country under Inez's name, so she couldn't have played the role of your mother," Macintosh says. "I guess, she planned to take you back illegally."

"Of course, I figured that much, too. She must have organized a false identity for me to smuggle me back. I wouldn't even exist down there. But I pretended to be the stupid girl who believed every promise, to make sure she'd come. Disneyland all over again. My plan worked."

The implications of my admission hang in the air between us until I can stand it no longer.

"I'm sorry. I should have told you."

He looks sad. Not surprised. Not shocked. Only sad. He must have known for some time. My God, he'd known my secret and had kept it safe.

"Weren't you mad at me?" I ask.

"Of course. Like hell."

"But you didn't withdraw your application to take me in?"

He looks even sadder now. "To be honest, there wasn't a chance in hell that the judge would accept."

"Then why try?"

He swallows hard. "I wanted to show you that I cared. That somebody cared. Even with you lying to me, I wanted you to know that I understand. We all have our secrets. "

Tiara

To see his eyes swimming brings tears into mine. How can I ever make up for this? "Honest to God, I hadn't planned to deceive you. When Stanley started working with me, I remembered nothing. I'd forgotten it was Gracie I attacked—didn't know until the day I remembered the rape. That's when it all came back to me. Only then did I remember who the Purple Shadow was."

"Even with that disgusting mask and the cape and the gloves you'd figured out it was Inez?"

"Actually, it wasn't." Silence. Another deep breath. "It was Gracie."

Macintosh does a double-take.

"What?"

"On the day they took the rape video, Gracie made a big mistake. She forgot to put her black gloves on. When I looked at the camera, I recognized the ring on her hand. It's always been Gracie. Always. At every single session, it was her who left the room, got changed and came back disguised as the Purple Shadow."

"Good Lord!" Macintosh shakes his head, huffs and grunts, has a really hard time digesting this ultimate betrayal by a person so close to me. At the same time, his disappointment in me evaporates into thin air. He goes all soft and limp and gentle. For once, I don't mind being pitied.

"That's what I tried to tell Mom when I came home that day."

"Oh shit," he says.

"She didn't want to hear it."

"And when you remembered again, you couldn't tell Dr. Eaton or me—"

"Exactly," I say. "You would have had to inform the judge that the attack was premeditated."

"I got the laptop a few weeks back already. But I put it away. Didn't want to check it out."

He's bent the rules to protect me. And I have lied to him. "Telling Stanley about Candy and the computer was my one big mistake. But then again, it wasn't really a mistake, I didn't know any better then. You have to believe me, I didn't know for a long time, and once I knew, I couldn't tell you."

Macintosh waves it aside. His detective brain needs to work out the snags. As if it mattered.

"Your laptop must have all your emails in it."

I keep quiet.

"The Texans will discover it. They're sifting through all the stuff on your aunt's computers right now."

"I used La Luna's internet account. I never signed the emails with my name, but identified myself to Gracie with small details only the two of us would know, until I established contact. Once I had her on the hook, I always called her."

"Disposable, of course?"

"Of course. They'll never figure it out. Unless you tell them."

Tiara

We fall quiet again. Telling them won't have any consequences. He didn't know, ergo, can't be held responsible, and as for me, I'm so dead inside, nothing will bother me ever again.

He can feel my dark mood.

"I can come visit."

I don't want to talk any more. Not even with him.

"I can take you up for a trip. You, and me, and Louise. I can't take you up there now, but we can all go on a holiday. While you're still with Louise. We'll go fishing. Like I told you."

His expression is so eager, so desperate. How much do I owe him? One last act of kindness, so he'll remember me fondly? I force myself to look interested.

"The lake with the best fish is close to my mountain cabin. About an hour's drive from my Squamish house. Beautiful, just beautiful. A day trip. Something to look forward to. Here, let me show you."

Show me what?

He takes an external drive from his pocket. "I downloaded a few pics from my camera." His voice trails off. "If you download them onto your laptop, you can look at them when…whenever…"

His voice dries up. Whenever I'm blue, he means. Whenever I need something to look forward to. He still doesn't understand how I plan to end this, but how could he? I certainly can't tell him that. But I can't bear to watch him break apart, either. I decide to humor him one final time, hold out my hand.

We insert the external drive. The computer is still working.

"I charged it," Macintosh explains. Of course, he would have. I realize it should still have internet access, too. Candy has paid a year in advance.

The scenery around the lake surpasses beautiful. A magical landscape, so serene. Pity the emptiness inside me can't be touched.

"Nice," I say. "Where exactly is this?"

He take a deep breath, goes into a lengthy explanation, glad to fill the waiting hours with something meaningful. I'm lost after the first sentences.

"Show me." I open Google Earth and we spend half an hour flying over British Columbia, its mountain ranges, lakes, towns and villages. He even finds his remote cabin by the lake. Above the lake, he explains, tucked into the mountain and only accessible by foot, but with a to-die-for view over the countryside. He's so pleased.

Then, the door opens, a servant of the court announces my grandmother arrived.

The end for Macintosh and me.

I want to hug him, but can't. He doesn't mind, thinks he will see me again soon.

My grandmother looks nervous. The way her glance shifts from me to the court servant, I can tell she hoped for a different outcome. Can't be helped. She thinks

Tiara

she's stuck with me for the next two years. I'll change my mind if she gives me the tiniest of indication that I'm reading her wrong. A smile. A kind word. A compassionate look.

"Did you hear about your mother?" is the first sentence coming out of her mouth. "After all I've done for her, she leaves me again."

We walk to her car parked three blocks away.

"Is my stuff still at the apartment?" After all, Mom only left a week ago.

Grandmother speeds up. "That's what I said. Leaves me to take care of everything. The landlord wants three months' notice, and she took all the money I had."

"Can we go there first? Pick up some of my things?"

We arrive at her car. The doors unlock with a push of the button.

"Don't expect me to drive you everywhere."

I get into the passenger side, hold on to my laptop.

"You got to put the seatbelt on."

Dear granny, so worried about my wellbeing.

Ten minutes later we arrive at the apartment block. All the way, I thought back to my drive in the cop car not even a year ago. Even then I've sensed what plays out now. This will be my last drive through the streets of Vancouver.

"If you prefer to wait here," I say when she stops the car. "It'll save you all those stairs. I won't be long."

She hands me the key to the apartment. "Take your time. I'll go get some groceries over there. Two people need more than one. Gets really expensive."

So I was right, she hadn't prepared for me. I get out fast so she won't see the hot tears I can't suppress much longer. I race up the stairs, arrive breathless and crying. Tears of joy, now that I know the misery will be over soon. Feel so light all of a sudden.

Take your time, she said. How long does it take to write a few lines?

Thanks for nothing, dear world. I'm done.

I stuff the note in my backpack, race back down and leave the apartment building through the back entrance.

The ocean isn't far. Still light, but darkness will engulf me soon. The ritual cleansing of my damned soul.

63

MACINTOSH was done. His final months over, right up to the last day. Early retirement would have been possible, but it wouldn't have been enough punishment for him.

When Louise called in on that fateful day of the verdict to report Tiara missing, he should have been upset but he'd been strangely pleased. Good for her to run away. He pictured her going into hiding until it was safe to contact him. He kept looking over his shoulder for three days, scanning the streets for secluded corners, expecting her to cower behind a dumpster. He had no plan what to do when he found her, but he knew he would help her stay away from her grandmother. He would help her any way he could because they had a bond.

Three days he waited, hoping, looking. Until someone walking on the beach found her backpack with the note stuck to its front flap. She'd placed the note in a plastic sandwich bag to keep it dry in case of rain. Tiara had thought it through, probably while they were sitting together waiting for Louise to arrive.

Tiara

For three days he had done his utmost to delay a search. Not difficult, as nobody gave a damn anymore, except him, and to some extent Harding and Dr. Eaton. The waste of her life, being missed by so few, made him understand why she had wanted to end it.

After that, he needed to punish himself. For the girl nobody wanted and everybody exploited. If he had searched for her sooner. If he had been more insistent with the judge. If he had given her a way out. He was all she had, and he had failed her.

His last day on the force was not a joyous occasion. They all knew how hard he took the outcome of his final case. After her, lots of paperwork, as expected. Three months of punishment wasn't a lot, but if he would ever see her again, somewhere in the after-life, he could tell her it had been agony.

Harding gave a little speech, so did his Sergeant, they all clapped, had a toast to his retirement, his miserable, lonely shithouse retirement. Then he was off.

He drove over the Lions Gate Bridge to the Sea-to-Sky highway that connects Vancouver with Whistler. The road wound along steep cliffs and most of the time the view was breathtaking. The sun came out, glittered on the ocean surface, the seagulls soaring until they flew next to him. He didn't pay any attention. He drove through the town where his country home was located. A quaint little town, harmless and peaceful, but too busy for him now. He craved the solitude of the wilderness.

When he arrived at the lake, the sun bathed the fir trees on the opposite shoreline in a golden glow. The lake was calm. He considered for a moment to walk in, keep walking until the ground gave way, keep swimming until his body gave way. But he was too good a swimmer. The opposite shore was not far enough. He wasn't desperate enough. Or brave enough. He'd make it across.

He walked over to the boat shed, picked up the key from its hiding place, unlocked it and pulled the fishing boat over the gravel until he reached the shallow water. He unloaded some of his supplies, as much as he could carry on his hike up to his cabin, and put the bags into the boat. He'd get the rest tomorrow. Enough to last him a few weeks. He didn't want to see anybody for a while. The wilderness had a way of healing, he was counting on it.

He pushed the boat in the water, jumped in and started rowing. Quiet. Until the sounds of the wilderness began to pierce through his acquired city deafness. It would take a while to adjust.

Already, the lake setting smoothed over the roughest edges.

Tiara. You poor thing, how I wish I could've shown you this place. How I wish you'd stand there, wave at me. Your giggle wouldn't have to be loud, the lake carries sounds like magic.

He squinted, looked, rubbed his eyes with one hand, holding on to both oars with the other. The image

Tiara

didn't go away. Tiara, standing there, waving. Then he heard her giggle. No. Couldn't be. He covered his ears, both hands, the boat began to turn. He grabbed the oars again, and there was the sound again.

He rowed fast. The opposite shore came closer, closer, closer. He was losing his mind. But why now. Tiara standing there, waving. Good enough to go crazy. She was only a few steps away when he heard, after a final push, the sand underneath grind the boat to a stop. He jumped out, holding his hands over his heart now because it was beating too fast.

A heart attack, right here, they wouldn't find him for months.

Why not. A good way to go.

"Hey, Macintosh," Tiara said. "Did I ever thank you?"

He stopped in his tracks. Her, right here, he was close enough to touch her. He did. Flesh and blood, she didn't flinch.

"It's you?"

"Of course it's me."

He sank to his knees. Heart still pumping.

She got down next to him, got comfortable. He shifted, they sat next to each other, looking over the lake surface. Ready for the long talk.

"Thank me for what?"

"For giving me all the info. I'd never have found that place without it. Took me three weeks to get here, and I still nearly missed it."

"I never—"

She looked hurt. She hadn't tricked him, not this time. She believed he'd done this on purpose. For her. He'd come to her rescue. Her knight in shining armor. Something they could hold onto in the coming months. She deserved this.

"I never stopped wondering if you'd make it," he said. Felt more perfect than the truth.

Giggle. Glorious giggle.

"Surviving in the wilderness you mean?"

"Yeah."

"I've survived worse."

He watched her draw lines into the sand. Lines and numbers. "Getting here wasn't easy. I knew I needed help and couldn't contact you. Not while you were with the force. So I went back to Candy. She lent me, well, with interest, close to a thousand dollars. She knows I won't pay her back until I'm of age. I can go back and give it to her, then, can't I? Or will they lock me up?"

He thought about it, slow and steady. This was all too much. But too much in a good way is never too much to handle.

"No, I guess you won't get into trouble. All you did was run away. There are a million runaways out there, nobody cares about them."

She stopped drawing her numbers. Wiped over the final tally. "You are the only one who knows my secret. You're a policeman. One day you might hate me for being a criminal. I'd die if you hate me."

Tiara

God, not that. Not her. He had to lift that burden off her. "I have a secret, too. One I never told anybody. I'll share it with you, if you want." Her eyes grew large. "That man who killed my daughter, I tracked him down, I found him—"

She placed her hand on his arm. "Don't."

But he couldn't stop now. He had to let it out. "I couldn't let him off the hook. He killed my daughter. He cost me my family. After Danielle was gone, Kathy died of a broken heart. I needed to revenge both of them. The new drug Fentanyl had just hit the market. I took some out of evidence, we had so much, nobody noticed. When I found him at a night club, I slipped a pill into his drink, waited until he went to the toilet and followed him. I was lucky, nobody was inside. But I wouldn't have cared. My mind was made up. I found him bent over a toilet, puking his guts out. Didn't even notice me. I injected the Fentanyl into him and left. He must have called for help, or somebody came in after me and saw him convulsing. I watched an ambulance arrive from across the street, hiding in the shadows. Most first responders didn't know how powerful that new drug was. When they transported him off, his corpse was already fully covered. He had died of an overdose, like so many others." Macintosh paused. It felt so good, after all this time. Josh had always suspected, but they had never talked about it. His confession was a secret only shared by Tiara. "Do you hate me now?"

"Of course not," she said, her hand still on his arm. "Will you stay at the cabin with me?"

"No way. And you can't stay here either."

"I have to. I won't go to my grandmother, and I can't go live with you in Squamish. Tell you what, this is another secret we share. I live in the cabin until I'm eighteen, and you come visiting and bring me supplies."

"Impossible."

"Nothing is impossible. Look how I found this place. All by myself. I found your boat, too. One of your pictures showed the shed."

"Obviously the key, too."

"You aren't very creative. Once I got all the supplies I bought over to the cabin, I put the boat back and swam across. Mountain lakes are pretty cold, I can tell you."

"But, how did you get the stuff here?

First time ever he saw her proud and pleased with herself. "You won't believe it."

"Try me."

"A cab," she said. "You know. One of those cars for hire—"

"I know."

She giggled from deep down. "It cost me three hundred dollars. I told the cab driver that I was planning a birthday party for my dad. She was so helpful."

A *she*? Then he understood. Tiara was smart, she would never have gone into the wilderness with a strange man.

"But you can't survive here for two years," he said. "You can't."

"Well, I did so far. Of course, I need you to drop by with stuff. Now that you're retired you can do what you want. I'll have to borrow money from you for this. But one day, when I can work, I'll pay you back, same as Candy."

She was thinking of working one day. The wilderness was already working on her. On him, too. His heart rate was nearly back to normal. No heart attack. He couldn't afford one. Not now. Not for a long time. What would happen to Tiara if he didn't show up? Surviving would be hard enough even with his help.

"You're a tough one," he said. "I think you can make it."

"We can, Macintosh. We can."

"Maybe it's time you call me Pete," he said.

"Pete? Really?"

"How about Mac, then?"

She gave him a smile that would light up the rest of his days.

"That'll do, Mac. That'll do."

Acknowledgement

I'm not ashamed to be judgemental when it comes to child beauty pageants. The idea of dressing up little girls like mini-adults, with make-up and all, seem preposterous, if not outright perverted, to me. What drives parents to expose their children to such a fake value system, and how do those kids cope later on?

Puzzling questions. Tiara is a fictitious character, but once she took shape in my head, I had to figure out what motivates participants and audience to create toddler beauty queens. Luckily I had the help of many professional experts when I started to explore, and later on write about, the dark side of this topic.

This is the place to acknowledge their contribution. A huge thank you to juvenile forensic psychiatrist Dr. Paul Janke for patiently answering my myriad of emails on the subject, to Anita McDonnell, Director of Burnaby Secure Youth Center, for allowing me an inside look into the institution, to my top-notch editor Toni Lopopolo for teaching me what words not to use and how to move the story forward, and to my final eyes Cynthia Lauriente for weeding out the dreaded typos. Also thanks to my numerous beta-readers who gave me valuable tips on what readers like, specially Val Ewald, and finally, a big hug and kiss to the best husband ever, Manfred, for his unwavering understanding and encouragement while I immersed myself into the creation of Tiara.

Of course, a story needs people who read it, love it, and talk about it. I therefore thank those of you—my dear readers—with all my heart for spreading the word about Tiara.

Thank you, all.

Printed in Great Britain
by Amazon